...Myles

CW00860276

A COLLECTION OF SHORT STORIES

CARLOS E. TIBBS

outskirts
press

This book is dedicated to my wife. My lifeblood. My wife of forty-one years.

Vernell Myles Tibbs

Table of Contents

Exodus—Stories from the Road

Jacob Franklin Myles picks up his father's rifle. There's still one round left. More than enough for what he has to do, he tells himself. He trains his gun on the beast, sitting with his back to Jacob and the rest of the God-fearing world guzzling away his useless life. Jacob cocks the twenty-year-old rifle. Wiping the sweat from his brow, he takes aim. The thug who attacked his daughter turns the bottom of his bottle to the sky. Weighing the consequences of his actions, Jacob trembles. Jacob Myles, one of the best hunters in Hopskip has bagged over fifty deer, a hundred or so mallards – maybe a dozen geese. Until today, no two-legged animal has ever framed the crosshairs of his rifle's scope. The young deacon is about to perform an act from which he knows he can never return.

Introduction of the Myles Family

BETWEEN THE YEARS 1940 and 1960, the African-American population of Chicago, Illinois exploded. The black population of Chicago grew from nearly three hundred thousand citizens to almost three times that amount. Receiving its' inhabitants from southerners becoming increasingly disenchanted with the racist policies of Jim Crow, Chicago, Cleveland, Los Angeles and other major metropolitan cities became the Mecca for African-Americans seeking a respite from the South and the inequities foisted upon them by its' bigoted environment. Today, Saturday, March 31st, 1962, the Myles family will add seven to that ever-growing number. The Myles clan, headed by Jacob, Sr. and his wife Dorothy (aka Dottie); homemaker and mother to their five children, are making that well-worn exodus to the windy city. Like so many migrants before them, the South no longer holds the promise of peace and tranquility once held in abundance in their little corner of the world. Certain elements in their hometown have made living there uncomfortable for Jacob and Dorothy; and even worse, dangerous for their elder children.

A red and gold paneled Ford Custom Deluxe station wagon makes its' way north along Interstate Highway 85. At the wheel of the twelve-year-old automobile, affectionately known as "Goldie", is Jacob Franklin Myles, Sr. - rancher, farmer and lifelong native of the rural town of Hopskip, Georgia. Jacob is leaving his place of birth after nearly forty years. An accomplished trainer of golden retrievers, Jacob Myles has trained and sold dogs to hunters throughout North Georgia and its' neighboring states for the last fifteen years. His reputation for honesty and fair play is known throughout the South. Even those who've run afoul of Jacob (usually a misstep of their own) respect his integrity. Clever and quick-witted, Jacob was always the man to turn to whenever there was a disagreement about sports, politics, and life in general. He's the man everyone stops to engage in conversation whenever he enters a room. Considered the unofficial mayor of Black Hopskip (the Negro side of town), Jacob Myles has only one regret in life. He never finished high school. He supplements that loss, however with a voracious appetite for anything worth reading. His favorite book? The Bible. His second? Any and everything pertaining to Negro League Baseball. Jacob Myles loves everything about 'America's Favorite Pastime'. Having never received his diploma, Jacob Myles, nicknamed 'Lightning' for his fastball and quick moves on the baseball diamond, is nevertheless determined to get his offspring through college. Armed with an unstoppable attitude and a desire to see his children fare better than himself, Jacob Franklin Myles – sometimes stubborn, a bit complex, yet always prideful- is making the move north for his children.

"If there's a Lord above…" Jacob frowns fidgeting with the radio.

"…and we all know there is!" Dottie exclaims finishing her husband's oft-quoted statement. "What's the matter, sweetheart?"

"…I'd be able to find a good jazz station," he replies. "Can never find a good station on the road. Let's hope Chicago has a good one."

"Let's hope so, baby!" Dottie responds with a pat on her husband's arm.

"Dottie," Jacob says to his wife. "Did the kids drink the last of the cranberry juice from the last stop?"

"'Fraid so, baby." Dottie looks around to see if her babies are asleep. They are, all but their eldest daughter, who's reading a magazine. Jacob's beloved reaches into her purse where she's hidden the last bottle of juice. It's okay. Jacob always waits until the kids are served before he even starts. Dottie saved it for him like she always does. She unscrews the cap and hands it to the love of her life.

"You're the best, baby!" winks Jacob saluting his wife with the bottle. He uncaps it and takes a swig. "Somebody should write a song about you, girl."

"Ha Ha! Anytime, handsome!" says Dottie going back to her book and winking back. "Anytime!"

Riding shotgun for the Myles family (as always) is Dorothy Rosetta Harris Myles; Jacob's faithful and supportive spouse. Although initially opposed to the notion of pulling up stakes, Dottie, as she's known to family and friends, supports her husband Jacob in his quest for a better life for his family. A high school graduate with a fondness for magazine recipes and a library of cookbooks, Dottie has always had a knack for creating scrumptious meals out of ordinary kitchen provisions. Unbeknownst to the prideful Jacob (or so she thinks), Dottie's culinary skills paid many a bill when money was scarce. A kind soul who was always ready with a pie when a church member passed or a pound cake when a child was born, Dottie Myles is loved by all who were blessed to make her acquaintance. With her eldest daughter's head for business and her love for baking, Dottie had hoped to parlay their talents into a catering business. *Rosie's and Josie's Cookies and Cakes and Other Things We Bakes.* (She's still working on the company name.) Dottie has accepted the move north and putting her dreams of catering on hold. For now. She hopes to once again pursue those dreams while "*up south*".

"Hey baby," says Dottie turning around and facing her pretty as a picture eldest. "How does *UpSouth Catering* sound?"

"Whatever you say, Mama," she answers nonchalantly. "Whatever you say."

"I kinda like it!" Dottie says proudly.

"Sounds like a winner!" Jacob chants.

"*Good Lord,*" their daughter thinks to herself. "*Don't they ever disagree?*"

Sitting behind her father in the second row of the family wagon stews an eighteen-year-old beauty named Jocelyn Dorothy Myles. Josie, as she's known to her family and friends, is the eldest (and to Jacob's chagrin the most rebellious of late) of the Myles children. In conflict recently with her father over her future and their decision to move north, Josie wanted instead to stay in Hopskip. Her father wants her to go to college and become a teacher. Tired of raising her little brothers and sisters – funny thing, she's never said that around Dottie – Miss Jocelyn has no plans to teach or further her education. A year out of high school and no real plans for the future, Josie wanted instead to get married and leave the home that's become her father's '*dungeon*'. Josie deplores her father's '*cowardly*' and sudden move from family and friends; particularly smooth talking Mack Hodges, whom she believes was about to propose and move her away from '*Daddy's Dungeon*'. A real beauty, suffering from her father's over-protection, Josie is unaware how much Jacob fears for her while growing up in an unapologetic and racist South. He hopes a change of scenery will persuade his daughter to change her mind about Hodges and concentrate on her future. Her mother hopes the two of them can start fresh with her plans for a catering business. Unbeknownst to her parents, Dottie's and Jacob's oldest has plans of her own.

'*Goldie*', the Myleses' station wagon hits a bump in the road.

"Whoa!" "Hey!" say the kids. "Daddy, what happened?"

"Sorry, family," says Jacob. "This highway. They really need to fix these potholes. And the reception."

"My God," marvels Josie to herself. She shakes her head incredulously staring at the sibling to her right. "My brother can sleep through an earthquake!"

Seated (sleeping actually) behind his mother is Dottie's pride and joy Jacob Franklin Myles, Jr. The eldest son and the apple of his mother's eye, Jacob is called '*L'il Daddy*' by family and friends. The spitting image of his dad, Jacob Jr. sees the rancher and ex-baseball pitcher as a hero and tries to pattern his own life after Jacob, Sr. If Jacob, Jr. could find a bumper sticker that read WWDD (What Would Daddy Do), he would display it proudly. Young Jacob has been "rocking the boat" with the local townsfolk of Hopskip (white and Negro) because of his collaboration with "northerners" and their recruitment of picketers for sit-ins and civil rights' marches. He was even seen seated in the white section of a lunch counter in a neighboring city two months earlier. Jacob, Sr. and Dottie have received veiled threats from so-called concerned citizens regarding their young son's safety. After the bombing at the old North Hopskip Church of Christ (which fortunately was empty), Jacob and Dottie believe the move north is their only hope of protecting their young crusader. Young Jacob defends his father's every decision… except the move north. In love with white landowner Marvin Brand's daughter Molly Beth, young Jacob secretly wishes his family had stayed in Hopskip. Pretty, sensitive, and miles away politically from her father, Margaret Elizabeth Brand is a secret sympathizer to the civil rights movement. With a passion for honesty and righteousness inherited from her absentee mother, Molly Brand has acquired an old copier with which she has been secretly assisting Jacob, Jr. in copying pamphlets for the voter recruitment drive. Although good friends with Josie as well, young Molly was kept at a distance by a perceptive Dottie who feared losing her son, her beloved *'L'il Daddy'* to Jim Crow.

L'il Daddy is awakened briefly by his baby brother counting the buttons on his shirt.

"One…two…three…four!" he says proudly. "*I'm* four!"

"Yes you are," big brother responds. He playfully pushes him toward Josie. "Where's *Bruno*?" L'il Daddy asks looking around. He finds Bruno, the baby's toy – a stuffed German shepherd doll L'il Daddy won at the county fair last year – and gives it to him before heading back to dreamland.

Firmly entrenched between his drowsy older brother and brooding big sister is Baby Terry. Terrence James Myles, the youngest of the clan, has just turned four. Terry adores his family and is happy wherever he goes. As long as he has his siblings, parents, and *Bruno* by his side, Terrence James is a happy camper. Terry will begin Head Start, a new program for children his age, in the fall. Terry loves puzzles, airplanes, and dogs (must be in the genes). Jacob promised to get him a real German shepherd as soon as they're settled in Chicago. For now, he has *Bruno* to keep him company. He turns around to the last row of the station wagon and taps his brother and sister on their heads with it.

"Hey, Terry!" says his middle brother from the back of the vehicle. "You're not big enough for a real German shepherd. How 'bout we get you a dog from another country when we get to Chicago? Like a Great Dane. They're from Denmark."

"Are you serious?" replies his little sister. "Great Danes are huge. Why do you think they call them *'Great'*? Hey, I know. Let's get him a French poodle. They're from France!"

"Are *you* serious?" her brother shouts incredulously. "Poodles are for girls!"

"Are not!"

"Are, too!" shouts the little chauvinist. "You never see a man with a French poodle. Do you, Daddy?"

"Not *this* one!" Jacob smiles.

"You're as bad as him," Dottie whispers.

"Yes!!!" Frankie shouts feeling redeemed by his father's concurrence. "Score one for Frankie J."

"Big Deal!" says his little sister.

"…and in honor of my victory, I will treat my little sister to a *song* about dogs."

"Frankie!" moan his female relatives already weary of what's coming next.

Frankie clears his throat. He stands up and starts snapping his fingers and twisting his legs like Elvis Presley.

"No, Frankie!"

"Aw, Mama."

Frankie!" shouts his mom. "Boy, sit down. This is a moving car!"

"Yes, Ma'am," he says slumping dejectedly in his seat.

"Ha, ha!" laughs little sister Savannah. "Now we all win!"

Bringing up the rear of the wagon is twelve-year-old balladeer Frankie and his compadre in mischief, Savannah. Franklin Joseph Myles is the middle child and the Myleses' second son. Charismatic and cute, young Frankie wants to be a singer. He sees the move to Chicago as a few miles closer to the motor city of Detroit – specifically Motown Records. Frankie is also hoping to put together a group - as long as he sings lead. Fancying himself as the next great singing sensation, young Frankie idolizes R & B artists Smokey Robinson and James Brown. He had pictures of Motown artists plastered all over his room back in Hopskip, and sometimes peppers his conversation with song lyrics. It's a habit his mother finds irritating but his proud father considers genius - a sign of *'genetic male intelligence'* he boasts playfully. Seldom seen without his portable radio, earphone, and a notepad for writing lyrics, Frankie takes a mostly nonchalant approach to life. He loves M&M's, likes spy movies and comic books, and gets along with everyone. Frankie is a tad chauvinistic toward girls. His mother is working on it. Frankie, like his sister Savannah, is unaware of the problems his family faced back in Hopskip but applauds any move that will get him closer to an audition with a certain music mogul named Gordy.

Cute little Savannah Vernell Myles was the baby of the family for seven years until Baby Terry *'swiped'* her position. She's forgiven him as big sisters often do and helps watch him while Mom is baking or taking care of their home. A happy, free-spirited soul, eleven-year-old Savannah looks forward to the move to Chicago. Ready to go out into the world to test the new 'rights' and 'freedoms' gained through the movement, Savannah mainly tests her family's patience as she sometimes goes to extremes in "outing" anything or anybody who appear the least bit conservative. Savannah salvaged her late '*Nana's*' old sewing machine for the trip north. She envisions making dashikis, short skirts, and other outerwear for her family emblazoned with black power symbols and the colors of the Black Flag. Having absolutely no problems with self-esteem, Little Miss Myles insists on being called Savannah. She says "nobody ever made it big being called just *Vanna*". Unlike big sister Josie, Savannah Vernell Myles can't wait to plant her flag (the red, black, and green one) atop the highest building in the Windy City.

Jacob, Sr. in particular hopes for a new start and a better life for this precious cargo - hopefully better than the one he left behind.

"Son, do you wanna take the wheel for a bit?" Jacob asks feeling a little exhausted by the long drive.

Silence.

"L'il Daddy?" Jacob says searching for his son in the rearview mirror.

"He's 'sleep, Daddy," Savannah offers. "Look, Frankie. He's smiling in his sleep. Must be a good dream. I bet it's about the Movement!"

Josie covers her brother with the blanket that slipped from his lap onto the floor of the car. She notices his smile.

"Glad somebody's happy," she mumbles to herself.

"Dream On, Big Brother!" sings Frankie digging up an old chestnut from his own repertoire of chart climbers. *"Sittin' behind your mother!"*

"Whose song is that?" Savannah asks puzzled.

"Mine. I just wrote it. What do you think?

"I'm thinking I wish I was 'sleep, too."

Jacob Myles, Jr.—Sweet Dreams

IT'S FIVE AFTER twelve. Friday, April 14th, 1961. The students of Beauregard James Whitehall Senior High are pouring onto the campus for lunch. B. J. Whitehall, one of the first schools in the south to integrate has so far accepted the state's two-year-old mandate without much difficulty. Although forced by the state of Georgia to integrate the city's two main high schools, the more enlightened citizenry of the sleepy little town of Hopskip has welcomed the change. Most of the town admittedly is still walking on eggshells hoping to avoid trouble with the state's directive. Though most of Whitehall's students still congregate with those of their own choosing, fifteen–year-olds Jacob Myles, Jr. and Margaret Elizabeth Brand take every opportunity they can to be together. The farmer's son and the rich girl from across the tracks have been sneaking off to the school's vacant library – *'the stacks'*, as they call it - to have a private lunch of their own. Their fathers, Jacob Myles, Sr. and Marvin Brand, of course, have no knowledge of their children's romance. Knowing that their friendship, much less their love for one another would never be accepted by their parents or friends, Jacob, Jr. also known as L'il Daddy and Margaret Elizabeth, who prefers Molly Beth, have been meeting in their secret hiding place for the last few months to have lunch in peace and to be together as friends. L'il Daddy's makeshift table – four books high and five books wide – hosts the couple's lunch. Molly Beth uses her scarf as a tablecloth. She grabs a slice of her boyfriend's dessert.

"Hmm! Nobody bakes a sweet potato pie like your mama," says Molly Beth. "What *does* she put in it?"

"Her finger," L'il Daddy responds laughing to himself.

"Excuse me?" she says.

"Yeah," says L'il Daddy. "Let my mother, Hopskip's answer to Betty

Crocker tell it, '*Mama's Finger*' adds a flavor you can't get in stores any-where in town …and Daddy wouldn't disagree."

"You're both just as silly as she is, Jacob Myles."

"I'll tell them you said so."

"Jacob!"

"Just kidding."

L'il Daddy gets up from his lunch on the floor and peeks out of one of the two windows facing the school campus.

"Come here, Molly Beth. I wanna show you something."

He points out the window toward the schoolyard where Whitehall students are having lunch and listening to their radios. He points to a table of black teens sitting under a shade tree reading, talking, and bop-ping their heads to Chuck Berry.

"Look out this window, sweetheart."

He directs his girlfriend's attention to two picnic tables of young white teens eating lunch and listening to a radio blasting the latest by Elvis Presley. Mr. Hennessey, Whitehall's wrestling coach stands guardedly between the two groups.

"See Cookie Abernathy with my sister at the '*black table*'?"

"Yep. She still fighting your daddy over being here at Whitehall?"

"Yep. It never stops."

"Too bad. What about Cookie? I like her."

"I know. She's good people. Did you know she's got a thing for Bobby Matthews over there doing that really bad Elvis impersonation? He's my man and all but he really should give it a rest. Ha! Ha!"

"Really? Bobby Matthews?" the pretty redhead asks wide-eyed. "They say his daddy's in the Klan."

"He's no Klansman. They tried but he shooed 'em off. Especially after they found that boy from Chicago in the lake. They say Mr. Matthews found God. Now watch," L'il Daddy says. "They're looking at each other but not looking at each other."

"What?"

"Directly, I mean," the teenager explains. "Look. She's patting her hair and pulling her ponytail. Now watch '*Mr. Presley*'. Tapping his watch, three fingers on his cheek. Clockwork! Seen it a hundred times!"

"So?"

"Sooo…" L'il Daddy says pulling his longtime love away from the windows. "My man Bobby and Miss Cookie are meeting behind *'Big Mama's Hair Emporium'* at three o'clock. If her daddy ever found out..."

"Meeting behind the Hair Emporium at three o'clock?" Molly Beth says astonished. "Jacob Myles, Jr., did you just make that up? You did, didn't you?"

"No, no, look! Mr. Hennessey just stepped in between them, aannnnndd...."

"Oh, my Lord!" Molly Beth exclaims. "They both moved to the left!"

"So they can still see each other," says Jacob. "Like instinct! Isn't Integration beautiful?"

"Delightful!" laughs Molly Beth. She pauses, takes a look out the window again, and then pensively at her young beau.

"Honey Dip," Molly Beth ponders with a smile. "Is it just me or are all the Negroes sitting in the shade and the white kids are sunning themselves trying to get a tan?"

The two teens look at one another and then back outside their windows at the two groups. They fall into each other laughing. They hug. Jacob, Jr. pulls away and stands, careful not to get too close to the window. He walks over to a stack of books and takes an old primer from the top. Molly Beth notices that her forbidden paramour's once joyful demeanor has suddenly turned sour.

"Honey, what's wrong?"

"What's wrong, Margaret Brand is I don't think your daddy would be too happy with how his baby girl's spending her lunch hour. Sneaking around the *'stacks'* with a..."

"L'il Daddy, don't!" interrupts Molly knowing what's coming next.

At that moment, the angry young man kicks over the stack of books and flings the primer across the room.

"JACOB!" Molly screams.

"Sorry, baby girl. It's just, I mean...Wow! These books are so old no one even comes up here anymore," L'il Daddy exclaims trying to change the subject. "Didn't have that problem at *my* school. Why do you suppose that is, huh?"

Molly Beth stands up and takes her beau's hand.

" Come on, ***baby boy***! Sit down."

"***Baby boy?*** Girl, you starting to sound like me!"

"I should. We been coming up here for two months. Sneaking, hiding out for what eight, nine years, now? The world's not ready for our kind of love, Mr. Myles. Hiding in the stacks. Winking in the hallways at school. Meeting behind the *Hair Emporium,*" Molly Beth says holding up her fingers 'quoting' her last sentence.

"Can't eat together. Can't sit together," L'il Daddy continues solemnly.

"Why, you can't even play football in your own school!" Molly Beth almost screams. "You were the quarterback at your old school, remember?"

"Course I do, baby girl. How can I forget?"

"Remember last year's homecoming?" Molly Beth says looking off into the distance. "Lincoln High vs. good ol' Whitehall - the school of the South. I'm still surprised we got to play each other."

"Me, too. I guess they figure if we can play football together…"

"Your team came running out on the field and you were right out front. Looking mighty handsome, Mr. Myles."

"Thank you! Thank you!" L'il Daddy says with a bow.

"…and when you threw that touchdown, my Lord! A Hail Mary, right? I almost cheered against my own team. Some cheerleader I was!"

"Yep. A Hail Mary," L'il Daddy responds smiling and reminiscing. "Surprised I pulled that one off."

"What do you mean?" the young teen says surprised. "You read that playbook of yours more than Brother Luke reads his bible. I see you sitting on the sidelines. Studying those X's and O's. You must know that book inside out."

"So I fooled you too, huh?"

Molly Beth looks at young Jacob, Jr. bewildered.

"What do you mean?"

"Margaret Elizabeth Brand! The only letters I was reading were on your sweater. Funny," he muses pulling her toward him. "Every paper shaker on your squad wore the same sweater. None of them looked as good as you."

Molly Beth sighs. She looks at her beau, a handsome young Negro from the other side of town. She melts in his arms.

'*Why can't people understand?*' she thinks to herself. '*Why don't they leave us alone?*' Molly Beth shakes herself out of her reverie and reaches across their makeshift picnic table for her purse.

"Jacob, I have something for you."

Molly Brand pulls out a locket. It's wrapped in a piece of stationery adorned with pink hearts – stationery she found in one of her mother's old purses. The locket itself is engraved with the words *Forever Yours*. Her fingers trembling, Molly hands the locket to her forbidden lover. His hands are trembling, too. Jacob Myles, Jr. slowly opens the locket. He's surprised by what he sees.

"Baby, I-,"

He starts to speak but Molly Beth puts her fingers to his lips.

"I hope I don't have to tell you, Mr. Myles," she says half-jokingly. "You must guard this with your life."

"No, honey you don't," he responds his voice cracking. He tucks the locket away in his jacket pocket.

The farmer's son and the rich girl from the other side of town –their love most likely wouldn't be accepted even if they shared the same hue. Molly Beth has fretted that likelihood since she was six, when she and L'il Daddy first met. Her mother, Elizabeth Brand allowed young Jacob to do *'chores'* around the house, sensing the special friendship between the boy and her daughter. L'il Daddy and Molly Beth played for hours – until Mr. Brand and his son Cletus came in from the fields. Mrs. Brand would sneak little Jacob out of the back door with a quarter, as proof to his own family that he actually did chores around her home. She loved Molly Beth and dreamed in her heart that someday she and L'il Daddy could be together as, in her words, *'as fate intended'*. Those days are long gone. Mrs. Brand mysteriously disappeared, leaving Margaret Elizabeth and Jacob, Jr. to seek seclusion in other ways. Now that their schools have integrated, the two friends use the old library to be together – as fate, they believe intended.

L'il Daddy pats the locket in his pocket. He moves toward Molly Beth for a kiss. She stops short to speak.

"So no one on my squad looked as good as me, huh? You have good taste, Mister Myles".

"Exquisite, Miss Brand."

The two lean toward one another. They're stopped when they hear a noise coming from behind them. At that moment, a fan belt falls from the sky.

"Hmm," says Molly Beth breaking away. "The motor mount's loose."

The Myleses' station wagon hits another pothole. The engine makes a squeaking, almost whimpering sound. Jacob, Jr., jolted out of his sleep, looks around and frowns. Sweet Molly Brand and her kisses are a distant memory - one that lovingly haunts his dreams.

"Daddy, what was that!" he asks. "Why are we pulling over?"

"Fan belt," Jacob answers knowingly. Jacob Myles, Hopskip, Georgia's very own shade tree mechanic, has always been able to diagnose and repair any problem with a car or truck just by listening to the engine - a handy skill to have when the only other mechanic in town started overcharging his customers.

"Sounds like the motor mount's loose, too," says Jacob.

"WHAT DID YOU SAY, DADDY?" Jacob screams remembering his dream girl's diagnosis.

"It's okay son, don't worry," Jacob replies. "Nothing that can't be fixed with a little elbow grease. There's a gas station at the next exit."

Josie taps her brother's arm smiling. She puts her finger to her lips and 'zips' them closed telling him he should do the same. Even when caught up in her own agony, Josie is always there for her little brother. He nods and smiles acknowledging his big sister's help.

Jacob looks in the rearview mirror at his children. Frankie and Savannah are asleep. So is Baby Terry. Josie pretends to read something so she won't have to talk to her father. She never agreed to the move north and she and her father have been at odds since his decision. Jacob decides to ease the tension by joking with his son who has now folded his blanket and placed it in the trunk area of the Custom Deluxe station wagon. Jacob elbows his wife Dottie and nods towards the rear of the car.

"Sounds like you were having quite a dream. You awake now?"

"Uhhh, yes, sir."

"Football or girls?" Jacob smiles winking at Dottie.

Josie looks out the window ignoring her father's attempt at humor.

"What?" asks L'il Daddy confused by his dad's odd request. "Were you talking to me, Daddy?"

"What do you think, baby girl?" asks Jacob, Sr. to his eldest. He calls both his daughters '*baby girl*' and somehow they always know which one he's talking to. "L'il Daddy looked pretty happy back there, don't you think?"

"I wouldn't know," Josie replies nonchalantly. If she could be any more disinterested…

"*Football, my eye!*" Dottie says to herself. "*If that boy talked in his sleep…*"

Dorothy Rosetta Myles—Catering to No One

WHEN SHE'S NOT meeting the demands of a growing family, Dorothy Rosetta Harris Myles can be found popping muffins out of a tin plate for her daughter's sleepover, icing a cake for new members of their congregation, or baking a sweet potato pie for the family of a sick friend. Dorothy Myles, also known as Dottie, loves to bake. Dottie has made cakes and pies for sale ever since she was old enough to turn on Mama Harris' old Chambers oven. She hopes to someday parlay her hobby into a real business. Today, the budding entrepreneur with youngest daughter Savannah are in the kitchen baking pies for members of her congregation. She's reading a clipboard she uses to take inventory of her sales and stock.

Ding!

"Yes! Another masterpiece," Dottie proclaims heading to the oven. "Hand me my oven mitts, Savannah."

"Sure, Mama."

Dottie lovingly takes the warm pie from the oven and places it on the window sill.

"Love the smell of lemon," she says. "Sister Hammer said Mrs. Murphy might drop by to buy one. Hope she likes it."

Savannah, inquisitive as ever poses a question for her mother.

"Mama," Savannah ponders looking over her mother's shoulder at her list of customers. "Why does Mrs. Appleby get the lemon pie and Mrs. Lemmon get the apple pie? Shouldn't it be the other way around?"

"Savannah, baby please, I'm trying to concentrate," Dottie says reading her checklist. "Mrs. Appleby, lemon meringue; the Lemmons, Brown Betty. Mrs. Hammer. Hmm. What did I make for the Deacon and Mrs. Hammer?"

"What else?" laughs Savannah. "Pound cake!"

"L'il girl, you are too much!" laughs her mother. "Get the wax paper out of the cupboard. I'm going to show you how to wrap these pies for delivery."

"Yes, ma'am."

Savannah goes to the cupboard for the wrapping paper. Looking out of an adjacent window, Savannah smirks when she sees Ethel Murphy and her daughter Jenny driving up the dirt road to the Myles' ranch. The Murphys are newcomers to Hopskip.

"Mama," Savannah asks innocently. "What's a Komodo dragon?"

"A Komodo dragon is a huge lizard," Dottie responds without missing a beat. "…found somewhere on the other side of the world."

"Wow, Mama. You and Daddy know everything."

"That's 'cause we read baby girl," says Mother Dottie always taking advantage of a teachable moment. "So should you and Frankie…and I don't just mean comic books. Now, why all these questions about the Komodo dragon?"

"'Cause one's about to ring the doorbell. It's the Murphys from church."

"Savannah, that's a horrible thing to say about a person."

"I didn't make it up. That's what L'il Daddy calls Jenny Murphy, the new girl in school. He says her face could stop a clock and her breath could light kindling. They call her…" Savannah pauses for effect. "THE KOMODO!"

Dottie almost drops the wax paper laughing at her daughter's antics.

"Now you stop it," Dottie tells her daughter trying not to laugh. "Nobody is that…*challenged*."

"Her breath is so hot she *coulda* browned the lemon meringue herself."

"I said stop it now, Savannah," Dottie says stifling her laughter.

Ding Dong.

"Open the door for our customers, Savannah. And be nice."

Savannah opens the door. Mrs. Murphy and her daughter Jenny step in. Dottie takes one look at Jenny and is speechless. Unintentionally, Dottie finds herself looking at the clock in the hallway. It's still ticking. She catches herself and directs the two women to the living room.

"Did we catch you at a bad time, Mrs. Myles?" Mrs. Murphy asks.

"Time?" Dottie says checking the clock again. "Uh no, no. Come in. Come in."

"Thank you, Mrs. Myles."

Dottie watches in disbelief as her two guests walk over to the couch. *"...and I thought God loved everyone,"* she mumbles to herself.

"Excuse me?" says her guest.

"Oh, nothing! Nothing!" Dottie says collecting herself. "Call me Dottie, everyone else does. Come in. Come in. Did you come for a pie? Mrs. Hammer told me you had a slice of my lemon meringue at the church potluck last week."

"No, no. Nothing like that," says Mrs. Murphy. "...and please, call me Ethel."

"Ethel, it is," Dottie beams. She takes off her apron and tosses it in the kitchen. "Have a seat."

"Thank you. I wonder, Mrs. Myles. I mean, Dottie..." Mrs. Murphy removes her gloves and hat. She places them on the coffee table in front of her. "Could the girls excuse us for a moment? I need to talk to you."

"Oh, I don't see why not," says Dottie. "Savannah, take Jenny up to Josie's room. Play some records for her. The grownups need to talk."

"Okay, Mama. Come on Jenny," Savannah says grabbing the young girl's arm. "...and don't be *draggin'* your feet."

"SAVANNAH!"

"Sorry, mama!" Savannah whispers.

Savannah leads Jenny down the hall to Josie's room. She leaves the door ajar.

"Close the door, Savannah," Dottie says without looking around.

"Yes, mama!" Savannah says wearily.

"That girl!" Dottie chuckles. "So Ethel, did you have some questions about our children's school? The town? Our church? You come to the right place. I've been here all my life."

"I'll get right to the point, Dottie," says Mrs. Murphy. She sits on the couch. "It's about your son, Jacob, Jr. I believe you call him *L'il Daddy*?"

"L'il Daddy, Junior, Choo Choo. We call that boy some of everything."

"Choo Choo?" says Mrs. Murphy stunned. "The boy likes *trains*?"

"The boy likes *football*, Mrs. Murphy," Dottie responds a little offended. "Charlie '*Choo Choo*' Brackins was a Negro quarterback a few years ago. My boy adores him."

"Okay! Well!" Mrs. Murphy says sitting up. "Rumors about uh, Choo Choo and a certain student have been swirling around the high school."

"*Swirling around the high school?*" Dottie says. "If my son is seeing a young lady, I don't see how that's anybody's business but ours. Who *is* this girl?"

"Well, I don't want to startle you…" Mrs. Murphy begins.

"What is it, Ethel," Dottie says getting anxious.

"All I know is…"

"*…is what?*"

"Wellll…"

"*Ethel, please!*"

"She's *white!*"

"*White?*" says Dottie shocked. "Who is she? Who told you this?"

"I don't know her name," she lies. "Dottie, I have a son, too. I don't want to see anything happen to Junior, uh Choo Choo, whatever! As a mother, I'd hate to think what folks around here might say. Or some folks might even do. If you get my drift."

"Mrs. Murphy, uh Ethel," Dottie says wringing her hands. "Are you sure about this?"

"Oh, I'm sure," Mrs. Murphy responds. "My little Jenny saw them in the old abandoned library with her own two eyes."

"Really?" Dottie says a little skeptical. '*Now what was **she** doing up there?*' Dottie thinks to herself.

"Oh, yes. My Jenny has been following them up to the library for the last two weeks."

"*Followed them for the last two weeks?*" Dottie says to herself. "*This little… they've only been here a month!*"

"Well! I thank you, Mrs. Murphy," Dottie responds calling on all the resources necessary to control her anger with the scheming woman. "I didn't mean to keep you so long. I'm sure you have other things on your schedule today."

"Oh, it's no bother," she says getting up from the couch. "We do have to look out for our own."

Ethel looks up as if she just remembered something.

"Oh! … By the way! What do you think of my Jenny?"

"*Your Jenny!*" Dottie says about to blow her stack.

"Well," Ethel says. "I was thinking, you know with your boy coming back to his own people…"

"*His own people?*"

"The junior prom's coming up."

"AND?"

"You know my Jenny was pretty popular at her old high school…"

"Is that right?" Dottie responds almost laughing.

"What with your boy not having a date and my Jenny… well, I'd hate to see a prize like her get away!"

"Who says he won't have a date?"

"Well, I figured since I helped you out…"

"You'd help yourself to my son?" Dottie says looking the old fraud in the eyes. "How do I know you don't want him for yourself, *Mrs. Murphy?*"

"EXCUSE ME???"

"Helping my boy. My God. I guess your altruism only goes so far."

"My what?" Ethel Murphy says flustered.

"Look it up!" says Dottie grabbing the old biddy's hat and gloves. She shoves them in her hands and points toward the door.

"Now, Dottie wait a minute. I didn't mean…"

"It's MRS. MYLES," Dottie says looking off toward the hallway. "SAVANNAH! JENNY! Jenny, honey your mother's ready to leave."

The girls come down the hall as the two adversaries stare one another down poised for battle. Savannah can tell something's wrong. She knows her mother. Poor Jenny doesn't have a clue.

"Go on out to the car, Jenny," Mrs. Murphy says adjusting her hat and pulling on her gloves.

"Did it work, Mama?" Jenny asks excitedly. "Am I going to the prom?"

"THE CAR, JENNY! NOW!"

"Yes, Mama," Jenny says sulking out the door.

"Good day, Mrs. Myles," Ethel says glaring at Dottie. She wipes the back of her dress and turns up her nose at what she apparently considers meager furnishings. "…and good luck with your pies," she says disparagingly.

"Good day, Mrs. Murphy," Dottie responds. "…and good luck finding your daughter a date for the prom!"

"Well, I never!" Mrs. Murphy says storming out of the house.

"You obviously did once!" Dottie snaps following Mrs. Murphy to the door. "NOT MY FAULT YOU GOT A KOMODO DRAGON FOR YOUR SORRY EFFORTS!"

Dottie slams the door just missing Ethel Murphy's rear end.

"MAMA!" Savannah screams shocked by her mother's remarks.

"Savannah!" Dottie says caught by surprise. "Oh Lord, I forgot you were here. Just go to your room, baby. I'll call you when I need you."

"Okay, mama," she replies scampering off. "Wait'll Frankie hears this!"

"*My son and a white girl!*" Dottie says to herself almost breathless. "*Why would she make up something like that?*"

Dottie walks back to the kitchen and tries to resume her baking. She takes a box of wax paper and slams it on the kitchen table. With one hand on her heart and the other waving at some imaginary gnat, Dottie catches her breath and glances upwards. She speaks.

"Forgive me, Lord," Dottie says. "Some people just make it so hard..."

Dottie grabs her apron from the table. While tying it, she recalls finding a pendant in her son's jacket two weeks ago while doing the laundry. She put it in his dresser drawer and forgot about it. She runs down the hall to his room and snatches his dresser drawer open. The pendant is right where she left it. Her hands shaking uncontrollably, Dottie picks up the trinket. It's a photograph locket – the kind that holds two pictures. Dreading the worst, she opens it. Her son's junior high graduation picture is in the left half. On the right is a picture of...

"*Molly Brand!*" Dottie gasps. "*Oh my Lord! Molly Brand!*" She drops in a nearby chair and screams for her husband.

"JACOB!"

Dottie looks at her son sitting in the middle row of old 'Goldie'. He's talking to his dad attempting to be vague about his dream. She heaves a heavy sigh.

'*L'il Daddy, you just don't know how I worry about you.*'

"I'm confused, Daddy," L'il Daddy replies feigning ignorance. He's not about to share his dream with the family. "What did I do?"

"Ha, ha!" laughs Jacob. "Here's the gas station. Hey, there's a diner, too. I could use something to eat. That garage better be open. Wake up the babies, son."

"Frankie! Savannah!" shouts L'il Daddy. "Wake up, babies. We're here!"

"I'm not a baby!" Frankie protests. He playfully pushes his big brother/idol.

"Sure you are," chuckles L'il Daddy trading pushes with his younger brother.

Baby Terry jumps in the fracas and trades shoves with his brothers.

"Enough, you too," says Jacob reprimanding his oldest sons. "You're being a bad influence on my favorite."

"WHAT?" says Frankie.

"He's playing with you, baby," says Dottie. "You know your Daddy."

"Yeah, yeah. I know," says Frankie relieved. "Hey, we're here!"

Jocelyn Dorothy Myles—The Experiment

JACOB PULLS UP to the first pump at the Mason Family Diner and Garage. He and L'il Daddy are the first to exit the car. L'il Daddy raises the hood of the family wagon. The garage mechanic, twenty-five-year-old John Mason runs out to the car. The name on his uniform reads *'Jack, Jr.'*. Jack holds open both doors on the passengers' side. He extends a hand to help an appreciative and exhausted Dottie exit the car. She thanks him and walks over to the building, a restaurant with the flashing sign – *Dora's Diner*.

Jack watches Josie as she slides over to the passenger side to exit the middle row of the vehicle. He reaches out to help her as he did with her mother. Jack greets her with a smiling *'Good morning, Ma'am'* only to have Josie give him a look that would sour even buttermilk. With Baby Terry in her arms, she ignores the young man's offer of assistance and steps out of the car on her own. She gently drops her little brother to the ground and walks him over to the steps of the diner. Dottie shakes her head at her daughter's insolence. So does Jacob, but his daughter pretends not to notice.

Frankie jumps out of the car.

'EEEOWWW!' He shouts terrifying the poor mechanic. Frankie does a spin like R & B vocalist James Brown (one of his many idols) and does the *Camel Walk*, Mr. Brown's signature move, halfway to the diner. He starts to do a split until he sees a rather stern expression on his mother's face. He knows that look. He smiles and turns to see both his daddy and big brother folding their arms and shaking their heads disapprovingly and at the same time. He sheepishly joins his family at the door. Dottie pulls Frankie over to her side.

"We're going to Chicago baby, not Detroit."

Savannah climbs from the back to the middle row. She steps out of the car and surveys the crowd – as a queen does when stepping out of a limousine and looking over her subjects - determinedly and with a grim and serious look on her face. Jack offers to take her hand. Instead of taking Jack's hand, she raises her fist in mock defiance.

"Umgowah! Black Power! Right On!" the little jokester smiles. She laughs and runs over to join her siblings and mom standing on the worn out welcome mat in front of the Mason family diner. A startled Jack Mason does a double take. He looks back and forth at Jacob and L'il Daddy and then the rest of the family standing at the door of the diner.

"Quite a family you got there," the mechanic says turning to Jacob.

L'il Daddy does a slow turn toward the mechanic. He glares at the hapless man. Jacob, Sr., a little heated himself looks the young man square in the eye.

"Like you said. They're *mine*."

"You're right. You're right," says Jack collecting himself. "I'm sorry. Mr. uh…?"

"Myles. Jacob Myles."

"Yes, sir! Mr. *Myles*." Jack says emphasizing their name. "Looks like you traveled a few getting here. Ha, ha!" Jack slaps the old car and looks around at the family.

No laughs. No smiles. Jack's feeble attempt at humor draws an audience unamused. They should be. They hear the reference only every other day.

"Ahem!" Jack says clearing his throat. "Sounds like you need a fan belt, Mr. Myles. I was just about to open up shop. Mama Dora's got the griddle fired up. Best 'cakes in town. OJ and milk for the little ones. This way, gentlemen," he offers as he motions toward the service area. "Let's say we take a look at some fan belts."

"Sounds good," says Jacob quickly turning his annoyance with the young man into a smile. "Dottie, Honey," Jacob yells toward the entrance. "Get the family something to eat would you please? We'll be in directly. Hotcakes for me and L'il Daddy."

"Okay, baby," Dottie responds while gathering the family and opening the door to the diner. "Don't be long, now."

"You see, Mama," says Savannah pointing at her father and big brother heading toward the garage. "Daddy made the right move. We're not even in Chicago yet and already white people are calling him sir."

"To his face," says a surly Josie.

"That's enough out of you, both of you," Dottie demands. "Savannah, find us a couple of tables. Frankie, take Terry to the bathroom. JOCELYN! Come with me!"

Dottie grabs her insolent daughter's arm and moves her out of earshot of the younger children. She shows remarkable restraint considering her daughter just slighted the man whom she's loved since the third grade.

"Jocelyn Dorothy Myles! I will not have you disrespecting your father. Why can't you be more supportive? There's nothing Daddy wouldn't do for us. You know that."

"But, Mama!" Josie begs.

"Quiet, young lady!" Dottie warns her. "This move is the right thing, for all of us. *All* of us, Jocelyn Myles. *Especially you!*"

"*Especially Me?*" Josie asks indignantly. "I didn't ask to come here. Mack and me…"

"Mack and I," Dottie corrects her.

"Mama. We was, I mean **we were** going to get married. Daddy had no right…"

"I said enough, Josie!" Dottie says to her daughter looking around at the suddenly attentive people in the diner. "Your **father** is the head of this family," she whispers. "Not Mack Hodges! Do you understand?"

Silence.

Dottie, getting more incensed with her daughter's impertinence looks directly into her face.

"DO…YOU…UNDERSTAND?"

"Yes, mama," she answers lowering her head. "I'm sorry."

Dottie could never stay mad at her firstborn very long. She hugs her. She even chuckles.

"Baby, you'll like Chicago," Dottie says trying to cheer up her distraught daughter. Aunt Lucy and Uncle Fredrick found us a nice place to stay. Big enough for all of us. You'll all have your own room, just like back at the ranch. Fredrick's gonna help your father find work and Lucy already got *you* a job at the restaurant downtown where *she* used to work. Honey, just give it a chance. For Daddy, OK. Can I have a smile, baby?"

Josie is silent. Dottie folds her arms anticipating her daughter's positive response.

"I have to use the bathroom," Josie says turning away from her mother. She walks past Dora Mason, short order cook, and owner of *Dora's Diner*. Up to now, Dora has been pretending not to notice mother and daughter arguing. She gives Dottie a shake of the head – the shake that says...

'I know what you're going through, honey. I have children of my own'.

She pours her a cup of coffee.

"On the house, sister," says a smiling Dora Mason.

Dottie nods her head thanks. She puts the cup to her lips and sighs. She shakes her head and returns a smile of her own. Every mother in the sisterhood knows that smile – it says...

'Ain't it the truth, honey! Ain't it the truth!'

"Wait for me, Josie," yells Savannah jumping out of the booth.

"Leave her be, honey," Dottie says grabbing her hand. "Your sister needs some time alone."

Passing by the ladies' room, Josie instead sits on the other side of the diner. She notices a young couple, about her age, feeding their young toddler. The baby girl points and smiles at a tearful Josie. Josie waves her pinkie at her. The toddler's mother looks up. Josie is startled. Her face is strangely familiar. It should be - she resembles Josie! The young man now holding the toddler takes on the features of Josie's beau back home, Mack Hodges. Josie gasps and quickly turns away. She then pulls out a picture of her and Mack from her purse. Sitting in Mack's car, a pink Cadillac with a convertible top, the two appear made for each other. A tear streams down the pretty teenager's face and falls onto the marble tabletop as Josie observes the clock on the diner wall.

Only ten more minutes before the bell. The calendar on the wall of classroom 309 reflects the day's date, Friday, May 12th, 1961. Some of the students are reading. A few are writing. Most of the boys, however, are ogling one of the new students – Jocelyn Dorothy Myles. Josie Myles, a little younger and a lot sassier knows she has an audience. Her knee-high pleated skirt shows off her legs – a little too much for her father's taste but his wife assured him 'that all girls these days dress like this'. She straightens her tight-knit top while touching up her makeup.

Evan Platt, Jr., a local boy and admirer of Josie's *fine brown frame* since before the city's two high schools integrated, shows a little more interest in the snugness of Josie's blouse than he should. He's had an unnatural craving for the young beauty for years. If he ever told his daddy, the old Klansman would kill him – and then *himself.* Josie is one of only five black seniors in a class of thirty. They all sit in the back. Their teacher, Miss Haynes wishes there were none. She makes this clear to them on a daily basis.

Two young white girls enter the classroom. Miss Haynes, obviously expecting them, perks up.

"Class! Class. Pay attention. We only have a few minutes," Miss Haynes says looking at the clock. "Our two candidates for prom queen, Miss Clarissa Perkins, and Miss Viola White are here to solicit your votes."

Josie, Miss Haynes' favorite scapegoat, rolls her eyes in disgust.

"Myles, my Lord, sit up!" Haynes yells rebuking the teen. "Heavens, one would think you were raised in a barn the way you slouch." She smiles motioning to the girls to begin.

"Miss Perkins…"

Josie mocks her teacher. *"Miss Frog Face!"*

"**Miss** Myles! …and I use the term loosely," Miss Haynes says berating her. "Those who *qualify* are trying to make their statements."

Some of the white children laugh. A few of them, like good-natured Bobby Matthews, resent their teacher's constant efforts to denigrate their new classmates. He and Josie's brother Jacob, Jr. (aka L'il Daddy) have been friends for years and he doesn't care who knows. He does, however, keep his feelings for Brittany 'Cookie' Abernathy, Josie's best friend, and his secret girlfriend, under wraps. Although Bobby's father has mellowed considerably over the years, Bobby's not completely convinced that his father would be open to his son exchanging vows with a girl from the *'other side of town'.* Cookie and the other black teens, repulsed by their teacher's loathing for *'all things colored'*, frown and shake their heads at one another. Their parents' complaints to the Principal and the School Board have fallen on deaf ears. The end of the school year and the so-called experiment in integration can't come soon enough for Josie and her friends.

Satisfied that she's thoroughly rebuked her *'special'* students, Miss Haynes re-directs her attention to the candidates.

"Now, Miss Perkins. If you please."

Clarissa nods her head approvingly of the teacher and begins to speak. She opens her notebook to read her *'heartfelt'* handwritten speech; the same one her sister read last year.

"Hello, everyone. My name is Francis, uh *Clarissa* Perkins and I'm here to solicit your vote for Beauregard James Whitehall Senior High School Prom Queen of 1961. Why should I be your Prom Queen…"

While Clarissa speaks, Josie mockingly mouths her speech word for word. She then looks at Cookie, her confidante and the only other black female in the class. They both shake their heads sickened by Miss Haynes, the school's racist policy of omitting its Negro students from extracurricular activities, and Clarissa Perkins who in their opinion couldn't win a dog show – even if she was the only hound in the running.

"Hmmph!" yells Josie aloud. "We'd all qualify if we didn't live in the 1800's!"

"You ain't never lied," Cookie whispers.

Miss Haynes rises from her seat. She comes from behind her desk reddened by Josie's last statement. Josie and Cookie sit at attention. Their expressions betray their thoughts.

"Who did she hear?" They wonder.

"MYLES! PRINCIPAL DAVIS' OFFICE. NOW!"

Some of the white students nod their heads in approval. Miss Haynes, despite her efforts, has never, ever told a funny joke in her thirty-year tenure at Whitehall. Many of the students; however, find her comments toward Josie – any comment – hilarious. A few of them slap their knees laughing.

'That colored girl complains way too much for a Negro who should be happy just to be in a school as good as Whitehall', whispers Chrissy Caldwell across the aisle to her boyfriend Kyle Griffin. He nods yes - although he and some of the other boys always felt the beauty quotient of good ol' Whitehall escalated a few notches the instant Josie and Cookie walked into the building.

"You're right, Chrissy" the young sycophant agrees. "She should be happy just to be here." If they only knew how often Josie fought with her father Jacob over her *transferring to that institution of Lily Whiteness'* in the first place. Josie's brother, Jacob, Jr. however (only two

CARLOS E. TIBBS

floors down) was more than happy to attend the school. He has his reasons.

Knowing she would be in hot water when her father finds out she's in trouble again, Josie reluctantly makes her way to the back of the room to leave. She grabs her jacket from the closet when Evan Platt, Jr., always boorish and offensive, makes a crude comment toward her gender. It's the one vulgarity that young women have abhorred since time began. The laughter stops. Even the most racist of students – particularly the girls who have been on the receiving end of that remark - finds the young degenerate's comment intolerable.

Josie looks at the student who called her the obscenity. She walks over to him and stares him right in the face. She speaks in a voice so serene and peaceful, one would never know she was about to retaliate with a comeback that would turn young Platt's world upside down.

"I don't know what your mother taught you she was but my mother raised a young woman!"

Evan Platt's face turns white – almost as white as the sheet and hood his father wears to cut the grass on Sunday. The entire class reacts favorably to Josie's remark. The black teens jump out of their seats jubilantly whooping and hollering - another victory for the browbeaten of the Haynes plantation. Even some of the white teens, led by Bobby Matthews slap each other five endorsing Josie's stinging comeback. A few of the girls, hiding their smiles behind their notebooks, nod approvingly in Josie's direction. Jocelyn Dorothy Myles, victorious and feeling redeemed, saunters back to her friend Cookie Abernathy's seat collecting hand slaps and *'you tell 'em girl'* from many of the white students along the way.

Miss Haynes; however, never one to give a Negro an even break retreats to her desk. She reaches into the back of her bottom drawer and pulls out a strap. The merriment in Room 309 comes to a screeching halt. She walks slowly in Josie's direction pounding the rubbery punisher in her palm in syncopation with each step. The mood in the classroom becomes somber. Clarissa Perkins, the Prom Queen candidate nods her head with a smirk in Josie's direction.

A few of the white students intercede on Josie's behalf. Bobby Matthews, ever mindful of his friendship with Josie's brother, jumps out of his seat to defend his friend's sister.

"Miss Haynes, Josie had a right. Evan Platt had no business…"

"Quiet!" she commands never taking her eyes off her target. She stops at Josie's desk and speaks to the frightened teen.

"Well?"

Josie looks around the room. Most of the teens that supported her turn and look the other way. They feel for her but are afraid to say anything. Miss Haynes has been known to write up any student, black or white, who rubbed her the wrong way. Josie gets up to leave out the back door of the classroom. Always one to kick a person when they're down, Clarissa Perkins, ever smug and never discerning, tosses a good-bye barb at Josie just as she turns the doorknob to leave.

"Prom queen? You? Humph! I would think you would be happy you wouldn't have to make the effort!"

"…like anyone would vote for you. Sit down, *Francis*!" shouts Bobby reminding her of her earlier *faux pas*.

The students laugh - all but Josie. She has her own way of handling racists.

"Thanks, Bobby. I got this. Oh, it's no effort, honey," Josie responds staring down the wannabe prom queen. "None at all."

Josie drops her jacket at her desk. She turns and walks toward Clarissa. Her gait is slow and seductive. The room is suddenly quiet. Josie runs a finger through her hair, shakes her head, stops to look back at her admirers, and then looks over her shoulder at Clarissa. She narrows her eyes and purses her lips revealing just the slightest bit of tongue. Clarissa gulps and shakes in fear as Josie slowly approaches the frightened girl. Chrissy Caldwell, upset with boyfriend Kyle Griffin for ogling the newly crowned runway model, smacks his hand as Josie nears his desk. Without looking his way, Josie places her forefinger under the boy's chin to close his gaping mouth. Still fearful and shaking, Clarissa turns and drops her head. She turns to the second candidate, Viola White mouthing the girl's name and looking for help. Viola steps aside. She wants no part of Clarissa's mess.

Josie stops just inches of the terrified teenager.

"You were saying?"

Clarissa bolts from the room dropping her speech on the floor in her wake. Viola puts her hand to her mouth to stifle her grin. She finds Clarissa's response hilarious. Maybe she'll use it in her campaign. Josie's friend Cookie Abernathy nods her approval to her friend. She slaps one of the black student's hands. Bobby Matthews smiles to himself but looks around to make sure Miss Haynes doesn't see him. He does, however, manage to steal a glance from his girl, Cookie who quickly winks back.

"MYLES!" shouts Miss Haynes.

"Yeah, right. Principal Davis' office," she smirks watching Clarissa in the hallway cowering in fear.

"On my way, Miss Haynes," Josie says grabbing her books and jacket. She looks back and speaks to Miss Haynes who is still boiling with rage.

"Same time, tomorrow?"

Four o'clock. Josie leaves the vestibule outside the principal's office. Seems he's off on a mission. Probably to get the state to release him from the experiment, she thinks.

'I hope it works', she says to herself. She'll have to deal with him tomorrow. She grabs her books and heads for the front door. Since all of her friends are gone already, Josie is making the walk home alone. She turns a corner at the end of the block before stopping at *Matthews' Groceries*. Taking a moment to look inside, she sees Bobby Matthews, her classmate, and friend, wearing an apron and stacking canned peaches. She smiles at him. Her way of saying thanks. He smiles back after he sees his father is busy elsewhere. She understands perfectly. You can't let everyone know where you stand in the South. Negroes and even whites have been lynched for less. Continuing home to the ranch, Josie decides to take a shortcut behind the store.

"AAGGHHH!"

Josie screams in agony. She's suddenly thrown to the ground. Blood streams from her leg. A huge brogaed foot holds her down.

"*My mama? My mama!!*" growls a familiar voice. Evan Platt, Jr., drunk and beside himself with rage, stares down at a shaken and frightened Josie Myles. Unbeknownst to Josie, she struck the boy's Achilles heel. Platt's mother died in childbirth. His father berates him on a regular basis and has been known to publicly blame him for the death of his wife. Platt spits a wad of tobacco at Josie just barely missing her torn skirt.

"You called my mama a…"

Afraid but refusing to show it, Josie screams at her tormenter.

"I called her the same thing you called me, Evan Platt!"

Platt backs away slightly from the terrified girl. He removes his belt.

"Evan, no," Josie begs rubbing her leg. "What are you going to do?"

"First, I'm gonna whup you like you stole something!" Evan retorts drooling spittle on Josie's pleated skirt. "Then, I'm gonna do something for that leg!"

Evan comes closer. Josie screams kicking at the ever approaching monster. Her kicks are useless against the would-be rapist. He raises his belt and swings it over his head. Josie screams. The poor girl closes her eyes afraid to imagine the worse.

Josie, fearful and dreading the sting of Platt's belt hears instead a different kind of noise – a thud. She slowly opens her eyes. She spies Evan Platt falling to the ground. A can of peaches with a huge dent the size of the bully's head rolls on the ground stopping just short of Josie's scattered books. Platt, groggy from the missile delivered by Josie's friend, Bobby Matthews, tries to stand. He staggers almost tripping over his own gigantic feet. He mumbles something about peaches and 'coloreds' before pulling a switchblade out of his sweat-stained overalls. He heads straight for Bobby.

Just then, Bobby's father exits the back of the store looking for his son. Running in the direction of the hubbub, he spies a young man running from behind and past him towards Platt. Appearing out of no-where it seems, the young man pushes Bobby aside and knocks Josie's assailant to the ground. Platt gets up and the two men fight – or at least Josie's protector does. He delivers a left hook to the intolerant racist's already bleeding jaw. A right hook immediately follows sending two of Platt's teeth flying through the air. By now, Platt is spitting blood, swinging at the air and hitting no one. His opponent knees Platt in the groin sending him spiraling to the ground. Bobby's father steps in and pulls the man off the crumpled mess that once resembled Evan Platt, Jr. now laying on the ground and begging for mercy. Bobby snatches off his apron and gives it to Josie, still laying on the ground and bleeding.

Platt stumbles to his feet mumbling obscenities at the crowd that's now gathered to see the town bully get his. He screams at Josie and her rescuers.

"The hell you looking at? I'm gonna tell my daddy! We'll be back! We'll gitcha! We'll git alla y'all!"

"You need to get your dumb ass home, Platt," Mr. Matthews warns him. "I don't care who your daddy is! Now! Before I call the sheriff. Bobby, go inside and get this girl a bandage."

"I'm okay, Mr. Matthews. Please! Don't tell my father! Please! Please!" Josie pleads with the grocer. She knows Jacob would kill the boy – or worse, get killed in the process.

"I just wanna go home."

"I'll take you home," the young man offers. He points down the alley toward his car, a bright shiny pink Cadillac.

Josie looks into her hero's eyes.

"Who - who are you?" she asks breathlessly. "What's your…?"

"Michael. Michael Hodges. Most folks call me Mack," he says helping Josie to her feet.

"Oh! Well, thank you! Thank you very much! My name is…"

"Josie! I know. Josie Myles."

"Do you know him, Daddy," Bobby asks his father.

Mr. Matthews answers his son but Josie's too caught up in her white knight's eyes to hear the grocer's response. She doesn't even notice the little girl from the crowd running behind her and handing her the books Platt knocked out of her hands when she fell.

Mack opens the door to his car. He gently sweeps a now very smitten Josie off her feet – literally - and places her safely inside his caddy, the car young Hodges boastfully refers to as the 'sweetest car in the Negro community'. Could have been a wheelbarrow for all Josie cared. With her hero, Michael 'Mack' Hodges by her side, the small town rancher's daughter felt like an African princess. Josie blinks. Mack moves in to kiss her. Josie opens her mouth slightly to return the proposal. Dottie puts her hands in the T-formation between them.

"Time out, Josie! Josie?"

"Josie!" shouts her mother from the other side of the diner. "Time to order, honey. Come on!"

"Coming, Mama!" Josie replies awakening from her dream.

Just three more weeks, Mack," she says to herself. "Just three more weeks."

Jacob Myles, Sr.—Crisis of Faith, Part 1

"DORA? WE'RE READY to order."

Dora walks over and refills Dottie's cup. She grabs a pen from behind her ear ready to take everyone's order. Baby Terry points out the window. He sees his father, big brother, and Jack Mason the mechanic pushing the station wagon towards the garage. Jacob steers the car from the driver's side while pushing it. Jack and L'il Daddy both push from the rear. They yell for Jacob to jump in and apply the emergency brake. He's way ahead of them. He jumps in and hits the brake suddenly, propelling both Jack and L'il Daddy to slide on the oily garage floor and lose their footing. Jacob smiles but he keeps his little joke to himself.

"Take care of this for me, L'il Daddy," he says helping the mechanic and his son onto their feet. He hands him the keys. "I'll be right back."

"No problem, Daddy," he replies getting up and giving the jokester the eye. "See you in the diner."

Jacob pats his son on the back. He then walks around to the back of the car to retrieve his jacket from the trunk. Seeming somewhat distracted, Jacob walks toward the road leading to the Interstate leaving Jack and L'il Daddy inside the garage. Jack proudly shows L'il Daddy his assortment of tires, oil, batteries, and his new tool cabinet.

"Sweet!" L'il Daddy responds. "Quite a setup you got here!"

"Somethin', ain't it?" says Jack. "Hey, L'il Daddy. L'il Daddy, right? Did you hear the one about the mechanic and the stewardess from New York City?" Jack says elbowing the boy.

"Uhhh, no, I haven't," says L'il Daddy laughing before Jack even finishes. He then checks to make sure his father is out of earshot. "What happened?"

Jacob walks behind an old silo out of sight of his son and his new friend. After he's sure he's completely hidden from view and his wife is busy with the children, Jacob reaches into his jacket pocket for a cigarette. He lights it, takes a draw and looks to the heavens. He half expects the smoke to turn into crystals and fall at his feet.

"Bit of a nip in the air this close to April," he thinks to himself. None of the Myles family is used to cold weather.

"This weather is gonna take some getting used to," he says to himself.

Jacob then peeks around the old structure watching for his family. He sees L'il Daddy and Jack in the garage slapping each other on the back and laughing. His beloved Dottie and the rest of his brood are inside and out of the cold. Dottie reads a roadmap while Josie gives Dora a half smile feigning interest in her attempt at banter. A light snow starts to fall as Jacob marvels at the wonder. Hopskip was always too warm for snow; at least in his forty years. Jacob turns his head again to the dark blue sky now dotted with snowflakes.

"Lord," Jacob says heaving a sigh. "Please tell me I'm doing the right thing."

His view of the heavens is suddenly interrupted by a flock of mallards heading south.

CRACK!

"Got him! Go get him, boy," shouts the man excitedly to the gray-haired terrier. "Let's see if all those stories I've heard about *'Jacob Myles, Dog Trainer Extraordinaire'* are true."

The man, dressed in his finest duck hunting regalia elbows Jacob and smiles.

"Oh, they're true, Mr. Matthews," Jacob smiles back. "You won't find no hunting dogs in Georgia trained better than mine. That is of course, unless you count my daddy's. Now there's a man who knew his dogs."

"Now I asked you before to call me Bob, Jake. Our boys get along. I don't see why we can't, too," he says extending his hand in friendship.

'Will wonders never cease," Jacob thinks to himself. *'A white man insisting I call him by his first name. I heard he found God, but this. Hmm. I bet he voted for Kennedy, too. I heard there were a few down here who did but I won't push it.'*

"Okay. Bob it is," Jacob replies tucking his Winchester under his left arm and shaking his new friend's hand with his right. "Scout should be back by now," muses Jacob referring to the terrier Matthews sent to fetch the felled mallard.

"Owwoooo!"

"What was that?" Bob inquires looking around. "Scout?"

"Sounds like him," Jacob responds.

"He went this way," says Bob heading north through the under-brush. "We better check it out."

"They're usually back by now," Jacob replies referring to his retriev-ers. "What do you bet he's got *two* ducks in his mouth?"

"My store," replies Bob confidently. "And if he's *got* two ducks, Bobby Jr. will work for you for free!"

"Deal, Mr. Matt.., uh Bob!" Jacob laughs. "You got a deal."

The two men laugh among themselves heading toward the sound of Scout's wailing. The terrier howls until he sees his owner trampling through the brush. He runs around in circles until his master calls.

"Scout, get over here. What's going... Oh my Lord," Bob says solemnly.

"Bob, what's wrong?" Jacob asks.

"Look here. A fawn. Shot dead. Can't be more than a year old. I know who did it. Nobody uses a crossbow in these parts but them damned Platts. Shooting for sport. And just left it here. No respect for life, Jake," shouts Matthews. "None!"

"Terrible," says Jacob shaking his head. "Beautiful animal like that, left out in the open to die. A sin is what it is. A sin against God."

"It truly is. We have to bury it. I have some shovels in my truck," says Matthews tying his dog to a tree. "Do you mind?"

"No, go ahead," Jacob answers kneeling and rubbing Scout's head. "I'll wait here."

"Jacob, I've been meaning to ask you. How's your daughter?"

"My daughter?" says Jacob suddenly rising. "What are you talking about?"

"Your oldest girl. Josie, right?"

"Matthews, why are you asking about my daughter?" says Jacob suddenly turning red.

"Now, now Jake. Take it easy. I was there when she was attacked. She's okay, isn't she?"

"Attacked!" Jacob screams incredulously. "My baby was attacked?!? What are you talking about?"

"My Lord. You don't know. I'm sorry," Bob says. "She didn't want to call the sheriff. That Hodges boy saved her. And *my* boy, Bobby. Jake, I thought you knew. I'm so sorry."

Jacob drops his rifle.

"I am SERIOUSLY, SERIOUSLY about to lose my religion. You wanna tell me what happened, Bob? You wanna tell me what happened to my baby? NOW!"

"Of course, Jake. Of course. Here, sit down."

The two men sit on a log felled by a bolt of lightning from years past. The look on Jacob's face says it all. He feels as if he was struck by that same bolt. He listens helplessly as his new friend shares some harsh realities. His baby girl - his and Dottie's first child - was attacked by a vicious bully. He thinks no one knows it, but anyone watching the interaction over the years between Father Jacob and daughter Jocelyn knows that Jacob Franklin Myles would give his right hand and every-thing he owns to ensure his little Jo-Jo's safety. *Jo-Jo.* He had almost forgotten. That was his nickname for his baby and he allowed no one else to call her that. This was the baby girl to whom he'd read bedtime stories after a long and tiring day in the fields – sometimes three stories in one night. She said no one did the Big Bad Wolf like Daddy. The same child he spent hours teaching to ride a horse – running alongside her to make sure she didn't fall. Precious little Jocelyn Dorothy Myles - the living proof of his wife's love – a victim of rape.

"He pushed her to the ground, Jake, that's all," says Matthews as-suring his friend that no other harm befell his daughter. "That's when my son and that Hodges boy intervened."

"But why…?" says Jake jumping to his feet and pacing back and forth. "Why didn't my baby…"

"Your daughter didn't wanna tell you, Jake," says Matthews antici-pating his distraught friend's inquiry. "She asked me not to. She was afraid of what might happen – to both of you. To your family. We've come a long way in Hopskip but we still got a ways to go. With God's help, well… I'm sorry, Jake. I really thought you knew."

Jake is uncontrollable. He walks around punching the air. He pulls off his jacket and throws it across the clearing into the brush. Scout tries to run toward Jacob but thinks better of it. He crouches in the fetal position and buries his nose in the leaves.

"Jake, sit down. I know it's difficult but try and be calm. The worse is over. Your daughter's strong. She'll pull through. I know it. You stay here while I get the shovels," Matthews says rising to his feet. He looks back at the fawn killed by Evan Platt. "We need to bury this poor animal."

Matthews straightens his jacket and looks off in the direction of the jeep left back near the road.

"I'll be right back, Jake," he says looking over his shoulder. "You try and stay calm."

Jacob is anything but calm. He is understandably beside himself. He jumps up and kicks an imaginary Evan Platt, Jr. Jacob looks to the heavens and asks for guidance.

"Lord, help me. I can't take this," Jacob screams wiping away a tear. "Help *him* if I ever see him again. Why my baby? Why?"

Scout jumps up from his hiding ground. He hears a noise. Jacob hears it, too. He grabs his binoculars from his jacket on the ground and peers in the direction of muffled shouting a few hundred yards away. Off in the distance is none other than Evan Platt, Jr. Apparently, one deer was not enough.

'...*must be out looking for more baby animals to kill,*' thinks Jacob to himself. "...*or someone else's daughter to...*'

Jacob tries not to think about it but the image of his baby girl cowering under a monster like Evan Platt, Jr. is more than he can bear. He takes another look at the thug who attacked his daughter. The boy's intoxicated. The drunken bully has his crossbow in one hand and a bottle of his daddy's moonshine in the other. He stumbles around aiming at nothing. He almost steps on a raccoon which runs back towards Jacob and Scout. Muttering something about high school football and his father, Platt throws his crossbow to the ground and takes to a nearby stump to have another drink.

Jacob steps back dodging the raccoon running past him. He almost falls over Matthews' dog, Scout. He can't believe his eyes - or his luck. Ready to be picked off like the piece of garbage he is, Evan Platt, Jr. the thug who tormented Jacob Myles' precious Jo-Jo, and turned his tranquil world into a living hell, sits only a rifle shot from glory. Jacob looks at his rifle lying on the ground; a Winchester .405 - a gift handed down from his father two years before he died. Papa Myles added the scope to help Jacob with his accuracy. Not that he needed it. The two men bonded on many a father and son outing discussing guns, life, and women and how precious they all are. Papa Myles taught his son that guns (and women, he would jest) are incredibly powerful. The old deacon taught him that rifles (like women) were to be handled with care and respect. Losing reverence for either of them, he would say is like losing respect for yourself.

'*It's a long road trying to get that respect back so don't ever risk it,*' Papa Myles would say. Jacob never forgot his daddy's words.

Jacob must have shot over a hundred ducks in the years since; felled nearly fifty deer and an elk on his son's fifteenth birthday with that very same rifle. Despite his Daddy's doctrine, today Jacob Franklin Myles can fathom only one purpose for Papa Myles' old Winchester – separating Evan Platt, Jr. from his heart.

"Why not?" Jacob rationalizes. *"The monster apparently has no use for it. Attacking my baby. My Jo-Jo."* Try as he might, he can't get it out of his head.

Jacob picks up his father's rifle. There's still one round left. More than enough for what he has to do, he tells himself. He trains his gun on the beast, sitting with his back to Jacob and the rest of the God-fearing world guzzling away his useless life. Jacob cocks the twenty-year-old rifle. Wiping the sweat from his brow, he takes aim. The thug who attacked his daughter turns the bottom of his bottle to the sky. Weighing the consequences of his actions, Jacob trembles. The young deacon is about to perform an act from which he knows he can never return. Never has any two-legged animal framed the crosshairs of his rifle's scope.

'*Never has any two-legged animal been more deserving,*' Jacob tells himself rationalizing his actions.

Jacob changes his mind and drops his rifle to his side. Just as quickly he raises it, taking aim at the unsuspecting Evan Platt, Jr. Peering through the crosshairs at the end of the scope, Jacob spies Platt's left ear in the center of it. His forefinger massages the trigger of the old Winchester. He blinks - once, then twice. His decision is made.

CRACK!

Jacob Myles, Sr.—Crisis of Faith, Part 2

"SO I TELL her, I said," laughs Jack Mason, the garage mechanic. *"'Lady, I only sell fan belts. You're gonna have to find chastity belts somewhere else!'"*

Jack and L'il Daddy fall onto each other laughing.

"Jack, that's hilarious," says L'il Daddy crying. "How do you know so many jokes?"

"Like the man said," says the mechanic shaking his head and doing his best Jimmy Durante impression. "I got a million of 'em. Hey, L'il Daddy how do you tell a fan belt from a chastity belt?"

"L'il Daddy," Frankie questions appearing out of nowhere and patting his big brother's shoulder. "What's a chastity belt?"

"WHAT?" L'il Daddy yells a little startled. "Where'd you come from?"

"Yes, son," says Dottie walking toward the two jokesters. "Why don't you tell him?"

"Oh, uh. Mama! Hi," says L'il Daddy flustered. "Jack and I was just…"

"Don't even try it," Dottie replies. "You two go on inside. Breakfast is ready. Where's your father."

"Over here, baby," says Jacob walking toward his wife. "Junior, take Frankie inside."

"Yes, Daddy. C'mon boy. You know you got me in trouble," L'il Daddy says to his bewildered sibling.

"Jack," says Jacob turning his attention to the mechanic. "How long before…"

"It'll be 'bout an hour - maybe less," says the mechanic rushing over to Jacob. "You folks go on and have your breakfast. I should be done right about then."

"Thank you, son."

Jack runs back to the garage as Dottie folds her arms.

"Well this is a sight," says Dottie sniffing her husband's clothes. "My son's out here playing Redd Foxx and my husband's smoking those God-awful cigarettes he *threw away* five years ago."

"Sorry, Dottie, I…"

"No need to apologize, my love. Now, the last time I remember seeing one of those… What did you call them?"

"Coffin nails," Jacob replies stomping out his cigarette.

"Right," Dottie responds. "The last time I saw you with a coffin nail between those beautiful lips was right before the baby came. I'm not pregnant - not that I know of, so you must be nervous about something else. It's the move north, isn't it?"

"You know your man, don't you Mrs. Myles?"

"I should, Mr. Myles," Dottie says reaching out for the cigarettes. "I've known you almost as long as I've known me."

"Now that's a long time!" Jacob winks handing over the contraband.

"Excuse me?" Dottie says pinching her husband's stomach.

"Just kidding, baby!" Jacob replies taking her hand in his. He looks deep into her eyes. His smile dissolves as his countenance grows dim. He drops his head.

"Baby, I'm so ashamed."

"Jacob, no! Don't," Dottie says knowing where her beloved is headed. "It's done, baby. No one would blame you. You were enraged. You did what you felt was right at the time. You did what you felt in your heart."

"That's just it, Dottie. I call myself a Christian. I'm a Deacon. A man of God wouldn't have even picked up the gun. I should know better."

"Baby, stop! Yes. You are a man of God. But Jacob, you're a man first - a father. That little…*beast*," Dottie says looking for the appropriate term instead of the one she knows describes the Platt boy best. "He attacked our baby."

"Yes, and I wasn't there!"

"Baby, you can't be everywhere. Now stop it, please."

"Dottie," says Jacob speaking slowly to emphasize his point. "A man, a real man takes care of his own. I should have been there to protect her. That's *my* Jo-Jo. Not Hodges'. My baby could've been…"

"But she wasn't!" says Dottie with relief. "Thank God she wasn't."

"Of all the people in the world to come to her rescue, why did it have to be that damned, no-good…?"

"Jacob!"

"That *peacock* Mack Hodges!" shouts Jacob. "Anybody but him, Dottie. ANYBODY!"

"Honey, please!" Dottie says trying to control her husband's temper. One doesn't see it happen often but when Jacob Franklin Myles loses his temper, it's not a pretty sight. "Jacob, please. You don't want the children to hear you."

"She's in love with *him?*" Jacob yells turning a deaf ear to his wife's pleas. "And mad at *me?* I could lose my baby girl over that piece of trash!?"

His rant continues.

"Ever since our baby was conceived…" Jacob reminisces. "We had *dreams* for our daughter. *Dr.* Jocelyn Myles. *Attorney* Jocelyn Myles. *Poet, Author. Not* Mrs. Mack Hodges! *Mack Hodges?* Looks like I wasted my bullet on the wrong man!"

"Jacob Myles!" says Dottie shocked. "You didn't just say that."

Jacob turns to look at Dottie as if to say, '***YES I DID***'.

"Oh, Jacob!" Dottie says taken aback by her husband's response.

Jacob grabs his wife and hugs her. He apologizes.

"I'm sorry, baby," he says. "I lost it. I'm sorry. It's just that when my children are concerned…"

"It's okay, honey," replies Dottie kissing his cheek. "I understand. I'm pretty sure the Lord does, too!"

Jacob drops his head in shame. Dottie lifts it and kisses the other cheek. He smiles and winks at her. She's always had this way.

"You're amazing, you know that?"

"I've heard talk," she says with a smile.

"Oh, you have?" Jacob chuckles then stops abruptly. He heaves a sigh. He then indicates to Dottie with his right forefinger and thumb as people do when measuring something.

"Honey…"

"I know what you're going to say…"

"I was this close."

"I know, baby," Dottie says anticipating her husband's words. "But you didn't!"

"I almost took a man's life," Jacob confesses. "The man who…"

"But you didn't, Jacob," Dottie assures him. "The Lord saved you from a heinous act. You asked him for guidance and he gave it to you."

"Dottie, if I had spent one more day in Hopskip…"

"I know, honey. I know. Let's not talk about it. Come on. The children are waiting for us. Your eggs are getting cold. And you know how you are about your eggs."

"Right!" says Jacob taking his wife's hand and leading the way. He stops just as abruptly to ask her a question.

"Dottie?"

"Yes, baby?"

"You think *that* piece of trash will stop drinking now?" Jacob says with a wink.

"After the way you shot that bottle out of his hand," laughs Dottie. "I'd bet on it."

"Yeah, me too." Jacob laughs. "I bet he's still pulling glass out of his hair. Baby, you should have seen that boy run."

"I wish I was there," she laughs. Dottie then looks at Jacob. She notices that he's still troubled. Thirty some-odd years of loving the same man will do that. She kisses him and rubs his back.

"Baby, you gonna be alright?"

"Dorothy Rosetta Myles. Will you ever stop?"

"I know my man," she whispers in his ear. "What's wrong?"

Jacob sighs. He couldn't keep anything from this woman if he tried. And why would he? If ever anyone was in his corner…

"Dottie," confesses Jacob. "I've been farming, ranching, and training dogs my whole life. I don't know anything else. Where do I get the nerve thinking I can leave all that and come North? It's cold up here. The kids will have to change schools. I have to find work. My oldest still won't talk to me - if she can help it."

"Give her time," Dottie says hugging her man. "She'll come around…and we'll make it honey. We always do. You'll do fine. *Shoot, I got mo' faith in my man than a l'il bit,*" she jokes. "So do they."

"What?"

"Over there, Mr. Myles."

Jacob looks over to the diner. The family waves at him through the window. Baby Terry kisses the window smearing the condensation forming on the glass. Frankie and Savannah, one always trying to show up the other, make funny faces for their parents. They then grab big sister Josie's hands and run outside when they see the snow - another family first for the Myles clan. Josie makes her first snowball and hurls it at little brother Frankie. She's in the middle of making another but stops when she sees her parents walking toward her. She quickly grasps her daddy's anguish when she sees her mother trying to hide his cigarettes. Josie knows that Jacob Myles, Sr. - *World's Greatest Father* - must be hurting too if he's gone back to smoking. She smiles her daddy's way, but her heart is still in Hopskip – with the name Michael 'Mack' Hodges indisputably imprinted in bold letters. Poor Josie – she just can't help herself. She's hooked. She will, however, make the effort, for her daddy – for now anyway. She turns and wipes a tear from her pretty face. Feeling a little guilty and ashamed, she smiles her father's way. She runs over to him and gives him a hug. She kisses his cheek. Father and daughter smile at one another for the first time in two weeks. What a feeling!

L'il Daddy, still inside with Baby Terry slices a bit of pancake, whirls it around in *Dora's Finest Maple Syrup* and shoves it in his mouth. He comically looks to the heavens as if he just ate manna from above. Josie throws a snowball and hits the window framing her brother's little sideshow.

Jacob and Dottie laugh at their children's antics. Frankie and Savannah run to Josie and their parents for a group hug. What a family, thinks Jacob to himself. Rejuvenated by his family's affection, Jacob takes the cigarettes from Dottie and shoves them in the trash can just outside the diner door.

"Let's eat, family," Jacob replies with a smile. "We got some driving to do."

Dora's Diner and the Story of John Mason

"**REMEMBER WHEN WE** all sat at one table?" Frankie says to Savannah and L'il Daddy, his breakfast companions. The rest of the family sits comfortably in the adjoining booth enjoying their pancakes, eggs, and Dora's famous biscuits and gravy.

"When was that?" Savannah says scratching her head.

"Oh right," says Frankie pointing his fork at his little sister. "That was before *you* came along. Ha! Ha!"

"Wow, Frankie," Savannah says dryly. "So funny I forgot to laugh."

"That's enough, Frankie," says Jacob. "Ummm. L'il Daddy's right. These pancakes are delicious. Could use a little whipped cream, though."

"Like mine?" Dottie says with a grin.

"Yep," Jacob says between bites. "Just like yours."

"The biscuits and gravy aren't bad either, Daddy," Josie says.

"Hey, Miss Dora," Frankie yells from the other table. "These pancakes are good. Mama, you should ask for the recipe."

"What did you say, boy?" Dottie says red-faced.

"They're good 'cause I got the recipe from your mama," Dora says coming to the poor child's rescue. She winks at Dottie as she pours Jacob another cup of coffee.

"How could she, Ma?" Frankie questions her. "You just met."

The rest of the family turns towards Frankie. Josie closes her eyes and puts her hand to her forehead.

'She must be having another migraine,' thinks clueless Frankie to himself. L'il Daddy shakes his head as if to say *'Does this boy ever learn?'* Savannah laughs almost spilling her juice. Even Baby Terry shakes his head in disbelief. If ever there was an award for putting one's foot in one's mouth, Franklin Joseph Myles would win it hands down. He means well. He just doesn't…

"THINK, boy." his father admonishes him. "What do I always say?"

"Think before I speak," says Frankie sheepishly.

"If he did that, he'd never talk," says Savannah keeping the pot boiling.

"You better be quiet, Savannah," Frankie warns her.

"No, *you* better keep quiet." his little sister dares him.

"Enough, you two," Dottie admonishes her babies. She winks at her hapless son and throws him a little smile.

Jack the mechanic rushes into the diner.

"Hey, Mr. Myles!"

"Over here, Jack," Jacob says to the mechanic. "What is it?"

"You could use an oil change, Mr. Myles. I know you guys got a ways to go. L'il Daddy told me y'all are going to Chicago. Oil change won't take long at all. Thirty minutes tops!"

"I knew there'd be something else," Jacob whispers to Dottie.

Back in Hopskip, Jacob Myles lent his mechanical skills (for a very small fee) to pretty much anyone who asked. Lester Smoot, the only mechanic for miles had a nasty habit of 'overestimating' repair jobs for the elderly females and Negro motorists in town. Jacob, in turn, became quite adept at diagnosing and repairing their old trucks. In return for his good deeds, Jacob became an enemy of Smoot and his cronies. Because of his run-ins with Smoot, Jacob has developed mistrust for auto mechanics in general.

"Be right back, Dottie." Jacob winks at his wife. "Frankie, behave yourself."

Jacob beckons to Jack.

"Let's go, son. I wanna see this oil change."

Leaning against an old workbench in the Mason Family Garage, Jacob watches intently as the young mechanic gathers supplies and tools for the oil change. He notices Jack has already taken the liberty of placing his beloved 'Goldie' on jack stands. He sees a pan underneath the car filled with oil.

"My Lord," Jacob says to himself. *"He's already begun the process."*

"You know what weight you need?" Jack asks pointing toward the many selections of motor oil displayed on the north wall.

"Pretty sure of himself," Jacob surmises with a hint of disgust. He

walks over to the far wall to choose the right weight for his car. He notices a wooden sign on the wall above the display. Underneath the sign is a picture of President John F. Kennedy. Next to it is a picture of a Marine in ceremonial dress, Jack's father John Mason. A pair of dog tags drapes the frame of the years-old photo.

"You like that," Jack says pointing at the two men on the wall. "I call it '*Two Johns, No Waiting*'. Two Johns, get it?"

"Hmmm," says Jacob reading the sign. "'*WE SERVE THE WORLD*.' What's that about?"

"How much time you got?" Jack smiles.

"According to you, thirty minutes," Jacob responds.

They both laugh.

"Well," says Jack shielding his eyes from the morning dawn. "The way mama tells it…"

Dora's Diner, formerly *Masons'* was established in Kentucky in 1946, shortly after its owner Sgt. John Raymond Mason, II was honorably discharged from the Marines. Using his G.I. bill to attend business classes, John decided to build a diner bearing the family name. John, like most successful businessmen, realized right from the start that location was everything. He decided the perfect location for his restaurant was right off the interstate. Success was immediate. Through word of mouth, John and Dora Mason's restaurant became known as the place to be for southern cuisine at a good price. With business booming, John decided the following year to build a motel next to the diner for the highway's lethargic motorists. Not only would he be able to feed them and the truckers trekking their loads north and south along I-65, he could offer them lodging for a quick nap between stops. The motel only accommodated six rooms on the small lot but John Mason was extremely proud of his accomplishments nonetheless. A motel and a diner bearing the family name – a legacy John, Dora and their six sons would maintain for generations to come. Anyone and everyone who had the fare were welcome, John decreed. That's when the trouble began.

One night in the spring of 1948, John Raymond Mason found himself with all six rooms occupied leaving a tired trucker from Florida without lodging for the night. John had just rented the last bungalow to a family travelling from Thyatira, Mississippi to East St. Louis, Illinois.

He apologized to the young man but told him he was welcome to park and sleep in his truck behind the diner for the night. He even offered him his first cup of coffee free the next day. The trucker took him up on his kindness and settled in for the night.

The trucker awoke the next day to see the occupants of Bungalow Six packing their belongings and heading for the highway. He flew into a rage. Storming into the diner, he found Dora, as promised waiting for him with coffee and a smile. He grabbed the cup of coffee from her and threw it on the floor. The occupants of Bungalow Six, he screamed were colored - Negroes. He couldn't believe that he, in his words, a white man was slighted for Negroes when he had to spend the night in his truck. Coming from behind the counter, John Mason, unbelievably calm and collected explained to him that it was his motel and that anyone with the fare is welcome in every part of his establishment. He also told the trucker that he was going to clean up the coffee on the floor – he could use a mop or his tongue, John told him. It didn't matter to him. The trucker, even more infuriated instead exited the diner but left a warning to John Mason. He assured him that he would inform his fellow truckers to take the Masons' Diner and Motel off their radar.

The trucker was true to his word. Business from the trucking firm and others fell off. The diner still did brisk business among the locals; however, but the motel was lucky to see even two patrons a week. John Mason held his ground. He refused to give in. Then an amazing thing happened. Business for the motel suddenly picked up. So did the diner's. John and Dora Mason also noticed a change in their clientele. More and more of their patrons were people of color. Word had spread throughout the South of John Mason's dispute with the truckers and his refusal to ban Negroes from his businesses. Negro families making the trek from the South to live north actually went out of their way to eat and sleep at the Masons' Diner and Motel. Travelling choirs stopped at the Masons' for Dora's biscuits and gravy. The men claimed it put bass in their voices. The restaurant and motel became an unofficial landmark. People from everywhere flocked to the Masons' establishments to get a look at a fair and honest man – a rarity they called him. The Mason family was exceedingly proud. John even had a sign made for the entrance of his motel –

WE SERVE THE WORLD.

"Shoot, my daddy wasn't no rarity," Jack said wiping the oil from his hands. "Plenty of good people in Kentucky. Just gotta know where to look. Hand me that oil filter wrench, Mr. Myles. If you don't mind."

"Not a problem, Jack," says Jacob reaching into the waist-high tool cabinet. He hands him the wrench. "Finish your story."

"Not a problem, Mr. Myles," Jack says wiping his brow. "Not a problem."

Life was good for the Masons and their part of Southern Kentucky. Even those who didn't stay overnight stopped for Dora's cuisine and to take a picture with her, John and the boys. The restaurant and motel went on for three years without incident. Then one day in late 1951, the unimaginable happened. John awoke one morning to find a cross burning on the lawn of his motel. No stranger to racism after having served in World War II, John realized that his motel, and possibly his wife's diner would be next. He was right. Later that month the Masons' Motel was torched, burned to cinders on the very land where John had hoped to leave his family legacy. The Masons' Diner, however was spared and no one was harmed. John Mason never rebuilt his motel. The ashen structure was never even demolished. He preferred to leave it as is, a monument to the hatred his family endured for simply living what he called *God's Way*. Sgt. John Raymond Mason, II, family man, decorated war hero, and entrepreneur, had a heart attack in 1959. He died later that year.

"His widow, my mama Dora," Jack continued as he returned his tools to the cabinet, "never remarried. Funeral could have lasted two days, all the people who came. Folks around here still talk about my daddy and how he stood up for what was right. What he felt in his heart!"

"Quite a story," Jacob remarks. "I do remember the old deacons back home talking about it, now that you bring it up."

"Yep. John Raymond Mason, the second. That was my daddy."

"Jack?" says Jacob.

"Yes, Mr. Myles?"

"Your sign? **WE SERVE THE WORLD**? There's not one scratch on it. No burn marks, no charring. Odd, wouldn't you say?"

"Hot dang!" Jack says dropping his head in amazement. "L'il Daddy *said* you was smart as all git out!"

"Jack, are you saying what I think…?"

"Yes, sir. You got it! John Mason, my daddy burned down his own motel."

"He did? Why?" asks Jacob already knowing the answer.

"Well, my daddy figured with the motel gone, the Kluxers would give him a pass on Mama's diner. He was right. They left us alone after that. Besides, he didn't wanna give *them* the satisfaction."

"…and he rescued the sign before setting the fire?"

"Yes sir, he did." Jack says before turning his attention back to his own personal wall of fame. "Mama found it in the basement after Daddy passed. I keep it here next to his picture and dog tags. I say '*Hello*' to Daddy every morning when I open up shop and '*Good Night*' when I shut it down."

Jack starts to well up with emotion. He whips out a greasy rag from his overalls and wipes his nose. Jacob drops his head to allow the young man a moment to grieve in peace. He pretends to check Jack's work on the engine until the young man collects himself.

"Thirty minutes, Mr. Myles," says Jack grinning and turning back to Jacob. "Did I call it or what?"

"You called it son," says Jacob beaming. He goes into his wallet and pulls out two twenties. "I believe this should cover everything."

"Right, Mr. Myles. Let me get your change."

"Keep it!" Jacob says. "…and thanks."

"Sir?" says the mechanic a little bewildered.

"For restoring my faith."

"Oh. In mechanics, huh?" Jack says. "I get that all the time."

"Them, too."

Jack smiles at Jacob now grasping his meaning. He nods as the two men look back at the picture of Jack's father.

Jack looks up to see the rest of the Myles family exiting the restaurant. L'il Daddy's carrying a very sleepy Savannah. He gently places her in the back of ol' Goldie.

"Here's your family. Right on time," says Jack. "You all have a nice trip."

"Thank you, son," says Jacob. "We will. Okay, family hop in. Frankie! Kick the snow off your feet before you get in the car, please."

"Okay, Daddy," Frankie says.

"Take the wheel, L'il Daddy," says Jacob. "Josie?"

"Yes, Daddy?"

"Mama and I are taking the middle. Keep your brother company up front."

"Okay, Daddy." says Josie smiling at her dad. "Whatever you say."

Dottie hugs her oldest and gives her a kiss. Jack holds the door open for Josie.

"Thank you, Jack," she says smiling this time. "You're very kind."

"Oh, no problem," Jack says a little smitten. "See ya, L'il Daddy." says Jack waving at his new friend.

"See ya, buddy. Hey!" says L'il Daddy laughing. "Let me know when those new belts come in."

"Hush, boy!" says Dottie.

Jack runs around and closes Jacob's door behind him. He reaches in and shakes his hand. "Good luck in Chicago, Mr. Myles."

"Thank you, son!" Jacob answers. "…and hey, say goodnight to your daddy for me. Sounds like my kinda guy."

"He would've liked you too, sir," Jack smiles. "He would've liked you, too!"

Franklin Myles—In Your Dreams

"**THAT** *IS* **QUITE** a story, Jacob," says Dottie patting her husband's lap. "I remember Daddy and Deacon Thomas talking about the restaurant once. Daddy and the choir had biscuits and gravy there right before a revival one year. Only it was called ***Masons'*** then."

"Jack *said* a lot of choir members used to come through," Jacob replies. He then turns his attention to his son behind the wheel. "L'il Daddy, how she running?"

"Never better," he responds. "Ol' Jack knows his way around engines. Knows a lot of jokes, too. He said..."

"Don't wanna hear it, Rudy Ray!" Dottie warns her son.

"Eyes on the road," Jacob tells his son. "Ten and two."

"Yes, sir."

"Well, Mama," Josie says reading a magazine Frankie bought from the restaurant. "That explains a couple of things."

"What's that, baby?"

"One, there were no facilities for separate toilets."

"...and two?" Dottie asks.

"How Frankie was able to buy his favorite magazine in a white restaurant." She hands it back to him.

"Well, now we know," Jacob replies with a chuckle. "Looks like John Mason *was* a little ahead of his time."

"Amen!" says Dottie. "Amen!"

"Hey mama, look!" says Frankie opening the magazine to the music section. "Misty Eagleton and the Sensations got a song in the Top 10. Boy, if I could be one of the Sensations. One day, Mama. One day."

Little sister Savannah, always on the ready blasts her brother.

"Frankie, if *you* were in a group that *would* be a sensation!"

"Now, now don't you start stepping on your brother's dreams," says

Dottie. "We got enough people doing that already. I think Frankie'll make it. One day."

"*Yeah*," Savannah thinks to herself. "*In his dreams.*"

"Wow, Mama!" says Frankie adjusting the crown on his head. "I can't believe we're at the Apollo Theatre. They got some of the greatest acts in the world here."

"…and we got some pretty good seats, too," says Dottie. "That seat isn't too high, is it?"

"Nope. Just right." says Frankie looking down at his little sister pouting. "Thanks for the throne, Daddy."

"Anything for the most intelligent son in the world," Jacob responds. "You deserve it! Sorry, L'il Daddy."

"Oh! No apologies necessary, Big Daddy," his son replies. He spikes his football after dodging two of the Georgia Bulldogs' biggest linemen. "When you're right, you're right. I feel so blessed just to be in my brother's presence."

"They don't have Mack Hodges here," says Josie looking around a little disappointed. "How great could it be if they don't have Mack Hodges?"

Jacob shakes his head.

"Josie, baby girl, baby girl, baby girl. Is that all you think about?"

"Yes," Josie responds blowing a bubble as big as her head. It pops leaving her hair a mess. "As a matter of fact, it is!"

"Well, tonight we're taking a break," says Dottie proudly. "We're here with the great Frankie J. to see the greatest group in the world. *The Sensations*. Right, my darling boy?"

"Right, Mama! Hey, look! On stage. It's that music guy, Very Wordy. Why is he running around like that?"

"I don't know," says Savannah. "…and that's strange 'cause I usually know everything."

"Oh no!" cries Frankie. "I hope nothing's wrong with Misty!"

"*Oh no!*" Savannah cries mimicking her brother. "*I hope nothing's wrong with Misty!* Ha! Ha! Ha!"

"Quiet, Savannah." Frankie admonishes his little sister. "This could be serious."

Josie jumps up and points toward the stage.

"Hey, look! It's that record producer Mack, I-I mean Very Wordy. He's coming this way. I wonder what he wants."

"No doubt wants to pray before the show," says Jacob. "Dottie, get me my bible."

"Right here, my precious," she says.

"Excuse me, young man," says the exasperated executive looking up at Frankie on his throne. "Aren't you Franklin Joseph Myles?"

"Wow!" Josie exclaims. "Very Wordy knows my brother! Ask him if he knows Mack Hodges."

"Son, I need you to come backstage," Mr. Wordy tells him. "Mr. Eagleton needs your assistance. It's an emergency!"

"Misty Eagleton wants to see Frankie?" Savannah says astonished. "Wow! My big brother's more important than I thought. I'm so jealous!"

"This way, son," says a grateful Very Wordy. "This way."

Frankie makes his way backstage. On the way to visit Mr. Eagleton, a young boy wearing sunglasses bumps into him almost knocking Frankie's crown off his head.

"Hey, watch where you're going," Frankie J. tells him. "I'm here to see Mr. Eagleton and he can't be kept waiting."

"I'm sorry, sir," the young man says. "I didn't see you."

"No problem," Frankie says. "…and pick up that harmonica before somebody trips on it."

"Yes, sir," the young man says. "No need to get uptight. Hmm. *Uptight?* Has a nice ring to it!"

Frankie is led by Mr. Wordy to a door at the end of a long hallway. Frankie can't help but be awed by the gold records plastered on the door. Nor is he prepared for what's ahead. When he's ushered inside by Mr. Wordy, he sees his hero lying sick in bed. Frankie's idol, the Great Misty Eagleton will not be singing tonight. He's sick and in his bedclothes. The appliqués on his pajamas (like the headboard and the bedspread) are also gold records. He has a steaming hot water bottle on his head and a huge thermometer in his mouth. The thermometer has a big, red throbbing head at the end of it. The number on the end of the thermometer reads 250 and growing by the second. A minister and a nurse are tending to the ailing crooner. The other Sensations are sobbing while Mr. Wordy clasps his hands in anguish.

"Wow, Misty Eagleton!" Frankie exclaims bowing to his hero. He takes off his crown and extends his hand to the sickly pop star. Misty coughs spitting out gold records.

"It's a pleasure to finally meet you, sir. Are you sick?"

"Of course he's sick, Frankie," says Dottie dressed as the RN at the singer's bedside. "That's why he called you back here."

"He needs your help, son," says Jacob flicking a piece of dog hair from his minister's robe. "...and only you can help him."

"Me?" says Frankie. "What can *I* do?"

"Son, we need you to go on for Mr. Eagleton," declares Mr. Wordy. "If we cancel another concert, I'll lose my hair. I'll lose my shorts. I'll lose Yotown Records and then who'll be around to sign *you* when *you're* ready?"

"Wow!" Frankie thinks to himself. *"I see now how he got his name!"*

Suddenly, Mr. Eagleton starts to move. The bedridden R & B singer rises from his bed. He raises his hand. It's adorned with rings bejeweled with gold records. The room is quiet as he beckons for Frankie to come nearer. He speaks.

"Say you'll do it, son," Misty whispers in young Franklin's ear. "For me. (*cough, cough*) For the Sensations. The entire industry depends on you."

"He'll do it!" Dottie says with her hands on her hips. "My baby can do anything!"

"What's your answer, Franklin?" says Jacob kneeling and patting the heads of two golden retrievers sitting beside him. "Your public is waiting."

"I'll do it!" says Frankie.

An 'APPLAUSE' sign over Mr. Eagleton's bed flashes on and off. Frankie hears the crowd from the auditorium cheering. Everyone joins in the applause. Even Jacob's retrievers give each other a high five.

Suddenly, the Sensations surround Frankie. Misty rises from his bed and waves his hand as if blessing the assemblage. When the Sensations move away, Frankie's jeans and T-shirt have magically changed into a bright blue velvet tuxedo. For good measure, Misty dons Frankie's noggin with a sparkling sequined blue velvet top hat. Needless to say, it's adorned with a gold record.

The Sensations push Frankie out on stage. The band starts to play Misty's latest hit. Frankie knows the song but he freezes. He opens his mouth but nothing comes out.

"Sing, Frankie, sing," yells big sister Josie from the crowd. "Sing so loud my Mack can hear you back in Hopskip where I belong."

"Frankie, I'm losing my hair! You have to sing, Frankie," cries Mr. Wordy. "Frankie, sing! I'm losing my hair!"

"Don't sing, Frankie! Don't sing," yells his big brother L'il Daddy. "Then I'll be Big Daddy's favorite again. Ha, ha, ha!"

All of a sudden, out of nowhere a huge hook seizes Frankie by the collar. The shadowy figure holding the giant hook is dressed as a clown and laughing maniacally from the wings. The specter walks slowly toward a very frightened Franklin Myles. Frozen by fear, Frankie stares at the apparition until its face is lit by the footlights beaming from the stage below. It's none other than his sister Savannah!

"AAAHHH, HA, HA, HA!" laughs Savannah. "I told you he couldn't sing, Mama. I told you!"

Savannah's laugh echoes throughout the Apollo auditorium. Mother Dottie cries into a bucket overflowing with tears. Jacob pats her back to console her but glares harshly at his son for making her cry. His dogs bark at the frightened boy.

"Don't cry, baby," says Jacob. "We have two other sons. I'm sure they'll make us proud."

"Get off my stage, you loser!" Savannah cries while pulling him with the hook. "Get off my stage, Frankie! Get off the stage, Frankie! Frankie?"

"Frankie, wake up!" Savannah cries. "Wake up, Frankie."

"Don't cry, Mama!" Frankie yells. "I'm sorry, Mr. Eagleton. Don't cry, Mr. Wordy. We can start another company."

"What in the world..." says Josie looking back at her brother. She and L'il Daddy start laughing.

"Okay, you two that's enough," Jacob admonishes his older children. He taps L'il Daddy on the shoulder warning him to stop teasing his brother but he has a hard time controlling his own laughter.

"Frankie!" says Jacob turning his attention to the middle child. "Wake up boy, you're having a nightmare."

Savannah looks at her brother and shakes her head woefully. She then turns to her parents.

"Mama, is a person supposed to have nightmares in the daytime? Will we have to leave Frankie at a hospital when we get to Chicago?"

Savannah never lets them down. Jacob, Josie, and L'il Daddy all try to suppress their laughter but with little success.

"Savannah, hush! Oh, you four are a big help," says Dottie admonishing her family. "Terry, sit in the back with Savannah. L'il Daddy, pull over at the next gas station."

"Yes, Mama," L'il Daddy says stifling a laugh.

"Honey," she says to Frankie. "You come up front with me."

"Yes, Mama!" Frankie says sobbing.

"Now, what's the matter, baby? Tell Mama about your dream."

Dottie hugs her child while he recounts his nightmare to the family. Baby Terry gives his troubled brother his stuffed dog, Bruno to cheer him up. Josie turns the radio down so she and L'il Daddy can hear over the old car's engine. Savannah kneels on the back seat and listens with interest as her brother tells all. He's careful to leave out the parts about his siblings' and his parents' less than flattering attributes.

"...and then," cries Frankie.

"Yes, baby?" says Dottie hugging her child.

"...and then. Oh, it was horrible, Mama."

"What happened, baby?"

"...and then," Frankie drops his head revealing the worst part of the nightmare.

"MR. WORDY LOST HIS SHORTS!"

"WHAT!!!" everyone screams. The station wagon, now parked at a gas station rocks with laughter. Everyone – even Baby Terry falls on the floor laughing. Everyone, that is except Dottie. Frankie, embarrassed by his admission buries his face in his mother's bosom.

"Frankie, I'm-I'm curious," says L'il Daddy catching his breath. "Mr. *Wordy's* drawers, were there gold records on *them*, too?" He and Josie fall on one another laughing.

Frankie drops his head red-faced. He starts to cry.

"Okay, stop it. Stop it you all," says Dottie. "Jacob, please."

"We're sorry, baby," says Jacob stifling his laughter. "Frankie, why do you think you had this dream, son?"

"'Cause I'm a loser," he says sobbing. "A failure. I'll never be anybody. *I'm the 'Great Pretender'.*"

Frankie's proud father smiles. Even in agony, Frankie can recall any song to fit any situation.

"I could never sing as good as Misty," Frankie laments.

"Savannah Myles!" says Dottie warning her daughter.

"I didn't say anything," Savannah protests.

"I know you!" Dottie says. She picks up Frankie's head and wipes his tears. She looks him right in the eye. "Frankie, you're putting too much on yourself. No one really gets famous overnight."

"They don't?" Frankie sobs.

"No, baby," Dottie says drying his tears. "You have to be patient. Getting a career started takes time."

"... and practice," says Jacob. "Lots of practice."

"Right," says Dottie holding up her son's face to hers. "Look at me, baby. You think your Daddy learned how to train all those hunting dogs overnight? No, baby. Of course not."

"Yeah, think about it Frankie," Josie chimes in. "You don't think L'il Daddy was born throwing touchdowns, do you?"

"Well," L'il Daddy says. "Actually I was."

"Be quiet, boy," says Jacob.

"Sorry, Daddy."

"C'mere Frankie," says Josie reaching across her seat to kiss her little brother. "I bet by the time you're Misty's age, he'll be begging *you* to join *your* group."

"You think so?" Frankie says wistfully.

"WE KNOW SO!" they all say in unison. Frankie smiles at his family – even Savannah, once again his partner-in-crime. Frankie hugs his daddy and kisses his mama. His big brother smiles at him through the rearview mirror.

"Hey!" says Dottie. "Who wants some M & M's?"

"Me!" says Frankie jumping out of his seat. "Come on, Savannah. I'll race you."

Jacob passes a quarter to his son.

"Share with your sister, Frankie. Get a big bag," Jacob yells as the two run into the little store connected to the gas station.

"I need to run to the ladies' room," Dottie says jumping out of the car. "Be right back."

"I'll come with you, mama," Josie cries out after her.

"That's okay, honey," Dottie says to her. "...be but a minute."

Dottie enters the ladies room. Placing her purse on the sink, she takes her comb out and begins styling her hair. She turns on the water to muffle any sounds coming from the bathroom. Suddenly, Dottie drops her head. Her comb falls out of her hand. She loses control of her faculties and starts to shake uncontrollably. She then looks at herself in the mirror and utters two words out loud:

"GOLD RECORDS???"

She bangs her fists on the sink and starts laughing. She did a magnificent job holding it in but couldn't any longer. She jumps up and down as if filled with the spirit of Mahalia Jackson herself. She tries to catch her breath but can't. She shrieks.

"Gold records!!!" she screams through tears of laughter. "On his drawers! Oh, my God! Lord, help that boy! AAAHHH, HA, HA!!"

Suddenly, a knock comes from outside of Dottie's personal sanctuary.

"Hey lady," a nasal voice yells. "How long you gonna be, I gotta clean up in there!"

"Coming. Just be a minute," Dottie says gathering her belongings. She fluffs her hair in the mirror, wipes away her tears and opens the door.

"Hi, baby!" laughs Jacob. "Ready when you are."

Standing right outside the door are L'il Daddy, Josie, and some old man who Dottie can't stand right now. Apparently, he thinks he's some kind of comedian. The three of them fall all over themselves laughing. They heard everything. Dottie collects herself and pushes past the jokesters.

"God don't like ugly, Jacob," she says with a straight face.

Josie and L'il Daddy catch up with her and hug her still laughing at their father's prank.

"…and he ain't all that happy 'bout you two either," Dottie says to her two oldest.

Jacob catches up with his wife and hugs her.

"You okay, baby?" he asks kissing her. "What went on in there?"

"Get off me before Frankie sees you," she laughs. "Gon' now!"

Poor Dottie. She couldn't be mad at this bunch if she tried.

Savannah Myles—Atlanta Compromise(s)

JACOB, DOTTIE, AND the children decide to take a few minutes at a park across the street from the gas station at their last stop. The parents both shoeless, sit underneath a tree next to an old picnic table while the rest of the family explores the landscape. Jacob takes this moment to massage his wife's tired feet.

"Now honey, you know once you get started I won't be able to walk - not after one of Jacob Myles' famous foot rubs," Dottie laughs. "You're gonna have to carry me to the car."

"I've never had a problem carrying you before," Jacob tells her.

"Hmmm!" Dottie says searching the sky. "Was that before or after five babies?"

"I'll take my chances, sweetheart."

Dottie rubs her husband's cheek. He gently kisses her hand and continues to rub her tired feet.

"You know, Jacob," Dottie thinks. "It's too bad we're not moving here to Kentucky. I'm sure Dora Mason would love a few pies from *UpSouth Catering*."

"I'm sure she would," Jacob assures her.

"Maybe we can get one of those refrigerated trucks to bring 'em down. I'm sure she'd be up for a couple thousand."

"A couple thousand, Dottie?" Jacob says looking at his wife and laughing. He knows when his wife gets an idea in her head, there's no stopping her.

"No one can ever say my baby thinks small," Jacob says rubbing the arches of his wife's feet.

"Ooh, that feels good," Dottie says glowing. "Daddy always said, *Think big!*"

Jacob rises to his feet. He stands next to the young businesswoman still sitting under the tree. Fingering a blade of grass between his teeth, he ponders his wife's dreams. Papa Myles told him on his wedding day that the secret to a happy marriage is to make *her* dreams *your* dreams. He never forgot his father's words. Tossing the blade of grass aside, he looks down at his wife as she retrieves her shoes from under the old table.

"Don't worry, baby," Jacob says assuredly. He takes Dottie's hands and helps her to her feet. She wobbles for a few seconds before regaining her composure. "We'll get your business up and running in Chicago. I promise."

"You're one good man, Jacob Myles. I love you."

"Iron sharpens iron," Jacob says citing the Old Testament. He looks lovingly into her eyes. "That goes for women too, you know!"

"I know," Dottie says blushing.

"I'll always be there for you, Dorothy Myles!" he says tapping the bridge of her nose. "By the way, have I kissed you, today?"

"Only three times," Dottie blushes. "My hand, my cheeks..."

"Just three?" Jacob says moving closer to his beloved.

"Um hmm," Dottie says feigning annoyance. "I think somebody's slipping!"

"Well," Jacob says. "Can't have that! Come here, woman!"

"Uh, I hate to interrupt this love fest," Josie says walking up to her parents. "...but I think one of us is missing."

"What?" Dottie and Jacob say in unison. Jacob hurriedly slips into his shoes. "Who?"

L'il Daddy, with Baby Terry on his shoulders, walks up to their parents and sits on the old table.

"Savannah!" Frankie says running up to the table and jumping on it. "Ten dollars says she's over by that swimming pool."

"Miss Olympic?" Jacob says tying his shoes. "I'll get her. We need to get back on the road."

"This one's on me, Daddy," L'il Daddy says winking knowingly at big sister Josie. She smiles back. "I'll get her."

"Drag her if you have to," Jacob jokes. "You know how she is about swimming."

"Yes, I do." L'il Daddy sighs.

The summer of 1960.

Nine-year-old Savannah Vernell Myles accompanies her mother Dottie to the exclusive Whitehall Country Club in nearby Atlanta to serve her *world famous* sweet potato pies at a banquet held by the local ladies club. The young businesswoman-to-be is ecstatic. Until now, Dottie has only sold her baked goods to church members and local clientele. Catering a function at Whitehall will be a big boost to her embryonic firm. She hopes the move *'across the tracks'* will get her struggling business off the ground. Margaret 'Molly' Brand, a friend of Dottie's eldest, sits on the social committee at Whitehall and has persuaded the head of the club's kitchen committee, Gretchen Davenport to purchase Dottie's pies for the function.

Dottie pulls Goldie, the family station wagon up to the front gate where Molly is waiting. Savannah, wary of all things Caucasian is none too pleased to see the young teenager.

"Hi, Mrs. Myles! How are you?" Molly says beaming. "Hey, Savannah! ...haven't seen *you* in a while."

"Do I know you?" Savannah asks bluntly. She points her rag doll Rosa in the girl's face.

"I'm Molly, Josie's friend."

"Give me that, young lady," Dottie says taking the doll. "Did you leave your manners somewhere I don't know about? We've talked about this. Now, sit up and behave."

Molly smiles at Savannah but only gets a frown in return. She turns her attention back to Dottie behind the wheel.

"If I can jump in with you, Mrs. Myles I'll be glad to show you around back."

"...and why can't we go through the front?" Savannah demands.

"Girl, hush!" Dottie tells her. "The kitchen is around back! I've already warned you, Miss Revolutionary. I'm not having that from you today."

Miss Revolutionary.

When Savannah Vernell Myles turned seven, she received a special birthday visit from her favorite aunt - her mother's baby sister Briana

Harris. Aunt Bree Bree, as Savannah calls her, spent a week with the Myleses and left an indelible impression upon young Savannah. Briana, a self-styled activist, and disciple of stand-up comedian/activist Richard Claxton Gregory developed a passion for the civil rights movement in her final year at Meharry Medical. To her family's chagrin, Briana dropped out of the prestigious HBCU in her last year and joined the civil rights movement. Impressed by the successful 381-day boycott of Montgomery, Alabama's segregated bus system, young Briana joined the up-and-coming Southern Christian Leadership Conference. Briana stirred a fire in young Savannah with her tales of boycotts, sit-ins, and protest marches. She even had the pleasure of sitting at the table of Coretta Scott King. Enthralled by Briana's travels and exploits, Savannah hopes to someday emulate her favorite aunt by making history of her own in the fight for civil rights. Unfortunately, to Mother Dottie's dismay, the little militant-in-training tends to get a little self-righteous in her quest for immortality.

"Did you hear me, Savannah? Not today!"

"Yes, ma'am," Savannah says sulking.

"I'm sorry, Miss Brand," Dottie says apologetically. "Please! Get in."

"That's all right, Mrs. Myles," she says. "...and please, call me Molly." Molly jumps in the front seat and directs Dottie down a side road toward the rear entrance of the club.

"Take a left at the end of the road."

"White folks!" Savannah mumbles. "...always giving orders!"

"Did you say something, young lady?" Dottie shouts.

"No, ma'am," Savannah says frowning.

Molly turns away from the two and smiles. L'il Daddy told her that his baby sister wasn't going to take to her right away.

'*Give her time,*' he told her. '*Savannah has a good heart. She'll soon love you as much as I do.*'

'*...as much as I do!*' Molly smiles thinking about Jacob Myles, Jr., her secret paramour, and their clandestine meetings. Molly is so smitten with the thought of the fifteen-year old's declaration of love for her that she loses her train of thought. Dottie almost passes the rear entrance of the building.

"Is this the turn, Miss Brand?" she asks

"What? Oh, sorry Mrs. Myles," Molly says. "Where's my head? Yes. Yes. Pull up behind that statue."

"...so nobody will see us?" Savannah barks.

"SAVANNAH!" Dottie shouts embarrassed.

"...so no other cars will hit us, honey," Molly replies jumping out. "Let me get someone from the kitchen to help with these pies. Um, they smell delicious, Mrs. Myles. Be right back."

Dottie turns to the audacious little girl sitting in the middle row of the family vehicle. She glares at the little pig-tailed radical. Savannah, defiant as always in matters of race refuses to back down.

"I didn't do anything, Mama," she protests. "I did what Aunt Bree Bree would do. I just told it like it is!"

"What you did is make a little fool of yourself. It's not always about race, Savannah. This function can be a huge boost to my new company, *Dottie's Cookies & Cakes.*"

"...*and pies*?" Savannah says wearily.

"I'm working on the name, okay. The fact is Miss Brand has been a tremendous help with expanding my catering service."

"She has?" Savannah says pretending to be interested. She half-listens to her mother's discourse on the politics of supply and demand.

"Oh yes! You see baby girl," Dottie continues. "In the world of business, an up-and-coming entrepreneur like yours truly can't survive by selling my product to the same old people. If I want to make some money, some *real* money, I have to increase my base. That means expanding my clientele - selling to people *'across the tracks'*. Like Miss Davenport. And who knows, when you're my age, *you* may even become a member here. That's what you want, right? Not *my* cup of tea, but today we can open those doors you're always talking about. You understand, don't you sweetheart?"

Dottie smiles at her baby girl waiting for her concurrence.

"Ohhhh!" Savannah says nodding her head up and down as if she finally understands.

'Ah, looks like I got through to her,' Dottie thinks to herself.

"Mama?"

"Yes, baby," Dottie says caressing her daughter's shiny black locks.

"YOU CAN CALL HER MOLLY," Savannah says condescendingly. "SHE GAVE YOU PERMISSION, REMEMBER?"

Time stands still for Dorothy Rosetta Harris Myles. She sits back stunned. Dottie looks at her daughter with what her children jokingly call elevator eyes. Up, then down. Down, then back up. She stops at Savannah's smug little mouth.

'*I know this child to whom I spent two days giving birth did not just...*'

Dottie takes a deep breath. She calmly steps out of the family wagon. Closing the door behind her, she directs the ungrateful little child to move over. She calmly opens Savannah's door and sits next to her. Folding her arms in front of her and tapping her left elbow with her right forefinger, she sits for a minute debating – debating how best to deal with her *husband's* child for no child of hers would dare speak like that to her. At least not twice. Dottie's mum. She doesn't say a word. Her demeanor; however, speaks volumes.

Savannah turns pale. Her once insolent smile disappears, the look of smugness running away from her face. Savannah starts to worry. Her mother's mysterious quietude prompts the wanna-be revolutionary to speak but she is prevented from doing so when Dottie raises her hand, a signal to her daughter that silence is not only golden but in this case beneficial. Savannah gulps, perspiring more and more with each second her mother remains mum. She wishes her mother would talk but she knows trying to get a word out of her now will only make matters worse. Savannah instead, steels herself for the worst.

Dottie takes off her pillbox hat and places it on the front seat of the car. She rolls up the window on her side of the family wagon. She deftly reaches over Savannah, now frightened out of her wits, and rolls up the window on the passenger side. One can't interrupt what one can't hear. Dottie again reaches toward Savannah. Panic-stricken, the nine-year-old instinctively ducks what she perceives to be a balled fist. No balled fist. Her mother simply wants to lock the door; a move that only serves to instill even more fear in her already extremely terrified child.

Savannah retreats to the other side of the car only to have her mother pull her little body closer to her side. Dottie is now nose to nose with her daughter. Kicking off her shoes, she leans in to '*impart some much-needed wisdom*' to the impudent child. The wisdom she shares? Her older children laughingly refer to their mother's technique as *Behavior Modification*. Needless to say, they weren't laughing when Dottie imparted that same wisdom to them in their own moments of brazen impertinence. *Discussions* on Behavior Modification, dispensed in the middle row of *Ol' Goldie*, have been known to work miracles with the Myles children. As of today, neither of Savannah's siblings has ever found the need to revisit Mrs. Myles for remediation.

"Who's that out in the car?" asks a young girl peeking out of a window of the kitchen. "What's she doing here?"

Her brother looks out an adjoining window to see Dottie Myles exiting and standing at the rear of her car. The little girl, wiping tears from her face, wisely remains inside.

"That's that Myles woman from the other side of town."

"Myles? You mean *Jacob* Myles' wife? From *Hopskip*? What business does she have here?"

"Molly Brand thought it'd be a good idea for the old gal to serve her sweet potato pies at the banquet. Why Miss Goody-Two-Shoes couldn't find somebody white is beyond me."

"Jacob Myles' wife," the girl says. "Interesting."

Wallowing in the misery of their own making are twin sister and brother, Jessica and Jedadiah Smoot. Born ten minutes apart, the Smoot siblings reside on the poor side of White Hopskip and resent every minute of it. The two begrudgingly wait tables at the Atlanta country club where their parents were once members. Jesse and Jed are the children of Lester Smoot, owner of Smoot's Auto Repair and the only body and car repair shop in the small burg of Hopskip. By over-charging for minor repairs and performing unneeded work, Smoot has made a career of cheating Hopskip's elderly women and all of its Negro constituents. Smoot disgusts Jacob Myles. Jacob, who learned car main-tenance from his father, performs the work himself for many of the women of Hopskip for a small pittance (sometimes for free). Negro or white, he doesn't discriminate. Word of Smoot's activities has black-listed him from the Atlanta country club and the hoi polloi of Georgia. Completely dismissing her father's behavior, Jesse blames Jacob Myles for their financial troubles. She abhors waiting tables and would do anything to be a *member* of Whitehall instead of a *'lowly employee'*.

"Who's the child in the back seat?" Jesse asks with a frown.

"Jesus, Jesse don't you know anybody colored?" Jed asks.

"I try not to get my hands dirty," she says nonchalantly.

"…girl's name's Savannah. Their daughter."

"Savannah, huh?" Jesse says watching the two. "Interesting."

"They say she's always talking 'bout Civil Rights and mouthing off at her l'il school," her brother tells her. "Civil Rights! I'll give her Civil Rights!"

"Civil Rights, huh?" Jesse says ominously. "Interesting."

"Yeah!" Jed says. "Miss Davenport says I have to help the Myles woman bring in her pies. …should toss 'em in the trash where they belong."

"Don't, l'il brother," Jesse tells him. "You go help the old gal. Git the retard to give you a hand. I'm gonna have a talk with Miss Savannah."

"OK! Hey, Saul," Jed shouts across the room. "Git yo' butt over here! Help the old lady take the pies out of her car. Gon' now, I'm right behind you."

Saul Krebs, the Smoots' toady, and ever available scapegoat jumps hearing Jed call his name. Saul has never attended school one day past the age of twelve. His widowed father Saul Krebs, Sr. literally dragged the poor boy from his desk at school to work in the fields.

'Bible's the only book you need to know', his father told him. Since then Saul, now seventeen and diffident has difficulty reading anything past the sixth-grade level. Lacking the most basic confidence, poor Saul is bullied by Jed and Jesse at the country club that kindly Gretchen Davenport owns with her sister Lila. Afraid of losing his part-time job as a dishwasher, poor Saul follows Jed's and Jesse's orders without question.

Saul runs over to the twins. He nods his head up and down and then runs out to the car. The two miscreants laugh at the poor boy. Jesse watches as Savannah gets out of the car. Her mother just as quickly directs her back into the vehicle.

"I'll be back for you later, young lady!" Dottie tells her.

Locking the car door behind her, Savannah sulks as she watches her mother open the trunk full of pies. Jed turns his attention back to his sister.

"What are you gonna do, Sis?" Jed asks heading for the door.

"Don't worry about it," Jesse says pulling off her apron. "Just know that it *will* be interesting."

Jesse Smoot watches the goings-on from the club's kitchen window. Molly Brand introduces Dottie Myles to Gretchen Davenport. The two women smile and shake hands. Miss Davenport hands Dottie a check which she proudly pockets in her purse. Miss Davenport then directs Jed and Saul to the rear of the Myleses' station wagon before taking off for other business. Each boy grabs a box of pies - ten each.

"Take these to the Preparation Area," Molly tells them.

Saul looks perplexed.

"The what…" he asks.

"Just follow me, retard," Jed tells him. "Got to be the dumbest white boy…"

Dottie runs back to the entrance to hold the door for the two boys. Jed frowns. He walks past the woman mumbling. Saul nods to her.

"Thank you, ma'am!"

"You're welcome," Dottie responds with a smile. She and Molly follow the boys inside.

No sooner than Saul and Jed have taken in the pies, Jesse Smoot sneaks out of a side door and approaches Savannah sitting in the car. She frowns watching her playing with her doll.

"A colored doll," she mutters to herself. "Will wonders never cease?"

Jesse knocks on the window of the old station wagon. She wipes her hand on the back of her dress as Savannah rolls down the window.

"Well, hello young lady," she says faking a smile. "You must be Savannah."

"What? Uh yes, I'm Savannah," she answers mindful of her 'session' with her mother. "Who are you?"

"Why I'm Jenny," Jesse lies. "Jenny Davenport. My mother owns the club, and *your* mama said I could take you for a tour. …if that's OK with you."

"A tour of the club?" Savannah says perking up. "She did? Are you sure it's okay?"

"I'm sure!" *'Jenny'* says. "Hey, my mama owns the club."

"Can I bring Rosa with us?" Savannah inquires getting out of the car.

"Uh, sure," *'Jenny'* says trying not to turn up her nose. "What's her name? Rosa?"

"Yeah," Savannah says proudly. "I named her after Mrs. Rosa Parks."

"Hmm. *Another* troublemaker," *'Jenny'* mumbles to herself. "Interesting."

Jed and Saul take the boxes of pies to a blue table in a corner of the large kitchen. Jed notices as Dottie smiles proudly watching him and Saul remove the pies from the boxes. In an attempt to erase the smile from the *uppity* young entrepreneur's face, Jed bumps into Saul causing him to drop one of the pies. Molly quickly catches it before it hits the floor. Jed smirks. He stares at Dottie, daring her to respond so that he can complain to Miss Davenport. Incensed, Dottie nearly obliges him until Molly stands between the two combatants.

"Well, Smoot," she says placing the pie on the preparation table. "Looks like you've found your station in life. Village Idiot."

The boy snatches a towel from his waist and throws it on the floor in front of Molly.

"Oh, I'm sorry, should I be afraid?" Molly says looking the boy straight in the eye.

"Now you look here, Molly Brand!" Jed barks.

"Saul, please get some saucers and the whipped cream," Molly says never taking her eyes off the bully. "Help Mrs. Myles prepare her pies. And if I see so much as a blemish on any of them, Jed Smoot, I'll have you fired! ...and you know I can do it. Go out and set the tables. Now!"

Margaret 'Molly' Brand is the daughter of Marvin Brand, reputed Klansman and owner of approximately 75% of all the land in Hopskip. Brand holds the mortgage on most of the businesses in Hopskip (including Lester Smoot's garage) and has connections throughout North Georgia. Marvin Brand has been known to destroy anyone who crosses him or anyone else with the Brand name. Although Molly abhors being associated with her daddy's so-called connections, the young beauty has never had to ask anyone anything twice.

Jed storms off. Infuriated, he takes a stack of plates out to the dining area. Molly, Dottie, and Saul hear the boy slamming the plates on the tables. Dottie grabs an apron from a hook on the wall. She quickly unwraps her pies. A little shaken, she grabs a knife from a drawer and begins slicing her pies into sixths. She then passes the pies to Saul to place onto the little saucers. Unfortunately, the poor boy's frozen in his tracks. Dottie notices that Saul hasn't moved since Jed left. He knows his tormenter will find a way to blame him for his run-in with Molly Brand.

"It's okay, Saul," Molly tells him. She pats the poor boy's shoulder. "You did nothing wrong. Go on and help Mrs. Myles with her pies."

Comforted by the pretty redhead's compassion, Saul pulls a pair of gloves and a spatula from the table drawer, smiles at Dottie and goes to work placing the slices onto the saucers.

"That's it, Saul," she says. Molly shakes her head, smiles and turns to Dottie, who's still overwhelmed by the fifteen-year old's moxie.

"Well," Molly says referring to Jed Smoot's antics. "Never a dull moment around here. I'll leave you to your work. If you need anything, just yell!"

"Ok, Miss Brand, uh Molly," Dottie says. "...and again. Thanks!"

"My pleasure, Ma'am! ...and don't worry about Jed," Molly says squeezing Dottie's hand. "He's all bark. Say, would it be okay if I took little Savannah on a tour of the club?"

"If you're sure it's alright," Dottie says. "I'm sure she'd like that very much."

"Not a problem at all," Molly replies. "Saul, Mrs. Myles is in charge. Be back in a bit."

"...and this is the tennis court."

"Wow, *Jenny'* this is nice! Wish I lived around here."

"Do you live in Atlanta, Savannah?"

"Nope, we live in Hopskip. Do you live in this club?" Savannah asks innocently.

"No, I'm in college in Philadelphia," *Jenny'* lies. "The city of brotherly love? You know I think it's horrible how white people treat the colored, uh Negro people down here."

"You do?" Savannah asks wide-eyed.

"Oh, yes, *Jenny'* lies. "We would never do that up north."

"Really?" Savannah says.

"Umm hmm. You know," *Jenny'* says baiting the unsuspecting child. "I just love that Rosa Parks. She really stood for something. Get it? *Stood* for something."

"Oh yeah. That's funny," Savannah laughs. "Wish I could do something like that."

"What do you mean, Savannah?" *Jenny'* asks feigning ignorance.

"You know, do something important," Savannah explains. "Something nobody's ever done before. Like Mrs. Parks."

"Oh, I don't think you could do anything like that around here," *Jenny'* says. "UNLESS..."

"Unless what," Savannah begs. "Tell me! What?"

"Well, you know they have a heated pool."

"What about it?"

"It's segregated."

"What?"

"Whites Only." *Jenny'* says with a phony look of shame on her face. "They say they don't even allow the poor colored, uh Negroes to even clean it."

"They don't?"

"'Fraid not, Savannah. But you know what? Oh, no we couldn't"

"What, Jenny? What?"

"Well, if *you* took a swim in it, you would be the first!"

Savannah beams.

"The *first*? The first ever?"

"Yep, the first ever," *Jenny'* says. "Mama Davenport always wanted to open up the pool to your people but she could never find anyone brave enough."

"I'm brave enough!" Savannah shouts. "I can do it. But, Jenny. I don't have anything to wear. I left my swimsuit back home."

"Don't you worry, honey," *Jenny'* says with a devilish grin. "I can take care of that."

"Why Saul, I don't think I've ever seen my sweet potato pies look so appealing!"

"Yes, ma'am," Saul responds holding a can of whipped cream in front of him as if he's peddling the product on TV. "I made 'em look like flowers."

"Yes, you did."

"Look at these over here, Mrs. Myles. They look like clouds. Pretty, huh?"

"*Very* pretty, Saul," Dottie says smiling. "You work wonders with the whipped cream."

"Wasn't my doing," Saul blushes. "Everything we have is a gift from God. Ol' Saul's just a vessel."

"Ah, a man of God," Dottie says noticing Saul coming alive for the first time since she arrived. "I'm impressed, Mr. Krebs."

"I read…what I can. Memorize a lot of it."

"You and my Jacob would get along like two peas in a pod. He'd be impressed, too."

"I'd like to meet him one day," Saul says beaming. "You're a very nice person, Mrs. Myles. Thank you very much."

"Oh, I should be thanking you!" Dottie says admiring Saul's work. "These flowers are such a nice touch. And the clouds. You have the soul of an artist. I bet you like to paint."

"As a matter of fact, I do," Saul responds showing a little confidence in himself. "Still lifes, rivers, sunsets, people fishing. People say I'm real good. I wanna go to art school someday. Maybe even own my own studio."

"I don't see why not!" Dottie tells him. "If your paintings look anything like my pies…"

"Wanna see one?"

"You brought one of your paintings?"

"You could say that," Saul says. He points to a painting hanging on the far wall of the kitchen. It's a portrait of the Davenport sisters posing in front of the club.

"I found it on an old program for a party they gave a few years ago," Saul says proudly. "Miss Davenport said it was okay to hang it up. Do you like it?"

"Saul, it's beautiful," Dottie says. "It looks just like Miss Davenport. Son, you are blessed. You really *should* go to art school. I think you'll be famous someday."

"SO OLD LADY DAVENPORT LET YOU HANG A PICTURE. BIG DEAL!"

Saul and Dottie look up to see Jed Smoot, standing in the doorway of the dining room and mocking poor Saul, who's now lost his confidence along with his smile. He pales at the sight of Jed Smoot walking toward him. Now nose-to-nose with Jed, Saul cowers in fear.

"FAMOUS? YOU?" The bully laughs. "Now how can a retard go to art school when he can't even fill out the registration form? *I'm gonna own my own studio!*" Jed roars with laughter. He grabs a container of silverware and heads back into the dining room. "Wait'll Jesse hears this! The retard thinks he can go back to school!"

"That boy!" Dottie shouts. "I'll never understand why some people find it so easy to be so mean. Saul, why do you let him…"

"He's right, Mrs. Myles."

"He's wrong, Saul!" Dottie insists. "Honey, you have to stand up to him. Who is he to say what you can and can't do?"

"Mrs. Myles. I-I'm fooling myself. Who's gonna hire a painter who can barely read?"

"Okay, Savannah. Come on out!"

"Here am I, Jenny!"

"Ready to make history?"

"Yep. Ooh, you got a camera!"

"Well, we need proof of your big moment, don't we?"

"Oh, yeah! Yeah! That's right! Okay, what do I do now?"

"Come with me!"

Toting a camera she swiped from the country club gift shop, Jesse Smoot sneaks the unwitting child into the pool area. The pool, although filled is closed for the ladies' club banquet. Savannah sports a swimsuit her duplicitous *'friend'* borrowed from the club. Oblivious to the pair running behind him, Ralph Hennessey, the club security guard, lounges in the guardhouse with a six-pack listening to his radio. After sneaking Savannah past the guard, Jesse rushes Savannah to the deep end of the pool.

"Okay, honey," *Jenny'* says. "First, we'll take a picture of you on the diving board. Then, we'll take a shot of you in the water. Ready?"

"Ready!" Savannah shouts climbing onto the beginner's diving board.

"Okay," *Jenny'* shouts. "Smile!"

Savannah smiles. She even poses for the treacherous girl.

"When I grow up, I'm going to the Olympics," Savannah shouts. "I'm gonna make history!"

"*Sure you are,*" *Jenny'* snickers. "Great shot, Savannah! Now let's get a shot of you in the pool. Jump in, honey!"

"Here I go!" Savannah screams. She jumps into the air, her knees firmly against her little chin. "Cannonball!" she shouts. Savannah hits the water. She surfaces, then plunges determinedly toward the bottom of the pool, touches it and swims effortlessly back to the top.

"Good!" *Jenny'* tells her. "Can you float on your back?"

"Like this?" Savannah laughs still unaware of the girl's plan.

"Perfect!" Jesse says snapping more pictures. She drops the stolen camera onto a nearby pool chair. "Stay right there!"

Jesse runs to the clubhouse and yells for the security guard.

"MR. HENNESSEY! MR. HENNESSEY! COME QUICK!"

Mr. Hennessey, who is also the Whitehall High School wrestling coach in Hopskip moonlights at the country club on nights and weekends. His wife just had their fifth child and money is very tight. Responding to the malevolent girl's cries, Hennessey is stunned to see Savannah floating in the exclusive country club pool. Even he's not allowed. Seeing a little black child in the Whites Only pool can mean only one thing to the poor man – his job. He rushes to the other side of the pool and into the maintenance closet. Snatching a net from a wall of the closet, he angrily drags a scared and confused Savannah Myles out of the pool.

Her little pigtails caught in Hennessey's mesh netting, Savannah screams for help.

"AAAHHH! Let me go! Let me go! Jenny! Help! Help!"

Savannah is shocked and speechless as Mr. Hennessey pulls her from the pool and throws her into a nearby chair.

"Little girl, what the hell is the matter with you?" Hennessey yells. "Don't you know this is a restricted pool?"

Jesse Smoot, her plan now in full swing, walks calmly over to the flustered security guard.

"Mr. Hennessey," Jesse says dispassionately. "I saw the whole thing. Why I even have pictures. How could you let this little pick-a-ninny get past you and swim in a Whites Only pool? What would the Davenports say?"

"Pictures? Now, wait a minute, Jesse!" Hennessey says nervously. "If the club finds out…"

"You could lose your job," Jesse says nonchalantly. "I know. What a horrible thing. …and you with all those mouths to feed."

"Jesse, wait…"

"Go on back to your radio," the deceitful teen demands. "I'll handle it."

"Jesse…" Hennessey says.

"Your beer is getting warm, Mr. Hennessey."

Mortified, Hennessey places the net back on the wall of the closet. He walks away mumbling obscenities about Jesse, her *no-good* father, and the proximity of apples falling from trees. Savannah, mystified sits on the edge of the pool chair shaking. She's also horrified.

"*Jenny!* Why did he call you 'Jesse'? What's going on…?"

"Shut up, you little fool! *I'm* talking, now! …and this is how it's gonna be!"

"First of all, let's get one thing straight, Saul. You're an artist, not a painter. Now there's nothing wrong with being a painter; however, there *is* a world of difference."

"It's not that important, Mrs. Myles."

"Saul…"

"Mrs. Myles, please," Saul says sadly.

"Saul, you know it's never too late…"

"For school? I don't wanna talk about it."

"Then I'll do the talking."

"Can I stop you?"

"Well!" Dottie says taken aback. "Maybe I should get back to my pies."

"No! No, Mrs. Myles," Saul says apologetically. "I'm sorry. I didn't mean that. It's just that… well, Jed…"

"Let me stop you right there," Dottie says raising her hand. "Come here, Saul. Sit with me."

Dottie covers her pies. She then directs Saul to a seat at a back table near the kitchen entrance – out of earshot of the diners in the adjoining room.

"What did you want to tell me, Mrs. Myles?"

"Nothing! Just that Jed Smoot's an old crab."

"An old crab?" Saul says a little puzzled.

"Um hm. Crabs in a barrel. You know the old story about the fisherman who left a bucket of crabs on the pier? He didn't bother to put a lid on the bucket because he knew that if one crab tried to get out, the others would just pull him back in. That's your friend, Jed."

"He's not really my friend," Saul confesses.

"No kidding!" Dottie says. "For a minute there, I didn't think you knew the difference."

"Mrs. Myles…"

"Honey, Jed Smoot knows he'll never be anything more than what he is now. So he does his best to keep everybody else down with him."

"You really think so? Jed?"

"I know what I'm talking about, Saul. Jed knows you got a chance of making something of yourself. He's jealous of you, baby. You're blessed and he knows it."

Just then, Jed bursts back into the kitchen. Wearing a busboy's jacket, he and two other busboys bring in the banquet's lunch dishes. Surprised to see Dottie and Saul sitting instead of working, he tosses a snide comment toward the pair.

"Well, well. Let me guess! Uhhh, you're discussing *Mr. Art School*'s new museum. No, no, what is it? Right! His great new art studio. HA! Only a real retard would go to something you'd put together, Krebs. The old lady is ready for the pies!"

Grabbing a pastry cart from the preparation area, Jed slams the trays of pies onto the cart. Dottie and Saul are still sitting at the entrance. Jed shakes his head. He looks at the pair and fumes.

"Oh, don't let me slaving like a… "

Dottie stands up daring the impudent boy to continue. He won't. Like most bullies, he knows who he can and can't push around. Instead, he heads back to the dining area mumbling under his breath.

As Dottie watches Jed and the others push the dessert cart into the dining area, she shakes her head pitying the boy.

"…ain't worth two dead flies!" Dottie tells Saul. "His sister anything like him?"

"Twins, Mrs. Myles. Cut from the same cloth."

"Lord, have mercy!"

"Jenny, what's going on? Why did that man call you *Jesse*'?"

"Savannah, you may not know me but I know you *and* your daddy very well."

"*My daddy? How do you know my daddy?*"

"Shut up and listen. Your old man's been fixing cars around town. Taking business from my daddy. Trying to put my daddy outta business. And you're gonna see to it that he stops!"

"Me? All my daddy did was fix Mrs. Green's flat tire. And Dr. Brown's engine that time. I don't know what you're talking about."

"Shut up, Savannah. You listen to me. I'm working here as a damned waitress 'cause of your daddy stickin' his nose where it don't belong. Well, today it stops. ...and *you* better make damned sure he does."

"Your mother makes you work in your own club?"

"Damn it, Savannah," Jesse scoffs exasperated. "Pay attention. There is no *Jenny Davenport*. My name is Jesse Smoot. My daddy owns the auto repair shop in Hopskip. Me and my brother work in the kitchen. Our parents used to be members here, but because *your* daddy took all *my* daddy's business, we can't be members. It's your daddy's fault. ...and if he don't stop, you're gonna be in real trouble."

"What am I supposed to do? I'm just a little girl."

"Shut up! If you don't tell your daddy to stop, I'll show everybody in town those pictures of you in the Whites Only pool. I'll put the Klan on your little 'Civil Rights' butt. And they'll burn your daddy's ranch to the ground."

"No, you can't do that!" Savannah screams. "Please Jesse. Don't burn down my house!"

Jesse smashes the camera into Savannah's face. She then grabs her arm and shakes the frightened child.

"Then you'll do what I said, you little..."

"Let me go!" Savannah shouts. "Let me go!"

"You gonna do it? Huh? Answer me, Savannah!"

"LET HER GO!"

"Molly!" Savannah screams. "Help me!"

"Stay outta this, Molly Brand!" Jesse shouts. "This don't concern you."

"I said let her go."

"This ain't your affair, Molly Brand."

Savannah breaks free. She kicks Jesse in the shin and runs to Molly.

"Go get changed, Savannah," Molly tells her. "Get out of those things before someone sees you."

"Too late, Miss Molly," Jesse says with a devilish grin. She holds up the camera she stole from the gift shop. "I got pictures."

"Molly!" Savannah yells. "She's gonna show 'em to the Klan. They're gonna burn down our house."

"No one's gonna burn down your house, Savannah," Molly says pushing the child toward the locker room. "Go on, baby girl. I'll take care of this."

Savannah nods her head and runs toward the locker room. She reaches the door of the building and stops. She looks back at Molly and Jesse now head to head – facing one another like two adversaries in an old Spaghetti western. Savannah blinks. Her little brow furrows. She heard something strange. Strange, yet familiar - from Molly Brand.

"Did she call me Baby Girl?"

"Well, those dishes ain't gonna wash themselves," Saul says. He heads over to the sink and grabs a few washcloths. Dottie takes one of the washcloths.

"You wash, Saul. I'll dry."

"Mrs. Myles, you don't have to…"

"Oh, I don't mind," Dottie says. "I find it relaxing."

"You do?" Saul asks incredulously. Besides art school, he has no other dream than to get out of washing dishes for the rest of his life.

"Yes, I do."

"Wow!" Saul thinks to himself.

"Saul, I want to tell you a story about my grandfather. Mr. Nathaniel Sanders."

"I know Mr. Sanders. Smart man," Saul says. He puts a stack of dishes under the running water. Dottie splashes a little dishwashing liquid into the sink. She then runs hot water in the adjacent sink to rinse the dishes.

"Thank you," Saul says. "Yeah, Mr. Sanders and my granddaddy sharecropped on Brand land when they was kids."

"Um hmm," Dottie says. "My granddaddy quit school in the sixth grade to help *his* daddy. He couldn't read very well, either."

"Mrs. Myles…"

"Now, now you said I could talk."

"Yes, ma'am," Saul says. He rinses a few plates in the adjacent sink and hands them to Dottie.

"Thank you, honey," Dottie says taking the plates and drying them. "Well, one night, when my mother Bea was about five years old, she heard my grandparents sitting at the kitchen table discussing of all things, the ABC's."

"ABC's?"

"Uh huh. Mama said that she thought they were talking about her homework. Turns out they were talking about *his*."

"Beg your pardon?"

"Um hm. Miss Bea, that's what we call her, found out later that after all of the kids went to bed, my Nana Yvonne was teaching Papa Nate how to read."

"Did you say she was teaching your granddaddy how to read?"

"I sure did!" Dottie exclaims stacking some plates on a nearby table.

"Isn't he on the school board on your side of town?"

"He sure is! My granddaddy went back to school and got *two* degrees."

"*Two?*" Saul says incredulously.

"Yes, sir!" Dottie says proudly. "Once Papa Nate got started... Well, that man was on *fire!*"

"Mrs. Myles, I'm almost eighteen. I can't go back to school."

"Well, how old do you think my granddaddy was?"

"I'm sure you're gonna tell me," Saul says smiling. He hands her a silver platter which she quickly immerses in the 'rinse' sink.

"My granddaddy was twenty-seven."

"Twenty-seven?"

"That's what I said."

"Really?"

"Really!"

"Praise the Lord!"

"...and the only reason it took that long is well, Papa Nate had a touch of the hubris. But, once he got over that..."

"Mr. Sanders was sick?"

"No, honey. Hubris. It means excessive pride." Dottie holds up the platter so that Saul can see his reflection. She looks the young man squarely in his eyes. "Someone in this room has it, too."

"You mean me, Mrs. Myles?"

"Um hm. You do recall Proverbs 29 and 23."

"I do," Saul proclaims with a smile. *A man's pride will bring him low, but a humble spirit will obtain honor.*"

"...and what were you saying before about God-given talent?"

Every good gift and every perfect gift is from above, coming down from the Father of lights with whom there is no variation or shadow due to change. James 1..."

"...and seventeen. Umph, umph, umph!" Dottie says marveling at young Saul's grasp of the good book. "Honey, you are much smarter than you give yourself credit for. Forgive the stranded preposition."

"Ma'am?"

"English 101. You'll see."

"Night school, Mrs. Myles? I don't know."

"Saul, I'm guessing it's gonna take you two, maybe three years to get your degree.

"Three years? Three years is a long time, Mrs. Myles."

"Honey, how are you gonna feel three years from now knowing you could have had a degree? ...and ready to go to Art School? That pesky old...!"

"*Hubris!*" Saul says with a smile. His posture straightens. His confidence returning, he looks at Dottie beaming.

"Saul, are you trying to blind me? ...'cause if you are..."

Saul chuckles.

"Mrs. Myles?"

"Yes, baby?"

"Would you like to see some more of my pictures? I got some in my truck!"

"I certainly would!"

"I won't ask you again, Jesse Smoot. Give me that camera!"

"Try and take it!"

Jesse backs away from Molly. She looks at her and then gives her a smile only Satan would love.

"Hmmm. Very interesting."

"What are you talking about, Jesse Smoot?"

"You think I don't know what this is about? Gittin' Miss Davenport to let the Myles woman cater her party? Taking up for that child? I know what's going on, Molly Brand."

"You don't know what you're talking about, Jesse Smoot. I want that camera!"

"Does your daddy know 'bout your boyfriend?"

"WHAT?" Molly says shocked.

"Fooling around with that…"

"You watch your mouth, Jesse Smoot!"

"You been sneaking around with that colored boy, Molly Brand! Jacob Myles, Jr. Hmmm. Interesting. Wish I had a picture of that!"

Savannah gasps. *L'il Daddy and Molly Brand?* Oh, my Lord!"

Molly is flabbergasted. She and L'il Daddy have always been so careful. She can't imagine how anyone discovered their secret.

"You keep your mouth closed, Jesse Smoot or I'll…"

"It's true! I knew it! Marvin Brand's daughter. A NIGGER LOVER!"

SMACK!

Molly Brand punches Jesse Smoot in her foul mouth. Her smack sends the devil's young apprentice flying through the air and into the same pool she tried to use to blackmail little Savannah. She hits the pool with a splash. Savannah runs to the pool and retrieves the camera from the water. After scrambling for what seems like an eternity, Jesse finally finds her legs and wades to the edge of the pool. She tries to get out only to have Molly push her back into the water. Savannah, awe-struck watches Molly Brand take charge.

"You'd be smart to stay in there, Jesse Smoot!"

"Or what, Molly Brand? What else do you want? You got everything! Money. Clothes. The club. Everything! *'CEPTING A MAMA!'*"

Incensed, Molly moves toward the pool. Savannah stops her. Feeling for her new friend, she gives her a hug. She remembers hearing a long time ago that Marvin Brand's wife, Molly's mother Elizabeth, disappeared without a trace. A tear falls from her eye. Molly brushes off her insult. She glares at Jesse still standing in the pool.

"Awww!" Jesse cries. "Poor Molly Brand! Your own mama don't want you so go looking for love 'cross the tracks! What's gonna happen when I tell your daddy?"

Molly looks at the foolish girl standing in the shallow end of the pool. She shakes her head pitying her. She actually feels sorry for the girl who would have easily turned her world upside down.

"You poor fool!" Molly Beth says shaking her head "You don't know. You just don't know."

"Saul, these are beautiful!"

"Thank you, ma'am."

"...and this bowl of fruit. I get hungry just looking at it."

Saul laughs.

"Daddy said the same thing. Mrs. Myles, you suppose I could ask you a favor?"

"Why, sure young man. What is it?"

"Well..."

"Say what's on your mind, Saul."

"You suppose I could borrow some of your granddaddy's books? Maybe I could get a head start on things. You know, before I go back to school. If he still has 'em, that is."

"It would be my pleasure." Dottie smiles and hugs Saul.

"Thanks, Mrs. Myles. If you ever need anything, I mean anything."

"Well, there's one thing," Dottie says looking around and pulling off her apron. "I want to talk to Miss Davenport. Could you find Molly and Savannah for me? They should've been back by now."

"No problem, ma'am," Saul says heading for the door. "I'll be right back."

"Thank you, Saul." Dottie picks up another painting. "I'll say it again. You are blessed."

Saul, feeling higher than he's ever been, turns to his new friend grinning from ear to ear.

"No ma'am!" he blushes. "That would be *Mr.* Myles."

"I don't know what?" Jesse Smoot cries. "What, Molly Brand?"

"You little fool. My daddy could've foreclosed on your daddy years ago. Your father couldn't make a go of his little shop. He was bleeding money long before Jacob Myles showed up. My daddy extended the loan, just to keep your daddy from going under. ...and you know why? 'Cause Jacob Myles felt sorry for him. The three of them were friends years ago. Good friends. Fishing buddies. He asked my daddy to give your daddy another chance. But that wasn't enough. Your daddy started cheating his customers. That's when Mr. Myles stepped in and started fixing people's cars. He felt responsible for talking *my* daddy into giving *yours* another chance."

"You're a liar, Molly Brand," Jesse shouts near tears. "A liar."

"Oh, it's true alright," Molly continues. "Who do you think keeps daddy's books? My daddy and Mr. Myles may not show much love for each other these days but hear this, Jesse Smoot. Marvin Brand respects the hell out of Jacob Myles. He's a man of his word, which is a lot more..."

Savannah tugs Molly's dress causing her to rethink her last line to Jesse. Even the young nine-year-old can see the girl has had enough. No sense in rubbing her nose in it. Molly nods her concurrence. She hastily changes her statement.

"...which means a lot to my daddy."

Jesses splashes angrily at the water.

"You finished? Can I get out now?"

"One more thing, Jesse Smoot," Molly says. She hands Savannah the camera.

"You wanna come after me? Or Jacob, Jr.? Or anybody I care about? Try it! See what happens! Come on Savannah."

"WHAT'S GOING ON HERE?"

"Stop her, Jed!" Jesse screams. "Stop her!"

"Stay right there, Molly Brand! You're not going anywhere!"

"She pushed me into the water!" Jesse shouts. She points an accusing finger at Savannah. "The other one stole my camera!"

"WHAT? That tears it, Molly Brand!" Jed shouts. "That tears it!" He grabs Molly's arm and shakes her.

"Leave my friend alone!" Savannah screams at the boy. Jed pushes her to the ground.

"Leave her alone! Get your hands off me, Jed Smoot!" Molly yells.

"...or what, rich girl?" Jed taunts her. "Whatcha gon' do? Huh?"

Jesse, finally finding the nerve to get out of the pool laughs at Molly Brand.

"Hold her, Jed!" Jesse gloats. "We got some unfinished business!"

"LET HER GO!"

"What? What?" Jed shouts. The bully looks around searching for the owner of that voice. He's heard it before, but never like this. Jed turns around to see Saul Krebs approaching the ruckus. Saul is now nose-to-nose with Jed. He's actually taller than Jed, but his fear of the boy and lack of confidence kept him slumped and appearing weak to the Smoots.

"I said let her go!"

"Hey, Jesse! Look!" Jed laughs. "The retard wants to fight. You think you can save this girl? Well, come on!"

Jed pushes Molly aside.

"I said come on, RETARD!" he laughs pushing Saul. "Let's see what you got!"

Jed and Jesse laugh. Their frivolity; however, is short-lived.

Saul steps up to Jed. He looks him square in the eyes.

"I hate that word!" he says.

SMACK!

Saul jaws the unsuspecting boy sending him flying into his sister. They both land with a splash in the pool. Molly's jaw drops. She pats Saul on the back and kisses his cheek. He smiles. She kneels at the pool to talk to Jesse splashing in the water.

"Hmmm. Interesting," Molly says mocking Jesse. She removes the film from the camera exposing the malevolent girl's so-called *'evidence'*. She tosses it into the water as Jesse watches helplessly as her evidence floats away.

"Interesting, indeed!" Savannah says, high-fiving Molly.

Remembering why he came to the pool area, Saul turns to Savannah.

"Your mother's looking for you, Savannah. She's a fine woman. ... wouldn't wanna keep her waiting."

"Uh, OK! Thanks!" Savannah says. "Thanks a lot!" She and Molly run to the locker room.

Jed and Jesse run toward the edge of the pool in an attempt to stop Molly and Savannah.

"I'd think twice before I got out of that pool if I was you," Saul tells them.

"Jesse?" Jed says with a whimper. "What do we do now?"

"Shut up, Jed!"

Inside the country club locker room, Savannah changes into her clothes while Molly stands guard. Savannah pulls off her swim cap, finds a towel and starts to dry her hair.

"Let me do that for you, honey."

"Okay, Molly!"

"Uh, Savannah?"

"Uh, huh?"

"Sweetheart?"

Savannah turns to face Molly. She can tell something's not right.

"Molly, what's the matter?"

"Savannah, you know you can never tell."

"…about me swimming in the Whites Only pool? I know," Savannah nods her head. "I could get in trouble. You could get in trouble for helping me."

"I wouldn't worry about that, honey. Jesse Smoot knows better. I meant…"

"Oh! You mean about you and my brother."

"Honey," Molly explains. "Your brother and I are in love. People just don't understand. We could get in a lot of trouble."

"I know Molly. I know. I'll keep quiet. If…"

"If? You wanna make a deal to keep quiet? Savannah, I'm surprised."

"No, not a deal. A co-promise."

Molly smiles.

"You mean a *compromise*, Savannah?"

"Yeah, that!"

"…and what are your terms, young lady?"

"Well," Savannah says. "I'll keep quiet about you and L'il Daddy…"

"If…"

Savannah starts to cry.

"…if you'll forgive me for being mean to you. I'm sorry." She hugs Molly.

Molly hugs her back.

"*L'il Daddy was right*," Molly thinks to herself. "*Savannah **does** have a good heart.*" She takes Savannah's towel and wipes a tear from her eye.

"We have a deal," she says hugging her special little friend. "I mean — a *co-promise!*"

Savannah looks at Molly and smiles. She grabs her shoes from the locker and quickly slips into them.

"You know what, Molly?" she says.

"What, baby girl?" Molly says stroking her hair.

"I see why my brother likes you. I kinda like you, too Molly Brand."

Molly almost chokes on her happiness. Savannah's sweetness is more than she can bear.

"I kinda like you, too Savannah Myles. Why don't you call me Molly Beth?"

"Deal!"

"You mean compromise, don't you?" Molly laughs. "We better go. Mrs. Myles is waiting."

"Ok, Molly Beth. Race ya!"

"So sleepyhead, that must have been some tour. You've been asleep for the last thirty minutes."

"It was okay, Mama," Savannah says yawning. "Seen one club, seen 'em all. Did the ladies like your pies?"

"I wasn't sure you cared, Savannah," Dottie says reminding her of her earlier comments.

"I'm sorry, Mama," Savannah says. "I know how much this means to you. I'm sorry."

"So am I, baby!"

Savannah leans over from the middle row of the station wagon and kisses her Mama. Dottie pats her baby's cheek and smiles.

"Well, to answer your question," Dottie says. "Yes, they did. Miss Davenport loved the pies. She said they have three more banquets next month and she might give me a call."

"That's great, Mama! I'm happy for you. I- AAAAHHH!!!"

"SAVANNAH! WHAT? WHY ARE YOU SCREAMING? WHAT'S WRONG?"

"Rosa!"

"Rosa? What? Your doll? What about her?"

"I left Rosa back at the club! We gotta go back!"

"Oh, Savannah," Dottie says. "We've been on the road for thirty minutes. We can't…"

"I can't leave Rosa, Mama! Aunt Bree Bree gave me that doll! Please!"

"Alright, baby. Alright. We'll turn around."

Dottie pulls the station wagon up to Whitehall Country Club. She drives around to the kitchen area. Savannah jumps out and runs to the pool. Dottie follows her. When she catches up to her daughter, she finds her standing motionless by the pool. It's empty. Miss Davenport and the Smoot twins are standing with Mr. Hennessey, the security guard. Molly and Saul are also in attendance. They all turn around when they see Savannah. Hennessey points at Savannah. She's horrified. Jesse and Jed, ever malevolent poke one another and laugh when they see the look on Savannah's face. Dottie walks up to Savannah.

"Baby, what's wrong? Did you find your doll?"

"Mrs. Myles, I'm so sorry," both Molly and Saul tell her.

"I'm sorry, Mama! I'm sorry!" Savannah starts to cry.

"Honey, for what?" Dottie asks her. "Would somebody tell me what's going on here?"

Miss Davenport walks over to Dottie.

"I believe this is yours, Mrs. Myles."

Miss Davenport hands her Savannah's doll. Drenched and smelling of chlorine, poor Rosa has seen better days. Unlike the sweet and unassuming woman Dottie met a few hours ago, Miss Davenport looks down at Savannah and turns up her nose. She then folds her arms and glares at Dottie.

"Mrs. Myles! Do you have any idea how much it costs to drain and clean the Whitehall pool?"

Dottie, fully grasping the situation reaches into her purse. She finds the check the old curmudgeon gave her. She rips it in two and shoves it into her wrinkled hands.

"You can bill me for the balance! Have a good day, Miss Davenport!"

"I made mama lose her contract."

"Are you serious, Savannah? You think Mama would make another pie for that old crone? After the way they treated you? I think not, little sister."

Savannah, somewhat relieved, smiles at her brother.

"I'm gonna miss her, L'il Daddy."

"Yeah! Me too, baby girl."

"She let me swim in her pool, you know? Just me and her."

"I know, Savannah," L'il Daddy says looking away. "She was sweet like that."

"Molly Beth should quit that old club."

"She did."

"She did?"

"Yep. After you and Mama left, Molly Beth tore her membership card in two."

"She did? For real? She tore it in two?"

"Um hmm. Gave half to that snot Jesse Smoot and the other half to her idiot brother. She told 'em, *'Don't worry. It's paid for!'* Hah! Wish I coulda seen that!"

"Molly Beth's cool!"

"Yep! My girl's got class!" L'il Daddy proclaims fondly. He hugs his little sister.

"Do you think we'll ever see her again?" Savannah asks wistfully.

"Well," L'il Daddy says crouching next to his sister. "Daddy used to say that sometimes people come into your life for a season."

"A season?"

"Um hmm. They walk into our lives, make some kind of impact, and then it's over. You have to know when that season is over, and let go."

Savannah looks at her brother. She wipes a tear on the sleeve of her blouse.

"Well, if Daddy said it, it must be true, huh?"

L'il Daddy smiles.

"Let's go, sweetheart. Family's waiting for us."

L'il Daddy picks up his sister and swings her around – helicopter style. She laughs. He then hoists the smiling child onto his shoulders.

"...and the winner of the silver for the butterfly," L'il Daddy shouts running down the hill to his family, "The great Savannah Vernell Myles! Yayyyy!"

"HOLD IT!" Savannah shouts. She quickly jumps off her brother's shoulders.

"What's the matter?" He asks.

"What do you mean, *silver?*" she asks. "BABY GIRL'S GOING FOR THE GOLD!"

The future Olympian tags her brother playfully and runs in front of him. L'il Daddy smiles. He gives chase to the sweet little Georgia peach.

"What was I thinking?" he laughs to himself. He knows his baby sister would have it no other way.

Fredrick P. Dupree, III—Light, Bright, (and Almost…)

Passé Blanc: a term used for the French Creoles of Color in Louisiana that were so light skinned and looked so white that they were called "Passé Blanc". Passé Blanc is French for "Passing for white".

"*M & M,* Daddy?" says Frankie from the third row of Ol' Goldie.

"I think I will, son. Thank you."

Frankie reaches into the box and passes his father a single piece of the candy.

"One?" Jacob says looking in his palm. "Won't have to worry about this one melting," Jacob replies sarcastically. He pops the single piece of candy in his mouth and shakes his head at his miserly son.

"Just kidding, Daddy," Frankie laughs. "You can have some more."

"Thanks, son," he says rubbing his head. "Junior, let me know when you get tired of driving. We still got quite a ways to go."

"I'm fine, Daddy," Jacob's namesake says from behind the wheel. "Relax. I got this."

"Good man!" Jacob responds. "Dottie, are you keeping a record of our purchases?"

"Down to the last M&M," she smiles looking over her ledger.

"By my account," Jacob says in a voice only his wife can hear. "We should be fine until the end of summer. Your brother-in-law said he could find me a job before then. Can't believe I'm putting my life in his…"

"Wait a minute!" Dottie says interrupting her husband. "*My who*?"

"You know who. *Mr. Dupree? Fredrick P?*" mimics Jacob in his best self-aggrandizing tone. "The boss with the hot sauce!"

"I don't know why you keep putting him off on *me*!" Dottie says increasing her volume. Poor Dottie. She loses it whenever the conversation turns to super-conservative and mega-snob Fredrick P. Dupree, the third.

"Fredrick Dupree is *your* brother-in-law, Jacob Franklin Myles. Not mine. *Your* baby sister married him, not mine. No way on earth I'd ever let *my* sister marry that condescending little..."

"The children, baby." Jacob laughs. "Not in front of the children."

"You love to get me started, don't you?" Dottie says taking an imaginary bat to her husband's head.

Frankie taps his dad on his shoulder from the back seat.

"How come you don't like Uncle Fredrick, Daddy?"

"I never said I didn't like him, son," Jacob responds looking around.

"Looking for lightning?" Dottie says.

"Dottie, please. Well, son," says Jacob. "You know that old saying, *'Once you get to know someone, can't help but love 'em'?*"

"I think so," Frankie says pensively.

"Well, with Fredrick P. Dupree the third, it works in reverse. The more *Mr. Passé Blanc* opens his sadity mouth..."

"Passin' blank?" Frankie says. "Is that what the 'P' stands for, Daddy?"

"Probably!" Jacob jokes. "Never looked at it that way..."

"Oh now there *you* go," says Dottie folding her arms.

"You know me, Dottie. I call 'em like I see 'em. Hey!" Jacob shouts to the family. "Who knows the difference between in-laws and outlaws?"

"JACOB!" Dottie exclaims failing to stifle her laughter. "Now don't you start..."

Friday, May 12th, 1960

"Pass me the drip pan, L'il Daddy," Jacob says from under his brother-in-law's car.

"Here you go, Daddy," says his assistant/son. "Hey, Daddy, I know you're not too crazy about Uncle Fred. So why are we working on his car?"

"'Cause he's driving my baby sister around, that's why," says Jacob. "Don't want anything to happen to your Aunt Lucy or the kids."

L'il Daddy kneels down to where his father has been lying on the ground for the last ten minutes. He hands him a handkerchief for his brow.

"What about Uncle Fred, Daddy?" L'il Daddy says elbowing his father. "Don't want nothing to happen to him either, right?"

"Never you mind," Jacob says wiping his brow. He smiles as he hands the handkerchief back to his son. Always the comic. Jacob hops on his feet and playfully punches his son in the breadbasket.

From underneath Hopskip's oldest oak (and the hood of his brother-in-law's 1959 El Camino), Jacob Myles; rancher, farmer, and today auto mechanic performs a much-needed oil change on a very overworked automobile.

"This thing is bone dry," Jacob says referring to the car's engine. "Nice car like this? I got more sweat on my forehead. Some people…"

Jacob looks up the road toward the hotel; Hopskip's own Old Oak Inn. The Old Oak Inn is the only Negro hotel in town and home away from home for the Duprees; Jacob's visiting sister Lucy, his detestable brother-in-law Fredrick, and their two children; Tamara and Freddie, the fourth. Lucy and the kids are sitting on the patio drinking lemonade and talking to some of Lucy's old friends from high school while Fredrick awaits the arrival of his business contact. Fredrick hasn't even said hello to Lucy's friends. He pretends to be more interested in his fob than his long-suffering wife's old girlfriends. Fredrick's in town to close a very important business transaction for his company, *Thompson and Thompson of Illinois* - nothing more.

'*Why should I engage in their country gossip?*' the snob tells himself. '*They're beneath me!*'

"What is keeping Mr. Brand?" he barks.

Jacob frowns at the sight of his sister's husband posturing at the top of the hotel steps in his overpriced three-piece suit. He shakes his head pitying his poor peacock of a brother-in-law.

"You would think he was the Great Pharaoh surveying the pyramids," Jacob muses. Fredrick P. Dupree the third, New Orleans' answer to Mussolini, stands regally (or so he thinks) at the head of the stairway of the Old Oak Inn. Collectively, his clothes cost more than all three of his family members' wardrobes put together. His wife Lucille, Jacob's baby sister claims that he's been known to smile and tell a joke every now and then but she seems to be the only human to have ever witnessed it. Dupree met Lucille (he refuses to call her Lucy) as a waitress thirteen years ago in the restaurant of that very same hotel. Despite warnings from Papa Myles, his daughter fell in love with the pompous Mr. Dupree while on one of his business trips. Two days after the wedding, Dupree immediately moved his young bride to Chicago. He earned the nickname '*Ol' Whisk Broom*' from Lucy's father after he 'whisked her away from the only family she's ever known'. Poor Lucy's loneliness in the Windy City is matched only by the regret she feels for allowing Fredrick to move her away, and keep her away from her family and friends in Georgia. Lucy's last trip to Hopskip was for Papa Myles' funeral later that year. Dupree refused to accompany his wife as there were '*matters more pressing at the plant*'. Needless to say, there is no love lost between Jacob and his brother-in-law. Dupree has made it clear to his wife that people of their caliber have no need to hobnob with the likes of '*Country boy*' Jacob Myles. Dupree, of course, has never made that statement in Jacob's presence.

Fredrick scowls as a couple of Deacon Talbert's boys walk by with fishing poles on their shoulders. They're shirtless. They speak and wave to the Duprees. Lucy speaks to them and asks about their mother. Dupree sneers at the two boys and turns his head.

"What a piece of work," Jacob thinks to himself. "You'd think he was an overseer on one of Massa's plantations."

"Father, look! They're going fishing, can we..."

"GOD, NO! Drink your lemonade."

"Yes, sir."

"Fredrick, there's no harm in Little Freddie going fishing," Lucy intervenes. "Why, when I was his age, Jacob and I used to..."

Dupree quickly turns to his wife with an icy glare that would rival that of literary villain Simon Legree. Poor Lucy. She's been here before, and she knows it's best to change the subject. Or in Fredrick's case, not talk at all. Embarrassed and hurt, Lucy drops her head. Her friends pity her. They turn away and pretend not to notice her husband's cruelty to her and her son.

"Your father's so focused on this business deal with Mr. Brand," Lucy says to Freddie. She then takes little Freddie in her arms to comfort him. She's been here many times before, too.

"Maybe another time, Freddie. Just not today. Okay?"

"Maybe Uncle Jacob..." Freddie says jumping to his feet.

"Fredrick!" Dupree bellows. "What part of NO don't you understand?!?"

"Yes, sir," little Freddie says crawling back to his seat. Most children would cry at this point. Not Freddie. Not because he's without feeling. Poor Freddie has long gotten used to his father's inexplicable revulsion for him. Fredrick Dupree the fourth doesn't cry because he's not hurting. He simply has no tears left. A luxury his poor mother doesn't share.

Fredrick Dupree, the fourth, a sensitive, caring, and sheltered child from the Pill Hill neighborhood on Chicago's South Side. Disregarded and ignored by his father, young Fredrick has his own way of dealing with heartache - thumbing through his book of piano concertos and practicing an imaginary keyboard. Dubbed the *Black Beethoven* by the younger members of the Myles clan, the young prodigy buries himself in his music to make up for his father's estrangement. Unbeknownst to the Myles children, Freddie is the love child of an affair between the senior Dupree and a woman who once worked for his company. She and Fredrick split before Dupree's marriage to Lucy. After a year of marriage, the Duprees were shocked to find a little boy with his father's eyes literally on their doorstep. Despite her husband's insistence that the child be shipped to an orphanage, Lucy insisted the boy move in with the Duprees. Although adopted by Lucy, Freddie is closer to her than he is to his father. Lucy raises young Freddie as her own. Sensing the coolness from his father and the tension between his parents, Freddie welcomes his Uncle Jacob as a surrogate dad; a relationship not lost on the elder Dupree - just one more reason why Mr. Dupree despises Mr. Myles and why Mrs. Dupree has been forbidden to travel south.

"Now, Fredrick," says his younger sister. "Why would anyone want to spend a beautiful day like today playing with worms and chicken livers? Why those boys weren't even wearing shoes. It's just not done, Freddie. It just isn't. Is it, Daddy?"

"Ha, Ha! That's my girl." Dupree chuckles. Even his laugh is sinister.

"Besides, Freddie," Tamara says with a wink to her Daddy. "I would think you've had *enough* sun!"

"TAMMY!" Lucy screams. "THAT'S ENOUGH!"

"Why mother," Tammy says feigning innocence. "What did *I* do?"

Freddie hangs his head. Dupree turns away from the gathering snickering at his only son's distress. Freddie gets up from the table and runs back to the hotel in shame.

"Oh, be a man already!" Dupree yells after his son. "Your sister was only kidding."

Tamara winks at her Dad and laughs as Freddie runs away.

"Good work, Lucille," Dupree sneers. "You'll make a girl out of him yet!"

Lucy shakes her head embarrassed by her husband's abuse of her and Freddie in front of her friends. They shake their heads and walk away feeling sorrow for Lucy and scorn for the poor woman's husband and daughter.

Tamara Lucille Dupree is the *light* of her father's life. Tamara or *Lady Jacqueline* as the Myles family calls her, (they seem to have a name for everyone) is a "bargained" child. Fredrick, who never wanted children, agreed to a child of their own for Lucy. Tammy is Lucy's "payment" from her husband for her silence and long-suffering regarding the younger Freddie's roots. Tammy, a ten-year-old fashion maven, and clotheshorse is spoiled by her father and grates on the nerves of the entire Myles clan – everyone that is except mother Dottie. She sees a heart under all that ribbon, lace, and sass. Dottie also sees the sweet little girl Tamara's mother Lucy was at that age. The complete opposite of her down-to-earth cousin Savannah Vernell, who never heard of anyone getting "paid for grades", spoiled yet pretty Tamara Dupree expects and usually gets money for every chore she does (or tricks poor Freddie into doing for her). Unlike young militant Savannah, Little Miss Runway would never give up her pillbox hat to go "protesting for other people's problems". To her mother's chagrin and her father's joy, Tamara is becoming a younger version of the high and mighty Fredrick P. Dupree. Apparently, the worst of his attributes has rubbed off on his daughter. Lucy has made it her life's work to turn her baby around and save her from her father's clutches - a task which seems to increase in difficulty each day.

"Tamara Dupree!"

"Yes, mother. I know, I know," the child says. She gets up from the table and heads for the hotel.

"*Find your brother and apologize,*" she says mimicking her mother. "Don't understand what made you think I'd enjoy myself in Hop. Skip."

"Amen!" Dupree says under his breath but loud enough to hear. Fredrick Dupree hasn't set foot in Hopskip since before he and Lucy married and moved to Chicago fifteen years ago. Whenever the Myleses attempted to visit the Duprees in Chicago, Fredrick had to work. Jacob doesn't doubt his sister's love. He knows her husband. He thinks he's too good for the likes of the Myleses and *'those of a darker hue'*.

"Color struck SOB thinks he's too good to stay at the ranch," says Jacob out of earshot of his son sitting on the trunk of his uncle's car. "I hope they overcharged him."

Lucy, distraught and embarrassed seeks shelter from her husband's abuse. She waves to her brother Jacob from the hotel patio. He blows his little sister a kiss, smiles and then turns his attention back to the car. Dupree frowns, throws his attaché case on the table and flops into his daughter's chair.

"Damn it, Brand! Would you please hurry so I can leave this God forsaken town!"

"So what's Uncle Fred doing here, Daddy," says L'il Daddy from behind the wheel of his uncle's El Camino.

"His company sent him down here. Wants to buy land to build a factory. Says he can bring new **BUS'-NESS** and *IN-**DUS**-TRI-A-LI-ZA-TION* to our little backwater town," Jacob says emphasizing his brother-in-law's arrogance. "Only people with that much land in these parts are the Brands. That should be interesting. Your Aunt Lucy confided in your mother that Fredrick could get a substantial raise and promotion if he pulls it off. Personally, I've never known Fredrick Dupree to do anything for anybody. Selfish, piece of work, your uncle…"

"The Brands are here?" says young Jacob glossing over his Daddy's last few sentences. The poor boy stopped listening when he heard the name Brand. He jumps out of the car and looks around.

"Did he bring Molly Beth?" he says staring up the road.

Jacob pauses. He drops an oil can on the ground near the toolbox. He looks up and notices his son fidgeting; looking around desperately as if he's lost something. His mind, no doubt thinks Jacob.

Jacob pauses. He watches his son looking around as if he's expecting a parade in his honor to come up the street any minute.

'Wait a minute! This can't be what I think', Jacob thinks to himself. *'I know the boy knows better!'*

"Why?" Jacob asks his son pointedly. "Why are you so interested in Molly Brand?"

"No reason, Daddy," L'il Daddy says collecting himself. "I see her at school sometimes is all. She's all right. We were friends a long, long time ago, remember?"

L'il Daddy picks up a wrench and hands it to his father. His hands are shaking.

"I didn't ask for this," Jacob says referring to the wrench. "Is that all? Just all right?" Jacob asks. He looks in his son's eyes for the truth but the boy wisely turns away.

"Son, I asked you a question."

"Well, Daddy…" L'il Daddy says staring at anything and everything but his father. "It so happens…"

"JACOB!" booms a voice from behind the elder Myles and his son. "Still fixing other people's cars, are ya? L'il Jacob, how's it going? Son, I'd like to talk to you if you have a few minutes. It's about my Molly."

Marvin Brand – landowner and childhood friend of Jacob Myles. At one time, Jacob Myles and Marvin Brand were close –like two peas in a pod. That is until Jim Crow, the code of the south dictated that they could no longer be friends once young Marvin 'came of age'. Marvin's father broke up the friendship between the two boys on young Marvin's thirteenth birthday. For two straight years, Jacob met Marvin on Saturday mornings at their own private fishing hole. The lake was on Brand property. Jacob bought Marvin a fishing pole with money he earned doing odd jobs around town. He expected his old friend to greet him with a smile and handshake as always when they got together; however, when he arrived Jacob was greeted instead by the barrel of Marvin's new rifle. Egged on by his father and a few of the old man's cronies, young Marvin told Jacob he was no longer welcome on Brand property and from that moment on, he was to refer to him as *Mister* Brand. Jacob refused. The senior Brand grabbed his son's new rifle and threatened to shoot Jacob's face off if he didn't *'remember his place'*. To save his friend, Marvin intervened and chased Jacob off his land. Later that day, Jacob pitched the fishing pole in the lake where the two *'buddies'* used to fish. Since then, there has never been a cordial moment between them. Jacob never fished anywhere without being reminded of Marvin's birthday and the humiliation he suffered at the hands of his *'best friend'*. The Brand family is said to own approximately 75% of the land in Hopskip. It is on this land

–called the North Forty - which *Thompson and Thompson of Illinois* plans to build a factory.

"What do you want to talk to my son about, Marvin?"

"Now, Jake there you go getting your feathers all ruffled."

"I think you know why," Jacob says confronting his ex-fishing buddy.

"Now Jake, I had nothing to do with that," Brand pleads with his childhood buddy. "You know how things are. Christ Almighty, I don't make the rules. Come on Jake, I just wanna talk to L'il Jacob. The boy hasn't done anything."

"I know that!"

"I'm just asking for his help is all, Jake. Christ Almighty!"

"Do yourself a favor, Marvin," Jacob admonishes him. "Leave the Good Lord's name out of your mouth."

Brand is shocked. He's speechless. He steps up to Jacob. Jacob stands his ground. The two men stare down one another until L'il Daddy breaks the tension.

"What is it, Mr. Brand," L'il Daddy says trying to temper the long-simmering crisis between the two ex-friends. "What can I do for you?"

"Son," Marvin says finally taking his gaze off Jacob. "You're in school with my Molly girl, right?"

"Yes, sir. I am."

"See her every day, do you?"

"Most days." L'il Daddy responds nervously. "Sometimes."

"Well now I'm sure this is just a vicious rumor, 'cause I trust my Molly."

"What is it, Marvin?" Jacob barks getting more irritated by the minute.

"I just wanna know. You see her with any of those new kids?"

"New kids?" L'il Daddy asks.

"You know what I mean. People saying since the school integrated… and guess what, I have no problem with that."

"You don't?" Jacob says reminded of Brand's reputation.

"No, I don't." Brand responds. "It's a new day. Anyway, people saying my Molly girl's getting real friendly with some of *your* friends, the new kids that got bussed in last month."

"Sir?"

"Would you know anything about that, L'il Jacob?"

L'il Daddy seems worried, but his nervousness is visible only to his father. Jacob steps up to his son's defense.

"Marvin!" says Jacob irritably. "What are you implying?"

"Now, now Jake I'm only worried about my baby's welfare. You would be, too if it was Rosie."

"Josie!" Jacob corrects him.

"Josie. Right, I knew that," says Marvin. "Good gal, er girl! Anyway, my Molly girl's softhearted – like her mother was. God bless her. I'm just asking you to keep an eye on her and those new kids. Big fellas, I hear. They might think my Molly's interested and you and I both know that could never be."

Jacob looks at the ignorant racist as if he'd just stepped off a spaceship.

"… and just what do you expect *my* son to do, Marvin?"

"Why, keep an eye on her of course. Make sure nobody gets too close. …know what I mean, L'il Jacob? You would be like, like my secret weapon. I'd even be willing to pay…"

"MARVIN!" Jacob starts to boil.

"That's not necessary, Mr. Brand," L'il Daddy says.

Oblivious to anyone's needs but his own, Brand ignores Myles and son and quickly switches gears.

"Okay, well let me know. Oh by the way," he continues. "Have either of you seen a white man in these parts looking for me."

"A white man?" Jacob responds. "Around here? Son, pick up these tools and put them in the truck. Toss these empty cans in the back while you're at it."

"Yes, Daddy," his son responds.

"Yeah, a white man." Brands answers. "Big shot corporate executive. Came all the way from Chicago with his family. That's in Illinois."

"I know where it is, Marvin." Jacob says annoyed by Marvin's pomposity.

"I heard he might be here at the Old Oak Inn."

"Now why would a white man be staying at the Old Oak?"

"Yeah, I know. I know," Brand responds scratching his head. "That's what they told me on the phone when I called his office. I figured he must've got lost. Have you seen him around?"

"Well, I don't know," Jacob responds. "What's his name?"

"His name?"

"His name," Jacob says even more annoyed than before.

Marvin Brand starts to chuckle. For some reason Jacob Myles' exasperation gives the old fool the giggles.

"Jake, you'll never change. Always in a hurry."

"Marvin?"

"Yeah?"

"His name?"

"Oh, yeah, yeah. His name. Got it right here." Marvin reaches into his pocket and pulls out a slip of paper.

"Ah, here we go." Marvin exclaims. "Dupree. Fella goes by the name of Dupree."

L'il Daddy drops the tool box and almost hits his father's foot.

"What?" L'il Daddy almost shouts.

"Son, please!" Jacob intervenes. He pauses a minute and turns his attention back to Marvin.

"Did you say a *white* man named Dupree?"

"Yeah! Fredrick P. Dupree." Brand says almost beaming. "Good ol' boy from Louisiana. Moved north about fifteen years ago."

Jacob turns away to stifle his laughter.

"Always knew he was passin'!" Jacob muses. *"Wait'll Dottie hears this!"*

"Dupree, huh?" Jacob says collecting himself. "Hmmm. Son."

"Yes, Daddy?"

"Got a little errand for you."

"Yes, sir?"

" Go tell your uncle his car is ready."

"Yes sir."

"...and while you're up there,"

"Yes, Daddy?"

" See if a..." Jacob stops and turns to Marvin to verify the gentleman's name.

"Dupree," Brand says proudly. "Fredrick P. Dupree. From Chicago, Illinois."

"See if a *Fredrick P. Dupree* from Chicago, Illinois is around. Let him know Mr. Marvin Brand is waitin' for him under the old oak tree."

"Got it, Daddy," his son responds fully aware of his daddy's prank. "Fredrick P. Dupree. Got it!"

"…and L'il Daddy,"

"Sir?"

" While you're up there…"

"Yes, sir?"

"Stay and visit with your Aunt Lucy and the kids."

"Aww, Daddy. Can't I…?"

"Now, son." Jacob says sternly. "Do as I ask. Mr. Dupree and Mr. Brand have important business to tend to."

"Whatever you say, Daddy."

"You're a good man, Jacob." Brand says patting his old friend on the shoulder. "Thank you, L'il Jacob. I appreciate it."

"No problem, Mr. Brand," L'il Daddy says walking toward the hotel. The young man then turns around as if he just remembered something.

"Oh, and Mr. Brand?"

"Yes, son."

"I'll be sure to keep an eye on Molly Beth at school."

Jacob blanches. Lucky for him (and L'il Daddy) that Marvin Brand is clueless when it comes to such things.

"Thank you, son. That means a lot to me." Brand turns to Jacob. "He's gonna be one of the good ones, Jake. You should be proud."

"Proud's not the word, Marvin."

Jacob and Marvin watch as L'il Daddy runs up the road to the hotel and straight up the stairs to Dupree standing at the top of the stairway. Jacob watches intently as his son speaks to his brother-in-law and then points to him and Marvin Brand standing beside his car.

"Little Lucy's back in town, is she?" Brand asks.

"Uh huh," Jacob responds. "Here with her husband and children for a visit."

"That a fact? Always liked your sister. She's a sweet girl."

"Uh huh. Husband's a nice fellow, too."

"Is he now?"

"Um hm."

Dupree looks up the road at the two men leaning on his El Camino. He puts on his hat and straightens his tie. Dupree then grabs his attaché case from the patio table where his wife and her friends had been talking and driving him mad with their *country gossip*.

"Good luck, dear," Lucy shouts.

Dupree ignores his wife and downs the last of her lemonade. He trots down the hotel stairway until he reaches the road. He then waves at Brand. Brand waves back to the enthusiastic sales representative. Dupree turns his brim down over his face to protect him from the sun. He walks with his head down.

"Probably afraid he'll step on a cow pie," Jacob laughs to himself. "Pompous little…"

"That must be Mr. Dupree," Brand says smiling.

"Yep, that's him all right," says Jacob. "You two should get along fine."

Dupree walks cautiously down the road toward Jacob and Marvin careful not to get any dust (or cow pies) on his brand new alligator shoes. Brand notices Dupree's finely tailored three-piece suit.

"Fancy fella, ain't he?"

"City folk," Jacob responds. "Must be professional at all times."

"Right, right," Brand concurs. He snatches off his baseball cap and shoves it in his back pocket. Brand then slicks back his hair and tucks his shirt in his pants.

"You don't have a tie in your truck, do you Jake," Brand asks looking to his one-time buddy for help.

"Sorry."

"You should always keep a tie nearby, Jacob."

"I'll remember that, Marvin."

Dupree gets closer to the pair standing under the old oak. L'il Daddy apparently left one of Jacob's tools on the ground when he dropped his daddy's toolbox. Dupree trips on it just as Brand steps forward to shake the *corporate bigwig's* hand. Dupree's hat falls to the ground. Instinctively, Brand stoops to pick it up. When he stands up, he's face-to-face with Fredrick P. Dupree, the third.

Brand turns pale.

"Who the hell are you?"

Jacob makes the introductions.

"Ahem. Fredrick Dupree, Marvin Brand. Marvin Brand, meet Fredrick Dupree; my brother-in-law."

Fredrick extends his hand. Brand retracts his.

"Brother-in-law?" Brand screams. "You're little Lucy's husband? The big shot CEO from Chicago? The hell you doing passing yourself off as a white man?!?"

"Now, now remember what you told L'il Jacob, Marvin," Jacob says stirring the pot. "It's a *new day!*"

"New day, hell!" Brand screams exploding with anger. He's almost nose to nose with Dupree. "You think I can't tell the difference? I'll ask you again, where do you get off passing yourself off as a white man?"

"Mr. Brand," Dupree yells reddened and flustered. "I assure you I'm not passing for any white man. I'm Fredrick P. Dupree, the third – Junior, soon to be Senior Sales Representative for *Thompson and Thompson, Inc.* of Chicago, Ill. I came here for business, Mr. Brand. To purchase *your* land to build a new a factory for *your* town. You stand to make a tidy little sum once we... Well, look. Mr. Brand. I have the blueprint right here..."

Dupree hurriedly places his attaché case on the hood of his car. He opens it and reaches into it for the blueprint.

"Really?" Brand screams knocking Dupree's attaché case to the ground. "Well, listen to me JUNIOR, soon to be SENIOR sales... whatever you call yourself! The deal's off!"

"OFF!?!"

"OFF, Dupree! O-F-F! OFF!"

"But Mr. Brand..." Dupree pleads. "If you'll just listen..."

"I've heard enough!" Brand continues. "You tell *Thompson and Thompson* of Chicago, Ill. to send me somebody I can work with – a white man. A *real* white man. Not some gussied up...whatever you call it, in a gaudy three-piece suit!"

Brand throws up his hands and storms off, but not before imparting a few choice words to Jacob.

"I won't forget this, Myles! Count on it!"

"I'm sure you won't, Marvin," Jacob replies calmly. "I'm sure you won't."

Lucy and L'il Daddy run to Fredrick and Jacob standing under the tree. The two men are arguing. Fredrick is obviously beside himself after the humiliation with Brand.

"Daddy, you OK," asks L'il Daddy.

"I'm fine, son. Nothing I can't handle."

"Fredrick, what's wrong?" asks Lucy distraught and anxious. "We heard Mr. Brand screaming all the way up the road. What happened?"

"Ask your precious brother!" Dupree screams.

"Me?" asks Jacob in mock bewilderment. "What did I do?"

"You set me up, Myles!" screams Dupree. "This is your doing. I know it."

"Set you up? How, Fredrick?" Jacob asks. "How did I set you up? All I did was introduce you..."

"...and you knew exactly what would transpire, didn't you? Apparently your little backwater burg has no need for INDUSTRIALIZATION."

"You're being irrational, Dupree. Get a grip!" Jacob says. "Not my fault Brand saw through you. Passing for white! Unbelievable!"

"I am not passing for white," Dupree shouts.

"Passing for white?" Lucy shouts.

"Uncle Fredrick's passin'?" L'il Daddy asks his father.

"I AM NOT PASSING FOR WHITE!" Dupree screams. "I've had enough! Lucille! Pack your things! Now! We're leaving."

"Leaving? Honey, please no!" begs Lucy.

"Now don't take this out on Lucy and the kids, Fred," Jacob says taking Dupree by the shoulders. "Just calm down."

"Fredrick, baby. We just got here. I haven't had more than a minute with Dottie and the kids! I haven't seen my family in years. Please!"

"REALLY?" Dupree says pulling away from Jacob. "Seems I did you a favor!"

"What's that supposed to mean, Dupree?" Jacob demands.

"I think you know. **COUNTRY BOY!**"

Jacob narrows his eyes. He takes off his gloves and throws them on the ground. Angered by his brother-in-law's obvious disrespect for his sister and the town he loves, he approaches the arrogant peacock until the two men are face-to-face. Anticipating a brawl, L'il Daddy takes it upon himself to step between the two men.

"Daddy. Uncle Fred..."

Jacob gently pushes his son aside. Though shaking inside, Dupree surprisingly stands his ground. No doubt expecting someone to break up the fracas.

Lucy grabs her brother's arm. She's seen Jacob upset before but never like this.

"Jacob, please. He didn't mean it."

"You don't speak for me, Lucille," Dupree says looking Jacob square in his eyes. "Go back to the hotel."

"You have two minutes, Dupree..." Jacob says approaching his brother-in-law and clenching his fists.

"Or what? Oh, of course! OF COURSE!" Dupree sneers. "Fisticuffs! Isn't that always the way? But then again, why should I be surprised? After all, what can you expect from a man who NEVER FINISHED HIGH SCHOOL?"

Dupree fires the first shot and as typical of men of his caliber, he hits below the belt. Jacob has always regretted never finishing high school and this jackal has the nerve to throw it in his face.

"Dupree," Jacob says calmly as he removes his shirt. "I'm going to do *you* a favor. I'm gonna take you out of your misery." Jacob removes his brother-in-law's glasses and gives them to his son. With just one hand, Jacob grabs his brother-in-law by the collar of his neatly starched shirt. Dupree tries to sucker punch Jacob but misses. He swings. Again. And again. His reach; unfortunately, is not as long as his opponent's and he misses each time. He tries to break free from Jacob's grasp but *Country Boy* Jacob Myles is much too powerful for the citified Fredrick P. Dupree. Poor Dupree is so thin and frail Jacob could easily choke his brother-in-law with one hand if he wanted to. Expecting the worst, Dupree closes his eyes and winces. After what seems like an eternity, he opens them again only to see a huge black fist circling the air. A crowd of onlookers has gathered. Some are actually placing bets on the odds-on favorite, *Country Boy Jacob Myles*.

With tears in his eyes, the cowardly sales rep looks to the crowd for help. Jacob Franklin Myles (and all of Lucy's friends and hotel staff who've now come down from the Inn to see the pummeling) has waited for this moment for years, since Lucy's wedding – the moment when Fredrick P. Dupree, the third, the prissy peacock from the big city gets his feathers plucked. Jacob draws his fist as far back as South Florida.

"Betcha he won't be passin' when Jacob gets through with him!" Lucy's old friend whispers to one of the onlookers.

"I know that's right!" he tells her.

Jacob swings!

Lucy screams.

"JACOB! NO! PLEASE!!!"

"...never get tired of hearing that story," Dottie says reminiscing.

"Daddy, did you really hit Uncle Fredrick?" asks Savannah from the back of the car.

"I thought you were asleep," Jacob responds looking back at his youngest daughter.

"Savannah is never asleep when there's a story to be told," Josie laughs.

"Amen to that," says Dottie.

"Daddy?" says Frankie.

"Yes, son?"

"What's *passin*?" Frankie says inquisitively.

"This should be good," L'il Daddy whispers to Josie.

"Hmmm. Passing…" muses Jacob. "How can I put this?"

"Get ready, Sis," L'il Daddy says.

Jacob turns around to the back seat to explain the word to Frankie.

"Well son, passing is when a ni-,"

"Daddy!" screams Josie horrified.

"I knew it," says L'il Daddy. "I knew it!"

"YOU KNEW WHAT?" Jacob bellows from the middle row of the station wagon. "When have you ever known me to use that word?"

Dottie steps up to support her husband. "…and girl, you know that word ain't even in your Daddy's vocabulary!"

"Thank you, baby!" Jacob says with a nod.

"Thank *you*, baby!" Dottie nods back.

"Sorry, Daddy." Josie and L'il Daddy say in unison. Jacob shakes his head at his two eldest.

"Frankie. As I was about to say. '*Passing*' is when a NIMCOMPOOP like your uncle Fredrick tries to be something he isn't."

"Something he isn't?" says Frankie.

"Um hmm. Remember when I told you that God gives us all a uniform to wear?"

L'il Daddy and Josie let out a collective groan. Their daddy's life lessons always come by way of one of his baseball analogies. Not very popular with Jacob's two oldest. Frankie, however is very attentive.

"Yes, sir," he responds. "…and we should be happy with the uniform God gives us."

"That's right, son."

"…and we should never try and change the color - even if others do."

"Right again. Well, some people like your Uncle Fredrick try to trade in their uniform for another one. One that doesn't really fit. They'll pull on the sleeves and tug on the collar this way and that trying to get it to fit but it won't. It never will. The day will always come when they'll see that God don't make no mistakes."

"Preach!" Dottie says.

Jacob continues. "He knew what he was doing when he issued him the uniform he was born with and that he should just do the best with it that they can. Do you see what I'm saying, son?"

"I do, Daddy," Frankie responds smiling. "Be yourself. Love who you are. Who God made you. And stop *passing*!"

"That's my boy," Jacob says hugging his smiling middle child. "That's why you're my favorite."

"Hey!" says L'il Daddy looking back at his father.

"Boy, watch the road," says Jacob. "You can be my favorite tomorrow."

The rest of the family laughs at L'il Daddy. He has to admit. It was funny. He soon joins in the frivolity with his family.

"Daddy," says Savannah.

"Yes, baby girl?"

"You never answered my question."

"What was that?"

"Did you really hit Uncle Fredrick?"

"What do you think?"

"Well, it doesn't sound like something you would do. You don't even hit us. Deacon Talbert back home hits his kids all the time."

"His kids deserve hitting!" Josie says under her breath.

"No, Savannah," says Dottie. "Your Daddy didn't hit Uncle Fredrick."

"I couldn't. The whole town was watching, his children. Besides, I couldn't do that to your Aunt Lucy," Jacob admits.

"She woulda been mad, huh Daddy?"

"No," says Jacob. "But if I hit Fredrick, your Aunt Lucy would've felt the pain, too. Maybe even more than your Uncle Fredrick. Do you understand what I'm saying, Savannah?"

"I think so."

"Besides, baby girl," Jacob continues. "There are better ways to handle arguments."

"But, Daddy!" Frankie says a little confused. "You taught *me* how to fight."

"No, I taught you how to *protect* yourself. There's a difference. Besides, with Fredrick P. Dupree, the third there wouldn't have been much of a fight," Jacob says winking at wife Dottie.

"I know that's right," says L'il Daddy at the wheel. "There woulda been only two hits." L'il Daddy loudly honks the station wagon's horn mimicking his father hitting his uncle. He hits it a second time – barely making a sound - mimicking his Uncle hitting the floor.

"Need I say more?"

"So very, very true," says Josie laughing.

They all look at their father with pride. Frankie and Savannah start to cheer. Baby Terry, awake from his nap chimes in.

"Yay, Daddy! Yay, Dad! Yay, Pop!" yell the three youngest of the Myles clan.

L'il Daddy smiles at Jacob through the rearview mirror. Savannah reaches over and kisses her dad. They soon stop cheering and go back to their books.

Jacob looks at Dottie and whispers in her ear.

"I didn't hit him, but it sure felt good watching him squirm!"

L'il Daddy snatches a peek at his dad in the rearview mirror.

"So Daddy," he says grinning. "What's the difference between in-laws and outlaws?"

"Simple, son!" Jacob says winking at the lovely lady next to him. "OUTLAWS ARE WANTED!"

The Myles Clan—Playing Favorites

Sunday morning, April 1ˢᵗ, 1962.

WITH ONLY A few hours to go, the Myles family decides to take another break. Jacob pulls over to a truck stop to rest. Jacob drove 'Goldie' the last 100 miles or so from Indiana while Dottie kept him awake with ideas for her catering business. L'il Daddy and Frankie, sitting in the middle row of the family wagon play War – a kid's card game and the only one Frankie knows. Unbeknownst to Mother Dottie - who abhors gambling in any form - they're playing for M & M's. Josie, Savannah, and Terry grabbed a few Z's for the last two hours in the back seat and are now anxious to see their new home.

"How much longer before we get to Chicago, Daddy?" says L'il Daddy? He zaps his little brother's forehead with the Ace of Spades.

Frankie playfully punches his brother in the breadbasket.

"Be patient," Jacob says. "By my calculations, we should get there this afternoon sometime."

"Okay, Daddy," L'il Daddy says smacking his cards on the seat between him and Frankie.

"Wanna see a picture of the house?" Jacob asks. He passes it to L'il Daddy but Josie snatches it out of her brother's hands.

"You know the favorite child goes first," Josie tells him.

"You wish!" her brother counters. Josie takes a look at the building her father has chosen for his family to live for the rest of their lives. She's not impressed.

"Hmmm. Kinda small, isn't it Daddy?"

"It looks small on the outside, I'll grant you that, baby girl," Jacob says taking back the Polaroid. He turns to her and smiles. "...but it's roomy. Once you get inside, you'll see it's pretty big. Everyone has their own bedroom. Frankie, I'll need you to bunk with the baby for awhile. At least 'til L'il Daddy goes off to school."

"School? You mean like college?" says Frankie winking at his brother. "Might as well get my own place."

"Cute, Frankie, cute," says L'il Daddy counting his books. "That's why I'm tanning that *butt*."

"Watch your mouth, son," says Jacob.

"Yes, sir."

"Frankie? Can you bunk with your brother?"

"Sure, Daddy. I can live with that," Frankie agrees. "But I get to choose the pictures we put on the wall. Deal, Terry?"

"Deal!" says Terry grinning.

"Wow! He understands," says Frankie.

"Ha, ha," laughs Jacob. "That's my boy."

"I assume all of our furniture made it in one piece," Dottie says. "Did you thank Milt Paulsen for lending you his truck?"

"I certainly did. Once we're in, the men will start moving everything to the right rooms."

"Milt's a good friend," says Dottie to her husband. "We have to invite him and Gloria up one day. How big is the dining room, Jacob?"

"Well, there's a room with a pool table in it," Jacob responds. "Me and L'il Dad- uh, L'il Daddy and *I* can move it down to the basement. I'll fix it up for you."

"The *basement*?" Dottie says.

"The dining room, I mean," Jacob smiles. "Cabinets and everything."

"A house with a basement," muses Dottie. "That's a first."

"Yep. Lucy says the previous owner once considered making it a bomb shelter."

"A bomb shelter?" Savannah says. "Daddy, is it dangerous where we're going?"

"Of course not, baby girl. I wouldn't have brought you here if it was."

Frankie jumps into the conversation. "A pool table? In our *house*? Now, *that's* a first!"

"Thought you'd like that," Jacob says enthusiastically. "...and I can teach you. We'll all learn."

"I didn't know you played pool, Daddy," says Savannah. "Were you a hustler? Like in that movie? Is that how you paid for this house, Daddy?"

"Leave the finances to the grownups, Savannah," Jacob admonishes his little girl. "…and yes, I played. In my youth. 'Til your mother came along."

"Thank God for that," Dottie says.

Frankie shakes his head piteously. "Boy. Marriage! Where fun goes to die!"

The family wagon at one time bustling with laughter and anticipation of their new beginnings suddenly grows silent. Everyone looks at Dottie - then at Frankie. Frankie looks around wondering what's going on. Dottie breaks the silence.

"WHERE FUN GOES TO DIE?!? What's that supposed to mean?" she says turning her head towards the little boy who's on his way to being her *ex*-son.

Josie and L'il Daddy stifle a giggle. Savannah; however, lets it all out. Franklin Joseph Myles, who apparently contracted *foot-in-mouth* as a baby has a knack for saying the wrong thing at the right time. Jacob shakes his head. L'il Daddy waves goodbye to poor Frankie.

"Good knowing you, Buddy."

"WHAT DID YOU MEAN, FRANKIE?" Dottie demands. "WHERE FUN GOES TO DIE?!?"

"Huh, uh nothing," Frankie says trying to wiggle out of his undoing. "I just meant that when two people get married, the man doesn't get to play with his friends anymore. He stays home and can't go nowhere. Marriage is like prison, only the food is better."

Josie and L'il Daddy drop their heads. Because of his mouth, their little brother is headed for the guillotine - again. Jacob's been here before – many times. Clouds are gathering from the east. The sky is dark and there's a storm brewing. It's name? DOROTHY ROSETTA MYLES.

"SO YOU THINK I CREATED A DUNGEON FOR YOUR DADDY?"

"NO! NO! Mama," Frankie says. "Not you! Your food is good!"

"For a prison?"

"Yeah! I mean NO! Aw, Mama!"

Frankie, known for interspersing his cheerful conversation with a song lyric or two is now at a loss for words. Savannah; unfortunately for Frankie, is not.

"Frankie's doing the Jailhouse Rock! Frankie's doing the Jailhouse Rock!"

Josie and L'il Daddy join in the hilarity by singing Savannah's little ditty and doing the twist in their seats. They both imitate the King.

"Frankie's doing the Jailhouse Rock! Frankie's doing the Jailhouse Rock!"

Frankie's siblings burst out in tears laughing at their poor brother's dilemma.

"Thank you very much! Thank you very much!" L'il Daddy says slicking back his imaginary pompadour and adding to the merriment.

"Okay, okay that's enough," says Jacob refereeing his crew as always. "A prison, Frankie? Boy, where are you getting these ideas?"

"Miles Wright," Frankie says dropping his head.

"There's no money on the floor of the car, son."

"Sir?"

"Hold your head up and look at the person talking to you. You're not in trouble," Jacob reassures him.

"Yes, sir." Frankie says licking out his tongue at Savannah.

"Miles Wright," Jason ponders. "Coach Charlie Wright's grandson?

"Yeah, I mean yes. Yes, sir," Frankie corrects himself mindful that his mom is sitting in front of him and still stewing over his latest *faux pas.* "His big brother got married."

"Who, Derek?" says L'il Daddy. *"Derek Wright got married?"*

"Yep!" says Josie. "He sure did. To *your* girl. Jennifer Murphy."

"Jennifer Murphy?" Jacob asks. "Isn't she in your class, son?"

"She got left back a few times at her old school." says L'il Daddy. "Wow. The Komodo got married."

"Well, you had your chance!" Josie laughs.

"Please!" L'il Daddy responds. "He has my condolences."

"Hmmm. So Ethel Murphy finally trapped a boy for her daughter," Dottie says to herself. She thinks back to their last and only confrontation. *"...a moment of silence for the dearly departed."*

"Yeah, Derek got married," Frankie continues. "...and his wife won't even let him come to the barbershop anymore."

"Yeah," says Josie laughing. "I heard that. They say *she* cuts his hair now. I think *some*body's whipped."

"JOCELYN DOROTHY MYLES." Dottie says firmly. "I don't like that term."

Josie knows that when her mother uses her whole name, it's best to be quiet and just say…

"Yes, Mama!"

"She's whipping him, too?" Frankie yells. "That's it. I'm never getting married."

"Oh, Frankie!" Dottie says annoyed by his naiveté.

"Alright, everybody. Calm down," Jacob says getting back on track. "Now, Frankie. You say marriage is like a prison. You see any handcuffs on me?"

"No, sir."

"Stripes?" Jacob says referring to the wardrobe of choice.

"No, sir," Frankie cries. "…but that's 'cause Mama's different."

"That's right, l'il brother," L'il Daddy whispers. *"Lay it on."*

"How am I different, baby?" says Dottie mellowing.

"You're pretty," Frankie says looking her way.

"There you go," L'il Daddy says holding an imaginary fishing pole. *"Reel her in."*

"…and *you* can cook!" Frankie says confidently.

"…and he's back!" L'il Daddy says clapping. "We have a winner, ladies and gentlemen. Franklin Myles is back in the family!"

"Boy, if you don't hush," Dottie warns her son.

"Okay, Mama. Okay."

"First of all, just because you think a woman is pretty and knows how to cook," Dottie says, "doesn't necessarily mean she's marriage material."

"Maybe not," L'il Daddy says. "But it's a good start."

"I'm going to pretend I didn't hear that," Dottie says.

"Sorry, Mama!"

"Frankie, how do you know this girl can't cook?" Dottie asks. "I mean it doesn't surprise me knowing her mother, but…"

"Oooooh, Mama," Savannah says laughing.

"Well," says Frankie. "Two weeks ago, Derek's wife told me and Miles she'd fix some snacks for us if we cut her mama's grass before she came home."

*"They're **living** with Ethel Murphy?"* Dottie says to Jacob. "That marriage doesn't stand a chance."

Jacob nods his head. "Talk about getting off on the wrong foot. Ethel Murphy? Go on, son!"

Frankie continues his story.

"I said sure. I'll do it but Miles said he had to go home."

"Smart boy!" says Jacob.

"It took me two whole hours to do it by myself," Frankie exclaimed. "…and I was getting real hungry. When I was finished, she gave me some greens and corn bread from the night before. She said Derek was on a diet."

"Diet, huh?" Everyone says to themselves. The family all give one another that knowing look.

Josie interrupts Frankie.

"I thought you *liked* greens and corn bread, Frankie."

"I do." Frankie says looking at Daddy Jacob for consensus. "…a little tomato, some vinegar, and onion. Oh yeah, I could *do* some damage!"

"TALK SON, TALK!" Jacob responds with his hands in the air.

"Jacob, you stop!" Dottie says trying to hide her smile. "Go on Frankie, what happened."

"Mama," Frankie continues with a puzzled look on his face. "Are greens supposed to crunch when you eat 'em?"

"If they're in a salad…" Dottie responds.

"This wasn't no salad," Frankie responds shaking his head.

"Oh no!" Dottie says. "She didn't cook 'em long enough. Poor thing!"

"Probably forgot to pick and wash 'em, too." Josie shakes her head pitifully.

Frankie continues his tale of woe.

"Derek's wife sat at the table the whole time watching me eat – smiling like they was so good. I didn't want to hurt her feelings – so I kept eating. It was horrible. I had to look at *her*, *and* eat those greens. I don't know which was worse. Derek stood over in the corner laughing. He finally gave me a quarter and told me to go home."

"So what did you do with the money?" Jacob asks his son.

"I went to the pharmacy and bought some of that pink stuff."

"What?" says Dottie puzzled. "I don't remember seeing a… Frankie no! You didn't! You drank the *whole bottle*?"

"EWWW!" Josie and Savannah scream.

"Yep," Frankie says rubbing his stomach. "I had to. I guess the Wrights have a bad marriage, huh?" Frankie concedes.

"Oh, I'm sure Jenny and Derek will be alright," Dottie says. "The Komodo just needs a few cooking lessons."

"Wouldn't hurt to find her own place, either," Josie concludes.

"Tell the truth and stay in the church, child!" Dottie says.

Mother and daughter both reach for the heavens and start laughing. Jacob's ladies – gotta love 'em. He looks to the Lord for relief before turning his attention back to Frankie.

"You two need help. Frankie, come here," says Jacob patting the seat between him and his wife. "I wanna talk to you."

Frankie climbs into the front seat.

"Don't take my cards, L'il Daddy," he says to his older brother.

Jacob takes Frankie in his arms. If ever a middle child needed attention…

"Son," Jacob begins. "I don't want you to get the wrong idea about being married. I like it. It's done a lot for me. Papa Myles once told me…"

"*Treat it like a part-time job!*" Dottie intervenes. She's heard it a hundred times – even used it herself a couple.

"A part-time job?" Frankie says scratching his head.

"Don't scratch, son," says Jacob frowning.

"Sir?"

"You're making *me* itch."

"Yes, Daddy," Frankie says.

"Yep, a part-time job," Jacob continues. "You have to be willing to work at it – make sacrifices. You have to be willing to make changes in your life for your mate and for yourself. It's not just *you* anymore. It's *Mr. and Mrs.* Your mother thought I played a little too much pool so I cut back. And it has nothing to do with being whipped, Josie."

"Yes, Daddy," Josie concedes. "I know."

"Frankie, I love your mother, and I love spending time with her. As long as you're willing to work on your marriage, the benefits you receive can be enormous."

"*All right now. Listen to my man.*" Dottie thinks to herself. "*Looks like all those years in the church's Marriage Ministry paid off.*"

"Benefits?" queries Frankie. "What kind of benefits, Daddy?"

Jacob looks at Dottie and smiles.

"Well, you for one." Jacob then grabs the M&M's that L'il Daddy tried to hide from his parents. He tosses one to each of his children while calling out their names.

"There's Josie, my first benefit."

"Daddy!" Josie blushes catching the candy.

"...your brother, *the riverboat gambler*. Benefit no. 2."

"Gambler?" Dottie exclaims.

"He's joking, Mama." L'il Daddy says hiding the cards. "He's joking!"

"There's goes another benefit," he says tossing an M & M to Savannah.

"Your *favorite* benefit, right Daddy?" Savannah grins.

"You wish," says Josie.

"No, **you** wish," says L'il Daddy to his big sister.

"...and everybody's favorite - Terrence James. You can have the rest," Jacob says passing the bag of sweets to his youngest. "L'il Daddy won't be needing them."

Josie laughs at L'il Daddy as he watches the candy he won from Frankie go to Terry instead. Jacob continues his story.

"Coach Wright and those other knuckleheads down at the pool hall used to laugh when I said I had a previous engagement and couldn't shoot a few with them. I simply weighed my options," Jacob said mimicking a scale with his hands.

"You weighed your options?" Frankie queries with a look of uncertainty on his face.

"I sure did," Jacob says holding up the palms of his hands as though he was weighing the merits of his situation. "Pool hall, Dottie Harris. Dottie Harris, pool hall. I think you know who won. Do you understand, son?"

"Yes, sir." says Frankie grabbing the *'pool hall'* hand. "If you made the wrong choice, we wouldn't be having this conversation."

"My man!" Jacob says proudly. He gives his son a big hug. "Didn't I tell you all he was smart? So much like his Daddy!"

Dottie shakes her head in wonder.

"So much like his Daddy? How did I ever get hooked up with this man?" she thinks to herself. *"Oh, that's right. I fell in love!"*

"So it didn't bother you what other people thought about you?" Frankie asks.

"Well son, I look at it like this. My real friends, they understand. The others? They don't count, anyway! Understand?"

"Yes, sir!" says Frankie. He thinks for a minute and then turns his attention to his mother. He approaches her gently.

"Are you still mad at me, Mama?"

"Oh no, baby. No. I'm sorry," says Dottie reaching for her son. "What with those greens and Jennifer Murphy, and losing all of your *M&M's*…"

Dottie glares a hole in her eldest son. He mouths the words *'Sorry, Mama'* and puts the cards away.

"…I think you've suffered enough."

Dottie hugs her son while Jacob pats his knee. Frankie beams. His mother's approval (not to mention her smile) is worth a hundred bags of M & M's.

"Thanks, Mama!"

Frankie, gleeful and energized turns to face his siblings in the back.

"Who's the favorite now?"

"Boy, please!" Josie tells him. "Everybody knows the firstborn is the favorite."

"The first born *boy!*" L'il Daddy bursts in. "I don't see anybody calling none of y'all Jacob, Jr.!"

"It's the cutest child," says Savannah. "…and we know who that is."

"Cute wears off quick, baby girl," Josie tells her. "You ain't even in the running."

Savannah, a little ticked off by her big sister's remark fires back.

"Oh yeah, then why does Daddy hold my hand when we cross the street?"

"So you won't get hit by a car, you little knucklehead," Josie tells her.

"Right! He holds *my* hand, not yours!" Savannah says triumphantly. "He don't care *what* happens to you! HA!"

Trying to hide their smiles, Jacob and Dottie turn away from the combatants. They're not very successful.

"Well, let me say that I'm proud to be *Mama's* favorite," Frankie announces to his siblings. "That's why our first big dinner will be greens and cornbread. Right, Mama?"

"Well…"

"Greens and Cornbread! Cornbread and Greens! It's the food of Kings and Queens!" Frankie sings.

"Well, Frankie…"

L'il Daddy interrupts his mother before she answers.

"Is you mad?" L'il Daddy laughs. "Everybody knows the baby of the family is the mother's favorite."

"Yeah, Frankie," Josie laughs. "You lost that battle two siblings ago!"

"All right, all right," says Jacob. "It's time we put this little mêlée to rest. We're going to settle this *who's the favorite* business once and for all."

The Myles children look at each other in horror. Josie and L'il Daddy are aghast. Daddy actually *has* a favorite? As the eldest of the siblings, they've never heard Jacob weigh in on the subject. Frankie and Savannah always assumed that those coveted positions, Mama's favorite and Daddy's favorite were theirs and theirs alone. Goldie, the Myles' family station wagon is quiet – even more so (if possible) than when Frankie called Dottie's home a prison. All eyes are on Jacob and Dottie. Even Baby Terry is attentive though he's not sure why.

"As it turns out, your father and I discussed this just before we left Hopskip."

"YOU DID?" they all say.

"YEP!" Jacob says winking at Dottie.

Jocelyn Dorothy Myles, commander-in-chief and self-appointed spokesperson for her siblings, sees the dismay in their faces. Afraid of what they may hear (or may not hear), Josie speaks up before her parents reveal their so-called true feelings about her siblings.

"Mama, Daddy," she says a little anxious. "We were just kidding around. We know you love all of us equally. Don't we, L'il Daddy?"

Jacob raises his hand before his son can open his mouth.

"No, no," Jacob says. "It's time you heard the truth."

The children all drop their heads afraid for one another. Watching the expressions on his siblings, even Baby Terry is a little saddened.

"Now, Josie," says Jacob. "You're right. You were my firstborn."

"Daddy, you don't have to…"

"…and for that reason, I became more convinced than ever of God's existence. He gave me you! … never saw anything so beautiful in my life. You were the spitting image of your mother. I used to call you L'il Dottie back then, remember? You were only a few hours old, but I could swear that you smiled and reached out to me every time I walked by the nursery. As if you knew I was your Daddy. Baby girl, your existence justifies my own. I don't know where, or what I'd be without you."

"Thanks, Daddy!" Josie says crying.

"L'il Daddy?"

"Sir?"

"Every man wants a son he can be proud of. A junior – someone to carry on his name. Someone he can give that name to who won't drag it through the mud. Do you understand?"

"Yes, sir," L'il Daddy replies. Jacob's son struggles to keep the bass in his voice but fails miserably. "I-I understand," he says his voice cracking.

"When you walk down the street, people say *'There goes Jacob Myles, Jr. Boy's gonna be just like his daddy.'* Shoot, I know some guys who named their sons after them and they turned out rotten. Horrible! Some of those men wished they could take their names back."

The children laugh. Dottie smiles at her son lovingly.

"Not you, L'il Daddy," Jacob continues. "You're becoming quite the young man. The fact that you want to be called L'il Daddy tells me *I* must be doing something right. You justify my own self-worth. I'm proud to call you son."

"Thank you, Daddy." L'il Daddy turns away from his siblings. He pretends to look out of the window so the others won't see him cry.

"Franklin?"

"Yes, Mama?"

"You work overtime to make me happy. You may say the wrong thing every now and then but I never have any doubt that you have a heart full of love. You ate Jennifer Murphy's greens because you didn't want to hurt her feelings. You barely know the woman. You have a good heart and that counts for a lot in this world. Not a day goes by that I don't point at you with pride."

Frankie smiles. His heart is pounding. He lives to make Dorothy Myles proud.

"Oh, Jacob," Dottie starts to laugh. "Remember when Frankie was about six? You got me flowers for Mother's Day?"

"Um hm," Jacob nods. "Frankie decided to pick some lilies for you out of Daisy Hargrove's garden."

"I remember that," Josie says wiping her tears. "They were mostly weeds but you said they were even better than Daddy's."

"That's Frankie," Dottie smiles. "Working overtime to make his mama happy. Do you remember that, baby?"

Instead of responding, Frankie nods his head. He knows if he tries to talk, he'll lose it. Dottie understands. She smiles and looks in the back of the station wagon where Savannah is patiently waiting.

"Savannah?"

"Front and center!"

The others laugh. They can always depend on Savannah.

"Savannah Vernell Myles!" Dottie says smiling at her youngest daughter. "You, my dear, are the jovial glue that keeps this family together."

"Jovial glue?" Savannah says puzzled. "What's that, Mama?"

"Whenever somebody's feeling bad for whatever reason," Dottie explains. "We can always depend on your good-natured joking to perk us up. You love your family, especially Frankie."

"Aw, Mama," Savannah cries.

"What?" Dottie says.

"Why did you have to go and ruin it?" Savannah jokes.

Dottie laughs at her baby girl.

"Don't even try and deny it, Savannah. As I was saying, you hate to see any of us sad, so you do whatever you can to get everybody laughing again."

"Like when you used your Christmas money to buy that joke book you kept hidden in your closet," L'il Daddy tells her.

"How did you know about that?" Savannah asks.

"You're no Redd Foxx, baby girl," L'il Daddy says playfully shoving her. "I knew you had to get those jokes from somewhere."

"Yeah," Josie says grabbing Savannah from the back and cradling her like an infant. "Whenever Daddy had a rough day in the fields…"

"…when I got grounded and couldn't play baseball," L'il Daddy remembers.

"…when I lost my marbles shooting *glassies* with Miles Wright," Frankie says.

"What?" shouts Dottie annoyed with her son.

"Uh, sorry Mama!"

"Serves you right!" Dottie tells him. She kisses his cheek and Frankie grins.

"…and I got a cold the night of my big date with Marcus King," Josie says reminiscing.

"You were right there, Savannah," Dottie says pinching her cheek. "…cheering us up! You keep us all grinning!"

"Like a chess cat?" Frankie says.

"Cheshire, baby! Cheshire!" Dottie says.

Baby Terry looks at his parents. He smiles at Jacob and Dottie as if he's waiting his turn.

"Come here, Terry," Jacob says holding out his arms. "Son, I'm not sure how you're going to turn out but I do know this! You got four of the greatest role models a kid can have."

Terry holds up his arms as if he's signaling a touchdown.

"YAY!" Terry yells. His siblings laugh.

Jacob looks at Dottie with a worried look.

"Baby, what's wrong," Dottie says.

"Dottie, we got a problem," Jacob tells her.

"What's wrong, Daddy?" they all say. "What's the matter?"

"Well, if Baby Terry turns out like these four…"

"Oh, oh," Dottie says hugging her youngest. "Looks like we got a new favorite!"

Movin' In

Dottie Myles closes the pamphlet she received from the kids' new school and heads home. She has a lot of work ahead of her and can't wait to start decorating. She looks up the block to see Jacob standing on the sidewalk and locking the gate behind him. She starts to wave until she notices something that almost stops her heart. He's standing in front of Mrs. Flores' fence and locking the gate to her yard. He then runs over to their gate, opens it and runs up the stairs to their home. He slams the door behind him, never noticing his wife coming up the block. Her heart in shambles, Dottie drops the pamphlet on the sidewalk and slowly makes her way down the block.

The Girl(s) Next Door

"LUCY AND FREDRICK should be pulling up any moment, now."

"Okay, Daddy," L'il Daddy says.

"When he gets here, he'll introduce us to the landlord, a Mr. J. Floors," Jacob says handing his son a business card.

"Flo-*rez*," L'il Daddy says emphasizing the last syllable. "Must be Espanol!"

"Makes no difference to me!" Jacob says.

"You didn't meet Mr. Flores when you were here last week?" Dottie asks.

"No, but he left the place open for Fredrick and Lucy," Jacob says. "Promised to be here today when we arrived."

"Little girl! Little girl!" yells a voice from the tiny kitchenette. "These breakfast dishes aren't going to wash themselves. Young lady, are you listening to me?"

"Abuela!" says the little girl. "There is a man outside throwing candy at his children."

"Throwing candy at his children? You and your imagination! Come away from that window."

"Now they're singing and dancing in their station wagon. They better be careful. That car looks old. Hmm. Papi in the back seat is cute. I can see *me and him* in Gay Paree!"

"What did you say, young lady?" says her grandmother.

"Nothing, Abuela!"

Twelve-year-old tomboy Carmen Clarita Hamilton is pretty as a picture and has a very vivid imagination. Carmen's flights of fancy take her all over the world. Whether it's the French Riviera, the snowcapped mountains of Alaska, the Australian Outback or just around the corner,

Carmen Hamilton has been there and back. Carmen's physical world collapsed when her mother, Clarita Flores Hamilton died of cancer six years ago. Her father, Master Sergeant Lance Hamilton, III allowed his daughter to live with her maternal grandmother until he returned from the war. Unbeknownst to Carmen, Mr. Hamilton has been recorded as MIA in the jungles of South Vietnam. Her grandmother is holding out hope that her father will return to his daughter. Until then, little Carmen uses her imagination to keep her busy and her mind off her problems. Her grandmother; unfortunately, feels her little princess has a bigger problem. Carmen's growing up a little too fast, she thinks and her growing infatuation with boys prevents her from progressing in school. Not a day goes by that her grandmother doesn't warn her to:

"…keep your mind off those boys and on your schoolwork, Carmen Hamilton."

"Yes, Abuela."

"Honey wait, did you say a station wagon? Can you see the license plate?"

Carmen takes another look out the window. She quickly puts on her glasses to read the license plate but stuffs them just as quickly into her dress pocket. Carmen is just making it in school because she refuses to wear them. She's fallen for that old adage that *boys don't make passes…*

"The Peach State, grandma. We have a state named after a peach?"

"Georgia, honey! Me and Papa were raised right next door - Alabama. Or did you forget?"

"You talk about Papa Hector every day. How could I?"

"You'd do well to listen, Carmen. Your Papa was a good man. … raised your Mama Clarita, your uncle Hector. We never wanted for nothin'. Big strong man, too. He didn't push nobody around…"

"… and nobody pushed him around!" Carmen says finishing the sentence she's heard all her life.

"You actin' grown now."

"Sorry, Abuela."

"That's the Myles family. All the way from Georgia," she says looking out the window at the old station wagon on the street. "Go get the keys off the coffee table. Our new tenants are waiting."

Johnnie Mae Flores, a fair-skinned beauty whose looks belie her years was a longtime native of Mobile, Alabama until she pulled up stakes and ran off with a very handsome and very headstrong oil rigger named Hector Flores. Hector, the first of his family to be born in the states convinced an eager and very smitten 18-year-old beauty named Johnnie Mae Jones to leave the cotton fields of Alabama for the oilfields of Texas. The two teens married and lived happily in the city of Corpus Christi for the next 10 years. Circumstances beyond their control, however soon forced them to leave Texas and move to Chicago. Upon their arrival, Hector discovered that his father was ill and dying. Hector and Johnnie Mae moved in with him with their two small children, Hector, Jr., and Clarita in tow. Hector soon took over his late father's apartment buildings and lived out the rest of his days as landlord to the two properties. Hector died in 1955. His daughter Clarita died of cancer the following year leaving her mother Johnnie Mae to raise Clarita's daughter Carmen while Clarita's husband served in the military. The property to be rented to Jacob Myles and family has been vacant for the last six months. Johnnie Mae Flores, widowed for the last seven years and desperate for some female company, is anxious for the new tenants to move in.

Mrs. Flores and her granddaughter Carmen walk briskly down the sidewalk approaching the Myleses. She waves as she approaches the family – everyone but Frankie that is – as they exit the car. Jacob looks back to see his middle child engrossed in a comic book.

"Frankie, let's go. You can finish *The Adventures of SuperSpy* another time. Let's meet our neighbors."

"Yes, sir!" Frankie says jumping out of the car. He walks toward the front of the old station wagon and positions himself in front of his big brother, Jacob Jr. Unfortunately for poor Frankie, he almost trips when he sees Carmen coming up the street.

"Hello, you must be the Myles family," Johnnie Mae says eyeing the children. "…didn't know there was so many of you."

"I beg your pardon," Dottie Myles says a little offended.

"Oh girl, I'm from the South, too. Texas! By way of Alabama - and there was 12 of us. I'm Johnnie Mae. Johnnie Mae Flores. …and this is my granddaughter, Carmen."

"Wow!" Frankie thinks to himself daydreaming. *"Princess Carmen! Just like in SuperSpy! I must be dreaming!"*

"Buenos Dias, Senorita," says the young man leaning against the jungle

gym. He reaches into his pocket and pulls out a yo-yo. He deftly performs an around-the-world, baby in the cradle, and the old walk-the-dog all while nursing a grape Slurpee. He does another around-the-world letting the yo-yo land in his inside jacket pocket. He smiles self-assuredly.

"The name is Myles. Franklin Myles."

The young lady is impressed. Not often does one so proficient in yo-yo-ology grace the schoolyard. In evening wear and gym shoes at that.

"Hello, Mr. Myles. It's rare that we get someone so suave and debonair on our playground. Rental?" she asks admiring the tuxedo.

*"Quite the contrary," young Myles tells her. "These are my play clothes. I have a dozen. And **your** name."*

"My name is Carmen. Princess Carmen. Of the Projects. Will you be staying in Chicago long, Mr. Myles?"

Franklin peers over the lid of his Slurpee - shaken, not stirred - at the vision awaiting his response.

"I will be here, Senorita. Until my mission is completed."

"Your mission, Mr. Myles?" she says breathlessly.

"Yes," he says taking a break from his drink. He pulls the yo-yo again from his pocket, utilizing the string to encircle the young princess' waist and pulling her toward him.

"Winning your heart, Mon Cher. That is my mission."

"Ohhhhhhh!" says the smitten princess. She melts into the sidewalk.

Frankie smiles – always the daydreamer. Unfortunately, his smile is unnoticed by his crush. The adults continue talking.

"These are my buildings," Mrs. Flores tells the family. "My Hector left them to me."

"Oh," Jacob says stepping up to shake his new landlady's hand. "*You're* J. Flores."

"I know. I know. I get that all the time. Mr. Flores was my husband, he's gone now."

"Where did he go?" asks Savannah.

"Quiet, child," Dottie says.

"Your sister called – Lucy Dupree - about an hour ago. Said she was running late and would I be kind enough to let you in. Well, here I am. You all must be tired. Such a nice-looking family. Nice-looking," she says extending her hand to Dottie. "...and you are?"

"Dorothy. Dorothy Myles," Dottie says suspiciously eyeing the overly friendly woman. "You met my husband Jacob."

"Jacob," Johnnie Mae responds smiling and looking his way.

"...and that's Josie," Dottie says dryly continuing the introductions.

"Hi, Josie."

"Nice to meet you, Mrs. Flores."

"My baby girl, Savannah."

"Savannah, oh that's pretty! Come here, honey," she says hugging the little girl.

"Hi, Mrs. Flores," Savannah says blushing.

"... And that's baby Terry, Frankie, and Jacob, Junior. We call him L'il Daddy."

"Good afternoon, Mrs. Flores," they all say.

"L'il Daddy, huh?" laughs Mrs. Flores. "Takes after his daddy, does he? Well, he *is* a handsome young man."

"*Of all the nerve*," thinks Dottie to herself. "*...and right in my face! She must not know who I am!*"

"Hi, Carmen," Frankie says smitten with his new neighbor. "I'm Frankie."

"Hi, Papi," Carmen says looking past Frankie and walking toward his older brother. "...so you're L'il Daddy. Welcome to Chicago."

"Carmen, get away from there. Take your fast tail back in the house!"

"Abuela, I want to help you show them the house."

"Then get over here and behave yourself!"

"Yes, ma'am," she says walking over to her grandmother. She sneaks a wink at L'il Daddy.

"Papi, huh," Josie whispers to her brother. "Wait'll Molly Beth hears about this."

Jacob drops his head hiding a half-smile. He looks over at his wife who's unmoved by their new landlady's charm. She's not at all amused with females flirting with her men. Jacob feels a storm brewing. He attempts to change the subject.

"Neighborhood looks nice. Wouldn't you say, Dottie?"

No response. Finally, Frankie breaks the silence.

"Abuela?" Frankie says puzzled. "I thought her name was Johnnie Mae."

"Correct me if I'm wrong, Mrs. Flores," Jacob jumps in. "Abuela! That's Spanish for grandmother isn't it?"

"Well, well," says Johnnie Mae. "A man of GOD, *and* a scholar."

"...and how do you know that?" Dottie says with an air of suspicion.

"Oh, it shows," she says patting Jacob's arm. "My Hector was the same way. Let's go see the house," she says opening the gate to the chain-link fence.

"*As long as you know the difference,*" Dottie mumbles grabbing little Terry's hand and walking toward the house. "*Light-skinned... Want all the men!*"

Josie stifles a giggle. She pulls her Mama back as Jacob follows Mrs. Flores into their new home.

"Don't worry, Mama," Josie whispers. "I got your back. We can take her."

"You be quiet, Josie Myles!" Dottie says unamused.

"What did I do?" Josie laughs.

The two Myles women walk up the stairs and through the front door. Everyone has entered the home but Frankie and L'il Daddy. Carmen waits at the top of the porch smiling at her '*betrothed*'. Her imagination is working overtime. Her grandmother, Johnnie Mae reaches out and pulls her inside.

Frankie grabs his big brother's arm and whispers in his ear.

"Just so you know, L'il Daddy. Don't be chasin' after Carmen. She's mine."

"What?" L'il Daddy says. He shakes his head and smiles at his brother. Frankie's naiveté has always been a source of amusement for him and the rest of the clan. He grabs Frankie's shoulder and whispers a word of warning into his ear.

"Chasing?" he says. "She doesn't look like the type who runs, Frankie. Let's go inside."

"So, Mr. and Mrs. Myles, how do you like the place."

"It's nice," Jacob says standing in the middle of the dining room. "I think we can turn this into a home. Dottie, baby, what do you think?"

"I like it," Dottie says coming from the kitchen. "Roomy... neighborhood seems nice. Josie? L'il Daddy? What do you think?" Dottie says to her two oldest.

"Looks good, mama," says Josie.

"It's nice. You're right, Daddy. I think we can turn it into a home,"

L'il Daddy says parroting his father. Josie and Dottie shake their head. '*Whatever Daddy says*', they both think to themselves.

"The previous tenant left some furniture," Johnnie Mae says leaning on the pool table. "There's even a barbecue grill outside. It's yours if you want it."

"Thank you, Mrs. Flores," Jacob says turning his attention to his new landlady. "That's very kind of you. Mrs. Flores, I understand this area is in transition,"

"What's transition, Daddy?" asks an ever inquisitive Savannah. "Oh, like a radio, right?"

"Let the adults talk, baby girl," Jacob says. "Why don't you and Frankie go check out the backyard? Take the baby with you."

"Okay, daddy," Savannah responds. "Come on, Frankie."

"That's a good idea," says Johnnie Mae. "Carmen, why don't you take our new neighbors and show them the backyard?"

"Be careful out there," Dottie cautions her three youngest.

Carmen and Frankie run to the back door with Little Terry. Savannah remains behind but out of sight of the adults. Placing her finger to her lips motioning for the others to stay silent, she hides just outside the door separating the kitchen from the dining room. Savannah; unfortunately, is never one to remain quiet very long.

"I understand this area just recently opened up to Negroes," Jacob says reiterating his last statement.

"Why, yes," says Johnnie Mae a little nervously. "I…"

"Black, Daddy, black," says Savannah interrupting Mrs. Flores from her hiding place. "We're up north now."

"Hush, Savannah, hush," Jacob warns his daughter. "Before I '*go south*', now."

"Ha! Good one, Daddy!" says L'il Daddy. "Good one!"

Jacob Myles go south? In the eighteen years since the birth of his eldest, Jacob Franklin Myles has never resorted to corporal punishment in reprimanding his children. Still, the mere threat of it works wonders. Savannah quickly joins Carmen and her brothers waiting at the back door.

"I knew she was still here," Josie laughs.

"So did I," says Dottie. "Savannah?"

"Ma'am?"

"Go on outside, girl before something happens to you!"

"Like what?" Savannah says puzzled.

"Like me!" Dottie warns her. "Go on now!"

"Yes, ma'am!" Savannah cries. She runs out the back with her two brothers and new neighbor Carmen in tow. Jacob starts to speak but Dottie cautions him to wait. Finally, they hear the back door slam with a reassuring click.

"That girl!" Dottie says. "Okay, we can talk now. Now, Mrs. Flores, you say the area just opened up to Negroes?"

"Yes," says Johnnie Mae cautiously.

"How long have you been here?"

"Well," Johnnie Mae begins. "Carmen and I..."

Suddenly, a car horn beeps from outside. Josie, sitting on the window sill looks out onto the street.

"Mama, Daddy, it's Aunt Lucy. Looks like she's by herself."

"Aunt Lucy can drive?" says L'il Daddy coming over to the window.

"...by herself?" says Jacob. "So Fredrick didn't..."

"Surprise," says Dottie snarkily.

Jacob's baby sister Lucy has been waiting for the Myles family to move north ever since she left Hopskip and moved to Chicago with her husband Fredrick nearly seventeen years ago. She comes running up the stairs and through the door.

"Jacob! Dottie! Hi, everybody. Josie! L'il Daddy! You made it!"

"Lucy!" yells Jacob hugging his sister. "Come here, girl!"

"Well," says Johnnie Mae heading toward the kitchen to get her granddaughter. "I'll let you folks get reacquainted. Carmen, time to go, baby! Let's leave these good people to their home. See you soon, Dottie."

"Um hmm," Dottie says as disinterested as she could possibly be in making friends with her new landlady. Carmen runs in and catches up with her grandmother. Frankie's right behind her. Just as Mrs. Flores turns the doorknob to leave, Carmen whispers in her ear.

"Oh, that's right," Johnnie Mae says stopping at the door. "Thank you, baby. Dottie, I can help you get the kids registered for school tomorrow. There is a good one just three blocks away. Carmen's been going there six years now. I can come by tomorrow morning and..."

"That won't be necessary," says Dottie.

"Oh, it's no trouble. I'll be glad to…"

"I can manage, Mrs. Flores!" Dottie says steadfastly. "Thank you."

"Well," Johnnie Mae says a little dejected. "The rent's due at the end of the week. Mr. Myles, you can…"

"I'll be sure to drop it off," Dottie says. "Have a nice day, Mrs. Flores."

...And in This Corner!

"JACOB, THE SOONER you and L'il Daddy get this pool table out of my dining room, the sooner we can get moved in."

"Almost done, honey. Soon as I get these legs off."

"Come on big brother, get a move on," Lucy jokes. "We don't have all day."

"I got it, ladies. I got it."

"I think *some*body's trying to get rid of us, Daddy," L'il Daddy whispers.

"You're learning, son," says Jacob smiling. "You're learning."

"What do you suppose they're up to?"

"I don't know, but I'm sure Mrs. Flores' ears are red pepper hot," Jacob whispers back. "Grab the other end, son. Frankie, get the pool sticks."

"No problem, Daddy. Hey, I wonder if Carmen plays pool." Frankie says aloud. "We can invite her over."

"*When pigs fly*," Dottie says under her breath.

Lucy watches Jacob and the boys as they maneuver the pool table down the basement stairs. Once they hit the pavement and are out of earshot, she closes the door behind them.

"Now, Dottie, what was that all about," Lucy asks running back to her sister-in-law. "Why were you so mean to Mrs. Flores?"

"Mama thinks Miss Johnnie Mae's got a thing for Daddy," Josie says.

"Johnnie Mae? Mrs. Flores? And Jacob?" laughs Lucy. "...my brother and Johnnie Mae Flores?" She laughs even louder.

"Yep," says Josie trying to hold back her laughter. "Daddy and Miss Johnnie Mae."

"Jacob and Johnnie Mae?" Lucy screams through her tears. "Boy, that old lady's quick!"

Lucy and Josie hold on to each other laughing at poor Dottie's dilemma.

"Well!" Dottie says feeling a little wounded. "...glad I made your day!"

"Oh, Dottie, I'm sorry," Lucy says stifling her laughter. "But you can't be serious. Big brother's been crazy about you since, since grade school."

"Him I'm not worried about," says Dottie trying to restrain herself. "It's that, that..."

"Now, Mama," Josie says trying to calm down her visibly upset mother. She's not very successful as Dottie starts to rant.

"She said her granddaughter attended the school up the street for six years..."

"So..." Lucy responds.

"But the neighborhood just opened up to minorities in the last few years," Dottie continues. "...and she never *did* say how long she's been here now, did she? What does that tell you?"

"What?" asks both Lucy and Josie.

"What am I missing, Dottie?" says Lucy.

"That old woman's passing!"

"Passing? Oh, Mama, please!"

"Passing for Mexican!" Dottie says shaking her head at the thought *"That's a twist!"*

"What? Oh, Dottie, you think everybody light-skinned is passing," says Lucy. "You used to say the same thing about Fredrick, remember? ...and I guarantee you my husband ain't passin'!"

"Jury's still out on that one," Josie thinks to herself.

"Dottie," says Lucy. "Why would you think Mrs. Flores is after Jacob? My Lord, you just got here!"

"Let's just say I know her type," Dottie snaps. "...and a grand-daughter? ...a granddaughter? ...at her age?"

"Her age?" Lucy asks. "Dottie, how old do you think she is?"

"She's about Mama's age, isn't she?" Josie asks.

"Not unless your mama's sixty-two!" Lucy laughs.

"Sixty-two?" Dottie screams.

"She's sixty-two?" Josie says incredulously.

"Mrs. Flores is sixty-two?" says L'il Daddy.

"Boy, what are you doing up here?" Dottie asks turning around.

"I came back for the table legs. *Don't wanna make no trouble for nobody or fight no causes,*" L'il Daddy says mimicking his cinematic hero Sidney Poitier. "*That's all I got to say about that. So Josie, my African Violet, what are we talking about?*"

"Get going, Walter Lee!" Josie laughs as she piles the legs into her brother's arms.

"These things are heavy," he says pretending to struggle with the pieces.

"L'il Daddy…" says his mama starting to tense up.

"It's gonna take at least two trips," the would-be comic says moving at a snail's pace.

"Boy, if you don't…," Dottie screams.

"Okay, Okay, you don't have to yell. Hey, Dad! *Big Walter*!" L'il Daddy says laughing as he walks down the stairs. "The ladies, they're talking about us!"

Josie slams the door behind him. "…should've never taken him to see that movie, Mama!"

"That boy is getting' too grown," says Dottie with a half-smile. She turns her attention back to her sister-in-law.

"Lucy."

"Yes?"

"Lucille Dupree."

"Yes, Dorothy?"

"*Sixty-two?*"

"Yep!"

"…and carrying on like that?"

"Like what?" Josie asks puzzled. "What did she do?"

"Playing in her hair," Dottie responds. "Switching her butt around like she's Lena Horne! More like a teenager in heat! No wonder her granddaughter…"

"Uh, Mama I didn't see that," Josie says.

"I know what I saw, Jocelyn!" Dottie says balling her fists and placing them on her hips.

"Wellll…" says Josie retreating behind her aunt. "Maybe I'm mistaken."

Lucy shakes her head piteously at her sister-in-law's rather peculiar behavior.

"Dottie, honey," says Lucy. "I admit that Miss Johnnie Mae can get a little familiar…"

"Lucy, please!" Dottie says. "I know the difference between *familiar* and flat-out flirting! *That hussy…*"

"Dottie!" Lucy screams surprised.

Suddenly Savannah runs into the dining room from the backyard with Baby Terry.

"Who's a hussy?" Savannah asks grinning. "Mama, what's all the… Aunt Lucy!"

"Hey, Savannah Vernell, come here baby girl!" Lucy says grabbing her niece.

"Who's a hussy, Aunt Lucy?"

"Nobody, honey!" Lucy changes the subject. "Savannah and Terry! Oooh, you two have gotten big. You better come here boy and give me a hug."

"Come see the backyard, Aunt Lucy," Savannah says pulling her aunt toward the kitchen.

"Okay baby. I'm coming. *Josie*," Lucy says whispering. "*Talk to your mama, please.*"

"There's nothing to talk about," Dottie says. "Lucy, where are those cleaning supplies?"

"They're outside. I'll get 'em. Come on, Savannah. Race you to the car."

"Oh, don't put yourself out," Dottie says raising her hand like a traffic cop. "I'll get it. You three stay here. Enjoy your little laugh-a-thon."

"What did I do?" Savannah asks puzzled.

"Nothing!" Dottie snaps. She turns up her nose at her home. "Too bad Miss Johnnie Mae and Miss Carmen didn't do as good a job of getting this place in shape as they are in flirting with the men in this house."

"Mama, what do you mean?" Josie protests. "The house looks…"

Dottie turns slowly to Josie. She gives her oldest a look that would curdle sour cream.

"Uh… like it could stand a little cleaning," Josie says backing away. She's never seen her mother this angry.

Dottie storms out of the house in a huff. As she grabs the box of cleaning materials from the trunk of Lucy's car, she looks up to see

Johnnie Mae seeding her front lawn. An aerosol can falls out of the box and rolls down the sidewalk stopping at Johnnie Mae Flores' feet. She drops the bag of seeds and runs to pick up the can. Dottie stands still. Her rigid frame and intimidating body language tell Mrs. Flores she'd be better off staying where she is. She does. Still and all, she attempts to be sociable with Dottie – from afar.

"…thought I'd get an early start on the yard," she says smiling. "How's the house coming?"

Dottie retrieves the can and quickly turns away ignoring her neighbor's efforts at small talk. She heads back to her home with her head down and mumbling to herself. She almost bumps into Jacob standing at the gate. He holds out his arms to take the box of supplies but Dottie refuses.

"Dottie…" he says.

"I don't want to talk about it, Jacob," Dottie says sidestepping her husband. "Have the boys unload the car."

"Alright, Mrs. Myles. Your children's papers appear to be in order." Natalie Kelly, the school's pretty new administrator comes from behind her desk to shake hands with her school's newest students.

"Franklin, Savannah, welcome to John Robinson Elementary. It so happens this is my first year, too. If you ever need anything, I'm always here."

"Thank you, Mrs. Kelly," they both say in unison.

"Now come with me," she motions to the two siblings. Peeking out her door into the outer office, she beckons two students to come inside.

"Franklin and Savannah Myles, this is Arnold Mayweather and Tamika Jefferson."

"Hi," say both Franklin and Savannah.

"Hi," say the pair returning the siblings' greeting. Tamika waves at Savannah.

"Arnold and Tamika will escort you to your classes, but remember tomorrow you're on your own. Franklin, you have Mrs. Massenberg. Savannah, Mrs. Adkins. Give these notes to your teachers. You have five minutes before class starts. Enjoy your day! Make your mama proud, now."

"Yes, ma'am," Frankie says. Savannah nods her head yes. The two children hug their mother goodbye and head for the door. Dottie stops them and hugs them even harder. She reaches into Frankie's shirt and takes his portable radio.

"Aw, Mama!"

"Have a good day, Frankie!" she says as they head for the door of Mrs. Kelly's office.

"Don't worry, Mrs. Myles," she says. "They're in good hands at John Robinson. Why don't you stay awhile and I'll tell you more about the school."

"That would be nice!" Dottie says smiling. "'bye, kids!"

"'bye, Mama!" both Frankie and Savannah say.

Tamika tags Savannah daring her to chase her. Savannah obliges and takes off after the little prankster.

"Stop running, you two," Mrs. Kelly yells after them. The two new friends freeze in their tracks. They turn and smile at one another.

"Yes, ma'am," they say giggling. They skip down the hall to Miss Adkins's room and go inside.

"So, Frankie where you from?" Arnold yells above the crowd of students.

"Georgia. *Georgia!*" says Frankie recalling one of his daddy's favorite songs.

"Country boy, huh?"

"Yep! *The whole day through…*"

"…kinda like Ray Charles, huh?"

"Uh, yeah. Just playing," Frankie says catching himself. "I'm from Hopskip, Georgia. Me and my family just…"

"Oh, Oh. Hold up, Country," Arnold says interrupting Frankie. "There's my woman."

"Your woman?" Frankie says aloud. "Who? Miss Kelly? Oh yeah. She's pretty. Kinda old."

"Naw! Right there."

"Where?" Frankie says looking around.

"There!" Arnold says turning Frankie's head toward a little girl walking into their classroom. "Right there! Carmen Clarita Hamilton!" Arnold says in a faux Spanish accent. "Finest girl in the sixth grade!"

Frankie is thrown for a loop. As much as he tries, he can't move his legs. He's frozen in his tracks. Two students almost run into him.

It can't be, Frankie thinks. Carmen Hamilton? Somebody's woman? It can't be. Miles Wright back in Georgia told him that when a boy calls a girl his woman… no, not Carmen. Could there be two of them? Nope… there's only one Carmen Clarita Hamilton. Frankie's crushed. His dreams dashed, poor Frankie summons the courage to ask Arnold Mayweather what he dreads in his heart.

"Arnold," Frankie says cautiously. "What do you mean she's your woman?"

"Whatcha think country boy? It ain't *but* one way!"

"Well, what way is that?"

"Well, what else," says Arnold. "Me and Carmen Hamilton…"

RIIINNNNNNGGGGG. The morning bell rings; unfortunately, it's not loud enough – nor long enough. Frankie heard every word.

Franklin Myles, dejected and brokenhearted, drops his Slurpee on the playground floor. He watches helplessly as Arnold Mayweather, dressed in black leather and sporting a black patch over his left eye escorts Princess Carmen off the playground in his helicopter. Mayweather, also known in the criminal underworld as Blohard, looks back at Frankie with that evil grin made famous by villains everywhere.

"Your mission in Chicago is over, Country Boy!" he screams maniacally over the noise of the blades. " Go back to Georgia! BWWAAAHAAAAHAAAA!"

"You and Carmen…?"

"Yep, it was good, too. Come on. You don't want to be late," Arnold says strolling into class. "Miss Massenberg is mean."

Frankie's broken heart drops to the floor. Fighting back his tears, he wishes he was *back* in *Georgia, Georgia*!

Dottie Myles leisurely walks the three blocks back to her new home. Reading some material given to her by Mrs. Kelly, and buoyed by her conversation with the administrator, she starts to smile.

"Hmm," Dottie says to herself. "*John Robinson* has a lot going for it. Maybe this move can work after all!"

She closes the pamphlet and picks up her pace. She has a lot of work ahead of her and can't wait to start decorating her new home. She looks up the block to see Jacob standing on the sidewalk and locking the gate behind him. She starts to wave until she notices something that almost stops her heart. He's standing in front of *Mrs. Flores'* fence and locking the gate to *her* yard. He then runs over to their gate, opens it and runs up the stairs to their home. He slams the door behind him, never noticing his wife coming up the block. Dottie is crestfallen. She wishes her walk was a little slower and that she never saw what she wishes was just a dream; her husband Jacob leaving her neighbor Mrs. Flores' home while she, Dottie was away. Her heart in shambles, she drops the pamphlet on the sidewalk and slowly makes her way down the block.

Where Heartaches Dwell

FOR THE NEXT few weeks, the new inhabitants of 9111 South Trendley Avenue work tirelessly to turn the forty-year-old bungalow into a home overflowing with love – a beautiful home worthy of House and Garden magazine.

The Myles family living room is just the right size for the plastic vinyl-covered sectional and end tables Dottie purchased last year. A coffee table with sliding drawers filled with old and new issues of Ebony and Jet Magazines (a must-have in most Negro households) sits in the middle of the room. A blue oblong porcelain vase with flowers adorns the table. Before the Myleses married and Dottie moved to the ranch, the Myles men (Jacob, Brother Joseph, and Papa Myles) adorned the tables with oversized ashtrays and table lighters. Papa Myles, an avid cigar smoker made good use of both. All three Myles men smoked until Dottie announced she was pregnant with little Josie. The men then took that opportunity to clear the whole house of any and everything that smelled of tobacco. The ashtrays and lighters were soon replaced by vases of flowers (which Dottie changed once a week), a Lazy Susan filled with colored marbles, and of course little Josie's baby pictures. The men all agreed. Nothing beats a woman's touch. Dottie also has pictures of each child on the coffee table in their new home. Each corner table has a lamp and one or two baby pictures of the children with their little bronzed baby shoes attached. Two three-foot pedestals with large round planters overflowing with chrysanthemums – Dottie's favorite – and accented with various ferns occupy the westernmost corners of the Myleses' living room. They both stand on either side of the picture window taking full advantage of God's bountiful warmth. Pictures of the Reverend Dr. Martin Luther King, Jr. and President John F. Kennedy occupy the foyer wall near the front door. Dottie also adorns the wall with pictures of Papa Myles (Joseph) and his wife Ruby; Joseph Myles, Jr. and wife Julia; Dottie's parents Henry and Beatrice Harris and all of Dottie's siblings; big brothers Lloyd and Nathaniel and little sister Briana.

Dottie embellishes the fireplace mantle and the surrounding wall with individual pictures of the family and a shot of the ranch taken years ago by her father-in-law, Papa Myles when he was alive and well and dabbling in photography. There's also an enlarged photo of Jacob and Dottie, happy as can be, on their wedding day. Many of the old deacon's photos survived the trek north and adorn the children's bedrooms as well. The obligatory picture of the entire family, taken by the local department store is centered on the wall above the mantle.

The Myles family dining room has a rectangular oak table with eight chairs. Dottie kept fresh flowers in the center of the dining room table back in Hopskip, too. Once she gets her garden going, she'll continue the tradition here in Chicago. A curio cabinet that Jacob, his brother Joseph and Papa Myles built when Josie was just a toddler is host to Dottie's bell collection. Her collection boasts a souvenir bell from every state in the union courtesy of big brother Nate. Nathaniel Harris - whose travels as an insurance adjuster take him all over the country - sends his sister a bell from every stop. Big brother's way of staying in touch. He jokes that he'll visit the Myleses as soon as there's a natural catastrophe in the area. The cabinet, stove, and a few other kitchen appliances survived the trip north in Mavericks' teammate Milt Paulsen's old truck. The cabinet suffered a few scratches but Jacob and L'il Daddy managed to smooth those out with a little sandpaper and Lemon Pledge. A silver platter given as a wedding gift by Jacob's baseball team holds a special place of honor in the middle of the cabinet. On either side of the platter sits two golden goblets, purchased by outfielder Johnny Hargrove and his wife Daisy. Jacob's oldest friend and his wife bought the items for their favorite pitcher and his wife when Jacob, Jr. was born. Johnny wanted goblets boasting the team's colors (black and orange) but common sense prevailed in the end. Daisy (with Dottie's gratitude) overruled Mr. Hargrove. God is everywhere, indeed.

Adjacent to the dining room is the Myles family TV/reading room. A 14-inch black and white set sits in the corner of the small room. Jacob jokingly agreed to purchase a color model *as soon as I see more than one color on that screen'*. He plans to buy one in a few years. A vintage floor model Westinghouse radio occupies the opposite corner. Jacob, older brother Joseph, and Papa Myles spent many evenings bonding over the adventures of Boston Blackie, The Green Hornet, and the Lone Ranger on the old set. Even little Lucy got in on the fun. These days only Jacob, a baseball fan from way back, takes advantage of the old set to catch up on the latest scores. A display case featuring the entire set of Encyclopedia Britannica occupies a corner of the west wall. A set of Negro History books collected by the entire family, plus a collection of plays by William Shakespeare occupy the top shelf. Jacob, a voracious reader since high school, developed a taste for the Bard after his oldest Josie appeared as Katharina in her junior high school's production of 'Kiss Me Kate' – a retelling of 'The Taming of the Shrew'. Jacob still raves about it today. A few of Baby Josie's books by Dr. Seuss handed down to each family member and now read exclusively by Baby Terry lay just within reach of the toddler on the bottom shelf. Lastly, an old rocker Jacob used to read to his children and which Dottie used to serenade her babies to sleep afterward holds a place of honor in the southwest corner of the room. Dottie also managed to find room for her late mother-in-law's sewing machine. Savannah plans to get plenty of use from the old but still operational relic just as her Granny Ruby did. The Myles' TV/reading room is literally dripping with memories.

An elliptical glass table with four matching chairs sits in the middle of Dottie Myles' favorite room – the kitchen. She keeps a bowl of fresh fruit in the middle of the table as an afterschool snack for the kids. A Chambers oven, the foundation of many a culinary masterpiece down south made the long trip *upsouth* to Chicago. Jacob knew there was no way the *'Black Betty Crocker'* was leaving Hopskip without it. A Frigidaire, purchased in neighboring Parker County occupies the west wall. Mrs. Myles fills her kitchen with recipe books, hanging flower pots, and pots and pans hanging from the ceiling. A cast iron skillet she got from her mother hangs on the wall just over the kitchen stove. A pink and gray Jersey cow with a clock in its stomach – a Mother's Day gift from Frankie – unfortunately, made the trip as well. Dottie didn't have the heart.

Dottie also graces the walls of her kitchen with pictures of fruit bowls, vegetables and old style kitchen appliances. On the corner of these pictures, she hangs the ribbons Savannah and Josie won in cooking contests given by the church back in Hopskip. Jacob's baby girls always said they *'couldn't have done it without Mama'*. Dottie adorns the counters with flour, sugar, and spice canisters of assorted colors. Little knickknacks amassed over the years peek out from behind the canisters offsetting the different colors. As promised, Jacob will build some cabinets to give the lady of the house extra storage space for her good dishes – her *'special guests only'* dishes. He's also promised to build Dottie a wall shelf for her collection of cookbooks. Happy wife – happy life.

The Myles family utilizes the western half of the basement as a recreation room for playing table tennis, board games, and billiards. A small area of the basement in the northeast corner is used for laundry. The corner hosts a wringer washer, a table for separating and folding clothes, and a dryer Jacob purchased for a song on Maxwell Street. Although Dottie preferred drying her wash in the Georgia sun, she's resigned to the fact that she'll be hanging a great deal of the family's laundry in the basement. Although Dottie and sometimes Josie is in charge of washing all the laundry, the children are expected to fold and put away their own clothes. The younger children store many of their toys and their bikes in the basement. Jacob has also set aside an area of the basement to cut the boys' hair. A well-stocked freezer sits tucked away in the southeast corner of the basement.

Jacob's and Dottie's bedroom lies at the end of the upstairs hall overlooking Trendley Avenue and the park across the street. Their bedroom is the only one with a transom over the door. The lady of the house opens it (and the windows) on hot days to allow air to circulate throughout the upstairs hallway. The lovebirds' bedroom boasts a four-poster queen-sized bed built by the master carpenter himself, (Jacob Myles, not the original) as a ten-year anniversary present for his wife. Where does he find the time? *'A queen-sized bed for a king-sized love'* – the male lovebird's attempt at romantic banter. Dottie likes it. That's all that matters. Mrs. Myles has a makeup table and mirror adjacent to the north window of the couple's bedroom overlooking their neighbor's tomato garden. Most of Dottie's wardrobe fills the entire closet so Jacob puts most of his clothes in a chifferobe that he built back in Hopskip. His friends were unable to transport the one from Hopskip whole so Jacob broke it down before the trip north. L'il Daddy and

Frankie, with Jacob overseeing the project, reassembled the closet in a matter of minutes. Apparently, the old man passed down his knack for carpentry to his sons. Jacob and Dottie share a dresser for the time being – two drawers apiece – although some of Dottie's smaller items have found refuge in the corner of one of her husband's drawers. He's happy to oblige. The couple both has nightstands on their side of the bed. Jacob has a lamp and an alarm clock on his table with a picture of his parents he had blown up at the local pharmacy - the wonder of to-day's technology. Dottie has a lamp on her nightstand as well. Her table sports a picture of her parents, an 8x11 of the children, and a drawer full of whatever she happens to be reading come bedtime – if Jacob lets her. As of late, he hasn't had much say in the matter. Needless to say, he's working on that.

Each of the Myles children is in charge of cleaning (of course) and decorating their own room. Two of the younger children, Frankie and Savannah have desks in their room. L'il Daddy does all of his home-work on the dining room table so he keeps his desk in the basement. Baby Terry will no doubt inherit it when he starts school. Each child (Josie included) has a dresser with four drawers. Each of the Myles sib-lings has a patchwork quilt on his or her bed that mother Dottie made in the ninth month of pregnancy of each child – a Harris family tradi-tion. When time allows – with the help of the girls - she adds a patch or two to each quilt. Each child has a display case built by Jacob and the boys. They also have their most recent diploma and/or certificates on the wall with pictures and posters depicting their own particular hob-bies and interests.

Josie has a picture of herself and her best friend Brittany 'Cookie' Abernathy in their graduation caps and gowns. It sits on the night-stand next to her bed. Her display case boasts pictures of her family, her high school diploma, books, fashion magazines, a shot of the ranch, and a playbill from her junior high school play Kiss Me, Kate. Her opening number in the ambitious little production brought down the house. Josie still has the clay statuettes of her mom and dad she made in art class in the sixth grade. Her Hopskip Spelling Bee certificate (First Place) along with other high school honors form a collage on the west wall of her room. On the east wall are pictures of Sidney Poitier, Leontyne Price, Nina Simone, and Italian actor and heartthrob Sal

Mineo. Josie fell in love with Mr. Mineo in her *'bad boy'* stage. The entertainers make quite a foursome. Miss Myles has a special place above her bed for her idol – singer/activist Josephine Baker superimposed against the Folies Bergere Music Hall in France. Miss Baker seems to lock eyes with anyone who enters the room. There's also a poster of Elvis, yes *Elvis Aaron Presley* posing with his guitar – a gift from Bobby Matthews. Josie developed an affinity for the *Pelvis* while hanging out with Bobby, Cookie, (his secret girlfriend), L'il Daddy and Molly Brand after school. Josie has a picture of her own secret paramour, Michael 'Mack' Hodges – not on her display case - on her closet shelf away from prying eyes. Daddy just wouldn't understand.

Not surprisingly, swatches of Kinte, Serpent, and other African-themed fabrics spell out the name of the cute little revolutionary across the hall. SAVANNAH VERNELL MYLES, in big, bold colors appears on the south wall of her room. Underneath it are pictures of Negro activists culled from the pages of her favorite magazines. The west side of her room is covered with pictures of Zulu and Watusi tribesmen literally fighting for space on the wall near her desk. Adam Clayton Powell, her hero, is placed lovingly over her headboard. For reasons unknown, Mother Dottie has never understood the attraction. Savannah's display case which she helped build (L'il Daddy let her hammer a few nails), overflows with her collection of Afro-centric dolls sent to her by her favorite aunt. A photo of Aunt Briana (also known as Bree Bree) posing with a group of activists at a peace rally in Memphis, sits atop the display case. Savannah's favorite doll, Rosa (named after civil rights activist Rosa Parks) sits alone on the top row front and center. Mrs. Parks, no doubt would be extremely flattered. A photo of her horse, a little pony she named Spirit sits on the bottom row of the display case. Savannah says a prayer for her every night. Jacob has assured her that God watches out for special pets and that her pony is in good hands.

L'il Daddy's room looks like the sports hall of fame. His old high school football made the trip north along with his old jersey, *Number 9* which he proudly hangs on the north wall over his bed. A copy of the quarterback's playbook from his Dunbar High School days sits in his display case with some old textbooks, a few bowling trophies, and a couple copies of a fairly new magazine called *Sports Illustrated*. Bobby Matthews told him he was wasting his money, but L'il Daddy likes them just the same. "Who knows?" he told Bobby. "Maybe one day they'll put football players in it." Next to a picture of his high school football team sits an autographed baseball signed by his father when L'il Daddy was just five years old. He caught the ball the young pitcher smacked out of the park in that game against the Parker County Pirates. Pictures of football and baseball heroes he cut out of old newspapers and magazines form a collage on the door of his room. Former Green Bay Packer Charlie 'Choo Choo' Brackins, L'il Daddy's idol occupies the center of the collage of athletes. He hopes one day to add a picture of himself. Like his sister Josie, he keeps a picture of his secret girl, Molly Brand hidden in his closet. Why? Because the boy knows *'Mama ain't having it!'*

The only room with bunk beds belongs of course to Frankie and little brother Terry. On Terry's side of the room is a display case his father built to house all of Terry's action figures and stuffed animals. Wanna stay on Terry's good side? Don't call them dolls. The boys' walls are peppered with family pictures and stage shots of the latest singers and dancers. A poster featuring Smokey Robinson and the Miracles that his Uncle Lloyd brought back from the Apollo Theatre in Harlem covers the two boys' east wall. Frankie played the Miracles' 45's until they were so scratched they were unintelligible. In a stroke of genius, the budding vocalist decided himself to tape the old records on the wall surrounding the poster. According to Jacob, you can't swing a dead cat in Frankie's room without getting permission from Mr. Robinson first. Needless to say, Frankie keeps a radio on his dresser – permanently dialed to the only R & B station in town.

Before the family left Hopskip, Frankie spent what seemed like a thousand Saturday afternoons at the old Hopskip Cinema watching cartoons, cowboy movies, and whatever else the old theater offered. When the theater closed, Frankie was able to salvage a few old movie posters from the owner. One he gave to his good friend Miles Wright back home. He kept his favorite, of course - *SuperSpy*. The story of an ultra-cool espionage agent who saves the world from a madman bent on destroying mankind. Such a novel concept!

"There'll never be a movie this good!" Frankie gushed. Fortunately for him, the poster of the British superspy made the trip north and adorns the wall of his new room. Frankie wanted to ask little Carmen next door for a picture of herself for his room. Not anymore.

'Why would I want that nasty girl's picture on my wall?' Frankie says kicking his little brother's toy dog Bruno across their room.

"Frankie!" yells his mom. "Time for school."

"Coming, Ma!" Frankie responds. He grabs his books and trudges out of his bedroom dreading another day at John Robinson Elementary.

On Thursday morning, Jacob and Dottie go shopping for furniture. Dottie needs a few pieces; end tables, a couple of chairs, a new lamp for Josie, a couple alarm clocks, school supplies for the kids, and a few items for the younger children's bedrooms. Since they're passing Frankie's and Savannah's school, they decide to give the two a ride. When they arrive, Savannah jumps out of the car and runs over to her new friend Tamika Jefferson. Tamika tags her and runs. Savannah joyfully runs after her. Frankie steps out of the car and trudges to the playground. Jacob and Dottie say goodbye to him. He doesn't speak. Apparently, he's in a world of his own. The parents take off and Frankie walks over to the fence separating the schoolyard from the street. Five minutes before the bell. Sitting on his pyramid of schoolbooks, Frankie eyes Carmen Hamilton at the other end of the playground playing baseball with some older boys.

"She can pitch?" Frankie says to himself. "...*and* catch?"

Carmen waves to Frankie. He starts to wave back. Remembering that he's supposed to be mad at her, he pretends not to see her.

"She expects me to say *'hi'* to *her*?" Frankie says to himself. "That little..."

"Well, hello young man," says a voice from above.

"Huh?" says Frankie looking around.

"Up here, Mr. Myles!"

Frankie looks up to see the school's administrator, Mrs. Kelly smiling down at him. He quickly gets up and says hello.

"Good morning, Mrs. Kelly. How are you?"

"Oh, I'm fine. Were those your parents?" she says looking up the street. "I wanted to talk to them."

"About what?" says Frankie defensively. "What did I do?"

"Calm down, son," Mrs. Kelly says chuckling. "You're not in any *real* trouble."

"Ma'am?"

"Walk with me, Frankie."

"Yes, ma'am," Frankie says picking up his books.

"Frankie, according to your transcripts you were the smartest boy in your classroom."

"I was?" Frankie says amazed.

"Um hm." Mrs. Kelly says smiling. "Your teacher, Mrs. Massenberg tells me you're not participating in class. You've even missed a few assignments. Are you having trouble with the work? Maybe you could use a little help."

"No, ma'am. I understand the work and all…"

"Just a minute, honey." Mrs. Kelly says interrupting him. "CARMEN! Come here a minute, sweetheart."

As if his day couldn't get any worse.

"What are you calling her for?" Frankie says.

"Carmen lives next door to you, doesn't she?"

"Well, yeah but… I mean yes, Mrs. Kelly…"

Carmen calls time out to the rest of the boys playing softball. She runs over to Frankie and Mrs. Kelly. Frankie hurriedly looks away as if preoccupied with something else. Mrs. Kelly turns a very hesitant Frankie around to face his crush.

"Yes, Mrs. Kelly?" Carmen says as she tosses the softball in the air and catches it.

"Frankie, if you're having trouble with your work, maybe you and Carmen can study together. What do you say, sweetheart can you study with Frankie?" Mrs. Kelly asks smiling.

Carmen hesitates.

"Well, honey," Mrs. Kelly reiterates. "Can you?"

"Well, I…"

Suddenly, appearing out of nowhere, Arnold Mayweather, the albatross around Frankie's neck shows up with a few of his friends. They're a few years older and Arnold would do anything to impress them. Emboldened by the boys, Arnold audaciously stands between Frankie and Carmen.

"Hey, Country Boy!" Arnold shouts in Frankie's face. "You ain't in Georgia. Whatcha doing with my woman?"

The other boys start to laugh and a few girls standing nearby start to whisper. Arnold high-fives Chester Cunningham. Chester's an eighth grader and apparent leader of the group. Carmen starts to cry. Embarrassed and hurt, she drops the softball and runs away. Mrs. Kelly looks down at Arnold with disdain. She turns back to see Carmen sitting in a corner of the schoolyard. She's wiping her tears and sobbing. Children are whispering and pointing at the poor girl. It seems the whole schoolyard is talking about her.

"*Poor baby,*" the concerned administrator thinks to herself. "*The world is always ready to think the worst about a pretty girl.*"

"Where you goin', Carmen?" Arnold shouts after her. "You can't run from your man!"

Frankie walks back over to the fence, sits on the ground and hangs his head. The rest of the students laugh while Mrs. Kelly takes off after Carmen.

"Frankie! Frankie! Frankie, wake up!"

Secret Agent Franklin Myles, a victim of Slurpee poisoning awakens to find himself and Princess Carmen tied to a giant pendulum. The pendulum swings back and forth over an over-sized pit – a pit full of screaming piranhas, hungry and snapping at the couple's heels.

"Where are we?" Frankie says disoriented. "What happened?"

"BWWAAAHAAAAHAAAA" screams a sinister laugh from below. A sliding door opens underneath the elementary school jungle gym. A tube rises slowly out of the ground until it is flush with the floor of the playground. Arch-criminal and chronic detention dweller Arnold Blohard steps out of the darkened tube. He slowly rubs the few hairs left on his mangy cat as he laughs at Frankie and Carmen chained to the giant pendulum in the sky.

"There is no use in trying to escape, Mr. Myles," Blohard laughs. "I'm afraid you've run out of time. You should have never come to Chicago, Myles. And you Princess Carmen, should be more discriminating in your choice of companions."

"Blohard, you will never get away with this!" the Princess cries. "Frankie, do something."

"He's helpless, Princess Carmen. A country boy. Straight outta Georgia. Unused to the ways of city folk. Blah, blah, blah! BWWAAAHAAAAHAAAA!"

"Wish I never left Georgia," Frankie says fighting back the tears.

"My Lord!" Jacob says pulling up to the curb of their new home. "I can't believe the prices on these pieces we picked up. It's like the whole street was on sale. Lucy *said* that if you get there early, you can get some good deals on just about anything."

Dottie is silent. Jacob notices that she hasn't said much of anything since arriving in Chicago. When confronted with her silence, she said that she was tired from cleaning and getting the kids off to school. Jacob decides to speak to her but she cuts him off instead.

"Dottie…"

"I'll carry in the groceries, Jacob. I need to start dinner."

"Baby, I can help with the…"

"Just get the furniture, please," Dottie says grabbing the bags. "I need to get started."

Just as Dottie exits the car, Jacob notices Mrs. Flores coming up the walk. Seeing Dottie struggle with the grocery bags and the gate, she rushes over to lend a hand.

"Hi, Dottie! Let me get that for you."

"I'm fine!" Dottie says abruptly.

"Oh, it's no trouble; let me take one of those bags…"

"I said I got it!" Dottie snaps. "Maybe you can help Jacob. You seem to be good at that! Goodbye, Mrs. Flores!"

Jacob, mouth agape looks at his wife and shakes his head. Dottie storms into the house, letting the screen door slam behind her. Dejected, Mrs. Flores walks back to her home and gently closes her gate. She reaches for a hankie from her pocket and runs inside. Perplexed, Jacob drops his head. He's never seen his wife behave like this – at least not since Lula Mae Crosby asked him to the junior prom – right in front of Dottie. As he heads to the rear of the car to take out the new furniture, something on the sidewalk catches his eye. He notices that Dottie dropped a small brown paper bag with a spice packet inside. He picks it up and nods his head. Mystery solved.

"*The A Cappella Regionals,*" he says with a nod of the head. "I should have known."

Twelve-year-old Dorothy Rosetta Harris was blessed with the sweetest voice in the little town of Hopskip, Georgia. In due time, her young heart believes, the rest of the world will come to the same conclusion. The *A Cappella Regionals*, an annual vocal competition held among the twenty or so sister congregations of North Georgia, is fast approaching. Dorothy, better known as '*Angel*' for her '*soaring soprano*', has been practicing for the *Regionals* since her eighth birthday. Determined to represent her church and win the coveted prize of *A Cappella Angel*, Dorothy Harris waits with anticipation to hear the results of her church's auditions.

After auditioning several candidates for the contest, Choir Director Irma Mae Prickly has narrowed the competition down to two finalists, Dorothy Harris and her best friend Tracey Ferguson. Tonight, the two friends have been asked to submit a second selection in front of a panel of judges selected by Miss Prickly. Tracey auditioned first. Although her selection of *Amazing Grace* has wowed most of the panel chosen to select the church's representative, those who have heard Dorothy Harris over the years have already cast their vote in her favor. Her rendition of *How Great Thou Art* has long been a favorite of the deacons and the congregation. Even Isaiah Lucas, the church's minister is secretly pulling for Dorothy to win. The Hopskip congregation has never won the '*Regionals*' but with Dorothy Rosetta Harris representing them, Brother Lucas feels destined for glory.

Dorothy Harris, for reasons unknown, has always been somewhat intimidated by the choir director and by her friend Tracey. She's intent, however, on putting that fear behind her and winning the second round of auditions. Nervous but confident, Dorothy approaches the podium. She sees her parents Henry and Beatrice Harris, beaming with pride and waving from the front pew. Their baby's four-year dream is about to come to fruition – not to mention the bragging rights that come with the win for Mr. and Mrs. Harris. Dorothy adjusts the microphone and clears her throat. She closes her eyes and begins to sing.

"*Oh Lord, My God...*"

From note one, Little Dorothy's audience is spellbound. Enthralled by the young warbler's intonation, they hang on her every note. Her mother cries. One of the panel members starts to sing along but is urged to remain quiet by Miss Prickly. Suppressing the urge to clap, Brother Lucas clutches his bible. Jacob, in love with Dorothy Harris since birth it seems, sits awestruck in the back pew.

"*Baby girl's got pipes!*" he thinks to himself.

Nodding his head to the young chanteuse's hymn, he's mesmerized by his heartthrob's lilting voice. Even *he* starts to get "*the ghost*". Tracey, Dorothy's best friend and opponent, is overwhelmed. She graciously concurs with the rest of the congregation.

"*Dorothy Harris is fantastic,*" she thinks to herself. "*She deserves to represent our town.*"

Dorothy hits the last note of the classic hymn. The church rafters seem to resonate with her voice. She receives a standing ovation. Jacob, the Harrises, and Brother Lucas all shout their approval.

'*Encore! Encore!*'

The entire panel of judges nods to one another smiling.

"Well, looks like we found a winner," says Judge No. 1.

"Miss Prickly?" says Judge No. 2 smiling and waiting for her concurrence.

They all look to Miss Prickly to give Dorothy Harris the '*OK*'. As Choir Director, Miss Prickly has the final word on the church's choice of representative. The old curmudgeon frowns. She disagrees with the parishioners. She steps to the microphone to speak.

"Nice, Miss Harris, nice. But I'm afraid there's more to winning the title than just your *soaring soprano*," Miss Prickly says sarcastically. "You're representing the church, the city of Hopskip. Most importantly, the Negro race. You're simply not ready. Miss Ferguson, you will represent Hopskip in the A Cappella Regionals."

"Dottie beat the pants off that Tracey Ferguson," Jacob says throwing the bag with the spice packet in the car. "Just couldn't pass that damned *brown paper bag test*!"

Josie comes out of the house just as Savannah and L'il Daddy come running up the street. Frankie walks slowly behind them.

"Humph! Doggone Irma Mae Prickly!" Jacob says pulling the furniture out of the car. "...always looked like she was smellin' somethin'!"

"Did you say something, Daddy," says Josie.

"No," Jacob responds obviously still peeved after all these years. "Did you want something, sweetheart?'

"Mama thinks she may have left something in the car."

"Here you are, honey," Jacob says handing her the spice packet.

"Mama's acting kinda funny," Josie says. "Is everything okay?"

"Don't worry about it, baby girl. I got my finger on it."

"Hey, Daddy!" Savannah yells. She runs up to Jacob and jumps in his arms.

"Hey, baby girl!" Jacob says. "Three o'clock already?"

"Hey, Daddy!" says L'il Daddy dropping his books in the station wagon. "Need some help?"

"Sure," Jacob tells him. "Grab a couple chairs. Hey, Frankie! Come here, son. How was school?"

Oblivious to his family gathered on the sidewalk, Frankie walks straight to the house. He runs up the steps, walks in and slams the door behind him.

"Frankie," Jacob calls after him. "I got a portable record player. You wanna help bring it in? Frankie? Frankie? What's the matter with him?"

"He got into a fight at school," says Savannah.

"A fight?" they all say.

"Yep!" Savannah says proudly. "I saw the whole thing."

"Did he win?" L'il Daddy asks.

"Junior!" Jacob says admonishing his son. "What happened, Savannah?"

"Her!" Savannah says looking over her shoulder.

Jacob and his kin turn around to see Carmen Hamilton walking toward her home. A few boys are walking behind her making catcalls. She tries to ignore them but the Myleses can see that she's taking the ribbing pretty hard. She runs into her house.

"Frankie beat up a boy over Carmen?" Jacob asks.

"Well, he didn't really hit him," Savannah confesses.

"He got beat up?" L'il Daddy asks. "Hey, I taught him how to fight."

"...fat lotta good, that did," says Josie.

"Alright, you two," Jacob says. "Savannah, did Frankie get beat up?"

"No, they was just talking."

"Talking?" says Jacob incredulously. "Then it wasn't a fight, was it?"

"I guess not," Savannah says bowing her head.

Josie and L'il Daddy try to stifle their laughter.

"*Savannahhhh...*" says Josie shaking her head.

"Girl, one day your imagination...," L'il Daddy chimes in.

"Enough, you two," Jacob cautions them. "Alright, Savannah. Tell us what happened."

"Well," Savannah begins.

"Without the usual embellishment!" Jacob scolds her.

"But, Daddy!" Savannah protests. "Do you want a good story or the truth?"

"SAVANNAH!" they all say.

"Ok, Ok," Savannah relents. "But it would have been better my way!"

Curlers and Cutthroat

"…**SO I GAVE** Mrs. Farmer a sample of my writing."

"She's your English teacher, right?"

"Yeah, Josie, English," L'il Daddy says after a couple of bites of Dottie's finest cuisine. "She asked everybody to do a report on someone in Negro History. Dinner's great, Ma."

"Um hm!" Jacob says looking at his wife. "After a week of burgers and fries, it's a real treat to get some of your mama's home cooking."

Dottie smiles but doesn't respond to Jacob. She instead asks L'il Daddy about his report.

"So who did you write about, son?"

"I wrote a couple paragraphs on the *'WEB'*."

"All right!" says Savannah raising a black power fist. "He was down for the revolution. Even then! Who wouldn't like a book report on ol' *WEB*?"

"Web? What are you talking about, spider webs?" asks Jacob. "Is this biology? I thought this was English."

"W.E.B. Du Bois, Daddy!" Savannah laughs. "Get with it, Daddy. Everybody calls him the *'WEB'*"

"Not in this house, young lady," Jacob says admonishing his brash young daughter. "I would think with all of his sacrifices, he deserves a little more than an acronym. Now eat your dinner!"

"Sorry, Daddy!"

"As I was saying," says L'il Daddy. "I handed in a couple paragraphs on *Mr.* Du Bois. The next day, Mrs. Farmer gives everybody in class a copy of the three best reports."

"She chose yours?" Josie asks.

"Uh, huh!" L'il Daddy says clearly displeased with his teacher's choices.

"Well, what's wrong with that?" Josie queries her brother.

"She had everybody check them for errors."

"For errors?" his sister asks.

"Yeah!" L'il Daddy scowls. "Apparently, she calls herself picking the three *worst* reports in class."

"Oooh, no she didn't!" laughs Josie.

"Yeah!" L'il Daddy says. "...says she wanted everybody to see how *not* to write a book report. ...says she wants to **incentivize** us to do better!"

"INCENTIVIZE!" says Jacob. "HA! I like her already."

"Well," Josie says recalling her last class on Du Bois. "Maybe she's a Booker T. fan."

"Excuse me?" her brother responds.

"*It seems to me, says Booker T...*" Josie laughs.

"*I don't agree, says W.E.B...*" Savannah chimes in. Everyone laughs but Dottie and Frankie, both despondent over the previous days' events.

"Funny, Josie!" L'il Daddy laughs. "*Real* funny, Savannah."

"Looks like you got your hands full, son," Jacob laughs.

"Nope!" L'il Daddy says confidently. "I'll show her. When I'm through with her class, they'll make me *her* teacher."

"Oh yeah," says Josie sarcastically. "That'll teach her! ...huh, Mama? Mama?"

"Um hm," Dottie responds barely looking up from her plate.

"Frankie, you barely touched your food," says Jacob noticing his son pushing his vegetables around his plate. "Frankie? Frankie?"

"*Frankie, do something!*" Carmen screams. "*The piranhas are getting closer!*"

"*Look again, Miss Hamilton!*" Blohard laughs. "*They're not piranhas!*"

Carmen and Frankie look down at the pit getting closer to their feet. The danger below them is not fish. They're tongues, wagging every which way but loose and shouting obscenities at the two children.

"*COUNTRY BOY! TRAMP! BARNEY FIFE! EASY GIRL!*"

Blohard laughs at the helpless children.

"*You should have stayed in Mayberry, Mr. Myles. You and Miss Hamilton are at my mercy and now you must pay the price.*"

"*BWWAAAHAAAAHAAAA!*"

"Frankie? Frankie, I'm talking to you, son. Aren't you hungry?"

"He doesn't have to eat if he doesn't want to, Jacob." Dottie snaps.

"Baby, I just..." Jacob says.

"Everyone, take your plates to the sink when you're finished," Dottie says getting up from the table. "Savannah, do the dishes. Make sure the kitchen's clean."

"Yes, Mama!"

"I'm going up," Dottie says to no one in particular. "Good night."

She kisses Baby Terry's head and walks upstairs.

"Good night, Mama!" They all say. The children watch in anguish as Dottie leaves the table without speaking.

"Daddy?" Josie says worriedly.

"Don't worry, baby," Jacob says getting up from the table. "I got this."

He pulls L'il Daddy aside and whispers to him and Josie.

"Remember what we talked about," Jacob says nodding toward Frankie whose apparently preoccupied with issues of his own.

"Gotcha, Daddy!" says Josie. "Hey, Frankie. Let's shoot some pool!"

Jacob heads upstairs. He sees that Dottie is already in her nightgown and bathrobe. She pretends not to notice him.

"That was quite a spread, baby," he says. "Mustard and Spinach, cornbread muffins, macaroni and cheese, candied yams, potato salad, beef roast... Sweetheart, you really outdid yourself."

"I promised Frankie," Dottie says curtly. She then picks up a bag of curlers and brushes by Jacob as she heads to the bathroom.

"Dottie, wait!"

"If you'll excuse me, I need to roll my hair," Dottie says avoiding her husband's eyes. "I may be awhile. You can go on to bed if you want."

"Honey, we need to talk."

"Good night, Jacob!"

"Okay, dear sister," L'il Daddy says racking the balls. "You may break. Probably the only shot you'll get tonight."

"Thank you, my brother," Josie smiles. "If you're lucky, I might let **you** get in a shot."

"OOOH, I'm shivering," L'il Daddy responds sarcastically.

Josie breaks sending the nine ball to the corner pocket. L'il Daddy feigns shock at his sister's prowess on the table.

"Oh, oh *somebody* got lucky," L'il Daddy jokes. "Frankie, grab a cue."

"What are we playing?" Frankie says nonchalantly.

"A little game I like to call Cutthroat," L'il Daddy says scanning the table for a shot. "Soon as I teach Miss Josie that women should be seen and not heard." He then banks the three into the side pocket.

"Wow, L'il Daddy!" Frankie says amazed. "Cutthroat, huh?"

"Yeah," Josie says hugging her little brother. "Daddy taught it to us."

"Daddy?" says Frankie. "I thought he stopped playing."

"Not completely," says Josie. She deftly kisses the cue ball with the six gently pocketing the ball into the far right corner. "…at least not before he taught us how to shoot."

"He could've gone pro," shouts L'il Daddy looking over the table at his younger brother.

"Daddy? A pro? Wow!" Frankie says finally coming to life. "What do I do? How do you play?"

"In time, little brother. In time. Well, I said well," L'il Daddy says imitating a certain cartoon rooster. "Looks like our big sister – with God's grace of course - was lucky enough to pocket two, did you hear me, I said *two balls!* Hmm. God is good!"

"God's grace?" Josie responds. "The audacity! Where I come from Foghorn, we call that skill."

"…and where is that? I never knew."

"Just play, Big Head," his sister laughs. "Just play."

"Now, Frankie you see that ball with the twelve on it?" L'il Daddy says chalking his cue.

"Right in front of the hole?"

"It's called a pocket, Frankie," L'il Daddy says correcting him.

"No, actually it's called a *duck*," Josie laughs. "Oh, wait! Is it duck hunting season already?"

"Duck hunting season?" says Frankie. "I'm confused."

"…when you have a shot that easy, Frankie it's called a duck!" Josie explains hugging her brother. "Now me? I only take the shots that call on my expertise as an artist of the cloth. I usually let the less experienced play the ducks. …not saying anybody's name but it does rhyme with *L'il Fatty*."

"Cute, Josie, cute!" L'il Daddy says tossing the chalk to his sister. "I was gonna take it easy on you but I see big sisters never learn. Frankie, see the seven in the middle of the table? I'm gonna bank twice and kick shot it into the side pocket."

"What?" says Frankie.

"Watch!" says L'il Daddy. L'il Daddy lines up the cue ball with the seven. He smacks the little white ball with all his might, connecting with the cloth on the left side of the table. The three siblings watch as the ball banks on the opposite side, connecting with the seven in the middle of the table and landing in the side pocket - just as L'il Daddy predicted. The cue ball then spins back, smacking the twelve – the duck Josie left for him – into the far right corner pocket. Frankie falls against the wall astonished. L'il Daddy looks at his sister with a very self-satisfied look. He struts over to her side of the table until they are nose-to-nose.

"You were saying, Miss Myles?"

Josie high fives her brother and bows; genuflecting to the master.

"Not bad, Minnesota! Not bad!"

"Wow," says Frankie. "You *gotta* teach me."

"No problem, little brother," L'il Daddy says. "Josie! Rack 'em up. Now Frankie, in Cutthroat, all the balls between one and five belong to you. Six through ten belong to me. That leaves the rest of the balls, eleven through fifteen for Josie. You have to sink all of your opponent's balls before they sink yours. Last man standing - and that should tell you something about Miss Josie's so-called abilities – is the winner."

"*So-called abilities?* That did it! Prepare to kiss my feet, l'il brother." Josie responds. "Your days of *trying* to shoot pool are officially over. Oh, and Frankie. There's one more rule in Cutthroat. No crying when you lose. I hate it when losers cry."

"Come on Josie," Frankie protests. "I wouldn't cry. I'm not a baby."

"She's right, Frankie," L'il Daddy concurs. "So embarrassing!"

"I wasn't talking to him," Josie says deflating her chauvinistic brother's ego. She winks at Frankie, pushes L'il Daddy aside and breaks. L'il Daddy's head spins watching the balls rotate on top of the green cloth. When the balls stop in place, L'il Daddy notices that two of his have found a home in the far corners of the table – pockets courtesy of Miss Jocelyn Dorothy Myles. Apparently, her father taught her well. For her next shot, she purposely scratches the cue ball leaving a duck – one of L'il Daddy's balls - at the far corner for little brother Frankie. He's impressed.

"You can have that one, Frankie," she says.

L'il Daddy leans his stick on the corner of the table. Frankie laughs as his big brother pretends to kiss his sister's feet.

"Good one, sis! Good one!"

"Thank you, Frankie," Josie says. "Okay! *Now* you see how it's done! Ready to play?"

"Ready!" Frankie says enthusiastically. "Let's play some Cutthroat!"

"First things first," L'il Daddy says tapping Frankie's stick with his own.

"What?" Frankie says bewildered.

Josie puts her arm around her little brother's shoulder and looks at him lovingly.

"What happened with you and Carmen at school today?"

Dottie comes out of the bathroom with curlers in her hair. She walks into the bedroom expecting her husband to be asleep. The bed is still made.

"What?" Dottie thinks to herself. *"Where is that man?"* Suddenly, Jacob jumps from behind the bedroom door and grabs his wife. She screams.

"AAAHHH!"

"Gotcha!" Jacob says. "...and I'm not letting go!"

"Jacob Myles!" Dottie screams trying to catch her breath. "What are you doing? This is not funny, Jacob. Please! Let me go."

"Nope. Not until you apologize."

"Apologize?"

"Yes," says Jacob caressing his wife's shoulders. "You were about to go to bed angry with me - again. We made a promise, remember? Never go to bed angry?"

"Apologize? I should apologize?" Dottie says breaking away. "I wasn't the one coming out of Johnnie Mae Flores' house yesterday morning!"

"What?" Jacob says incredulously. "Is that what this is about? Dottie, come on. You know better."

Deep in her heart, she does. Jacob Myles has never been anything less than faithful to his adoring wife, their family and the home they made together. But for some reason she can't fathom, Dottie is starting to doubt herself and the man she loves.

"Well, Jacob!" Dottie continues. "Why were you over there yesterday morning?"

"Dottie…"

"Jacob…"

"I had to handle some business."

"Handle some business?" Dottie screams. "What kinda business you got with Johnnie Mae Flores?"

"Dottie, what are you talking about?"

"I asked you a question, Jacob Myles. What do you mean handle some business?"

"Woman, do you hear yourself?" Jacob asks with a broad grin. "Oh, I am loving this!"

"Do you see me smiling, Jacob Myles? WHAT BUSINESS DO YOU HAVE WITH THAT HUSSY?"

"THE UTILITIES, Dottie!" Jacob says a little insulted. Dottie blanches.

"Utilities?" She says embarrassed. Her volume level is barely audible.

"Baby, I had to get the utilities switched. From her name to mine. Gas, lights, the telephone. Mrs. Flores let me use her phone to get the utilities taken out of her name and put in mine."

Dottie flops on the bed. Humiliated by her actions, she covers her face. Jacob sits on the bed next to her. Taking her hand, he kisses it and then hugs her. She buries her head in his chest and sniffs.

"Jacob, I'm sorry. I don't know what got into me!"

"Dottie, you know I would never…"

"I know, Jacob," Dottie says trying to hold back her tears. "I know. I'm so sorry."

"Dottie," Jacob says breaking away to look into his wife's moistened eyes. "I know what this is about."

"What? What are you talking about?" Dottie says dropping her head.

Jacob raises her chin before speaking. They're now face-to-face. Jacob wipes her tears and then kisses her cheek.

"Don't you know what's going on?"

Perplexed, Dottie furrows her brow and shakes her head no.

"Irma Mae Prickly," Jacob reminds his wife. "Remember her? The queen of colorism?"

Sitting between his older brother and sister in the Myles family basement, Frankie tells all. He pours his heart out over the recent days' traumas with cute little Carmen Hamilton next door and Frankie's schoolyard nemesis, boorish Arnold Mayweather.

"Got three words for you, little brother," L'il Daddy says. He gets up, walks over to the pool table and picks up the eight ball. Josie eyes the eight ball and gives her brother a knowing look. She drops her head and laughs to herself.

"Smelly Jelly Jackson?" she asks.

"Smelly Jelly Jackson!" L'il Daddy says twirling the ball on the green cloth. "Boy used to tape mirrors to the front of his shoes. I won't say why!"

"Smelly Jelly Jackson?" Frankie asks puzzled. "Who's that?"

"His real name is Jefferson Davis Jackson," Josie says. "Why his ol' man named him that…"

"Um hm." L'il Daddy says. "Smelly Jelly Jackson. Bald-headed, five foot nothing and acne for days. Even on his back."

"Eww!" Josie screams shivering at the thought.

"Smelly Jelly was the water boy for the junior varsity," L'il Daddy continues. "Boy couldn't get a girl to save his life."

"So he lied on 'em instead," Josie says shaking her head.

"Uh huh," L'il Daddy says thinking back. "Fool told anybody who would listen that him and Anna Mae Pendleton…, remember her Josie?"

"Um hm. Pretty girl."

"Yep! Jelly told the whole football team that him and Anna Mae was *doing the do*. …if you know what I mean."

"For real?" Frankie asks.

"Yep. See Jelly figured nobody on the team would actually go up to the girl and ask if she was messing around like that."

"…and they believed him?" Frankie asks.

"Yep. See half of them was lying on girls, too," L'il Daddy explains. "If they busted Jelly, then Jelly would bust them. It's a game some guys play."

"Yeah, a stupid one," Josie says joining her brother at the pool table. "Only Anna Mae found out."

"Anna Mae was not happy!" L'il Daddy laughs.

"Anna Mae was steaming!" Josie laughs. "She wondered why nobody ever asked her out. She was Jelly's girl for two years and didn't even know it."

"So what happened?" Frankie asks.

"Well, Anna Mae's big brother Marcus got wind of what Jelly was doing," L'il Daddy says thinking back.

"*Master Sergeant* Marcus Antonio Pendleton!" Josie says swooning. "Broad shoulders. Six feet two. Muscles for days. The boy's muscles had muscles! HAVE MERCY!"

"Okay, Josie. Back to earth," L'il Daddy says laughing.

"Wow," Frankie thinks to himself. *"Girls are nuts!"*

"Sorry," Josie says collecting herself. "Anyway, the Sarge just got back from Korea. He approached Jelly on the sidelines in that game against Webster. Ol' boy threatened to shove that football down his throat if he didn't come clean about his sister."

"Did he take it back?" Frankie asks encouraged.

"Sort of!" Josie laughs.

"Sort of?" Frankie asks.

"Yep!" Josie responds doubled over with laughter. "Jelly crapped his pants in the third quarter."

"For real?"

"Yep!" says L'il Daddy laughing. "How do you think he got the name Smelly Jelly? He 'fessed up on the spot!"

Frankie smiles. He can picture his nemesis, Arnold Mayweather, crapping his pants on the playground.

"I'm sure Arnold's lying about Carmen, too Frankie," Josie tells her little brother.

Franklin Joseph Myles is not easily convinced. Little Frankie has always been the type that has to have a building literally fall on him before he believes it's a building. Not entirely sold on Carmen's innocence, he turns to his brother.

"L'il Daddy, if that's true," Frankie says. "How come she flirted with *you?* Soon as we got here? Remember?"

"Ooh, ooh, Professor Myles," says Josie raising her hand as if she's in a classroom. "I know! I know!"

Playing along, L'il Daddy points his cue stick toward his sister.

"The chair recognizes the pretty pool shark in the blue dress. Miss Myles. Why don't you give our young friend here the answer?"

Josie clears her throat.

"Well," Josie says breathlessly. She's mimicking movie star, Marilyn Monroe. *"Sometimes when a girl gets a bad reputation, whether they deserve it or not, they figure well why not? If everybody thinks I'm a trollop, I might as well act like one."*

"Excellent, Miss Monroe. Excellent!" L'il Daddy says to his curtseying sister. She then bows to an imaginary audience. "Give that girl a gold star!"

"What's a trollop?" Frankie asks innocently. "...and who's Miss Monroe?"

"Never mind," Josie says. "I think you know what I mean. Even good girls get tired of defending themselves. So they play the role."

"Seen it a million times," says L'il Daddy.

Josie continues her impersonation of the screen idol. *"If they wanna treat me like a tramp, I might as well be one!"*

"Poor Carmen," Josie continues. "I figured she was going through something. I mean, who would be interested in L'il Daddy?"

L'il Daddy laughs until he realizes his sister just zinged him.

"Yeah. Hey, wait! What?"

"Ohhh," Frankie says. "So a trollop is like a tramp?"

"Boy, are you even listening?" L'il Daddy says.

"Yeah, yeah," Frankie says. "I hear you. But what about Arnold Mayweather?"

"What about him?" says Josie.

"How do I know he's not lying? He told everybody at school about it and she didn't even deny it!"

"Frankie, you are a hard nut to crack!" Josie says resignedly. "Tell you what. Ask your friend Arnold if..." Josie whispers in his ear.

"What?" says Frankie. "That's crazy! Girls don't..."

"That's right," says L'il Daddy aware of his sister's plan.

"Ohhh!" Frankie says elated. "Yeah! Yeah! I get it!"

Frankie dances around the pool table. Using his cue stick as a guitar, he starts to belt out a tune. Josie and L'il Daddy high-five one another congratulating themselves - mission accomplished. Frankie hasn't been this cheerful in days. Just as quickly as he started, Frankie suddenly stops dancing. Turning to Josie and L'il Daddy with a horrified look on his face, he acts as if he just remembered the house was on fire. He throws his cue stick to his brother and runs upstairs.

"Frankie, what's the matter?" Josie asks. "Where are you going?"

"To get something to eat, I'm hungry. I gotta get some of Mama's greens before Savannah puts all the food away."

Frankie runs up the stairs humming the tune he created a few days ago when the family first arrived at their new home.

"Greens and Cornbread! Cornbread and Greens! It's the food of Kings and Queens!"

"Looks like Frankie's back," Josie says hugging her brother. "By the way, how was my *Marilyn*?"

"Greens and Cornbread! Cornbread and Greens!" L'il Daddy says running up the stairs. *"It's the food of Kings and Queens!"*

"Real funny, L'il Daddy," yells Josie running after him. "That's why I tanned that butt on this table."

"Did you have to remind me about Irma Mae Prickly?" Dottie says.

"Foolish ol' woman!" Jacob says looking back. "Color struck. Trying to keep my baby out of the Regionals! ...lady's got a lot of nerve! ... talking 'bout sending that Tracey Ferguson 'cause she's light-skinned! She'd risk losing the Regionals, thinking 'cause you're brown-skinned, that somehow makes you inferior. Jesus Christ. Sometimes we're all own worst enemy."

"I liked Tracey Ferguson, Jacob." Dottie reminds him. "It wasn't her fault. We were friends."

"But you won that audition hands down. Everybody knew it! Tracey knew it. Prickly knew it! Everybody!"

"Yes baby, but remember Tracey fought for me," Dottie says smiling. "I'll never forget her for that."

"*I'll* never forget how Mama Harris came to your defense," Jacob counters. "I thought for sure Miss Bea was gonna snatch that ol' fool bald."

"I'm glad she didn't."

"What? Why!"

"As I recall, she never had that much hair to start."

"Dottie!" Jacob laughs. "Well, it was a good thing your daddy stepped in."

"Everybody did," Dottie says proudly. "Brother Luke. Deacon Fred. All the judges. Everybody. If it wasn't for them…"

"My baby would've never become A'Cappella Angel."

"Three years running!" Dottie says proudly.

"Longer than that, Angel!" Jacob winks.

"You always know what to say, don't you Romeo?"

"I'm not just talking, Dottie. I mean it."

"I know baby, I know. And I'm sorry for the way I behaved these last few days," Dottie says kissing her husband's cheek. "I shouldn't have gotten so jealous. I guess Mrs. Flores brought all those old demons back to the surface."

"Honey, please. You will always be my one and only."

"Oh, Jacob I know that. It's just that…"

"What, honey?"

"For a few seconds, I actually believed that somehow I was lacking. I almost lost it, Jacob."

"Lost what, baby?" Jacob says taking his wife's hand.

"Confidence. In myself," Dottie says looking away. "Jacob, I was horrible to Mrs. Flores."

"Yes, you were," Jacob says tongue in cheek. "I've *never* been so embarrassed."

"What?" Dottie says looking at her husband.

"Appalled," Jacob says trying not to laugh but failing miserably.

"Oh, you stop!" Dottie says laughing along with her husband.

"So undone."

"I'm gonna hurt you, Jacob Myles!"

Jacob laughs.

"I'll speak to Johnnie Mae tomorrow."

"Maybe invite her to dinner?"

"Sure!" Dottie says. "I'll break out the paper plates!"

"My baby's back," Jacob shouts. "I knew there was a reason I fell in love with you. So smart, so pretty, so sensitive to the needs of others."

"Hilarious, Jacob Myles." Dottie laughs. "Oh, and by the way, we've been calling Mr. Du Bois *'Ol Web'* for years. You need to catch up."

"Oh, I do?"

"Yes, you do!"

"Well, I know somebody else who needs to do some catching up," Jacob says taking his wife in his arms.

Jacob starts to get that look in his eyes. With five children between them, Dottie knows that look only too well.

"I'm listening," Dottie says.

"Do you realize we've been in this house for days and haven't 'christened' it yet?"

"Is that all you think about," Dottie says trying to play coy.

"Yeah. Pretty much," Jacob says slyly. "Still tired?"

"Jacob, my head's full of curlers…"

"I've never seen you more beautiful," Jacob says. "My A'Cappella Angel!"

"Mama looked upset tonight, Josie," says Frankie devouring a second plate of greens and cornbread. "Think she'll be alright?"

"I saw that too, Josie," says Savannah. "She was mad at everybody."

"Dottie, my angel," Jacob says pulling off his shirt. "Do you think you can still hit some of those high notes like you used to?"

"Hmmm," Dottie says winking at her husband. "Maybe. With a little help."

The children hear laughter from above. L'il Daddy smiles to himself. Josie blushes. She covers her mouth trying to hide her smile.

"Don't worry about Mama," L'il Daddy says to his younger siblings. "Daddy's on the case!"

The Life and Times of Johnnie Mae Flores

"**GOOD MORNING, MRS.** Flores," Dottie says running down the steps.

"Mrs. Myles," Mrs. Flores says responding nonchalantly to her neighbor. Still stinging from their confrontation from the day before, Dottie's landlady doesn't even bother to look up. She continues to water her flowers.

"My Lord," Dottie persists. "Your tulips are coming in nicely. They're gonna be beautiful by the time summer arrives. ...and your hydrangeas, Mrs. Flores. Prettiest on the block, I must say."

"You know your flowers. I'm happy for you."

Carmen walks out of the house with her head down. Still humiliated from the recent days' events, she walks slowly toward the gate to leave for school.

"Hi, Carmen!" says Dottie. "How are you, sweetheart? That's a beautiful dress. Did your grandmother pick that out?"

Johnnie Mae rolls her eyes and frowns. She looks the other way ignoring her neighbor's compliment.

"Good morning, Mrs. Myles. Thank you. Bye, Abuela."

Josie, helping Savannah and Frankie off to school, sees Carmen, Mrs. Flores and her mother talking in their neighbors' front yard. She suggests to Frankie that he catch up to Carmen and talk to her when he comes out. Josie then rushes outside with a platter of fresh-baked pastry.

"Hey, Carmen," says Josie uncovering the platter. "Have a cinnamon roll. Mama always makes too much."

"Abuela?" Carmen says looking for permission.

"Sure, baby," Mrs. Flores responds. "I have to admit they look good."

"Thank you," Carmen says taking a piece of the still warm pastry.

"Careful, they're a little hot," Josie says. "Why don't you wait right here, Carmen? Frankie and Savannah will be right out. You can walk to school together."

Carmen nods OK. Josie then waves the platter under Mrs. Flores' nose.

"Mrs. Flores, would you like a cinnamon roll?" Josie says tempting her neighbor. "Nobody, I mean nobody makes 'em like Mama. She brags about 'em all the time."

"JOSIE!" Dottie says her face reddened.

"Well, Mama. You do!" Josie says. "Mrs. Flores?"

Mrs. Flores smiles at Dottie. Dottie smiles back. Josie's successful. She's demolished the middle wall of partition between the two battling neighbors.

"Well," says Mrs. Flores. "They'd probably go real good with some chamomile. Would you join me, Mrs. Myles?"

"It would be my pleasure, Mrs. Flores!" Dottie says beaming.

Frankie, Carmen, and Savannah walk the three blocks to school. Running ahead of her brother and their new neighbor, Savannah grabs a stick from a trash barrel on the street. She starts tapping the sidewalk making music as she hums an old hymn she learned in her church's children's choir. She then runs the stick along their neighbor's wrought iron fence – creating the same noise that kids make by sticking a playing card in the spokes of their bicycle tires. Little Savannah's oblivious to the two friends talking behind her.

"So, Carmen. How long you been living in Chicago? What's it like up here?"

"Frankie," says Carmen disregarding his questions about the city. "You ever think about running away? Living in another country?"

"Another country?" Frankie says perplexed. "What's wrong with this one?"

"I just think sometimes I should be somewhere else. Jamaica. Paris. Switzerland."

"Switzerland?" says Frankie listening to Carmen's rambling. "I hear its cold all the time. Nothing but snow. I hope you know how to ski."

"Anything's gotta be better than this," Carmen tells him.

"So this is Hector," Dottie says taking a picture frame from the fireplace mantle. She hands it to Josie.

"That's my Hector," Mrs. Flores says pouring hot water for her guests.

"Ummm, I love chamomile," says Dottie. "Please have a roll, Mrs. Flores."

"Thank you!" She says taking one of the tasty treats with a napkin.

"Your husband is very handsome, Mrs. Flores," Josie says.

"I know," Mrs. Flores says still blushing after all these years.

"...and this has to be Carmen's mother," Dottie says holding a picture of a stunning young woman in a burgundy dress. She's holding a bouquet of lavender orchids and standing next to a soldier who bears a striking resemblance to young Carmen.

"Um hm, that's my Clarita," says Mrs. Flores sadly. "We lost her to cancer. Carmen was only six when my baby passed. I agreed to watch her until her daddy comes home," she says nodding toward the picture. "If he comes home."

"If?" Dottie asks.

"Missing in action. A year now. Carmen doesn't know," says Mrs. Flores as she dabs her eyes with the napkin. "...but I keep a light in my window. Good Lord's been known to work miracles, so..."

The room is silent as the three women drop their heads in sorrow. Dottie starts to get a little misty herself. She understands Mrs. Flores' pain all too well. Her older brother Lloyd was missing in action in World War II. The agony her family felt until his return was unbearable. Dottie puts the picture frame back on the mantle and consoles her new friend with a pat on the hand.

"Stay prayerful, my sister," Dottie says. Mrs. Flores nods thank you and smiles.

"Who is this, Mrs. Flores?" asks Josie holding up a picture of a young man in scrubs.

"I was wondering when you'd get around to asking, young lady," Mrs. Flores says smiling. "That's my grandson, Marcel. He's an intern downtown at *The County*."

"I didn't know Carmen had a brother," Dottie asks sipping her tea.

"Oh no! Carmen's an only child!" says Mrs. Flores. "That's my junior's boy! Quite the young man. He ain't just handsome. He's smart.

Real smart. Graduated two years early. I think you and Marcel would make a fine pair, Josie."

Josie blushes.

Dottie jumps in winking at her landlady.

"Oh, I'm sorry, Mrs. Flores but Josie has her heart set on a certain young buck back in Georgia. What would she want with a doctor?"

"Mama, please!" Josie says trying to look unconcerned. She turns away but snatches another glimpse of the future doctor.

The two women laugh at poor Josie's lame attempt at indifference.

"How's the cinnamon roll, Mrs. Flores?" Dottie asks.

"Delicious," Mrs. Flores says with a smile. "Dottie, I'd appreciate it so much if you'd call me Johnnie Mae."

"Johnnie Mae," Dottie nods. "I'd like that, too."

The two women hug. Josie smiles.

"So, Johnnie Mae…" Dottie says with a grin. "How did you and Mr. Flores meet? Even though he's gone, I can see you're still very much in love with the man."

"Oh, it shows, huh?"

"Um hm," Dottie laughs.

"Mama oughta know," laughs Josie.

"You hush, girl!" Dottie laughs blushing herself. "This is Johnnie Mae's story."

"Well," says Johnnie Mae sitting back on the couch and thinking back. "It was the spring of 1919. Seems like yesterday. How come stories always start like that? *'It seemed like yesterday.'* Ha!"

"Good question, Johnnie Mae," Dottie says with a smile looking at her new friend. "When you find out, let *me* know!"

"Well, anyway," Johnnie Mae laughs. "Hector's parents were migrant farm workers. The Flores' traveled all over, wherever there was work. …picking cotton, corn, apples, whatever. That year, Hector's mother was pregnant with Juanita, Hector's little sister. She was in no shape to travel or do any manual labor, so Hector Flores the first, my soon to be father-in-law brought Hector instead. Well, we were out in the field sowing cotton for Mr. Larry when a voice from heaven came up behind me and said those magic words."

"What was that," Dottie asks anxiously.

"He said," '*Senorita, the air is so hot. You look tired. Come with me. We'll get some water and maybe talk a little.*'

"Oh, oh," Josie grins.

"Girl, I was hot, but not as hot as I was when I turned around and connected the face to the voice."

"Was he fine, Johnnie Mae?" Josie asks.

"Josie!" Dottie says. "You better *put* a handle on that!"

"Sorry!" Josie says embarrassed. "I mean *Mrs. Flores*. Was he?"

"Yes, he was!" she says. "Honey, he was standing there perspiring with the heat, and girl I envied every bead of sweat on that gorgeous head. It took everything I had not to ravish him right there on the spot."

"All right now!" the Myles ladies say in unison. They look at one another and fall on each other laughing.

"Don't tell your father!" Dottie admonishes her daughter.

"Oh I won't, Mama," says Josie. "What happened then, Mrs. Flores?"

"How old are you, honey?"

"She's not *that* old," Dottie intervenes.

"Mama!" Josie protests.

"Don't 'mama' me, Jocelyn Myles!" says Dottie. "You're only eighteen. Johnnie Mae?"

"We fell in love and got married," Johnnie Mae tells the inquisitive teen. "Josie, would you get us some more tea, dear? Top shelf, over the stove."

"Sure," Josie says getting up from the couch. "Be right back!"

Johnnie Mae waits until the door closes behind Josie. She and Dottie lean into one another. When she's sure Josie's out of earshot, Johnnie Mae whispers in Dottie's ear.

"*Let's just say we planted more than cotton that year.*"

The ladies howl with laughter. Josie runs in with the box of tea and a bowl of sugar cubes.

"What I miss, Mama?" Josie asks. "What I miss?"

"Oh nothing, honey. Nothing at all," Dottie says smiling at Johnnie Mae. She pats her landlady's wrist. "Just two old ladies talking."

"Hey Carmen," Frankie whispers. "Watch this."

Carmen takes a moment from daydreaming and looks at her new neighbor. Frankie points at his sister now balancing the stick she found in the trash on her head.

"Hey, Savannah!" Frankie shouts. "Girl, you don't know where that stick came from. A dog coulda messed on it."

"Aaaahh!" Savannah screams slamming the stick to the ground.

Frankie laughs. Carmen tries to hide her smile.

"Hey Carmen," Frankie says. "Why would you want to move all the way to Switzerland? You'll freeze up there."

"I really don't care where I go, Frankie," she responds. "I just want to be away from here. To live with my father."

"Your father's in Switzerland?" Frankie asks confused. "Is your mother there, too? Why do you live with your grandmother?"

"Frankie!" shouts Savannah. "That's rude. You have to forgive him, Carmen. Josie says he was born with his foot in his mouth."

"You be quiet, Savannah," Frankie says red-faced.

"That's okay, I don't mind," Carmen says.

The three children walk slowly as Carmen tells her story.

"My mother died in Miami when I was in first grade. She used to go to the hospital a lot when I was little. She would always come home but then she would go right back. One day I came home from school and Daddy told me she wouldn't be back. That's when Abuela, my grandmother came and got me. She brought me here to live with her here in Chicago."

"What about your father?" Frankie asks.

"He's in the Marines," Carmen says sadly. "Vietnam. They let him come home when my grandfather and mother died but then he had to go back."

"Go back?" Savannah says.

"Yeah," Carmen responds looking away. "He said they still needed him. He says he'll see me soon as his hitch is up. Whenever that happens."

"Well," says Frankie smiling at Carmen. "You wouldn't wanna be off skiing down some mountain when he comes back. Looks like you're stuck here with us."

Frankie runs back and picks up the stick his sister threw on the ground. He breaks it in two and pretends to ski around his sister and Carmen. They two girls laugh as Frankie schusses up and down Trendley Ave. Frankie and Savannah smile at their new friend. For the first time in days, Carmen smiles back - mostly at Frankie. A love struck Frankie blushes. Nothing like having your crush return the favor. Frankie takes her books while Savannah hugs her. The children hear the school bell ringing in the distance.

"Better put your skis on!" Frankie says leading the way. "I don't want Mrs. Massenberg mad at me!"

The three children laugh as they ski all the way to school.

Johnnie Mae Flores continues her story about the love of her life and the fateful summer she fell in love.

"It's a good thing there's more to this world than picking cotton," she says stirring her tea and reminiscing. "My Hector hated it."

"…wanted something more, huh Mrs. Flores?" asks Josie.

"Um hm." Johnnie Mae says adoringly. "Hector loved getting his hands dirty. He wanted to be an oilman. Said one day he was gonna own his own oil well and name it after me. *The Johnnie Mae.* He was funny that way. We settled for him being an oil rigger."

"Ohhh!" Dottie says engrossed in her landlady's tale of love. "That's why you moved to Texas."

"Yep! Corpus Christi!" Johnnie Mae says nodding her head. "Hector even taught me Spanish."

"Really?" says Josie.

"Oh yeah, and I was a quick study. I learned so much that summer," Johnnie Mae says smiling. "It's amazing what you can pick up when you have a good teacher."

Dottie almost chokes on her tea. She turns away from Josie and smiles.

"*Tell me about it, girl,*" she thinks to herself. "*…learned a thing or two from my man last night!*"

Dottie and Johnnie Mae pretend to be engrossed in the figurines on Mrs. Flores' coffee table. They both snatch knowing glances at one another as they reminisce about their respective husbands. Their smiles, however, give them away.

"Soooo…" Josie says interrupting the daydreamers. "You two got married and moved to Texas."

"Yep! And in that order!" Johnnie Mae says pointing a cautionary finger to her young neighbor.

"Yes, Ma'am," Josie responds smiling.

"I don't have to tell you about that summer do I, Dottie?"

"No you don't," Dottie says grasping her meaning.

"What, Mama?" Josie says "What are you talking about?"

"They called it *Red Summer*," Dottie tells her daughter. "The Red Summer of 1919."

"The Red Summer of 1919," Johnnie Mae says shaking her head. "Horrible time! The papers said race riots sprung up in nearly forty cities. They were mostly up north but we saw a lot of rioting going on down south, too. Negroes pulled off streetcars, out of their homes… They even killed some soldiers marching in a parade. Killed just for being black."

"We studied the Red Summer in school," Josie says. "The Negro soldiers came home from World War I looking for jobs."

"… and equality," Dottie says dabbing her chin with a napkin. "They didn't get either. They hoped to be treated like real Americans after fighting overseas, but…"

"Wasn't meant to be, I guess," Johnnie Mae chimes in. "Those poor people. A lot of black businesses were destroyed, too."

"A real shame," Dottie says.

Johnnie Mae grabs the teakettle and pours her guests another cup. Dottie and Josie take a teabag from the box Josie brought from the kitchen. Josie offers Johnnie Mae another cinnamon roll.

"Thank you, honey," she says. "These *are* good, Dottie."

"I thank you," Dottie nods to her landlady.

"Well," Johnnie Mae says. "After the cotton was all picked, we decided to head for Texas. Hector and I made a stop in a little town in Arkansas. A couple of rednecks approached Hector when we stopped to fill up. Told us they didn't appreciate aliens in their town. Can you believe that? They actually called us *aliens*. One of 'em asked us if we were strikebreakers."

"Strikebreakers?" Josie asks.

"Scabs, honey," Dottie explains. "Sometimes companies bring in Negroes to do the work when their regular employees go on strike. Then they send them on their way when the strike is over. Not even so much as a thank you."

"Strikebreakers," Josie says nodding her head. "Hmmm. Life just keeps on getting better."

"Not that it really mattered," Dottie continues. "They were just looking for a reason to harass you and your husband. Am I right, Johnnie?"

"Right as rain, honey. ...and Josie," says Johnnie Mae turning her attention to the young woman. "I did something I hope you never have to do."

"What's that, Mrs. Flores?"

Johnnie Mae drops her head. She's obviously still despondent over what transpired years ago. She takes a breath, gathers her courage and confesses what she considers her transgression.

"I denied my heritage."

"Ma'am?" says Josie.

"What Mrs. Flores means, baby girl," Dottie intervenes. "...is that, well considering the times, Mrs. Flores pretended to be something that she wasn't. Johnnie, you don't have to..."

"I want to, Dottie," Johnnie Mae says. "I want to."

"I don't understand. What did you do, Mrs. Flores?" Josie asks.

"I told them I wasn't black," Mrs. Flores says head bowed.

"But how..." Josie asks.

"Let Mrs. Flores talk honey," Dottie intervenes. "Johnnie Mae..."

"Well, I was fair-skinned like my father and his mother before him," Johnnie Mae says. She picks up a picture of her father from the mantle and hands it to her guests. "I told those foolish rednecks that I was Spanish and that me and Hector were from Mexico. I told them that we were run out of Chicago ourselves 'cause Negro strikebreakers stole our jobs. I didn't think that they would believe us but they did. They gave us five minutes to get out of town."

"Oh, Mrs. Flores, that's terrible," says Josie. "You had to be scared to death."

"I was sweetheart. I was," Johnnie Mae says continuing her story. "When we got to Corpus Christi, we weren't exactly welcome there, either. Because of the rioting going on, nobody would hire Hector if they thought a colored girl came with the package. Once again, I pretended to be something I wasn't. Fortunately, Hector had taught me enough of the language to get by. We weren't proud of what we did but we had no choice. We were tired of running. We were down to our last dime and *little* Hector was on the way."

"You were pregnant, Mrs. Flores?" Josie asks.

"I was."

"So what happened when little Hector arrived?" Dottie asks.

"We were on pins and needles," Johnnie Mae responds. "Not knowing if the color of my baby would give us away? Would Hector lose his job? Would we have to head back to Alabama? Carrying my first child was supposed to be the happiest days of my life, but living under the shadow of fear and deceit, they were the worst. Those were some of the hardest months I ever had to endure."

"So what happened," Josie and Dottie ask on pins and needles themselves.

"What happened was that my little Hector was the spitting image of his father," Johnnie Mae says with a smile. "He was gorgeous. We couldn't be happier. We built a beautiful home in Corpus Christi. Big Hector loved his work on the oil wells. Little Hector loved school. Life was great. I never told anybody about my real life or who I really was. I convinced myself that I was doing the right thing for our son. It hurt, though. I never got to see Mama, Daddy, or my family because I was afraid that if they visited our secret would be out and we would lose everything we worked for. Some nights I cried myself to sleep wishing that I could see them and praying that they would forgive me and understand what I did."

"My God," Dottie thinks to herself. *She **was** passing! ...and here I am thinking she was better off because ... Oh my Lord!"*

"So what made you come to Chicago, Mrs. Flores," Josie asks.

"It was Clarita, honey," Johnnie Mae says picking up her late daughter's picture from the mantle.

"Carmen's mother," Josie says.

"Um hm. The three of us lived happily in our little bungalow in Corpus Christi," Johnnie Mae says. "Just the three of us for eight years. I never thought I'd get pregnant again. Then one day, well let's just say we got a surprise package."

"They have a way of doing that," Dottie says. She's referring of course to her last baby, little Terry who was born seven years after Savannah. Jacob, surprised beyond belief was still the doting, happy father.

"Clarita Marie Flores. My baby girl was beautiful. She looked just like my mother. Mama and Clarita had the same dark complexion. My Daddy loved Mama. He used to call her his African Violet."

"Like the flower," Josie offers.

"Um hm," Johnnie Mae concurs. "Mama was proud of her skin tone. Loved it. She said it made her feel regal. There were some people, however who weren't as kind. Said some awful things. ...and I knew the same would happen to my Clarita."

"But she was just a baby," Josie says. "Who would...?"

"Everybody, just about," says Mrs. Flores. "People started putting labels on me and Clarita. Some said she was a dark-skinned Mexican. Too dark. As if my Hector was worried about that. One man even asked Hector if he was gonna throw me out in the street. Said I must've been puttin' out to get a child looking like that."

"Oh no he didn't," Dottie says.

"He did," Johnnie Mae recalls. "My man got into a bar fight and almost got thrown in jail defending me and our baby. He almost lost his job on the rig because people kept picking at him. Everybody had an opinion. ...as if it was anybody's business but our own."

"So, Mrs. Flores," Josie interrupts. "After all this time, no one knew about your background at all."

"Oh, I'm sure people suspected," Johnnie Mae says. "With a name like Johnnie Mae Jones, I couldn't keep that secret forever."

"I would think not," Dottie laughs.

"...and none of them defended you?" Josie says sadly. "That's terrible."

"Nobody really wanted to get involved," Johnnie Mae says sadly. "They just wanted to work, get their paychecks and come home. Tell me this, Dottie..."

"Yes, dear."

"Why is it that those who *do* get involved, it's always something negative."

"Human nature, honey," says Dottie. "Folks love to see mess get stirred. If it ain't their way, then it shouldn't be at all."

"Um hm," Johnnie Mae concurs. "But Josie, honey. Don't get us wrong. That's not everybody. There's a lot of good people around. Just not enough of 'em speaking up."

"Oh I know, Mrs. Flores," Josie says putting down her cup for emphasis. "Dr. King said it best. He said as long as good people stand by and do nothing, racism and injustice will continue to flourish. He wasn't lying."

"JOSIE!" Dottie says. "Watch your language!"

"Sorry, Mama," Josie says looking away and rolling her pretty eyes. "Fibbing."

Johnnie Mae laughs to herself.

"When Clarita started school," she continues. "…it seemed like little Hector was fighting over something somebody said about her every day. I couldn't blame him. He loved his little sister. He even got expelled once."

"EXPELLED?" the Myles women say almost shouting. "For protecting his sister?"

"Um hm," Johnnie Mae says. "Like father, like son."

"How do you mean," Dottie says perplexed. "Wait, you mean Hector…"

"Remember that bar fight I told you about," Johnnie Mae says. "The man in the bar was the son of Hector's boss."

"Oh no!" Dottie says.

"Um hm," Johnnie Mae says. "We knew things were coming to an end. My man really loved that job. It broke his heart. You know the old saying, *'When it rains, it pours?'*"

Both ladies nod their heads.

"Well, Hector's mother had passed away the year before. His father asked us to come to Chicago. A new start, he said. We would take over the buildings his father bought and raise the kids here. It turned out to be the best move we ever made. My family saw us more often and Hector took over as landlord for his father. I told you he was good with his hands. Got a job at a gun shop across town fixing rifles."

"Rifles?" says Josie. "Mr. Flores and Daddy woulda got along great, huh Mama?"

Dottie nods her head and smiles.

"They would indeed!" she concurs.

"When Hector's father called, we pulled up stakes and came up here. We were fortunate. People in this neighborhood… They don't too much care what you look like. Long as you cut your grass and keep your dogs out of their trash," Johnnie Mae laughs. "Everybody gets along just fine."

"Good to hear," Dottie says sipping the last of her tea. Johnnie Mae turns to Josie and places her hand on her shoulder.

"Josie, could you let us have a minute? There are more figurines in the kitchen that are just lovely. They're from Paris - real pretty. Would you like to see them?"

"Oh, sure," Josie says as she heads for the other room. "I'll give you ladies some privacy."

Josie exits the room and closes the door behind her. Dottie and Johnnie Mae are left alone with her old pictures and a half pot of hot water. Johnnie Mae picks up a picture of an old woman with a saddened, compulsory smile.

"A lot of memories in those old photos," Dottie says.

"Um hm," Johnnie Mae says sternly. "...and if you don't mind, I have one more I'd like to share with you."

Schoolyard Justice

RIIINNNGGG!!!

The morning recess bell rings for the students at John Robinson Elementary.

"Class! Pay attention, class!" says Mrs. Massenberg. "Morning recess. Pencils down."

"Hey, Mrs. Massenberg," Arnold Mayweather shouts. He points a finger at Frankie Myles. "You want me to make sure *Country Boy* gets back on time? I don't think they have clocks in Georgia!"

A few of the children laugh along with Arnold and the would-be comedian's attempt at humor. Not a good idea.

"Quiet, Mayweather!" Mrs. Massenberg responds. "The rest of you, would you rather stay inside?"

"Noooo!" the children exclaim.

"Twenty minutes, class!" Mrs. Massenberg tells them. "Not one minute later!"

"AWWWW!!" the children moan.

"...and be prepared to take this week's spelling test." Mrs. Massenberg continues. "I hope you studied. There will be no do-overs in my class! Are we clear, Mr. Mayweather?"

"Yes, ma'am," Arnold says dropping his head.

Twelve-year-old Carmen Clarita Hamilton, Johnnie Mae Flores' granddaughter is not having as happy a day as her grandmother. Humiliated by bad boy Arnold Mayweather's lies, she watches forlornly as the other children run out to the playground with her classmates. She strolls slowly toward a lonely corner of the schoolyard and waits for recess to end. She starts to speak to Mrs. Kelly who's on playground duty but stops abruptly when she sees Mayweather nearby boxing with his idol, Chester Cunningham. She drops her head and turns away hoping he won't see her. Frankie Myles runs by Mrs. Kelly standing in the middle of the yard. He waves at her before sneaking up behind Carmen.

"BOO!"

"Hi, Frankie," Carmen says with a half smile.

"Hi, Carmen. Boy, Mrs. Massenberg don't play. *There won't be no do-overs in my class*," he says mocking their teacher. "Did you study for the test?"

"It's not like I have a lot of friends, Frankie. What else would I be doing?"

"What do you mean?" Frankie says earnestly.

"Frankie, if you wanna play with the other kids, it's okay."

"What are you talking about, Carmen?" Frankie asks.

"Frankie, I know what everybody's saying at school."

"Aw, that," Frankie says. "Nobody believes that. Who listens to Arnold Mayweather, anyway?"

"You did, Frankie."

"…and I was wrong, Carmen. I'm really sorry," Frankie says apologetically. "But if you don't defend yourself, they're gonna keep on saying it."

"…and if I *do* defend myself, people are gonna say I got something to hide."

"Aw, forget them," Frankie says. "Hey, you wanna go skiing again?" Trying to cheer the miserable child, Frankie circles her pretending to ski. Not even a smile.

"Frankie, please…" Carmen begs.

"HEY! COUNTRY BOY!" yells a voice from across the playground. Frankie and Carmen look up. It's Arnold Mayweather with Chester Cunningham and his crew walking toward them. Arnold looks around to make sure he has the whole playground's attention.

"What I tell you 'bout hangin' 'round my woman?"

Many of the children stop their various activities and circle the two boys. Savannah runs over and stands behind her brother – a position she's held since birth. Carmen tries to leave but Savannah grabs her hand to keep her from running away. Refusing to be bullied again, Frankie stands up to Mayweather and his buddies.

"The name's Frankie!" He tells him. "Franklin to you."

"Frankie, please do something," Carmen says as the pendulum swings closer to the pit of wagging tongues. "The tongues are getting closer!"

Agent Myles hears beeping from his watch/mini-television. He hears his sister's voice imitating Marilyn Monroe. Josie, wearing a platinum blonde wig speaks to him.

"Don't forget what we told you, Agent Frankie," she says breathlessly. "The playground is counting on you!"

Frankie nods his head.

Suddenly rejuvenated, Frankie shakes off the poison the evil Blohard used to spike his Slurpee. How else could he outwit the agent and tie him to the pendulum?

"Don't worry, Princess," Frankie says. "I got this!"

"The name's Frankie!" He tells him. "Franklin to you."

"OOOOOHHH!" the playground chants on cue. Looking to start a battle between the two adversaries, a couple of older boys push Arnold toward Frankie.

"Yeah, yeah whatever. Country!" Arnold responds. Some of the girls on the playground whisper and point at Carmen. The poor girl starts to walk away until Frankie stops her.

"Don't go!" Frankie whispers to her. Recalling his talk with Josie and L'il Daddy from the night before, Frankie approaches his nemesis. He's now nose-to-nose with him. Mrs. Kelly, watching the boys from a distance, prepares for a confrontation.

"Hey, Arnold!" Frankie says looking back at Carmen.

"What's up, country?" Arnold says laughing with Chester and some other eighth graders.

"Hey, Man," Frankie says. "When you and Carmen, uh you know, did the '*do*', did her ears turn red?"

"What? Huh?" Arnold asks perplexed.

A few girls look at Carmen and shake their heads. A few others point and laugh at her.

"Frankie!" Carmen screams surprised at her friend. "What are you doing?"

"I got this, Carmen," he whispers.

"Did her ears turn red?" Frankie asks a very puzzled Mayweather. "They did with me. When we was through, she couldn't even hear! Her granny was calling and calling her. She couldn't hear nothing. I had to tell her to go home!"

Frankie laughs. Some of the older children, onto Frankie's plan, laugh along with the clever boy. Arnold looks around at the crowd – especially Chester Cunningham. He lives to impress him and Chester's buddies. Cunningham and the other boys fold their arms waiting on Mayweather's answer.

"Oh yeah, yeah," he says anxiously. "That happened with me, too. She was like *'what, what'*. It was funny!"

Cunningham and his crew look at each other shaking their heads.

"You idiot," Chester laughs. "Girls don't go deaf when they... Boy, I shoulda known you was lying. Franklin! Come here dog."

Chester hugs Frankie and slaps his hand. He pushes Mayweather aside.

"You alright, l'il brother," Chester tells him. "You can hang with me, anytime. MAYWEATHER!"

"Yeah, Chester?" poor Arnold answers red-faced.

"GET LOST!" he orders him.

Mrs. Kelly hears everything but pretends to focus on some of the younger children on the other side of the schoolyard. She turns away so no one sees her smiling. Arnold's and Carmen's classmates point at Arnold and laugh. A few girls go over to Carmen and invite her to jump rope with them. A few even apologize. Carmen happily accepts both offers. As it turns out, she's pretty good at double-dutch. She winks an appreciative *'thank you'* to Frankie, hugs Savannah and runs off with her new friends.

His confidence renewed, Frankie breaks the chains restraining him and Princess Carmen to the swinging pendulum. Using his yo-yo string as a lasso, he wraps it around the laughing Blohard's tongue. The intrepid agent pulls his nemesis off his feet leaving him dangling between him, Princess Carmen and the pit of wagging tongues. Just as quickly, the tongues wagging below the trio change their tune.

"LIAR, LIAR! PANTS ON FIRE. STRING HIM UP WITH CHICKEN WIRE.

Blohard screams.

"NO! NO! I'M ARNOLD BLOHARD! YOU CAN'T TURN ON ME!"

"What's the matter, Blohard?" Myles says drily. "You're looking a bit down in the mouth!"

With that, Frankie cuts the string as Blohard sinks screaming into the pit of tongues. Agent Myles takes what's left of the string from his yo-yo and lassoes the see-saw on the other side of the playground. He then ties the other end to the pendulum. Taking Princess Carmen in his arms, the intrepid agent deftly slides down the string until they're both on the ground and out of danger. Frankie and Carmen walk away listening to the once powerful Arnold Blohard begging for mercy.

"What was that you said about looking down in the mouth?" Carmen winks.

"Hey, give me a break," Agent Myles laughs. "I'm only twelve. I'm still working on the witticisms. Cafeteria, Mon Cher? It's Taco Tuesday."

Princess Carmen kisses Frankie's cheek as they head gleefully to the school cafeteria. The ladies at John Robinson make some pretty good enchiladas.

Mission accomplished, Frankie thinks to himself. He slaps five with Chester and a couple of his friends. He then looks up at the sun and takes in the fresh April air. He smiles at Mrs. Kelly who slyly winks back.

"Maybe this Chicago thing will work after all," Frankie tells himself.

Savannah, watching the whole show with pride, pats her brother on the back. If Frankie could, he'd do the same. He and Savannah playfully shove one another.

"I don't know what you did, Frankie but you got that boy Arnold looking silly!"

"Ha!" Frankie laughs content with himself. "Yeah I did, didn't I?"

Suddenly, Frankie's bliss comes to a screeching halt. Out of nowhere, he hears his nemesis yelling across the playground. He turns around and sees Arnold Mayweather push his crush, Carmen Hamilton to the ground. The bully, embarrassed and dismissed by his friends, stands over poor Carmen, frightened and shaking. Mayweather points an accusing finger in her face.

"CARMEN HAMILTON! YOU AIN'T NOTHING BUT A…" RIIINNNGGG!!!

"Well, Josie's in the kitchen. What did you want to tell me, Johnnie Mae?" Dottie asks anxiously.

"Dottie," Johnnie Mae says picking up a picture of a middle-aged couple. "This is my Aunt Johnnie Mae and Uncle Duke. They were married for twenty-five years."

"You were named after your aunt," Dottie says.

"Um hm. My Daddy's baby sister. Loved me some Aunt Johnnie Mae. Can't say the same about Uncle Duke."

"Oh? Why not?" Dottie asks.

"Uncle Duke strayed. …with Auntie's so-called best friend. … broke her heart. I was about fifteen at the time."

"What happened?" Dottie asks.

"She stayed with him," Johnnie Mae says looking at the once beautiful woman with the angelic smile. "Figured after twenty-five years with the same man, she couldn't do any better. Thought nobody else would want her."

"Johnnie, that's awful!" Dottie says commiserating with her landlady. "I'm so sorry."

"Coming from a small town," Johnnie Mae says. "It wasn't long before everybody heard about it. My aunt tried to be strong. We all knew she was hurting inside. She died later that year. Doctor said it was a broken heart. I don't know how true that is. I do know she was never the same after that…rat cheated on her."

"What happened to your Uncle Duke?"

"Don't know. Don't care," Johnnie Mae says. She places the old photo back on the mantle. "Would you believe that witch he was messing with had the nerve to think Duke was gonna marry her?"

"Marry *her*?" Dottie says. "Funny. Do they ever?"

"Nobody I know," Johnnie Mae concurs. "…but my mama wasn't having it. Willie Bea - that's my mama – had quite the talk with *Little Miss Homewrecker*."

"Did she now?" says Dottie. "What happened?"

"Well, we were at the cemetery saying goodbye to my aunt," Johnnie Mae says thinking back. "…when Miss Willie Bea Jones walked up to

Miss Thang and assured her that if she wasn't leaving on the next thing smoking, the next hole in the ground would be for her."

"Oh, Oh!" Dottie says slapping her knee.

"...ANNNDD," Johnnie Mae continues. "She *wouldn't* need no coffin. Last I heard, she was tricking her way west."

Dottie laughs. Johnnie Mae retrieves the picture from the mantle.

"After what she did to my auntie," Johnnie Mae says solemnly. "I couldn't help but wonder."

"What's that, Hon?" Dottie asks placing her cup on the coffee table. She gives her full attention as her landlady and new friend, Johnnie Mae Flores continues her story.

"How," Johnnie Mae says looking straight at Dottie. "...could a woman, a so-called friend, hurt another woman... like that heifer did my aunt?"

Dottie starts to get the hint. She insulted this poor woman yesterday. Called her everything but a child of God. This grand old lady wanted nothing more than to be her friend but she let her insecurities get the better of her. Dottie starts to regret her words. She puts down her cup and takes a napkin to her face.

"I could never do that to another woman," Johnnie Mae says sitting next to her new friend. "Especially you, Dottie."

"Especially me?" Dottie says.

"Um hm," Johnnie Mae says. "Honey, you remind me of me."

"How's that?" Dottie says fidgeting nervously with her napkin.

"*How's that?*" Johnnie Mae says a little surprised. "Girl, don't you know?"

Dottie shakes her head no.

"Girl, I was in your shoes. Throwing all caution to the wind – going all the way to God knows where for the man I love. But you and your Jacob, you did it. ...and you did it together. I admire you, Dottie Myles. You two always got each other's back. Just like me and my Hector. He would have been proud to know you. I know I am."

Dropping her head in shame, Dottie chokes. She grabs another napkin and wipes the tears from her eyes.

"Mrs. Flores...Johnnie Mae, I'm so sorry," Dottie says sniffling. "I – I..."

"It's alright," She tells her. Johnnie Mae pats her hand and snatches another napkin from the table to dry her own eyes. "I come on kinda strong, I know. Shoot, that Jacob's a fine man. Fine man! It's a wonder you didn't scratch my eyes out the first day!"

The two friends laugh. They hug one another. Just then Josie bounces in holding one of the figurines - a small statuette of the Eiffel Tower.

"Mama, these figurines are beautiful. Look at... Mama! Mrs. Flores! Why are you crying? What's wrong?"

"Oh, this room," Johnnie Mae says dabbing her cheeks. "I forgot to dust this morning. Allergies. It's my fault."

"Josie," Dottie says getting up from the couch. "I think it's time to go."

"Oh, you don't have to leave so soon do you?" Johnnie Mae protests. "We were just getting to know one another."

"Well, I do if you're coming over for supper," Dottie says smiling. She grabs Johnnie Mae's hand and squeezes it. "Girl, I got to get my pork roast on."

Dottie picks up the empty platter her daughter brought over.

"Besides," she says. "It takes time to make Dorothy Myles' famous cinnamon peach cobbler. I only make it for friends, family, and *special* people."

Johnnie Mae smiles. She clutches her new friend's hand.

"Dottie, are you sure you'll have enough? I could bring something over."

"Girl, I'm from the south," Dottie replies. Josie and Johnnie Mae look at one another and smile.

"THERE'S ALWAYS ENOUGH!" they all say in unison.

"We sit down at six," Dottie says. "Jacob and I would be proud to have you."

"We'll be there. Dottie," Johnnie Mae says holding back the tears. "Six o'clock."

RIIINNNNGGGG.

Johnnie Mae runs and answers the phone.

"I'll let you get that," Dottie says. "Come on Josie. We have work to do."

"Yes, Mama!"

"Dottie, wait!" Johnnie Mae says stopping her at the door. "Honey, it's for you. Mrs. Kelly from the school."

"Mrs. Kelly?" Dottie says grabbing the phone from her landlady.

"Hello? This is Mrs. Myles. Mrs. Kelly?"

Dottie opens her mouth in shock. Josie and Mrs. Flores look at each other. After a moment of silence, Dottie finally speaks.

"FRANKIE DID WHAT? TO WHO?"

"...so Frankie said, '*Come on, punk! Ain't nothin' between us but air and opportunity!*'"

"Savannah, quit!" Josie laughs. "Did Frankie really say that?"

"Well, not really," Savannah admits. "But that's what I woulda said!"

"Girl, just tell the story!" L'il Daddy laughs.

"Okay! Okay!" Savannah says mimicking her brother's movements. Or at least the way she saw it. "...next thing you know, Frankie flew through the air like Superman. He dived right at that punk Arnold Mayweather and started swinging. You shoulda seen it, L'il Daddy!" Savannah says twirling around. "He looked like that white tornado on TV!"

Josie and L'il Daddy look at each other laughing to themselves. Nobody. Nobody embellishes a story like Savannah Vernell Myles.

"What happened next, baby girl?" L'il Daddy asks.

"First, Frankie popped Arnold in the chest."

"Did?" Josie says imitating her father.

"Yep! Knocked him down. Then he picked him up."

"What?" L'il Daddy says howling with laughter.

"Then he hit him in the jaw!"

"Oh, oh!"

"...in the shoulder!"

"Go'n Frankie!" Josie screams.

"Then he stepped on his foot!"

"His foot?" The two older siblings say perplexed.

"Yeah!" Savannah concurs. "He said it was something he saw on TV. Arnold didn't even get one lick in. Mrs. Kelly made the big boys break it up."

"All right, Frankie!" L'il Daddy says slapping five with Josie.

"All the kids said Frankie was the bomb!" Savannah says proudly.

"I assume that's a good thing," Dottie says coming from the kitchen. She places a roast in the center of the dining room table.

"The bees' knees, Mama," Josie says winking at L'il Daddy.

"I'm not that old, young lady. Savannah," says Mother Dottie. "How many times are you gonna tell this story? The fight's over. Your brother's lucky he didn't get expelled. Get the good silverware out of the cabinet and help your sister set the table."

"Yes, Mama!" Savannah says swinging in the air like a boxer. "My brother was baaad!"

"Frankie did the right thing, Ma," Josie says placing her mother's favorite china on the table. "That kid's been messing with Frankie since we got here – and Carmen longer than that. You shoulda heard the stories he was telling about that poor baby."

"…kid got what was coming to him," L'il Daddy says co-signing his sister's defense of their brother. "He won't be messing with Frankie no more! Or Carmen!"

"You hush, L'il Daddy," Dottie says removing her apron. "You know how your father feels about fighting. I just hope he's not too hard on Frankie."

Upstairs, Frankie unfolds the events of the last few days. He tells his attentive dad about his crush on Carmen Hamilton, their next door neighbor. How Arnold Mayweather lied on his crush and turned the entire school against her. How the boy tried to make him feel insignificant because he was from the south. He also tells his dad how Josie and L'il Daddy helped him regain confidence in himself and how he tricked Mayweather into telling the truth. Jacob raises his hand for a timeout.

"My Lord," Jacob says astonished. "All that happened in two weeks?"

"Yes, sir," Frankie responds out of breath.

"Two weeks?"

"It wasn't my fault, Daddy."

"I know," Jacob says patting his son's knee reassuringly. "Finish your story, son."

"Well, we was…"

"Were!" Jacob says correcting his son.

"Were," Frankie says. "We were on the playground messing around. Me and Savannah…"

"Savannah and I…" Jacob says ribbing his son.

"Come on, Daddy!"

"Ok, Ok," Jacob says smiling. "What happened next?"

"Well, we were messing around on the playground waiting for the bell. That's when Arnold Mayweather called Carmen a bad name."

"A bad name?"

"Yes, sir!"

"Well, what did he call her?" Jacob asks.

"Well, you remember when you told us how that boy called Mama a name 'cause she wouldn't ask him to the Lady Hawkins' dance?"

"SADIE Hawkins, son," Jacob says correcting him. "Wait, what! He called her... that boy *needed* his..."

"Um hm," Frankie says nodding his head in concurrence. "I did just what you did."

"Uh, Frankie..."

"I knocked his butt into the middle of next week!" Frankie says proudly. He takes a swing at an imaginary Arnold Mayweather.

Embarrassed that his son chose that particular incident to emulate him, Jacob attempts to calm Frankie down.

"Uh, son..."

"First, I popped him in the chest..." Frankie says reenacting the fight.

"Frankie..."

"Then I hit him in the jaw!" he says taking a swing at himself in the dresser mirror.

"Son..."

"...in the shoulder!"

"Frankie, wait."

"Then I stepped on his foot!"

"Did?"

"Uh, huh," Frankie says. "...something I..."

"...saw on TV. I heard." Jacob says finishing his son's incredible story. "Come here, son. Sit down. We still have a problem."

"Sir?"

"A conundrum, actually."

"A conundrum?" Frankie asks. "Is that one of those things that's good and bad at the same time?"

"You could say that," Jacob says laughing to himself. "Now Frankie, although the boy clearly deserved it, I can't condone fighting."

"Yes, sir." Frankie says dropping his head.

"…no matter how proud I am!" Jacob says under his breath.

"Sir?" Frankie says.

"Nothing, son. Nothing." Jacob says catching himself. "Now, tonight after dinner, I want you to clean out the attic. That's your punishment."

"Sir?"

"The attic, son. No buts."

"Yes, sir."

DING DONG!

Both Jacob and Frankie turn their attention to the sound of the doorbell downstairs.

"Company's here! Come on son. Let's eat. You're gonna need your strength to clean out that attic."

Jacob gets up to leave but is stopped by his son.

"Yes, Frankie?"

Frankie, sitting on the bed looks up at his dad and smiles. He hugs him – harder than he ever has before. Frankie starts to cry. Apparently the weeks' events have finally caught up to him. Jacob hugs his son and rubs his head.

"It's OK, Champ. You had quite a week. Hey," Jacob says. "You know I'm in your corner, right?"

Frankie nods yes.

"Let's go, son. Race ya!"

Jacob and Frankie run downstairs. Johnnie Mae and Carmen are seated at the far end of the dinner table with an empty chair between them. Everybody cheers when they see Frankie.

"ALRIGHT, FRANKIE!" His siblings shout. Dottie shakes her head but can't help but smile at her son's happiness. Frankie actually takes a bow playing along with his family and friends.

"Sit here, Papi," Carmen says patting the seat next to her.

"There's my hero," Mrs. Flores says beaming. "Frankie, I'm gonna fix you a plate fit for a king. I'd heard you like mustard and spinach."

"Yes, ma'am," Frankie says.

"Let me butter your bread for you, Frankie." Carmen says.

"Don't worry, L'il Daddy," Josie whispers to her brother. "Maybe Carmen can fix you up with one of her girlfriends."

"Hilarious, Josie," L'il Daddy says playfully shoving his sister. "Hilarious!"

"Hey, Carmen!" Josie says. "I didn't know you wore glasses. They're so pretty."

"Thank you!" Carmen blushes.

Dottie takes her husband aside and whispers in his ear.

"Poor Frankie," she says ribbing her husband. "I hope you weren't too hard on him."

"Did what I had to do, honey. I see you brought out the good China," Jacob says returning the joust. "...ran out of paper plates, huh?"

"OK, OK you were right!" Dottie admits as she watches her neighbor and new friend fuss over her son. "Johnnie Mae's good people."

"Is that right?" Jacob muses. "Hmmm. Think she'll give us a break on the rent?"

"Ha, ha! Funny, Mr. Myles. Extremely. Have a seat."

Later that evening, Frankie grabs a broom, dustpan, and a garbage bag from the kitchen closet. He heads upstairs to the Myles' family attic.

"Guess I better get started," he says to himself.

He climbs the stairs expecting the worst.

Frankie's taken aback by what he sees. Save for two or three magazines, the entire attic is spotless. Frankie goes down to his parents' bedroom and knocks on the door.

"Hey, Dad..."

"Goodnight, Frankie!" his father says through the closed door.

"But, Dad..."

"See you in the morning. ...*champ!*"

"Goodnight, Dad," Frankie says silently as he heads to his room. "Love you, too!"

Totally exhausted, Frankie joins his little brother on the bottom bunk. Barely able to keep his eyes open, Frankie looks up at the SuperSpy poster on the wall. The agent in the poster seems to smile in his direction. He winks at Frankie lying comfortably in his little brother's bunk.

"*Congratulations, Agent Myles!*" he seems to say. "*Good job!*"

"*Backatcha!*" Frankie says between yawns. "*Backatcha!*"

Movin' On

With one eye on the clock, Mack grabs Josie and kisses her passionately. He stops, rubs her shoulders and looks poor Josie in her pretty brown eyes. Josie looks at her suitcase and then the kitchen door. On the other side of which are the people who've stood behind Josie her whole life – just a few feet away.

"I – I should talk to my parents, Mack."

"Honey, look at me," Hodges says. "…if you leave this room, then I know that I don't have a woman but a frightened little girl. I need my Princess to be my queen."

Mack kisses Josie again. She melts in his arms.

"What's it gonna be, Mrs. Hodges?"

Josie's Dilemma, Part 1—Daddy's Dungeon

Wednesday, May 30th, 1962

MINISTER ISAIAH LUCAS, wiping his brow and reading from his late father's fifty-year- old bible, leads the funeral march for the late Brother Joseph Leroy Hodges. Master Sergeant Hodges' coffin, adorned with the nation's flag is carried by six pallbearers all in military dress. The six pallbearers – with three on either side of the proverbial pine box between them – follow Brother Lucas as they descend the stairs of the town's oldest black church. The men, all veterans of World War I, march slowly to the cemetery adjacent to the fifty-year-old structure. Several of the congregation's parishioners, handkerchiefs dampened by sweat from the blistering hot day, follow in procession. Two of the parishioners, Deacon Ed Talbert and his daughter Marilyn, clutching her three-week-old son, follow the brethren carrying the deceased. The two pallbearers at the head of the casket observe three men; Evan Platt, Sr., his son Evan, Jr., and Floyd Watts watching the proceedings from the Senior Platt's old truck. Floyd Watts has one of the biggest peanut farms in North Georgia and is the former employer of the late Mr. Hodges.

"A military funeral. For Joe Hodges," Evan Sr. says shaking his head in disbelief. "Hell of a way to be celebrating Memorial Day, huh Mr. Watts?"

"Boy worked for me for fifteen years," says Floyd Watts. "Never knew he was in the army."

"Were you in the service, Mr. Watts?" Evan Jr. asks.

"Quiet, Evan," his father tells him. He's still holding on to the story Watts has been telling for years. Floyd Watts, who with his father's help acquired a student deferment to avoid the draft, told anyone who would listen that he was unfairly labeled 4F. He watched shamelessly as Joseph Hodges and others like him, followed their conscience and joined the war effort.

"Military ain't everything, boy!" Watts bellows. "The real war is right here! Damn it, Platt! It's hot out here. We been waitin' 'round this hellhole for two solid hours. Thought you said that boy would be here."

"I know the boy's not trustworthy, Mr. Watts. ...and I'm sorry! ... real sorry!" says the elder Platt scratching his head. "...but damn! Who misses his own daddy's funeral?"

"A no-account monkey, that's who!" the younger Platt shouts. "Right, Mr. Watts?"

"Shut up, Evan," his father tells him. "Mr. Watts is talking." He directs his attention to Floyd Watts sitting behind him. "Are we gonna hurt the boy, Mr. Watts?"

Watts is silent.

"We're not gonna hurt him, right?" Evan, Sr. beseeches him. "You know. Just talk to him, right? Mr. Watts?"

Floyd Watts, second lieutenant to the Grand Wizard of Humble County contemplates his response. The old Klansman drums his fingers on the back seat of Platt's old truck. He furrows his brow at the parishioners leaving the church and then at Evan Platt and his son seated in front of him. He's burned a couple of crosses with these boys, went to a few meetings, but as far as he knows they've never committed to anything serious.

"These boys can't handle it," he tells himself. *"Damned fools don't even know the real reason we're here."*

"Mr. Watts," Evan, Sr. asks. "What's your answer?"

Watts remains tight-lipped, his icy silence intimidating Platt and his son. He has never seen them do anything beyond marching and telling stupid jokes. Unsure whether his countenance will betray his true feelings, he turns away from the men awaiting his response. Staring off into the distance, Watts breaks his silence.

"No, boys," he lies. "We won't hurt him."

"Looks like we have company," the first pallbearer tells his brother on the other side of the casket. "What do you suppose they want?"

"Ol' 4F Floyd probably figures poor Joe here's got a drop of blood he forgot," the second man says nodding toward the deceased.

"4F, my foot!" the third pallbearer laughs. "Poor Joe must've share-cropped that old draft dodger's land his whole life!'

"Wouldn't doubt it," says the fourth man nodding his head in concurrence. "...*and he* got the nerve to show up *here?*"

Pallbearer number five knocks on the pine box with his free hand. "Y'all hear that? Joe says hurry up and bury me 'fore he try to take my shoes, too!"

"That ain't *no* guarantee!" jokes the last pallbearer. "Y'all know Floyd Watts. Better git a move on 'fore he come after *our* shoes, too!"

They all laugh until they notice the minister, Brother Isaiah clearing his throat and frowning their way. In an effort to regain their composure, the old veterans walk hurriedly to a freshly dug grave, smiling but failing miserably to stifle their laughter. Watching the pallbearers' little sideshow, Deacon Talbert can't help but chuckle.

"My Lord, my Lord," he says wiping the sweat from his brow. "Brother Joe always kept us grinning one way or another. He's gonna be missed. Wish I could say the same for his son."

Marilyn Talbert, the deacon's daughter calls to her father. She stops just short of the cemetery gate surveying the area.

"Daddy," she says looking around. "Have you seen...?

"No!" the deacon yells. "...and I better not! Get your baby and come on! Let him say goodbye to his grandfather."

"Yes sir," she says cradling her infant. "C'mon Little Mackie. Time to say goodbye."

"...and stop calling him that!" her father screams. "Little Mackie! God knows the boy deserves better!"

"So I tell her, I said, *'Lady, I only sell fan belts. You're gonna have to find chastity belts somewhere else!'* Get it? Chastity belts? Haa!"

"Look, Buddy!" the young man says impatiently. "Just change the tire, OK. I need to get out of here."

"No problem, sir. Almost done," says the mechanic checking the air pressure on the brash young man's tire. "You were lucky to get here when you did. Let me get some air in the others. Won't take but a second."

"Look, Jake…"

"Jack!" the young mechanic says smiling. He jumps up and extends his hand. "John, actually. John Mason, the third. And you're?"

"Don't you get it?" he screams ignoring the good-humored mechanic's offer of friendship. "I'm in a hurry! I wanna make Detroit sometime tonight!"

"Oh, you won't hit Michigan today," Jack tells him.

"No I guess not," he says condescendingly. "Not at this rate."

"I'm on it, sir," Jack says. "Almost done. Hey!"

"Hey, what?" the man says rolling his eyes.

"You're in high school?"

"Do I look like I'm in high school?"

"Well, I was just looking at your bumper sticker."

"It's my girlfriend's, OK? Was, anyway."

"Hmm. Whitehall Senior High. Now, where have I seen that sticker?"

"*Can't imagine this hayseed even **seeing** the **inside** of a high school*", the young man thinks to himself.

"Oh yeah, I know. 'Bout a month ago."

"What? You've seen this sticker before?" the man says finally showing some interest in something other than himself. He follows Jack frantically as the mechanic inflates the other tires.

"When? Where?"

"Yeah, family drove through here back end of April. No, March. Yep, it was March all right. Buggy needed an oil change."

"March? What kind of car was it?"

"…station wagon. Custom Deluxe. Wood paneling. I never forget a car… *or* a nice family," he says looking the young man up and down.

"Hey, I'm sorry," the slickster lies. "I'm a little on edge, here. Got real important business up north. I apologize. Now, you say you saw the sticker before? On a station wagon? You remember their name?"

"Oh, sure. Myles. Jacob Myles. Good man. Decent. Pretty wife. Five kids, I think. The oldest boy? Now he knew a good joke when he heard one."

"Was there a girl?" the man pushes him. "…about eighteen?"

"Oh, yeah. Won't be forgettin' her anytime soon. Josie. Real looker. Pretty. I believe they were headed to Chicago. Yep, Chicago, Illinois."

"Chicago, huh?"

"Yep! Good people!" Jack says finishing up. He wraps the hose around an old air pump. "Well, you're done!"

"Well, well!" the young man says with an ominous smile. *"The ol' bible thumper took 'Baby Girl' to Chicago. Hmmm. Feds won't be looking for a couple."*

"Uh, sir?" Jack says perplexed. "You alright?"

The young man rudely pushes Jack aside and runs back into the diner.

"Hey, where's the phone?" he demands of the fortyish strawberry blonde pouring coffee.

"Over there," owner Dora Mason responds sarcastically. "On the wall? Black? Bunch of numbers on it? Can't miss it."

"Thanks, lady," the man says rushing to the phone. "...whole world's a comedian."

The young man hurriedly picks up the phone, dials the operator and speaks into the receiver.

"Long Distance? Hopskip, Georgia. HOP. SKIP. Right." The brash young man gives the operator the number of a friend back in Georgia. "Yeah, I'll wait."

The young man turns to Dora Mason standing behind the counter. Above her head on the wall is a picture of her husband, Sgt. John Mason the second. Mason's in uniform. It's the same picture Dora's son Jack keeps in the garage. The young man sneers at the picture offending Dora and a few of Dora's regulars watching him with disdain. He turns away from the patrons. After a brief silence, he yells into the phone.

"TURNER?"

"Speaking," says an indistinct voice on the other end. "Who is this?"

"Don't act like you don't know who this is," the young man barks into the phone. "What are you still doing there?"

"'Cause Floyd Watts don't scare me like some people I know!"

"Oh, really? Boy, I will come back to Hopskip and dismantle you. Is your sister home? I need you to ask her something. Now!"

"Excuse me," Dora says sidling between the young man and the counter. The young man presumptuously takes that opportunity to snatch a pencil from Dora's hair. He tears a slip of paper from Dora's receipt book.

"I need to borrow this," he says without asking.

"Don't let me stop you!" Dora says.

"Alright, Turner. Give it to me."

Jack Mason walks into the restaurant holding the keys to the young man's car.

"What's his problem?" Dora asks her son.

"No idea, Mama," Jack responds. He sits at the counter, takes off his cap and wipes his brow. He turns back to the man now heading toward him. "You're all ready, Mr. -"

The man snatches the key before Jack is able to finish his sentence. He takes ten dollars from his wallet, slams it on the counter and takes off.

"I don't know *what* his problem is, Mama," Jack says. "…just glad to see him go."

"Amen! Coffee, baby?"

Thursday, May 31st, 1962

Waitressing at the Breakfast Nook in downtown Chicago, Jocelyn Dorothy Myles - newly transplanted to the Windy City - readies herself for the day ahead. The young beauty slips into her waitress' uniform and combs her hair. Applying some lipstick and dabbing a little blush to her cheeks, she steps back from the mirror to take a look at her handiwork.

'*A bit much,*' she thinks blotting her lips. '*Deacon Myles will surely blow a gasket*', she jokes half-heartedly. Josie searches her reflection in the mirror looking for a smile. Nothing.

'*Why do I even try?*' she tells herself. '*This just isn't working.*'

Josie's referring to the talk she had with her mother back in Kentucky. She promised her parents that she would stop sulking about leaving Hopskip and give her new home a chance. She tried to put on a happy face with the lipstick and blush this morning but unfortunately, she fell short. Poor girl. She's miserable and it's getting harder every day to keep up the pretense. Apparently, something - or someone is missing in her life. Josie flops on her bed and buries her head in her hands. Fighting back the tears, Josie screams.

"It's not fair, Daddy! I deserve better than this. God knows I deserve better than this!"

Sitting up on her bed, Josie looks over at her dresser on the far wall of her room. The lovelorn ex-rancher's daughter dabs a tissue to her pretty brown eyes and smiles. She jumps up, opens the top drawer of her dresser and pushes a few clothes aside. Camouflaged under an old nightie is the something - or someone missing in her life. She gently pulls out a picture of a young man – a young man to whom she says goodnight every evening and hello every morning. Josie kisses the man in the picture and gently caresses its frame.

"Good morning, my love," she says. A tear falls down her pretty cheek onto the frame. She takes a tissue and wipes it clean away. If only heartache was as easy.

"It's been two months," she says to the year-old photo. "… and you haven't answered my letters – or my prayers. What's the matter, baby? Don't you love me no more? I'm just playing. I know you love me - to the moon and back. That's what you said. I just miss you, that's all. I hate to tell you this, my darling but *you* better hurry up. Lotta brothers up here – *fine* brothers asking your girl out every day. Our landlady next door wants to introduce me to her grandson and he's a doctor. A *doctor*. Not that that matters, mind you. I love you for you. Nothing else matters. Couple of my customers at the restaurant asked me out but I told them no, too! Told 'em I was spoken for- by the finest man in Georgia. So don't you worry, baby. I know you're coming. You're just waiting 'til you can get enough money saved to come and get me. But you, you said three weeks. Oh, I'm sorry, baby. I don't mean to pressure you. I know you hate that. I know we'll get married as soon as you get here. …and you'll get me out of Daddy's dungeon. Just like we planned. Ain't that right, baby?"

Josie sits on her bed reminiscing. She recalls the time she first met the love of her young life – Michael 'Mack' Hodges. The young man saved her from a vicious attack by town bully, Evan Platt, Jr.

"I'm okay, Mr. Matthews. Please! Don't tell my father! Please! Please!" Josie pleads with the grocer. She knows Jacob would kill the boy – or worse, get killed in the process. "I just wanna go home."

"I'll take you home," says her rescuer. He points down the alley toward his car, a bright shiny pink Cadillac.

Josie looks into her hero's eyes. She's in love.

"Who are you?" she asks breathlessly. "What's your...?"

"Michael. Michael Hodges. Most folks call me Mack," he says walking her to his car.

"Oh! Well, thank you, Mack! My name is..."

"Josie? Josie?"

Knock! Knock!

"Yes, who is it?" Josie says coming back to earth. She leaps from the bed, pats her hair and straightens her uniform. She slips the picture frame under her pillow.

"Savannah, if that's you..."

"It's Mama, honey," Dottie yells through the closed door. "Daddy's waiting for you, baby. He's got some business downtown. He wants to drop you off at the restaurant. Josie?"

'The dungeon master calls,' Josie says to herself. "Okay, Mama! Be right down," Josie says retrieving the picture from its hiding place. Closing her tear-soaked eyes, she presses the picture to her bosom and rocks back and forth imagining the love of her life sweeping her off her feet.

Mack opens the door to his car. He gently sweeps a now very smitten Josie off her feet and places her safely inside his caddy, the car young Hodges boastfully refers to as the 'sweetest car in the Negro community'. Could have been a wheelbarrow for all Josie cared. With her hero, Michael 'Mack' Hodges by her side, the small town rancher's daughter felt like an African princess.

Josie sighs. It was that very day - a day etched permanently in her heart – that young Jocelyn Dorothy Myles kissed a man, not a boy for the very first time.

"I don't care what Daddy says," Josie whispers to her beloved. "Soon as you get here, "BABY GIRL IS GONNA BE YOURS – ALL YOURS!"

"Josie, did you say something baby?"

"No, Mama!" Josie says dabbing her face with a tissue. "I'm coming!" She carefully places the photo back in the drawer and covers it with her bedclothes. As an afterthought, she pulls the picture back out of the drawer.

"See you tonight!" she says smooching her beloved. "Your baby is waiting!"

Evan Platt, Sr. and his son, Evan Platt, Jr. quietly pull up to the farm of Turner Abernathy and family. Two generations of farmers have resided in the old ramshackle structure purchased for a song in the early thirties. Like many of the homes on the outskirts of Black Hopskip, it's seen better days. Corn no longer grows on the land since Turner Abernathy the second, now in his sixties and in poor health no longer tills the land bequeathed to him by his father, Turner Abernathy the first. Grandson Turner Abernathy, the third sees no future in selling grain when he and his friends can make money selling a more *lucrative* product. It is the younger Abernathy the Platts have come to visit.

Evan, Jr. nervously puts the vehicle in park. He watches his father fidgeting, looking around apprehensively at the town's bleak surroundings. Apparently, neither of them is too anxious to be there. Evan, Sr. grabs a bottle of whiskey from the glove compartment and takes a swig to calm his nerves. He passes it to his son who drinks almost half.

"Paw," the teenager says between guzzles, "I still don't understand what we're doin' here."

"Boy, you ain't got the sense God gave a Billy goat," says the older man. "Can't you see Mr. Watts is testing us?"

"What do you mean, Daddy?" Junior says wiping his mouth with his sleeve. "I don't do too good with tests."

"Shut up, boy and listen. Did you see how Mr. Watts was looking at us yesterday? Like we was sissies or something. He don't think we got what it takes. ...and you bringing up him not going to the army didn't help none."

"Well, P -Paw," Evan, Jr. stammers. "I just thought a man like Mr. Watts..."

"Men like Watts don't go to the army. Boy, you got a lot to learn."

"You never said why we're here, Paw."

"If you'll shut up a minute, I'll tell you. Mr. Watts is looking for that other boy. If we get this boy Turner to talk, he can lead us to him. Then Mr. Watts will believe in us. ...start showing us some respect. Hell, he might even invite us out to his house."

"That would be nice, Paw!" Junior says grinning.

"You want him to believe in us, don't you?"

"Yes, sir!"

"Then come on!" the old man says exiting the truck. "We got work to do."

"You want me to bring 'Ol Bessie'," Junior says pointing to his father's rifle hanging on the gun rack.

"Leave it!" his father says. "How the hell we gon' git the boy to talk if'n he's dead. I swear sometimes, boy... Just leave it!"

"Right, paw!" his son says. He throws the bottle in the glove compartment and jumps out of the driver's side of the truck. "...'sides. I owe that other boy something."

"What, Junior?" his father says. "Another chance to whip your dumb ass in front of the whole town? Shut up and come on!"

Evan, Sr. pushes his son up the steps of the old 'shotgun' house that's served as the Abernathy home for the last thirty years. Evan, Sr. motions for his son to knock on the door. The younger Platt opens the outside screen and knocks on the Abernathys' front door. Their quarry, Turner Abernathy the third, sitting on a couch near the door, spies the Platts standing on his porch through an adjacent window. He leaps over his late granddaddy's old easy chair and sprints toward the back of the house. He's unnoticed by his sister Cookie doing laundry in the back room.

"Paw," says Junior looking through the window. "He's running out the back door."

Platt senior and junior stare at one another until the older man breaks the silence.

"Junior?"

"Sir?"

"He ran out the back?"

"Yes, sir."

"Um hmm."

Silence.

"Ran out the back door, you say."

"Uh, yes sir."

Evan, Sr. slaps his son's hat onto the ground.

"WELL GO GIT HIM, YOU DANG FOOL! HE'S GITTIN' AWAY!"

"Oh! Yes sir, Paw!" Junior says retrieving his hat. "Yes, sir!"

The Platts run around to the side of the little frame house. The two men spot their prey running through the Abernathy's long-abandoned cornfield and into the woods. They take pursuit. Evan, Jr. catches up to Turner and tackles him. His lumbering two hundred fifty pound frame sends Turner flying headfirst into a tree stump. Turner bashes his head on the stump and is knocked unconscious.

"I got him, Paw! I got him!" the younger Platt yells. "Alright, boy, get up!"

Turner doesn't move.

"I said get up, boy!" Junior shouts kicking the man.

The older man catches up with his son. He's grinning and out of breath.

"Good work, Junior," his daddy says. "You did good, boy! Mr. Watts is gonna look at us with some respect now. All right boy, get up from there."

The younger Platt steps back from Turner. He starts to cry.

"Junior, what's the matter?" Platt, Sr. asks. He looks at Turner unresponsive and laying on the ground. He kicks Turner's seemingly lifeless body and yells.

"Get up, boy! I said get up, boy!"

"Paw..."

" Junior, he's not moving! What did you do? Get up, boy. Get up, I said!"

"I killed him, paw! I killed him!" Junior says leaning over Turner. "What do we do, Paw? What do we do?"

"Shut up, boy!" his daddy yells.

"I killed him, Paw!"

"...and I said shut up, dammit! You want somebody to hear you?"

Platt, Sr. slaps his son, grabs his arm and drags him away from Turner's crumpled body.

"Come on, we gotta get out of here."

"But, Paw..."

"I said shut up, you idiot! Let's go!"

Thomas James Abernathy, little brother to Turner the third, and his partner-in-crime Miles Wright toss their textbooks onto the back porch of the Turner homestead. The two twelve-year-olds, taking advantage of their lunch hour from Carver Elementary to sneak a quick smoke, have been waiting for this moment all morning. Thomas James, better known as T. J. looks in the back door window to find his sister Cookie folding fresh laundry on the kitchen table.

"You have to be quiet, Miles," he whispers. "Cookie's in the back room."

"Okay," Miles says.

T. J. reaches under the porch to retrieve a package he hid before taking off for school. Looking around to make sure no one sees him, he stuffs the package under his shirt as he and Miles take off for the woods.

"Got the matches?"

"Yeah! I brought some potato chips, too."

"For what?"

"Well, my big brother says it makes you hungry!"

"Hungry enough for his wife's cooking?" T. J. laughs.

"Nobody's that hungry!" Miles laughs. "Man, when is Jennifer gonna learn how to cook?"

"Yeah, I know," T. J. laughs. "I heard about those crunchy greens. Frankie Myles had me laughing so hard I was choking."

After the boys have walked a few hundred feet through the Abernathy family's desolated cornfield, Miles asks his friend a question about some wild plants he saw hidden behind a row of corn stalks.

"Hey, T. J.," Miles says. "Is that poison ivy?"

"Yeah, be careful!" T. J. says laughing at his friend's naiveté. "Let's go!"

The two boys run through the Abernathy's cornfield and into the woods behind the Abernathy farm. They have a seat on an old tree stump.

"Hey T. J.," says Miles opening the bag of potato chips. "You ever get high with Frankie Myles?"

"Nah!" T. J. says waving his hand. "Ol' Deacon Myles would have all kinda fits! I ain't got time for l'il scaredy cat Frankie anyway. Gimme the matches, Miles."

"Frankie's cool. I wonder how he's doing. Boy, they sure left in a hurry!"

"Whatever. Matches, please. Let's light this baby up. …unless *you're* a scaredy cat, too."

"I ain't no scaredy cat," Miles replies. He hands T. J. the matches from his back pocket. He looks off into the woods while T. J. lights up. T. J. takes a puff, coughs, and passes the illegal weed to his friend. Suddenly, Miles' face turns pale. He sees something in the distance that almost stops the twelve-year old's heart. He lets the chips fall out of the bag and onto the ground.

"What's the matter, Miles?" T. J. says looking at his friend's ashen face. "Don't tell me *you* scared, too?"

Miles, unable to speak shakes his head no.

"Then take a hit! Whatcha waitin' for?"

"T. J.…"

"What, man? C'mon, take a hit!"

"Wait! Stop!" Miles says. He stands up and points at a tree stump a few yards away. "Look!"

T. J. stands up and turns around.

"Man, what is wrong with…?"

T. J. gasps. He drops the marijuana cigarette onto the ground. T.J. runs in the direction of what he hopes is laundry his sister Cookie somehow left in the middle of the forest. He stops at the bloodied tree stump and almost faints. Miles grabs him before he falls. Thomas James Abernathy, uncharacteristically speechless stands frozen in his tracks. Inside his head, he screams the name his heart won't allow him to say.

"TURNER!!!"

"Another cup, Daddy?" Josie says blandly. She pours her father a cup of the Breakfast Nook's special brew while he scopes the want ads.

"Thank you, baby girl," Jacob says smiling. "Kinda slow for lunch-time, isn't it?"

His daughter doesn't answer. After an entire morning of dreaming of her absentee boyfriend, Josie Myles is not in the mood for small talk – especially from the man she blames for her loneliness. If she can help it, she'll keep to herself. She walks two tables over to wait on her only other customers - the Johnson sisters. The forty-something Johnson sisters noisily devour their club sandwiches - and just about every man who passes by. The two come by every day for lunch and a little gossip. By the lascivious looks on their faces, it appears they would like to have Josie's father Jacob for dessert.

"More coffee, Miss Johnson?" Josie asks nonchalantly.

"Thank you, baby," Ellie, the older sister responds. She pushes her cup toward Josie's hovering pot. "Hey, who's that gentleman in the corner booth? Lord, he's fine!"

"What?" Josie says taken aback.

"You heard her," says Doris, her lunch companion. "That's *her* man. You heard her call him '*Daddy*'."

"Wait, what?" Josie says almost dropping the pot. "He's not - "

"He *is* handsome," Doris says almost salivating. "When you're through with him honey, send him over to me!"

"Well," Josie says recovering. "I think my mama would take issue with that!"

"What?" Ellie says. "You and your mama got the same Sugar Daddy? All right now!"

"No," Josie says flabbergasted. "That's not what I meant. I mean - oh, never mind!"

"Keep it in the family, girl! That's what I say!" Doris screams slapping her sister five. "AIN'T THAT RIGHT, DADDY?"

Doris winks salaciously at Jacob. He continues to read his paper. He couldn't be more disinterested in the two women flirting with him so bodaciously. Jacob Franklin Myles, Hopskip, Georgia's answer to Harry Belafonte has been here before – many times. Unfortunately for the women who would seek to separate the ebony screen idol from his common sense, Jacob has eyes for one woman and one woman alone. Unbeknownst to Josie, that woman, Dorothy Rosetta Myles is the reason for Jacob's visit to the Nook.

Josie leaves the women laughing among themselves. She walks over to her daddy's table expecting him to be a little unnerved. He's unmoved.

"Now, Daddy! You're gonna tell me you didn't hear that?"

"Pay 'em no mind, baby girl," Jacob says. "Sit down a minute if you're not too busy."

"Yes, Daddy!" Josie says a little unnerved herself. "I – I mean sir!"

"Daddy's fine, baby girl," Jacob says laughing. "You know honey, watching you wait tables reminds me of when you were five years old."

"Five years old?"

"Um hm. You got your first '*Majestic Hostess*' tea set. You couldn't wait to have your first tea party."

"I remember, Daddy," Josie says trying not to smile. There is nothing about her life her father doesn't remember – with pride at that.

"If I remember correctly," Jacob says reminiscing. "…me and Winnie the Pooh were your first guests. He drank almost as much as me. Ha Ha!"

Josie watches her father laugh. She finds it hard to join him although she does manage a half-smile. For his sake, she tells herself.

"Everything ok, honey?"

'Is everything okay?' Josie says to herself. *'This man's got mama at home, strange women on my job - and I do mean strange – flirting with him and I got nobody. My daddy's got women coming out of the woodwork and I - Careful, Josie. Remember your promise.'*

"Josie, I asked you a question."

"I'm okay, Daddy," Josie says collecting herself. "Just not my day, I guess. How's the job hunt?"

"Got a few nibbles," Jacob says.

"Oh? Think you can find something for me?" Josie says nodding toward the two hens still cackling over her father. "I don't know how long I can take this."

"*Hmm,*" Jacob thinks to himself. "*This is going to be easier than I thought.* Uh, honey, did you ever stop to think that there's more to life than waiting tables?"

"Of course I have, Daddy. I'm just not too sure what I can do about it."

"Remember when you were about six, maybe seven? I took you to the hospital for a flu shot. You actually got to see your Aunt Julia at work. You were beyond impressed."

"I remember!" Josie says excitedly. "She was giving orders, signing important documents. Aunt Julia was running things!"

"Yep! My brother's wife was the youngest head nurse Black Hopskip General ever had. She had an offer from the other side of town, but…"

"Aunt Julia said no way," Josie says continuing an oft-repeated story.

"*…her people came first!*" father and daughter say in unison. Josie smiles for the first time today thinking of her favorite aunt.

"Yep! Aunt Julia was something else, Daddy."

"Baby Girl! Do you remember about four, five Christmases ago, the whole family got sick?"

"What is this?" Josie says to herself. *"This Is Your Life?"*

"Everybody got sick but you!" Jacob continues. "...and you took care of all of us. Running back and forth with soup, medicine, whatever we needed. I got the feeling you enjoyed what you were doing."

"You know, Daddy," Josie smiles reminiscing. "L'il Daddy and Frankie weren't as sick as they were making out."

"They weren't?"

"Nah, those two rats just liked having me waitin' on 'em."

"What? I never knew that."

"I really didn't mind. I liked it. Gave me a chance to take charge. ... like Aunt Julia."

"You were my little Florence Nightingale."

"Oh, Daddy!" Josie says mellowing.

"You're a natural, baby girl. I think you'd make a wonderful nurse yourself."

"You do, Daddy?"

"Look here, baby girl," Jacob says pointing at the want ads. "There's a nursing college only two blocks away from here. *Amlin School of Nursing – A Division of Middleton College.* Might be worth looking into, Josie."

"...and you just happen to have it right here?" Josie says.

"Well, sometimes miracles fall in your lap."

Josie's customers – the Johnson sisters - get up to leave. They pass by father and daughter reading the paper. Doris stops her sister, flabbergasted by what she sees.

"Ellie, look!"

"What, girl?"

"He's got the want ads out!"

"So?"

"So he's making her get a part-time job!"

"A part-time job? I bet he makes her mama work, too! Come on, we're outta here!"

"Don't forget my tip!" Josie yells but expecting nothing in return.

"Oh, no problem, honey!" Doris sasses back. She flips Josie a dime. "With a man like that, you need all the tips you can get!"

"Wow! Two more and I can get the special," Josie says shaking her head. Jacob drops his head and smiles.

"This is what I have to deal with, Daddy!" Josie says. She goes over to clean the mess left by the sisters. She sighs. "Hmmm. Nursing. Daddy, you really think…"

"I sure do!" Jacob says getting up from the booth. Josie clears the table while Jacob puts on his jacket. He leaves the newspaper open to the ad for Middleton College. He kisses Josie's forehead and gives her a hug. He then pats the ad he left on the table.

"God knows my baby girl deserves better!" he tells her. "See you tonight."

Josie almost drops the dishes she cleared from the Johnson sisters' table.

"Wait! Did he just say…?"

"Josie!" yells a voice from the back of the restaurant.

Josie turns to face another waitress, Millie Cooper. She's just starting her shift.

"You have a phone call, honey. He sounds cute. You can take it upfront."

"Thanks, Millie," Josie says grabbing a phone near the register. "Hello?"

"Hey, Princess."

Josie's lonely heart skips a beat.

"Mack?"

"Look outside."

Josie turns around to see a pink Cadillac parked just outside the Breakfast Nook. A young man standing in a nearby phone booth slowly turns to reveal a very handsome and smiling face. He throws her a kiss. Josie drops the phone and runs outside. She jumps into his arms.

"MACK!"

"Hey, Princess. I'm home."

SMACK! Josie slaps Mack.

"OWW, PRINCESS! WHAT'S THE DEAL!"

"PRINCESS, MY FOOT!" Josie yells. "MACK HODGES, WHERE THE HECK HAVE YOU BEEN?"

Mack laughs. He kisses Josie. She melts in his arms. Poor Josie. She could never resist his smile. He takes her in his arms and hugs her; all the while staring at Josie's co-worker Millie. She's standing at the door of the restaurant admiring the young man. The scoundrel winks at Millie. Taken aback at first she gasps. Millie then recoups, smiles and returns the wink.

"He *is* cute," she says to no one in particular. "Way too cute for Miss Josie!"

"…and bless the hands that prepared the black-eyed peas and corn bread for the nourishment of yours truly."

"FRANKIE!" Jacob says admonishing him. "That's not a prayer."

"…for the nourishment of our *bodies*. Amen."

"Amen!" Jacob, Dottie, and family all say in unison.

"*… and bless you Lord for bringing Mack Hodges back into my life,*" Josie thinks to herself. "*All I have to do is play along one more night. Tomorrow, Mack it'll be you and…*"

"Pass the chicken, Josie!" Frankie says. "…and don't hold back…"

"…on the black-eyed peas!" Josie responds. "Got it, Frankie!"

"So, Josie," Dottie says. "How was your day, baby?"

"Fine, Mama!"

"Mama!" Frankie interjects. "I got a home run at recess, today."

"That's good, baby. So Josie, how was…?"

"…and there was three men on base!" Frankie says jumping up and swinging an imaginary bat. "I got a grand slam!"

"You mean *boys*!" Savannah says.

"What?"

"You said *men*, Frankie," Savannah says deflating her brother's already delicate ego. She never even looks up from her plate. "You mean boys."

"Stay out of this, Savannah!" Frankie says.

"Just stating the obvious," she says nonchalantly.

"You be quiet, Savannah!"

"What did I do?" Savannah looks up feigning innocence.

"Both of you be quiet," Jacob intervenes. "Your mother was talking. Dottie?"

"Well, before *Mr. Banks* interrupted us…" Dottie says.

"Ernie Banks' a first baseman, Ma," says Frankie. "…don't get me wrong. He can hit all right, but…"

"Frankie," Jacob says.

"Actually, he's good in a lotta positions," Frankie continues.

"Frankie!" Dottie says.

"...so I guess you *could* call me *Mr. Banks*! Hey, thanks, Ma!"

"Enough!" Jacob says slamming his silverware on the table. "Now, no one else talks! Nobody opens their mouth unless I see food going in it. Josie, tell your mother how your day went!"

"*...aanndd here it comes*," Josie says to herself. "Uh, great Daddy."

"Did you go downtown?"

"I work downtown."

"Josie, I meant did you go to the school?"

"School?" Frankie asks bewildered. "Josie's going back to school? I thought you graduated."

"Boy!" Jacob says wearily. "What did I say about opening your mouth?"

"I was gonna put some food in it," Frankie laughs. "I figured it would be okay to talk while the food was on its way."

Frankie's siblings drop their heads. They're laughing but they know their parents are not in the mood.

"*Ernie's battin' a thousand!*" L'il Daddy whispers to Josie.

"Frankie," Jacob says exasperatedly. "We're trying to have a conversation. Josie..."

"I went to the school, Daddy," Josie says. She whips out a pamphlet from the purse in her lap. "TA-DAAA!" she says with a flourish.

"Oooh, baby," Dottie says. "Let me see."

Jacob gently taps his wife's foot under the table - his covert way of saying *Mission Accomplished*. Dottie squeezes his knee, motioning for him to stay calm. Yes, he convinced their daughter to consider attending school up north. Yes, she brought home a pamphlet about a nursing college. Yes, she's excited. Is she still talking to that bum Mack Hodges' picture every morning? Unfortunately, that's also a YES!

"*We're not out of the woods yet, honey,*" Dottie's eyes tell her husband. In a good marriage, couples can say a lot with one or two words. In a great one, like Jacob's and Dottie's, couples can say volumes without muttering a sound. Still, Jacob can't help looking a little full of himself - a look not lost on his eldest.

"*I'm onto you, Daddy,*" Josie says to herself. "*If you think some school will make me forget about Mack...*"

Dottie reaches for the pamphlet. She lays it on the table between herself and Frankie.

"Hmm," Dottie says. "*Amlin School of Nursing*. Sounds nice."

"Medicine?" Frankie asks.

"Yes, Frankie," Josie says trying not to look at her smug father. "I'm going to be a nurse."

"Oh!" says Frankie relieved. "For a minute there, I thought you were gonna try and be a doctor or something!"

"Excuse me?" Josie says her hands on her hips.

"My Lord!" Jacob says to himself exasperated. *"How does he even get food in his mouth when his foot takes up permanent residence?"*

"I blame myself, Jacob," Dottie says frowning at her chauvinistic offspring. "…not enough vitamins in my last trimester."

"Good one, Ma!" L'il Daddy laughs. "Good one!"

"Some-bo-dy's in trou-ble!" Savannah sings.

"What did I do now?" Frankie says between bites.

"…besides talking with food in your mouth?" Josie says.

"Is that all?" Frankie says sheepishly.

"IS THAT ALL?" Dottie almost shouts. Jacob pats her knee. She calms down. "You don't think a woman can be a doctor? Boy, where are you getting these antiquated ideas?"

"I know what that means," Savannah shouts proudly.

"I didn't ask!" Dottie snaps back.

"Ha!" Frankie laughs. "Who's in trouble, now?"

"I'm not done with you, Mister," Dottie says. "Where are you getting these crazy ideas?"

"Well," Frankie says looking to the ceiling for an answer. "You never see any lady doctors on TV! Just nurses!"

"TV?" Jacob interjects. "Boy, if I began to tell you what you don't see on TV and what's really going on in the world…"

"…we'd never leave this table." Dottie continues. "Frankie, baby there are plenty of Negro women doctors in this world."

"Rebecca Lee Crumpler!" says Savannah. "Oh, I'm sorry, Mama."

"It's okay, baby," Dottie says encouragingly. "Go on!"

"Rebecca Lee Crumpler was the first black woman to earn a degree in medicine."

"…andddd!" Josie adds. "She started as a nurse."

"Is she a friend of yours, Mama?" Frankie asks innocently.

"Wellll…" Jacob says laughing. Josie hides her smile. Her daddy always had a direct connect to baby girl's funny bone.

"Oh, don't you even start," Dottie says taking a playful swipe at her husband's head. "No Frankie, that was during the civil war. You're gonna pay for that, Mr. Myles."

"I'm sorry, baby," Jacob says hugging his wife. "Hey, don't forget Dorothy Ferebee, M.D. Southern girl, born in Virginia."

"Mary Eliza Mahoney," Dottie says looking at a now very attentive Frankie. "She was the first Negro woman to become a professional nurse in the United States."

"That was in 1879," L'il Daddy joins in. "Definitely not a friend of Mama's."

"I said I was sorry," Jacob laughs. Josie can't help but smile.

"How did you know that, L'il Daddy?" Frankie asks.

"Well, l'il brother," L'il Daddy says putting his arm around Frankie. "There's more to Jet Magazine than the top songs of the week. Really, l'il brother, you should read more."

"I don't think it would hurt to leave the TV off some nights, Frankie," says Jacob. "Time you started reading some of those Negro History books we got for the family."

"Yes, sir!" Frankie says nodding his head. "I will."

"Good man!" Jacob tells his son. He reaches over and rubs his head.

"Well, Frankie I hope you learned something," Dottie says. She lovingly rubs his head.

"Yes, Ma'am! Women can be just as good a doctor as men can."

"I'll forgive the grammatical errors," Dottie says smiling.

"Yes, ma'am," Frankie says. "Uh, Mama?"

"What is it, slugger?"

"Do you forgive *me*?" Frankie asks wide-eyed.

"Of course, baby," she says. "Give Mama a hug!"

Everyone at the table stops to watch Frankie hug his mother. They all know the approval of Dorothy Rosetta Myles is worth a thousand grand slams to little Franklin Joseph Myles. Josie almost cries. She catches herself before anyone sees her. Frankie runs over to her side of the dinner table.

"I'm sorry, Josie," Frankie says. "I guess if any woman can be a doctor, it would be you."

"Well, thank you, little brother," she says kissing his cheek. "But why do you say that?"

"'Cause you know everything," he says confidently and without hesitation. "You're *almost* as smart as Mama. Hey, all the cornbread's gone!"

"Check the stove, baby," Dottie says. "I saved you some!"

Savannah jumps out of her chair and runs to the oven.

"I'll get it for you, Frankie!"

"Thanks, Savannah."

"...and while baby girl number two's handling cornbread duty," says Jacob with a smile. "Let's not forget Baby Girl number one. Congratulations, Josie! Great career choice."

"Yes, baby," Dottie says. "Congratulations. I'm so proud of you."

L'il Daddy lifts his glass. "A toast! ...to Nurse, soon to become *Dr.* Jocelyn Myles."

The entire family - even Baby Terry, who's been quiet up to now - lifts their individual glasses to Josie. They get out of their seats and run over to hug and kiss the woman of honor. She starts to cry.

"Oh my God," Josie thinks to herself. *"This has gone too far. I can't leave like this. Mack's coming for me tomorrow. What am I gonna do!"*

"...kids in bed, baby?"

"Yep, everyone's turned in for the night," Jacob says. "I do believe I saw a light on in L'il Daddy's room."

"I think Josie's down there," Dottie says. "No doubt sharing her plans for the future."

"Um hmm. Another crisis averted," Jacob grins. He pitches an imaginary ball to the coat rack standing in the corner of their bedroom. "Strriiiike three! Hit the showers, Hodges. You're outta here!"

"Not so fast, Lightning!" Dottie warns the ex-pitcher. "Game's not over yet! She hasn't even registered for the classes."

"What do you mean?" Jacob says crawling onto the bed in his pajamas. "You saw how happy she was. She's staying. She wants to be a nurse. Maybe even a doctor. She's ecstatic."

Dottie smiles.

"My baby *did* look happy."

"L'il Daddy, I got a problem. A big problem."

"What are you talking about, Sis?"

"Oh, this is huge. I mean do you believe Mama and Daddy? I can't believe they fell for it."

"Fell for what? Josie, what are you talking about?"

"I'm not going to college. I only brought that pamphlet home to get Daddy off my back."

"Wait, wait, hold up, Sis. What do you mean you're not going to college? …and get Daddy off your back about what?"

"Can you keep a secret?"

"Sure!"

"I think Mama and Daddy's been eavesdropping. They must've heard me talking to Mack."

"You called Mack Hodges from the house? Long distance? Are you crazy?"

"Not on the phone, L'il Daddy! Calm down. I mean his picture."

L'il Daddy looks at his sister in disbelief.

"Lord help her! The girl's gone mad!"

"Baby, when you told me you heard Josie talking to that picture she keeps hidden in her dresser…" Jacob says. "I have to be honest. I was getting a little worried."

"So was I," Dottie says. "Eight hundred miles away and she's still hung up on that man. Mama Harris used to say you don't always get to choose who you fall in love with. I guess the heart wants what it wants."

"…and her heart wants Mack Hodges?" Jacob shouts. "Not while I'm living!"

"You talk to Mack's picture every morning?"

"Never mind the look, l'il brother. I've seen you look at that picture of Molly Brand in your wallet."

"Yeah, but I don't talk to her! You're nuts."

"We'll see who's nuts tomorrow. I saw Mack today."

"You saw Mack Hodges? He's in Chicago?"

"Yep!" Josie says happily. She dances around the room smiling. Her brother doesn't share in her excitement.

"Chicago?" L'il Daddy says incredulously. "Mack Hodges is in Chicago?"

"Mack came by the restaurant today. L'il Daddy, my man will be here in the morning to take me away from here. We're leaving, and I can finally say goodbye to Daddy's dungeon!"

"Daddy's dungeon? Josie, are you sure? We've been here two months and Hodges never called. He's never even responded to your letters. Every time you called him from work, he was never home and now he just pops up? I don't mean to sound like Daddy, but…"

"Mack Hodges is not the man for my Josie, Dottie!" Jacob says jumping out of bed. Dottie puts her finger to her lips. She motions for Jacob to settle down.

"I'm sorry!" Jacob says apologetically. He whispers to his wife. "I get a little excited…"

"…*where my children are concerned!*" Dottie says continuing her husband's oft-heard sentiment. She smiles. "It's alright, Jacob. I know. Come back to bed, baby."

Jacob rejoins his wife in bed.

"The sooner she sees that low-life for what he is," he whispers. "The better off we'll all be."

"No argument there," Dottie says.

"Once Josie starts school," Jacob reiterates. "…she'll get her mind off that bum and start dating real men. Not… *boys*, who skip out on their own father's funeral."

"I have to admit even I was shocked when your brother called with that piece of news," Dottie says shaking her head.

"I wasn't!" Jacob says. "Joseph says the police have been asking around town about Hodges. …and the Platts showed up at the funeral looking for him. With Floyd Watts. Floyd Watts of all people. What could that boy be into?"

"The Platts were looking for him?" Dottie asks. She looks at her husband with a knowing wink. "You mean Junior Platt's come outta hiding?"

Jacob and Dottie look at each other and laugh. She's obviously referring to the younger Platt almost getting his head blown off by parties unknown - unknown to everybody but the couple sharing the Myleses' master bedroom.

"Baby," Jacob says after a good laugh. "Our plan worked like a charm. I have no doubt Baby Girl No. 1 is staying in Chicago."

"So Mack's father Daddy Joseph died. Sorry to hear that."

"So was I," Josie sighs. "But Mack said that watching his father die, watching him suffer made him realize just how precious life is…"

"Really?" L'il Daddy asks somewhat surprised.

"Uh huh. I shoulda been there for him. I feel so bad that I wasn't."

"Do Mama and Daddy know? Do they know Mack Hodges is here in Chicago? Do they know he wants to take you away?"

"Who are you?" Josie asks her brother. "Walter Cronkite? What do you think? Daddy would have a conniption."

"He's not by himself."

"You mean Mama!"

"I mean me, Sis!"

"L'il Daddy!"

"Josie, come here." L'il Daddy directs his love struck sister to a near-by chair. He sits on his bed across from her and holds her hand.

"Josie, you're not making sense. Why after all this time does Mack Hodges show up? Without even calling? What are you two gonna do for money? Far as I know, he never worked a day in his life."

"That's not fair, L'il Daddy!" Josie says rising from her chair. "My man…"

"Josie, you keep saying your man?"

"I love Mack!" Josie confesses. "I can't do without him. I don't know about you but I'm miserable up here. Mack wants me to go with him."

"Go where Josie?"

"If I tell L'il Daddy we're going to Canada, he'll never go for it," Josie says to herself. *"I hate lying to my little brother, but Mack says it's for the best."*

"Talk to me, Sis. Where are you going?"

"Mack and I are going to Detroit," Josie fibs. "He's gonna use his Daddy's insurance money to buy a gasoline station."

"A gasoline station?" says L'il Daddy. "You never said anything about any relatives up north. I thought Daddy Joseph was an only child."

"It's his mother's folks," Josie says thinking on her feet. "Right, he and his cousin are going into business together. Mack says I can keep the books."

"Sis, have you really thought this through? I don't trust him. It sounds fishy."

"You never trusted Mack!" Josie almost screams. "You're as bad as Grandma Harris. She claimed Mack was a liar because he had a gap in his teeth!"

"Josie. Sis. Come on. Think about this. Mack Hodges…"

"L'il Daddy, I'm not completely in the dark. I know Mack has had some issues in the past. He never goes to church, never finished school. I know he and Daddy Joseph fought a lot. But once we get married, my Mack will be a new man!"

"A new man?"

"Um hmm. This is his chance to start fresh, L'il Daddy. He just needs a change of venue."

"Venue?" L'il Daddy says joking. "Somebody swallowed a Thesaurus."

"Boy, please! Now come on, L'il Daddy. I need you to have my back on this one. Mack will be here tomorrow and I'm gonna need all the help I can get."

"Tomorrow, huh? You ain't never lied."

"Now," Josie says putting her plan together. "…if we work on Mama first…"

"She'll help bring Daddy around," L'il Daddy says.

"Uh huh!" Josie says. "Mama's a soft touch."

"Jacob, do you think Hodges would bring his narrow tail to Chicago? That rat might try and contact Josie."

"Not if he's smart," Jacob says. "You don't have to worry about Hodges showing his face around here, honey. That boy is on the run, and he knows I have no use for him."

"Ain't worth a damn!" Dottie concurs.

"Dottie!" Jacob says stifling his laugh.

"Sorry, sweetheart but that boy brings out the worse in me," Dottie says apologetically. "I'm not one for turning Negroes over to the police, but in his case, I'll make an exception."

"You're a mess, Dottie Myles!" Jacob says laughing. "Get the light, baby! Time for bed."

"So you'll help me talk to Daddy?" Josie says.

"I got your back, Mrs. Hodges!" L'il Daddy says hugging his sister.

She turns the doorknob to exit her brother's room but stops to say goodnight – just enough time to give an eavesdropping younger sister time to run across the hall to Frankie's room.

"Good night, Josie."

"Good night, l'il brother! …and thanks!"

"Yep, our plan worked like a charm," says Jacob his glee piercing the darkness. "I'm so happy I can't sleep!"

"Good night sweetheart," Dottie laughs. She hugs her husband. "You have an interview in the morning."

"Good night, baby!"

Savannah switches on the light in her brother's room. She dances around the room singing the favorite song of little sister's everywhere.

"I KNOW SOMETHING YOU DON'T KNOW! I KNOW SOMETHING YOU DON'T KNOW!"

Josie tiptoes to her room and gently closes the door behind her. She looks back toward her brother's room.

"I'm sorry I lied to you, L'il Daddy. I can't help it. I have to be with Mack."

Friday, June 1st, 1962

"Finish your cereal, Savannah. I don't want you late for school."

"Yes, ma'am."

"Savannah, come on," Frankie tells her. "Carmen's waiting for us."

"Hurry up, baby," Dottie says. "It's not nice to keep people waiting. Jacob, I fixed a couple sandwiches for you. Good luck with your interview."

"Thank you, baby. Is Josie down yet?"

"I think she's still getting dressed, Daddy," L'il Daddy says covering for his sister. When he passed her room earlier, she was packing for the trip to 'Detroit' with Mack Hodges.

"Hey, Daddy," Savannah says. "When Josie gets married, will she keep her name?"

"Oh my God!" L'il Daddy tells himself. He spills his milk on the dining room table. *"How does she…"*

"She's gonna tell!" Frankie says looking at his big brother. *"She never could hold water!"*

"Keep her name?" Jacob asks. "What are you talking about, Savannah?"

"Lots of liberated women these days keep their last name," she says. "I know I am."

"You won't have to worry about keeping your last name, Savannah," Frankie says. "Who would be nutty enough to marry you?"

"I was talking to Daddy, Frankie!"

"So?" Frankie says.

"So this is an *'A' and 'B'* conversation," Savannah says shaking her head. "*'C'* your way out of it!"

"Alright you two," Jacob says in his daily job as referee. "Enough of that. You're gonna be late."

"Hey, Daddy!" Savannah says. "When Josie gets married, will you walk her down the aisle?"

"Of course, baby girl," Jacob chuckles. "But that won't be for awhile. What with Josie going to med school and all…"

"Med school?" Dottie says pulling her husband's sleeve. "Jacob, aren't you jumping the gun. She only brought home a pamphlet. Let her get through nursing first."

"…so that means we'll be going to Detroit for the wedding?"

"Detroit?" Dottie says a little perplexed. "Who's going to Detroit?"

"I am, Mama!" Frankie shouts. He grabs his sister, shoves her books in her arms and drags her from the table. "I'm gonna meet Smokey Robinson! Remember? Savannah, let's go!"

"Savannah! You're gonna be late," L'il Daddy says frantically. "Where're my books?"

Jacob places his lunch on the table. He looks at Dottie and then nods towards his son frenetically trying to rush his younger siblings out the door. She nods her head in concurrence.

"Yes, you two get going," she says hurrying her children out the door. She closes the door behind them and then turns her attention to her very nervous son. "Have a seat, L'il Daddy!"

"Ma, I have to go…"

"IT'LL WAIT!" Dottie says sternly. "JOSIE! COME DOWNSTAIRS, PLEASE!"

Jacob pulls out a chair for his son to sit. He wisely obliges. Jacob looks his son square in the eye.

"What's all this talk about marriage? …and Detroit? JOSIE! GET DOWN HERE, NOW!"

Dottie calmly turns her son's head to face her.

"Your father asked you a question. Did your sister say something about getting married and moving to Detroit?"

"N-No!" L'il Daddy says crumbling under his parents' interrogation. "Not exactly."

"Uh huh!" Jacob says circling his son's chair. "Then you know what *exactly* she *did* say!"

"Uh, I object," L'il Daddy says jokingly.

"YOU DO WHAT?" Jacob screams.

"Nothing. Nothing." L'il Daddy says slumping in his chair.

"Jacob?" Dottie says.

"WHAT?" Jacob screams. "I mean yes, honey. What is it?"

Dottie points to the stairs leading down to the dining room. Jacob looks up. His mouth is agape. With all of his and Dottie's machinations of the last few days, he hadn't planned on this moment. No father ever does.

"JOSIE! WHERE ARE YOU GOING WITH THAT SUITCASE?"

"Honey," Dottie says approaching her first born. "Where are you going? Why aren't you dressed for work?"

At that moment, Savannah runs back into the house. She's excited.

"Savannah," Dottie says. "What are you doing back here?"

"Mama, Mama. Look who I found outside!"

Savannah drags a very reluctant Mack Hodges by his sleeve into the Myles' home.

"Mr. Myles. Mrs. Myles. L'il Daddy. How is everyone?"

Jacob is flabbergasted. Dottie drops into the nearest chair. L'il Daddy drops his head in his hands and shakes his head.

"It's Mack Hodges, Mama!" Savannah shouts. "He's looking for Josie. Does this mean we're going to Detroit for the wedding?"

At this point, Jacob says a prayer of thanks. Dottie and L'il Daddy are on the same page. If Mack Hodges knew what they were thinking, he would say a prayer as well – a prayer of gratitude that Jacob keeps his old Winchester packed away in the basement and not above the fireplace, as he did back home.

But, if looks could kill...

Josie's Dilemma, Part 2–
As Easily As He Breathes

Friday, June 1ˢᵗ, 1962

WHEN JACOB MYLES was just a lad, his mother taught him to treat a visitor in their home like a member of the family. Jacob's mom taught him to welcome your guest with open arms. Offer them a chair - the most comfortable chair in the house. Always ask your guest if he or she would like something to drink – maybe even a snack. If you're watching TV, offer to change the channel or turn it off giving your guests your undivided attention. Treat a caller to your home as you would want to be treated – like royalty. Jacob learned his mother's lessons well, so well that he's passed on these rules of etiquette to his own children. Today; however, Jacob Franklin Myles has dispensed with his mother's teachings for the visitor standing in his doorway. In Jacob's mind, today's visitor is not a guest but an intruder - a cancer. A cancer he traveled eight hundred miles to escape. Its' name? Mack Hodges.

Michael Hodges, nicknamed Mack by his disreputable circle of friends, is an arrogant young man who's won Josie Myles' heart and her parent's disgust. After a two-month separation, Michael Hodges has come to Chicago to marry Josie. Michael loves Josie in his own way. Mr. Hodges; however, loves himself and the finer things in life a little more. Unbeknownst to the residents of Hopskip, Mack Hodges, along with his buddy Turner Abernathy had been selling information about civil rights meetings and marches to Klansman Floyd Watts. The civil rights workers of Hopskip have come home to broken windows, torched porches and fiery crosses on their lawns. They have no idea how the local Klan always knew their strategies. Michael's father Joseph sharecropped on Floyd Watts' peanut farm his entire adult life. Although the senior Hodges remained in debt to and fear of Floyd Watts until Mr. Hodges' recent death, his son Mack received a 'salary' from Watts not only for the information regarding the civil rights workers but for other misdeeds as well. Crimes none of which the senior Hodges nor the local sheriff are aware. Mack spends his so-called salary on flashy suits, jewelry and the "sweetest car in the Negro community". With clearly no visible means of support, Mack Hodges has earned the distrust of not only Jacob and Dottie Myles but of the reputable citizens of the small town of Hopskip, Georgia. Unfortunately, their disgust only endears the scoundrel to Jacob's lovelorn and impressionable daughter. She sees only the 'handsome prince' who saved her from a brutal attack by town bully Evan Platt, Jr. Jacob and Dottie see the most despicable man who ever walked the earth – Michael 'Mack' Hodges - a cad who lies as easily as he breathes.

Jacob Myles, teeming with anger maintains his distance from the cancer that would dare cross his threshold. Sensing his father's anguish, L'il Daddy steps between the two men. Smart move! Any closer and Michael Hodges would surely feel the wrath of the man who would dismantle anyone who would dare harm any of his precious brood. Just ask Evan Platt, Jr.

"Dottie, take Josie upstairs," Jacob says watching Mack like a thief in a jewelry shop.

"Daddy!" Josie begs. "Please! I need to see Mack!"

"Now, Dottie. Please."

Dottie grabs her eldest by the arm. She motions to her son L'il Daddy to remain with the men.

"Come on, baby," she tells her. "The men need to talk."

L'il Daddy watches as his mother directs his sister upstairs to her bedroom. He smiles nodding to his big sister. His smile reassures her that all will be fine. He won't let Daddy kill the boy. She manages a smile as she climbs the stairs to her room.

"Well, well, Ol' Grizzly," Hodges says to himself. *"Looks like it's just me and you."*

Ol' Grizzly. Mack Hodges gave his adversary this disparaging name the first time the two men crossed swords. He felt Jacob smothered his young daughter whenever Hodges showed his face – like a bear does his cubs when strangers get too close. To his credit, Hodges has never used the term around Jacob - probably more to his own safety.

"Well, I may as well get started if I want to dodge the Feds," he tells himself.

"You're looking well, Mr. Myles," the faker says extending his perfectly manicured hand. "Mind if I sit down?"

"I see the pretty boy still gets his nails done," Jacob tells himself. *"Is there no end to this boy's vanity?"*

L'il Daddy starts to offer the young man a seat until Jacob raises his hand in defiance. He also ignores Hodges' offer of a handshake.

"Hodges," Jacob says staring down his adversary. "Do you honestly think I'm gonna let my daughter take off with the likes of you?"

"Sir," Mack begins his lies. "Josie means the world to me. I have nothing but your daughter's best interests in mind. Now I know you've never cared for me…"

"That's an understatement, Hodges! There's never been anything to care about!"

"I see winning this old man over won't be as easy as his daughter," Mack thinks to himself. *"…but if I wanna throw the Feds off my tail…"*

"Sir," Hodges says continuing the charade. "I'm only asking you to be fair."

"Tell me, Hodges," Jacob says ignoring the man's disingenuous pleas. "What kind of man misses his own father's funeral? I know you two had your issues, but…"

"I had my reasons, Mr. Myles."

"I BET!" Jacob tells him. "Did you know the Klan came to your father's funeral looking for you?"

"The Klan?"

"Oh, yeah! Floyd Watts! Evan Platt and that ignorant…" Jacob pauses. He's careful not to speak out of turn about the boy he almost killed. "…that ignorant son of his! What was that all about?"

"Could be a number of things," Hodges tells himself. *"…the dope, those so-called peace marches, that stupid Turner Abernathy skimming off the top!"*

"I don't know sir," Hodges lies. As easily as he breathes.

"Oh, and let's not forget the police. I understand the local cops have been turning Hopskip inside out looking for you! You think I want my baby girl mixed up in all that? Oh, you've been real busy haven't you Hodges?"

"That wasn't the police, Mr. Myles."

"…so you never had any intention of going into nursing," Dottie says standing over her frightened daughter fidgeting nervously on her bed. "Answer me, Jocelyn! Did Hodges put you up to this?"

Afraid of her mother's reaction, Josie drops her head.

"You don't have to answer!" Dottie says pacing her daughter's room. "I guess you two thought you'd just take off, get married, and the rest of us be damned!"

"No, Mama," Josie protests. She starts to cry. "I would never do that, Mama. Mack wanted to leave yesterday but I told him I had to say goodbye to the family first. I told him about Daddy coming to the restaurant and he said I should go ahead and get that pamphlet. …to show that I was serious about…"

"…and you made up that story about going to school to buy yourself some time. Wasn't that clever of him? Jocelyn Myles, I am so disappointed. The boy's got you lying to your parents! Your family! You've never done that!"

"No, Mama," Josie says through her tears. "You don't understand…"

"What, Josie? What don't I understand? That you're in love with someone the rest of the world can do without? The boy's no good, Josie! There's no getting around that!"

"That's not fair, Mama!" Josie says jumping to her feet. "Mack can change. Just like Daddy did."

"WHAT DID YOU SAY?" Dottie shouts incredulously.

"Daddy changed and you married him," Josie says standing her ground. "Mack can change. Why can't you give him the same chance you gave Daddy?"

Dottie looks at her daughter standing up to her. She almost laughs.

I know this child doesn't have her hands on her hips!" Dottie tells herself. She slowly approaches her spirited, yet misguided daughter until the child she birthed regains her composure (i.e. common sense) and sits back on the bed.

"Now you hold it right there, young lady," Dottie says after she's calmed down a minute. "Your daddy had some issues coming up but nothing like this boy. Do us both a favor, Jocelyn Myles. ...and never, ever let me hear you compare that lowlife to **my** *husband,* **your** *father, ever again!*"

"Mama!" Josie begs.

"THERE IS NO COMPARISON! DO WE UNDERSTAND ONE ANOTHER?"

"Yes, Ma'am," Josie says retreating to her bed. "I'm sorry, Mama.!"

"Good!" Dottie tells her. "Besides, that Mack Hodges is only up here for one thing!"

"MAMA!" Josie says astounded. "You can't believe..."

"Oh, child calm down!" Dottie says. "I meant that he's *up here* 'cause they're looking for him *down there.* Back home. Your precious Mack is wanted by the law."

"It's not the police, Mama," Josie says almost inaudibly.

Dottie's taken aback.

"It's not the police? Then who..."

"It's the army, Mr. Myles. The MP's." Hodges says telling the truth for the first time since arriving in Chicago – quite possibly his life.

"The army? Boy, what in the world..."

Jacob looks at Hodges. He's stunned, and then he's not. Jacob has always remarked that with men like Hodges, all the manicures in the world won't hide the dirt under their nails. L'il Daddy, who's re- mained quiet until now poses a question to the man who would be his brother-in-law.

"Why is the army looking for you, Mack?"

"Isn't it obvious son?" Jacob says sarcastically. "Mr. Hodges here is on the run. Somebody got their draft notice and decided to skip town. Tell me I'm wrong."

"I was supposed to report two weeks ago."

L'il Daddy is stunned. He drops into the nearest chair.

"You've been hiding out for two weeks?" he says. "Josie never said anything about that."

"Like I said, Hodges," Jacob tells him. "You've been very busy."

"This man is wearing my last nerve!" Hodges says to himself trying to keep a civil tongue in his head. Instead of lashing out, he tries de- fending himself.

"Mr. Myles," Hodges says. "Do you know how many black soldiers die in Vietnam every day?"

"The military is after Mack, Mama. They wanna send Mack to Vietnam! Vietnam, Mama. He'll get killed over there!"
"If the army's after him, he can get killed over here! Baby, you're not thinking this through."
"Mama, I have thought it through! Mack can't go to Vietnam! I can't let that happen!"
"You can't let that happen?" Dottie says. "What can *you* do about it? Oh, Josie no! You're not thinking about…"
"I have to Mama. I'm going to Canada with Mack."

Realizing that his sister hasn't been completely truthful with him, L'il Daddy's demeanor toward Mack starts to change. He approaches Hodges with a question – actually more of an accusation.
"So you're not taking my sister to Detroit to open a gas station."
"A gas station?" Jacob says. He shakes his head.
"You're running to Canada. To hide."
"More lies!" Jacob says getting madder by the minute.
"Mack," L'il Daddy continues. "Your father served in World War I. We talked about him and his regiment in school. He was a hero. Daddy Joseph proved that Negroes can do more than cook, wash dishes, and clean toilets. He fought for this country and he made a difference. He wasn't welcomed as a hero when he came back. I know that was wrong, but…"
"Wrong?" Mack says feigning anger. "He couldn't even march in the city parade. …and when Black Hopskip had a parade…"
"The city fathers put a stop to it," Jacob says. "We all know the story, Hodges."
"Still," L'il Daddy continues. "Your daddy followed his conscience. He came back with honors. Black Hopskip still appreciated him even if the rest of the world didn't. What would he think about you running away?"
"My father came back with a bum leg and a bad back," Mack says his voice cracking. Nice touch. His scam is almost believable. L'il Daddy and Jacob listen as Hodges continues his tale of woe.

"Somehow, L'il Daddy, my daddy missed out on those GI benefits the white man's always talking about. He spent the rest of his life stooped over, picking peanuts for Floyd Watts. Not me! I know my father. He wouldn't want me to go. He said so."

"He said so?" Jacob demands.

"Yes, sir. He also said any black man who goes to Vietnam is a damned fool!"

"This is a Christian home, Hodges. You watch your mouth."

"Is it Christian to kill someone you don't even know?" Hodges asks. "Someone you never even met? I mean what are we even fighting for, anyway? Can you answer that one for me, Mr. Myles? L'il Daddy?"

Father and son are at a loss for words. Jacob gazes at the floor pondering a response to the hypocrite standing before him.

"Ha!" Hodges thinks to himself. *"What do you say to that, old man?"*

Hodges smirks puffing his imaginary chest thinking he's gotten the best of his adversary. Jacob, though temporarily quieted by Hodges' commentary isn't easily swayed. He knew Joe Hodges. The pair fished off Miller's Creek on many a Sunday discussing the topic of the day. Despite the 'unwelcome wagon' he and his compatriots received after the first World War, the man never mentioned regretting his actions, going to war, or sacrificing his life for his country and his people. Mack Hodges obviously will say anything to get his way. Jacob despises him all the more and would be delighted if this heathen never darkened his door another day in his life. Unfortunately, this heathen has a hold on his baby girl and Jacob Myles will do anything (and has) to keep her from being hurt. He walks over to Hodges, points a finger in his smug face and responds.

"You are not taking my daughter to Canada, Hodges!"

"We'll see about that, Ol' Grizzly!" Hodges tells himself.

Josie sits on the edge of her bed crying. She doesn't want to leave her family, but she can't imagine life without Mack Hodges. Dottie sits on the bed next to her daughter, takes her in her arms and rocks her. She is dumbfounded. She's never seen her baby so distraught.

"What is the hold this boy has on my baby?" she thinks to herself. Imagining the worst, Dottie Myles suddenly stops rocking her baby. She looks to the heavens. Her mind runs in a thousand directions contemplating what she prays isn't true.

"Oh God, please don't tell me she… not with that creep Hodges. Josie would never… Would she… If that boy's anything like Jacob… Okay, Dottie Myles get a hold of yourself! You taught your daughter better. Still, I'll never know until I ask."

"Uh, Josie…" Dottie says hesitantly.

"No, Mama," Josie says anticipating her mother's question.

"No?" Dottie says meekly.

"No," Josie reassures her.

"YESSS! Thank you, Jesus!" Dottie says to herself. She squeezes her daughter and looks to the heavens once again. Her smile is as wide as all outdoors.

"Mama?" Josie says.

"Yes, sweetheart?" Dottie says trying to hide her joy.

"I can see you in the mirror."

Mother and daughter laugh for the first time this morning. Score one for the home team!

"I never figured you for a conscientious objector, Mack." L'il Daddy says.

"I've never supported the war, L'il Daddy," Mack says. "It's unjust. Ungodly…"

"Unbelievable!" Jacob laughs despite himself.

"Daddy!" L'il Daddy says surprised.

"Don't be fooled by this charlatan, son!" Jacob says.

"I *am* a conscientious objector, sir." Mack protests.

"You have to have a conscience first, don't you Hodges?" Jacob tells him.

"Daddy!" L'il Daddy says again. He's truly surprised. So is Jacob. It just hit him that his son should be in school.

"Son, what are you doing here? Why aren't you in school?"

"I'm here for Josie, Daddy. I can't leave her right now. I promised my sister I'd stand by her side. No disrespect, sir."

Jacob smiles. His son never lets him down.

"None taken, son!" Jacob says patting his son's shoulder. He hugs him. "I guarantee your sister will be okay. I'm proud of you, son. You're supposed to have your family's back. It's what men, *real* men do."

Jacob stares Hodges square in the eye emphasizing his last words.

Hodges turns away from the familial display of affection with sadness in his eyes. He's reminded of his father's final words of contrition to his wayward son. With his last dying breath, Joseph Hodges begged his son to straighten out his life. Although Mack envies L'il Daddy's and Jacob's relationship, he still refuses to acknowledge that the elder Myles could be on to something – just as he refused his father's wishes on his deathbed.

"I got your 'real men', Deacon!" Hodges says to himself. *"Um hmm. I can see right through you. Well, think again, old man! Your daughter's coming with me!"*

"Baby, look at me," Dottie says sitting up on her daughter's bed.

"Yes, Mama?"

"Josie, have you asked Hodges about Marilyn Talbert's…"

"IT'S NOT TRUE!" Josie screams jumping off the bed. She becomes irrational and paces the floor waving her hands wildly in the air. The brief mother and daughter laugh they shared a few minutes ago dies on the vine at the mention of Josie's archrival Marilyn 'Jezebel' Talbert.

"Marilyn Talbert's lying!"

"Josie!" Dottie says grabbing her daughter. It's apparent she's becoming unhinged at the thought of her beloved with another woman.

"Marilyn Talbert has always hated me."

"Josie, honey calm down."

"…ever since grade school. Remember, Mama." Josie says. "I dusted her l'il raggedy tail in the fourth grade talent show. She's hated me ever since. She would do anything to get back at me!"

"Honey, do you hear yourself?" Dottie says. "She got pregnant to get back at you? Over a talent show that nobody even cares about anymore?"

"You don't know Marilyn Talbert!" Josie says shaking her head.

"Okay, let's say that's true," Dottie concedes. "What about Mack?"

"What about him?"

"Well, he's no innocent bystander, honey. Have you talked to him about it?"

Josie turns away. Unable to form an answer, she waves her mother away.

"Answer me, baby," Dottie says ignoring what would have normally been cause for regret in an insolent child. "Josie, you have to talk to him about Marilyn Talbert!"

"I don't have to," Josie says. She turns away embarrassed unable to face her mother's prying eyes. "Mack wouldn't lie to me. We're gonna get married. He would never lie to me. I'm his princess."

Dottie sighs. She understands. Poor Josie. She's never asked. She's afraid of the answer she may hear.

"If somehow I can get her to ask…" Dottie tells herself. *"She'll see this man for what he is!"*

"Sir I'd really like to sit down," Hodges pleads. "Uh, L'il Daddy, can I get some water?"

"Son, ask your mother and sister to come downstairs," Jacob says ignoring his visitor's request. "We need to iron this out so Mr. Hodges can be on his way."

"Yes, sir. Uh, Mack, I was sorry to hear about your daddy. He was a good man."

"Thank you, L'il Daddy."

"Go on, son."

"Yes, sir." L'il Daddy takes his books and runs upstairs. Jacob walks over to Hodges and looks him square in the eye.

"I'm sorry about your father. It's sad what happens to our soldiers overseas. It's no better here at home. There's no question about that. But, no man with a conscience leaves his own."

"His own? I'm not sure what you mean…"

Jacob waves his hands. He's tired of the lies.

"Don't even try it, Hodges. I've heard the rumors, and I've heard the truth. Marilyn Talbert has your son."

"Sir, you can't believe all the rumors you hear."

"Oh, but I do. I still have eyes in Hopskip, Hodges. Don't stand there and tell me you didn't leave Deacon Talbert's daughter to take care of your son by herself."

"This old man," Hodges says under his breath. He's fuming but wisely understands that at this juncture, there's very little he can say. Realizing he has no other recourse, he tries another tactic - one foreign to his very soul – the truth.

"Okay! So I've been with Marilyn Talbert a few times. What's the big deal?"

"My God! Is that the truth, Hodges? I'm shocked!"

"Oh come on Jake," Hodges says with a phony laugh.

"JAKE?" The Deacon says checking the young man. "My son has left the room! Who are *you* talking to?"

"MISTER Myles, sorry," Hodges says. He tries to appeal (or so he thinks) to Jacob as a man.

"A man's gonna be a man, right?" Hodges laughs. "Marilyn Talbert offered it up, so who am I to say no? A real man don't turn down nothin' but his collar. Know what I'm saying?"

"No, Hodges. I don't."

"What! Oh come on, Deacon," Hodges says strutting like the peacock he is. He places an unwanted hand on Jacob's shoulder. "I seen some of the sisters in your church. You gonna tell me Dottie Harris was the only chicken you ever plucked?"

BAM!

Looking up from the floor, Michael Mack Hodges finds himself on the receiving end of the wrath of the man he so callously refers to as Ol' Grizzly. Who, on God's green earth don't know that the surest way to get on this grizzly's bad side is to besmirch the girl he's loved since the third grade? Now Hodges knows – apparently too late for his own good. Jacob walks over to Hodges, flabbergasted and shocked beyond words. Always ready to give Hodges a piece of his mind, Jacob looks down at his adversary. His words are measured and concise.

"Michael Hodges. As long as you are black… If you ever speak of my children's mother in that manner…"

"Y-Yes, sir?"

"I will skin you alive. Do we understand one another?"

"You're gonna pay for that, old man. If it's the last thing I do – one way or another – your precious baby girl is coming with me!"

Josie, Dottie, and L'il Daddy hear the noise from upstairs. They all rush downstairs to investigate. They find Hodges sitting on the floor and holding his jaw. Josie is stunned by her father's actions.

"DADDY! WHAT DID YOU DO?"

Dottie rushes to Jacob's side as Mack rises from the floor.

"Jacob, honey what's going on?"

"Our guest asked to sit down," Jacob says sheepishly. "I obliged his request."

"You didn't have to hit him, Daddy," Josie says reprimanding her father.

"I slipped, honey," Hodges says getting up from the floor. "I'm sorry."

"Mack, are you…"

"I'm fine, Josie," Mack says. The arrogant young man is not about to admit he was decked by a man almost twice his age. "Your father's right. I spoke out of turn. I slipped."

"DADDY!"

"Sit down, Josie!" Jacob tells her. "We need to talk."

Jacob, Dottie, L'il Daddy and Josie all head for the Myles' family dinner table. Jacob can't help but recall that only a few hours earlier, at this very table, the entire family celebrated his daughter's decision to be a doctor. It was the highlight of their move north. Now he and his wife have to convince her to simply stay home and not run off with Mack Hodges, the blight ruining his family's very existence. Everyone takes a seat at the table. Hodges wisely waits until Jacob nods his concurrence before taking a seat. Hodges takes Josie's hand in his left while rubbing the sting of Jacob's wrath with his right. L'il Daddy sits between his sister and his father while Dottie takes a seat next to her husband.

"You could've called first, honey," Dottie whispers. *"Would've liked to have seen that!"*

"Alright, let's get to it," Jacob says. "Josie, please tell me you do not intend on running away with this man."

"I – I love Mack, Daddy," she says. "I have to be with him. We're in love."

"Josie, he's a wanted man," Jacob explains. "Military police are looking for him. Baby girl, we're criminals just talking to him. We could be arrested for harboring a fugitive."

"Daddy…"

"Let me finish. If you go with this man, you could be arrested for aiding and abetting. The man's a fugitive."

"Josie, we talked," Dottie says. "There are just too many reasons why you can't go with this man. Baby, we talked about it. You and Mack need to talk about it."

"Mama, Daddy, you don't understand," Josie pleads. "L'il Daddy…"

"Josie," L'il Daddy stumbles. It breaks his heart to see his sister like this. "I'm sorry Sis, Mack. You can't go to Canada. You'll never be able to come home. Don't do this."

"Mama, Daddy you can come see me," Josie pleads.

"That's not about to happen, Josie!" Jacob says staring down Hodges.

"Josie, you need to talk to Mack," Dottie says firmly. "Would you like a minute?"

"Mrs. Myles, if I could…" Hodges butts in.

"I'm talking to my daughter," Dottie tells the interloper. "I'm gonna trust you on this one, Josie. Jacob, L'il Daddy. Let's go," she says getting up from the table. "Give them some privacy,"

"Dottie, are you sure?" Jacob says.

"I trust my daughter, Jacob. Let's go."

Jacob, Dottie, and L'il Daddy head for the kitchen. L'il Daddy looks back at his sister and winks. Although somewhat uneasy, L'il Daddy gives her a thumbs-up. He knows she'll do the right thing. She smiles as L'il Daddy closes the door separating the two rooms. Dottie makes a pot of coffee while the men of the house sit at the table. L'il Daddy suddenly starts to worry about his sister. He knows Josie can be irrational where Mack Hodges is concerned.

"Mama, Daddy, you have to do something. She wants to go to Canada!"

"We know, son," Jacob says. "This is her decision. We can't make it for her. If we intervene, she'll never forgive us. We've said our piece, your mother and I. It's up to Josie, now."

Mack looks at the clock on the wall of the Myles' dining room.

"Jesus, it's almost twelve o'clock? If we don't get out of the here, I'm toast. The MP's are probably circling the block as we speak."

"Uh, Josie honey if you're packed we need to go!"

"No, Mack. I have to ask you something first."

"You want to know if I love you. I do."

"No, Mack."

"To the moon and back, Josie Hodges."

"Mack…"

"Baby, we discussed this. What we have is real. We were made for each other. I knew it the moment I laid eyes on you. Are you packed?"

"Mack, please…" Josie begs trying to get a word in edgewise. Anticipating Josie's question, Mack continues to play on the poor girl's weakness.

"Baby. My princess! This is the opportunity we've always waited for. To fulfill our dreams. Have our own place. A castle for Princess Hodges. We can say goodbye to your daddy's dungeon. …and sweetheart if you're worried about me, don't. I can change. Doesn't the bible say that the love of a good woman can change even the lowest man? Baby, I've changed already. I'm here. And I need you. Baby, please!"

"Yes, but… Mack, my parents…"

"Baby, didn't you tell me your neighbor married a man that her parents didn't like?"

"Yes, Mack…"

"…and they stayed married until he died. Their parents were wrong and so are yours, God bless 'em."

"Mack, please. I have to know something."

"Anything, Princess."

Josie hesitates.

"What is it, baby?" Mack asks. He snatches a quick glance at the clock.

"Why did my father hit you?"

Mack stares at Josie as if her question belittles him. He stands and walks away. With his back to the guileless girl, he fabricates another tale. After he's sure his lying heart has generated just the right amount of deception to continue his con, he turns back to an anxious and hopeful Josie.

"Your father hit me…"

"Yes?" Josie says anxiously.

"Your father hit me… because the old man's afraid," Hodges lies. "…afraid that'll I'll replace him in his daughter's heart."

"Oh Mack, that doesn't make sense," Josie tells him. "My father's not like that."

"All fathers are like that, Princess. Even *my* father didn't want us to get married."

"I thought you said your father liked me."

"Right, right," Mack stumbles. "…that is until I straightened him out. He loved you just as much as I do."

"Oh, Mack!" Josie says falling for the liar's tale of deceit. "Oh honey, I'm so sorry. I should have been there for you when Daddy Joseph passed."

"It's okay, baby," Mack says. "I forgive you."

"Daddy got it in his head that we had to move north."

"It's okay, baby!" Mack tells her smiling to himself.

"...and you know Mama. Whatever Daddy wants, Daddy gets."

"Ha, that's right, baby!" Mack laughs to himself. *"You still got it, Hodges!"*

"I – I still can't believe Daddy hit you."

"Well, bless his heart," Mack says. "Your father was just defending his own."

"His own?" Josie asks.

"Baby, no real man in good conscience leaves his own without a fight," the hypocrite says stealing the same line that started the altercation between him and Jacob. Mack continues to hoodwink Jacob's poor love struck daughter.

"I told Ol' Grizzly..."

"Mack, please! He doesn't like that. He might hear you."

"Uh, yes! You're right! I'm sorry!" Mack says remembering the last time he upset his nemesis. "Well, anyway baby, I told him I loved you and that's that. You're gonna be my wife and he can't stop us. We were meant to be. He got mad and hit me. God's honest truth!"

"Oh Mack that's horrible," Josie says rising to her feet. "I've got to talk to him."

"No, Josie don't," Mack says stopping her. He takes her in his arms. "If you do, they'll just try and talk you out of getting married. They wanna keep you a child forever. Trapped in this house- your daddy's dungeon. Forever your daddy's baby girl. You're a woman, Jocelyn Myles. My woman, ...and I want you...as my wife."

With one eye on the clock, Mack grabs Josie and kisses her passionately. He stops, rubs her shoulders and looks poor Josie in her pretty brown eyes.

"What do you say, honey?"

Josie looks at her suitcase and then the kitchen door. On the other side of which are the people who've stood behind Josie her whole life - just a few feet away.

"I should talk to my parents, Mack."

"Jocelyn Dorothy Myles," Hodges says kissing her forehead. "We have to do what's right for us. We're the only two that matter now."

"Mack, I'm scared."

"Honey, look at me," Hodges says continuing his con. "…if you leave this room, then I know that I don't have a woman but a child. A frightened little child. I need my African Princess to be my African Queen."

Mack kisses Josie again. She melts.

"What's it gonna be, Mrs. Hodges?"

"Say that again!" Jacob says somewhat skeptical. "Marilyn Talbert got pregnant to get revenge?"

He holds out his cup for a refill from Dottie. L'il Daddy grabs a cup from the rack over the kitchen sink. Dottie pours him a cup of orange juice instead.

"Marilyn Talbert's pregnant?" L'il Daddy asks. "That girl!"

"*Was* pregnant," Dottie says. "Your Aunt Julia was there for the delivery. She gave birth about three weeks ago. Deacon Talbert's daughter and Mack Hodges have a son."

"Boy, she did a good job hiding it," L'il Daddy says. "Does Josie know?"

"She knows, baby," Dottie says. "I just can't get your sister to accept it. She thinks the Talbert girl's lying to break up her and Mack."

"Are you serious, Dottie?" Jacob says almost dropping his cup. "Our baby girl actually thinks this girl got pregnant to steal her boyfriend? That's the dumbest thing I ever heard."

"Ha!" says L'il Daddy. "You don't know Marilyn Talbert."

"…and this girl would actually…"

"It's been known to happen!" L'il Daddy says. *"They don't call her 'round heels' for nothing!"* L'il Daddy says to himself.

"… Lord have mercy!" Jacob says shaking his head.

"Daddy, what are we gonna do about Josie," L'il Daddy says. "We can't let her run off with Mack. We'll never see her again if she runs away to Canada."

"We can't make her stay either, son. She'll always hate us for it. It has to be her decision. She'll have to make up her own mind."

Dottie sighs.

"Well, I told her that she had to confront the boy. Make him tell her the truth about Marilyn Talbert. Josie's smart. She would never get involved with a man who would walk out on his child. We raised her better…"

"Well," L'il Daddy says swirling the juice in his cup. "How do we know it's Mack's?"

"Your uncle was at Joseph Hodges' funeral," Jacob says. "He clearly heard Deacon Talbert refer to the deceased as the baby's grandfather. Marilyn even called the boy 'Little Mackie'."

"She did?" L'il Daddy says.

"Hodges pretty much confessed the boy could be his. That's when I threw him on his butt."

Dottie elbows her husband.

"About that, Jacob Myles."

"Yes, baby. I know. I know," Jacob laughs. "Call you next time so you won't miss it! L'il Daddy, you can bring your camera."

The family breaks into raucous laughter. Dottie tries to shush her men lest Josie hears them.

"Alright, you two. Enough! Quiet. Josie might hear you."

"Uh, Daddy?" L'il Daddy says getting up.

"Yes?"

"…kinda quiet in there."

Jacob turns to Dottie. She shakes her head.

"No, she wouldn't…"

Just as Jacob and Dottie get up, Frankie and Savannah enter the kitchen.

"What are you two doing here?" Jacob asks.

"It's lunchtime, Daddy," Frankie says. "Everybody goes home for lunch. Do we have any black-eyed peas left from last night?"

"I didn't realize it was that late," Dottie says.

"Where's Josie, Mama?" Savannah says. "I wanna show her my new…"

"JOSIE?" Dottie yells. "SHE'S NOT…"

Jacob, Dottie, and L'il Daddy rush into the adjoining room. Josie's gone. L'il Daddy runs outside and into the street. He yells for his sister but she and Mack Hodges are long gone. Dottie drops into a chair.

She's distraught. Jacob holds her hand. Frankie comes back into the dining room with an empty plate.

"Hey, Ma! Did you hear me? Do we have any more...WHAT'S THE MATTER?"

Josie's Dilemma, Part 3—Flight

JACOB FRANKLIN MYLES would give his life and everything he owns to protect his baby girl. Jacob made the best decision of his life the very day his precious daughter, Jocelyn Dorothy Myles was born. Jacob vowed that for his daughter, he would be the greatest role model on earth – even better than Papa Myles, the man who taught him that women were to be respected and children were to be molded in the way that they should go. Jacob Myles taught his daughter Josie how to ride a pony when she was only two years old. He gave her an appreciation for the environment by taking his daughter mountain climbing, camping and on nature hikes. He even taught her to fly her first kite. The Deacon even initiated the first father-daughter social at their church when Josie was just five years old. As Jacob saw it, if the man who meant the most in a young girl's life takes the time to show her how women should be treated by men, then they wouldn't be so easily swayed by the charlatans and players of this world. The charlatans and players who would lie to them so easily and dare keep score of the broken hearts they've collected like so many seashells on the shore. No wonder he feels cast aside like one of those seashells. His baby girl left without so much as a goodbye.

The best days of young Josie's life were spent with Daddy. Even when Jacob, Jr. arrived, Jacob Sr. took time out to have a cup of tea with his baby girl.

"Sit down, Daddy. We're having a tea party."

"Okay, baby girl," Jacob says playing along. He squats on the floor next to Josie's collection of stuffed animals. He takes a cup to his lips and sips his daughter's imaginary brew.

"Not that one, Daddy!" Josie laughs.

"Oh! What's wrong with this one?" Jacob asks perplexed.

"That's the sugar bowl, Daddy!" Josie laughs. "You're not supposed to drink the sugar!"

"Sugar? I thought it was kinda sweet!" Jacob laughs. He takes another cup. "Is this one okay?"

"Yes, Daddy. Now, M'Lord," Josie says affecting a funny cockney accent she likely picked up from one of her Saturday morning cartoons. "If you would like another cup, guv'nor..."

"Thank you, M'Lady!" Jacob says. He takes a sip, dabs his chin and looks over to the stuffed teddy bear to his right.

"Theodore, my good man! How'd you do in the stock market today?"

"Sock market? Daddy! You're silly!"

Jacob continues to sip his 'tea' and talk to the other dolls. Dottie - watching from another room- smiles as she cradles Jacob, Jr. She winks at her husband approvingly. He winks back as his 'baby girl' pours him another cup.

Jacob points to Josie's giant stuffed Winnie the Pooh doll sitting on the floor next to him.

"Is this your husband?"

"No, Daddy! You're silly. You can't marry a teddy bear!"

"You can't?" Jacob asks in mock shock. "Then where do little teddy bears come from?"

"I don't know!" Josie laughs. "The zoo?"

"Possibly. Possibly. Are you gonna get married someday, baby girl?"

"Sure, Daddy. but not to a doll."

"Oh?"

"No, when I grow up, I'm gonna marry a 'daddy'."

Jacob smiles. He looks over at Dottie holding little Jacob. He's bursting at the seams with the news his daughter just dropped on him.

"Another spot of tea, gov'nor?" Josie says as cockney as a three-year-old can.

"I'd like nothing better, baby girl."

Jacob Myles sits quietly with his wife and oldest son at the dining room table. Baby Terry, who spent the bulk of the morning watching game shows and soap operas (normally a no-no in the Myles household) plays on the floor with his building blocks. Dottie offers Jacob another cup of coffee. He signifies no by waving his hand over the empty cup. He fingers the rim of the mug thinking of his daughter's tea parties. Jacob's heartsick. They all are. Josie's gone – possibly forever. She's left the loving home her parents created for her to be with a man who cares nothing for her - a man who cares more about himself than anyone or anything else. Dottie and Jacob left their baby in the hands of a jackal hoping that she would see the liar for what he is, and decide for herself that his fabrications no longer have any effect on her heart. Jocelyn Dorothy Myles, heart-stricken and blinded by love, has left the only home she knows to marry a scoundrel – Michael Mack Hodges.

"What do we tell Frankie and Savannah when they come home from school?" L'il Daddy asks.

"That's the least of our worries," Jacob says holding back his anger. "That boy's no good. He's gonna break my baby's heart. I know it."

"Probably run out on her," Dottie says through her tears. She flings a potholder Josie made in grade school across the table. "Leave my baby like he did Marilyn Talbert!"

"Daddy, we need to find her!" L'il Daddy says. "I hate to say it but Josie doesn't think when it comes to him. There's no telling what she might do!"

"Son, if you're suggesting she would hurt herself…" Jacob says.

"Our baby is stronger than that," Dottie tells her son. "She may have been waylaid by that, that parasite but she'll come around. …and she'll come home. I have no doubt my baby will come to her senses and come home."

L'il Daddy is angry. He wants his parents to do more.

"Well, we can't just sit here waiting for that time to come," he says.

"What do you want us to do, son?" Jacob says. "Drag her back? We don't even know where she is. They may not even go to Canada. We don't know."

"Mama, Daddy." L'il Daddy beseeches them. "Suppose something happens to her. What if he *does* leave her like he did Marilyn Talbert? What then?"

"Then we'll love her even more," Dottie says. "…*and* the baby. You wouldn't have a problem with that would you, son?"

"Of course not, Mama," L'il Daddy says. "She's my sister. She put up with me when *I* was born."

Jacob and Dottie manage a smile for the first time since Josie left.

"Yes, she did," Jacob chuckles. "Your sister protected you. She really loved you."

"Um hmm," Dottie smiles reminiscing. "When you were born, she used to bring her friends out to the ranch to show you off. She really... WAIT!"

"Dottie, what's wrong?" Jacob asks.

"L'il Daddy!" Dottie shouts. "Call your girlfriend!"

"What? Huh?" L'il Daddy can't believe his ears. *"I know she didn't just ask me to call Molly Beth. She must be delusional."*

"Uh, Mama did you say..."

"Call Brittany, son!" Dottie says hurriedly. "If Josie calls anyone, it'll be *your* girlfriend Brittany 'Cookie' Abernathy. Cookie's her best friend. They tell each other everything."

"Oh, right mama. Right!" L'il Daddy says. The poor boy's sweating bullets. "I'll call her right now!"

Back in Hopskip, L'il Daddy and Cookie pretended to be a couple as a means of hiding their true relationships with Molly Beth Brand and Bobby Matthews from their parents. Molly Beth and Bobby both live on the other side of town and are forced to hide their true feelings as well. L'il Daddy came up with the ruse after Molly's father Marvin Brand asked him to keep an eye on his daughter. As far as the Brands are concerned, Molly and Bobby are a couple.

"That was close!" he says under his breath.

"Good idea, baby," Jacob says. "...and son, find out what she knows. If we can get to Josie, we may be able to convince her to come home. We'll talk to her again. Try and get her to see through that low-life Hodges."

"Yes, sir!" L'il Daddy says. "Josie left her address book next to her phone on the nightstand. I'll go get it."

L'il Daddy runs upstairs to his sister's room. Jacob's brow furrows.

"He doesn't know his girlfriend's phone number?"

Dottie shrugs.

"Strange, huh?"

L'il Daddy runs back downstairs with his sister's pocket directory in hand. He sprints past his parents, jumps over his little brother's tower of blocks and plops onto the living room sofa. Opening his sister's directory to 'A', he picks up the telephone receiver and dials Cookie's number.

"Son, you could've used the phone upstairs…"

"Jacob…" Dottie says touching her husband's shoulder. She waves her hand telling him to let it go. He's fighting a lost cause. No way on earth would Hopskip's answer to star quarterback Choo Choo Brackins be caught dead using his sister's Princess phone. Not even if the NFL called to offer him first string with the Chicago Bears and Josie's phone was the only working unit in the house. And why, L'il Daddy's asked himself a thousand times did she have to pick pink?

The phone rings on the other end.

"Hello?"

"Hello." L'il Daddy says stoically. He looks at his parents out of the corner of his eye. "Hi, Cookie. It's me. Your *boyfriend*, Jacob Myles, Jr."

Jacob, confounded by his son's conversation turns to look at his wife.

"Did he just introduce himself?"

Dottie is just as perplexed as her husband.

"Um hmm. Something's going on."

"Did they break up?" Jacob asks.

Dottie shrugs her shoulders.

"Don't start me…" she says. "Hey, Terry. Come here, baby. Go listen in on your brother."

"Dottie!" Jacob laughs.

"Well, you wanna know, don't you?"

"One problem at a time, baby. One problem at a time."

"Hey, L'il Daddy," Cookie says. "Your parents listening?"

"Probably!" L'il Daddy chuckles. "How's Bobby?" he whispers. "He make an honest woman of you yet?"

"Boy, shut up!" Cookie chuckles. "Bobby's good." Cookie's demeanor suddenly changes. "I was about to call. Is Josie there?"

"Uh no. She took off with Mack Hodges. Is everything OK?"

"She did? She ran off with Mack Hodges?"

"Yeah. That's why I'm calling you. We were hoping you could help us find her!"

"I was afraid you'd say something like that. You better sit down."

Cookie Abernathy sadly recounts the incident involving her brothers. She explains to L'il Daddy how her younger brother T. J. found her older brother Turner beaten and left for dead in the forest.

"Left for dead? My God Cookie, I'm so sorry," L'il Daddy says. "Does anybody know what happened?"

"T. J. saw the Platts driving off in their truck."

"The Platts? Why would they beat up Turner? Did they catch 'em?"

"Oh, they got caught alright," Cookie says. "They won't be bothering nobody."

"Cookie, what – what's going on?"

"Well, Sheriff Yates thinks…"

Two days ago, Wednesday, May 30th

"Junior, what's the matter?" Platt, Sr. asks. He looks at Turner Abernathy unresponsive and laying on the ground. "Get up, boy! Get up, I said!"

"Paw…"

"Junior, he's not moving! What did you do? Get up, boy. I said get up!"

"I killed him, paw! I killed him!" Junior says leaning over Turner. "What do we do, Paw? What do we do?"

"Shut up, boy!" his daddy yells. He slaps his son, grabs his arm and drags him away from young Abernathy's body.

"Come on, we gotta get out of here."

"But, Paw…"

"I said shut up! It was an accident! Now come on, boy. Let's go!"

The two men run to their truck parked behind the forest and out of sight of the Abernathy farm. Evan, Sr. pushes his son aside and jumps under the wheel. Evan, Jr. runs around to the passenger side and hops in tripping on the gravel underneath.

"Hurry up, you damned fool," his father shouts.

Evan, Jr. finally gets his footing and hops in the truck. The two men take off leaving a trail of dust from the gravel. Choking on the dust – and his guilt – the younger Platt starts crying. Platt, Sr. grabs the whiskey bottle from the glove compartment and shoves it in his son's chest.

"Drink this! It'll calm your nerves!"

The junior Platt shakes his head no. He starts bawling like a baby.

"What the hell are you crying for, dumb ass? It was an accident."

"You stop calling me dumb!" Junior cries. He grabs the bottle and throws it on the floor of the truck. "I ain't no dummy!"

"You ain't? Well, who told you to tackle that boy anyway? God Almighty. You couldn't even play high school football 'cause you was too dumb to remember the plays and you wanna tackle somebody? High school football! They was gonna pay you to go to college, but nawww! We stuck here cause you too stupid to remember a bunch of stupid X's and O's. Lawd Almighty. I had plans for you boy. Big plans – but you... You did what you do best. You let me down! You always let me down! What's Mr. Watts gonna say, huh? What's he gonna think of us, now? Stupid, clumsy..."

"Shut up, Paw! You stop it, Paw! You shut up!"

"Shut up?" Evan, Sr., holding on to the steering wheel with his left land, strikes his son repeatedly with his right elbow and then his fist. He then grabs the magazine left in his truck by Floyd Watts. He rolls it up and beats his poor son like an errant puppy.

"Who you telling to shut up? **I** raised you, boy. **I** raised **you**! Ignorant, fat...You never do anything right! Why you think your mama died, huh? 'Cause a your big useless butt! You killed Amanda! You killed my wife!"

Evan Platt, Sr. lost his beautiful wife Amanda Jean the day Evan, Jr. was born. Not a day goes by that the egregious old man doesn't –in some form or fashion – attribute his wife's death to his son's girth. On his better days, he blames Amanda for giving him a useless and ineffectual son.

"Your mama was just as weak as you!" the old man says berating his son.

Young Evan pulls his cap down over his face. He stares at the old man next to him as if he's never laid eyes on him. The culmination of twenty years of abuse finally taking its' toll, Evan, Jr. looks at the bottle on the floor of the car.

"You got one more time to talk about my Maw."

Evan, Sr. laughs. He pulls over, turns off the truck and faces his son.

"Feeling your oats, are you boy?" the old man dares him. "Well, come on, Evan. Do something. Do something, You fat piece of...!

Evan, Jr. grabs the bottle by the neck and swings wildly at the abusive old man. The senior Platt grabs the bottle from his son and breaks it across the boy's head. Drenched in alcohol and his own blood, Evan, Jr. disoriented and enraged reaches for his daddy's rifle hanging in the gun rack behind them. He points Ol' Bessie at his lifelong tormenter.

Evan, Sr. stares down the barrel of the old Winchester pointed less than *six inches from his face. He laughs at his namesake trembling next to him.*

"Well, look at you!" the old man laughs derisively. "You wanna kill me, boy. Well, go ahead. Do it! I got nothing to live for. You took everything! Go on boy, do it!"

Evan, Jr. has never taken a stand against his sadistic father. He stammers.

"I-I'm warning you, Paw. I'll do it."

"You –You - You are?" Evan, Sr. says mocking his son. "Ha! Ha! Ha!"

"Please, Paw!" Evan, Jr. begs. "Stop!"

"You ain't got the guts. You're weak!"

"SHUT UP, PAW!"

Evan, Sr. starts up the truck. He puts it in gear and takes off. He looks over at his crying son and shakes his head.

"...stupid fat weakling. Just like your mama!"

BAM!

L'il Daddy is mildly shocked. All of Hopskip knew the hateful Platts would come to some dreadful end sooner or later. *"Just a matter of time"*, was the general consensus throughout the small burg. Evan Platt, Jr., the thug who attacked his beautiful sister is dead.

Cookie Abernathy continues her story.

"You remember how Evan and his daddy was always in town fighting over something. Maybe Junior got tired of the beatings and shot the old man, lost control of the truck. I don't know. Who cares after what they did to my brother? ...and Josie? The sheriff found the truck this morning over in Sherman's ravine. Been dead about two days."

"Evan Platt, Jr. dead," L'il Daddy tells himself. *"...and his father! Wait'll everybody hears this. Hmmm. Daddy always said hate the sin, not the person. I wonder if that goes for rapists, too."*

Remembering his father's Christian philosophy, L'il Daddy tries to muster some sympathy for the Platts.

"That's life, I guess," L'il Daddy says quickly. Well, he tried.

"Stuff happens, huh?" Cookie says dryly. No love lost with Cookie, either. L'il Daddy changes the subject.

"Cookie, did you say this had something to do with Mack Hodges?"

"'Fraid so, L'il Daddy," Cookie says. "Turner confessed."

"Confessed? To what?" L'il Daddy almost shouts.

"Well, son," Jacob says playing with little Terry in his lap. "Was your day as interesting as mine?"

"I want a pet!" Terry says oblivious to his family's woes.

"Oh, that's right," Jacob says smiling at Dottie. "I promised you a dog after we settled in. Been going through so much, I almost forgot. German Shepherd, right?"

"I want a rabbit!" Terry tells his father.

"A rabbit?" Dottie says. "What happened to the dog?"

"I changed my mind," Terry affirms. "I want a rabbit!"

"Okay, son if that's what you want," Jacob says. "Hmmm. Now, what's a good name for a rabbit? Bugs? Jack? Hank?"

"Hank? Don't talk about my father, Jacob Myles!" Dottie laughs.

"Well, we gotta name him something," Jacob says. "What do you think, Terry? What's a good name for a rabbit?"

Terry, never missing a beat offers a suggestion.

"JOSIE!"

Jacob's and Dottie's youngest jumps out of his father's lap and runs upstairs. He stops midway and looks back at his parents with a discerning frown.

"I WANT JOSIE!"

Terry runs upstairs and slams the door to his room. First Josie leaves, now Baby Terry is upset because of it. Not a good day for the Myles clan.

"Jacob…" Dottie says.

"I know, baby. Time to swallow a little pride."

L'il Daddy comes in at that moment to share the news from Cookie.

"What's wrong with him?" L'il Daddy says after watching his youngest brother storm off. He takes a seat with his parents.

"Nothing we can't handle," Jacob tells him. "Does Cookie know anything?"

"Oh yeah!" L'il Daddy says. "Cookie had quite a story to tell."

"Oh?" says Dottie and Jacob in unison.

"Um hmm," their son says. "Guess who they found in the bottom of Sherman's Ravine?"

"…so this is where you spent the night? The *'Sneakaway'* Inn?"

"It's not so bad," Mack says to Josie. He pulls the caddy into the adjoining parking lot of the old hotel. He pulls Josie to his side of the car and plants a kiss on her trembling lips. Josie takes another look at the meager surroundings.

"Why are we here, Mack?" she asks nervously. "Don't we have to leave the country before the MP's show up?"

"We have a little time," Mack tells her. "Look at me, baby!"

Mack Hodges, always careful to cover his tracks, has parked in the lot across from his motel room. He stays in the car with Josie until young Belle the cleaning lady, gives him the OK to enter his room.

"You gonna be okay, Josie?" Mack asks pretending to be concerned. "Baby, you cried all the way here."

"I didn't even say goodbye, Mack. Daddy looked so hurt this morning…"

"Come here, baby."

Mack takes Josie in his arms. He hugs her. Not that he's feeling any rush of emotions, he just doesn't want Josie to see the look of disgust on his face. He hates Jacob Myles. He knows the man sees right through him. Getting his daughter to forget the Deacon and his family will be no easy feat.

"Don't worry, Josie. We'll see your family again. I promise."

"When pigs fly!" Mack says to himself.

"I didn't even say goodbye to Terry, or Frankie," Josie continues. "Savannah is gonna be crushed. Oh Mack, what's she gonna think?"

Josie buries her head in Mack's chest. If she only knew how much this man didn't care.

"Okay, okay honey," Mack says tiring already of his girlfriend's outburst. He looks up to see Belle give him a thumbs-up.

"We'll be sure to call them. Let's go to the room."

"Uh, Mack…"

"I just need to check out and pick up the rest of my things, honey. That's all."

Mack grabs Josie's hand and runs to his room. Pushing the door open, he tells her to close her eyes. She obliges. Mack sweeps her off her feet and into his arms.

"Mack, what are you doing?"

"Remember, when we first met? I picked you up and carried you to my car?"

Josie bows her head blushing.

"How can I forget?" she says kissing her hero.

Mack gently lays her on the bed.

"I'll be right back," he says kissing her. "I'm gonna go check out. Unless…"

"Plenty of time for that later, Mr. Hodges," Josie says winking at Mack. "I'm gonna freshen up."

"Okay, baby. I'll be right back!"

Mack rushes out the door just as Josie remembers that she left her luggage in the car. She opens the door and runs to Mack's Cadillac. No sooner than Josie retrieves her luggage, she sees Mack talking to Belle. He hands her what looks like five dollars. She kisses his cheek as they both head for the main office. Josie's crestfallen. She stands frozen for a moment, just having taken in the sight of her man being kissed by another woman. Someone he apparently just met kissed him as if she knows him – well. She falls back on the pink Caddy as memories of her and Mack's first meeting come rushing back to her.

"I'm okay, Mr. Matthews. Please! Don't tell my father! Please! Please! I just wanna go home."

"I'll take you home," says the young man. He points down the alley toward his car, a bright shiny pink Cadillac.

Josie looks into her hero's eyes.

"Who are you?" she asks breathlessly. "What's your…?"

"Michael. Michael Hodges. Most folks call me Mack," he says carrying her to his car.

"Oh! Well, thank you! Thank you very much! My name is…"

"Josie! I know. Josie Myles."

"Do you know him, Daddy," Bobby Matthews asks his father.

"Yeah, I know him. I think your friend is in over her head. Boy's quite the ladies' man."

Suddenly, Josie's world comes into focus. Mr. Matthews's words to his son that fateful day are now as clear as a bell. *'Quite the ladies' man.'* Why didn't Josie hear Mr. Matthews before? Was she so taken in by her knight in shining armor that she never saw the chinks? Poor Josie was so enamored with her champion that she never heard anything disparaging that was said about the man – even by her family.

Josie hurries back into the room before she's seen. Her stomach in knots, she drops to her knees in tears. Grabbing a tissue from the nightstand, Josie dries her eyes. She tosses the dampened napkin into a nearby wastebasket. As if Mack's lies weren't enough, her moistened eyes espy something especially familiar in the wastebasket. She moves forward for a closer look.

"Oh my God!" she says. "Oh my God!"

"…and the sheriff believes Evan, Jr. shot his own father? How awful!"

"Well, Mama," L'il Daddy says. "According to Cookie, they found a broken whiskey bottle in the Platts' truck. Cookie says Sheriff Yates figures one or both of 'em had been drinking before they attacked her brother. They got into an argument, Evan shot his father, and they crashed into the ravine."

"No surprise there, Dottie!" Jacob intervenes. "Evan, Sr. picked on that boy from the day he was born."

"He did?" L'il Daddy says.

"Oh yeah!" Jacob says. "Evan Platt's wife died in childbirth. Platt told anybody who'd listen that Amanda Jean – that's her name – died 'cause of Evan, Jr. He blamed Amanda's death on his son. No wonder that… *boy* turned out the way he did. Still…"

Dottie squeezes her husband's hand. She knows whenever the conversation turns to Evan Platt, Jr. that her husband is likely to fume and go into a rage. Who would blame him? The boy tried to rape his daughter. L'il Daddy notices the interaction between his parents. His daddy always stiffens and turns red whenever the Platts are mentioned.

"Everybody loved Amanda Jean," Dottie says. "Just never understood what she saw in Evan Platt, Sr."

"Excuse me!" Jacob says abruptly. He pushes away from the table in a very uncharacteristic, very *unJacoblike* manner. He heads upstairs talking to himself.

"Damned Platts!" he mumbles.

L'il Daddy is shocked.

"Well, I'll be!" L'il Daddy says to himself. He's flabbergasted. He finally puts the pieces of the Platt puzzle together.

"Oh my God! It was Daddy! Daddy shot at Evan, Jr.!"

"Oh my God!" Josie says to herself. She wipes her face as she stares at herself in the bathroom mirror. "How could I have been so stupid?"

"Stupid? Who's stupid?"

Josie turns around to see Mack standing behind her. She pushes past him and stands at the doorway.

"Baby, what's wrong," Mack asks. "Are you still crying over Ol' Grizzly? Ha, ha---"

"You don't get to call him that!" Josie screams. "Ever!"

"Okay, honey," Mack says. "I'm sorry. Hey, I'm all checked out. Let's go."

"Mack Hodges, *the ladies' man!* All this time…"

"What? Josie, honey. Calm down," Mack says. He grabs Josie's shoulders only to have the distraught young woman snatch away from him. "Baby, what's the matter? What's going on?"

"Is it true?" Josie demands.

"Is what true?" Mack says dumbfounded.

"Marilyn Talbert!"

"What?"

"Is it true, Michael? Do you have a son with Marilyn Talbert?"

Mack is stunned. For months he's been able to stave off Josie with a kiss and a few well-placed sweet nothings in her ear. Now she's demanding the truth – and she won't take no for an answer. Mack resorts to his favorite option. He lies.

"I don't know, Josie. I don't know for sure."

"Oh, Mack!"

"Well, you know Marilyn Talbert. Could be anybody's. I don't know."

"You told me you never touched her. Why would you lie to me? I loved you. I was ready to give you everything, Mack. Everything. Why? Why her?"

"Josie, I'm sorry. She – she caught me at a weak moment. Last year, I asked you to leave town with me – to drive up to Atlanta for the weekend. I really needed you. But you said no!"

"Yes, I said no! I guess Marilyn Talbert said yes!"

"Well…"

"How many times did she say yes, Mack? Couldn't have been just the one?"

"Josie, I made a mistake. I'm sorry…"

"You made a lot of mistakes, Michael Hodges."

"Honey, please. I made one mistake. I'm sorry. Can't we…?"

"Why did that cleaning lady kiss you just now?"

"What? Belle?"

"Yeah, Belle. Why did she kiss you? What was that for? Services rendered? You could've done a lot better for five dollars, Michael Hodges."

"All she did was clean the room, Josie. I tipped her."

"You tipped her?"

"Yes!"

"For doing her job?"

"Josie," Mack says moving toward her. "Honey, nothing happened. I didn't want you coming back here to a pigsty. I know how you are. Honey, you couldn't possibly think I would…"

"Oh, I don't," Josie says walking away.

"Good!" Mack says sighing.

"But I think you should get your money back," Josie tells him. She angrily grabs the wastebasket from the side of the bed and shoves it into her startled boyfriend's chest.

"Your Belle didn't do a very good job!"

"Terry okay?" L'il Daddy says. He knows his father needed an excuse to leave the room. It's starting to dawn on L'il Daddy that his father blows his stack whenever Evan Platt, Jr. is mentioned. He's convinced that his father was the man who shot at the boy some months back.

"Terry's fine," Jacob says rejoining his wife and son at the table. "One of the advantages of being the baby."

"Yeah, all the bad stuff falls on us grownups," L'il Daddy says.

"Us grownups?" Dottie says.

"Yeah, the adults," L'il Daddy says.

"Boy, you are in too big a hurry to be grown," his mother laughs.

Jacob smiles. He remembers that their previous conversation got off track with the news about the Platts.

"Son, you never said if Cookie heard from your sister."

"Well, no," L'il Daddy says. "...but the rest of the news. It's not good, Daddy."

"What do you mean the rest of the news?" Dottie asks.

"Well," L'il Daddy says. "If the sheriff wasn't after him before..."

"What?" Dottie says.

Jacob quickly rises from his chair.

"What are you talking about, son?"

L'il Daddy shakes his head at the news he's about to deliver.

"Like I said. If the sheriff wasn't after Mack before, they are now."

"L'il Daddy, please!" Dottie beseeches him. "Just tell us!"

"Well, Turner Abernathy confessed to Sheriff Yates that he and Mack was growing marijuana in the Abernathy's abandoned cornfield."

"Marijuana?" Dottie says shocked. "Did the rest of the family know?"

"Cookie says no," L'il Daddy tells his parents. "They were living off Daddy Turner's social security and Turner supposedly had a job in Atlanta."

"I knew that boy was no good!" Jacob says slamming his fist against the table.

"There's more, daddy," L'il Daddy says. "Floyd Watts was behind it all."

"Floyd Watts?" his parents say in unison.

"Yep. Turner told everything. He said him and Mack and a couple of others was growing 'weed' on those old abandoned farms on the edge of town. They gave it to Watts who sold it to some good ol' boys down in Atlanta. Mack and Turner was selling some on the side. What do they call it on TV? Skimming off the top?"

"Something like that," Jacob says.

"So that's why ol' 4F Floyd was at Joe Hodges' funeral," Dottie surmises. "He was looking for Mack. That boy's got the Klan *and* the law looking for him."

Jacob shakes his head and looks at his wife trembling. He takes her hand.

"...and our baby girl is right in the middle of it! Jesus Christ!"

"Look in the wastebasket, Mack."

"Josie, Princess…"

"Look in the wastebasket, Mack!"

Mack takes the receptacle and places it on the bed. He looks inside. His heart stops. For a player who's always so careful, Mack Hodges has made one huge mistake. He left someone else to clean up after him.

"Damn it, Belle!" he mumbles under his breath.

"Take it out, Mack," Josie demands. She's almost in tears.

Mack slowly reaches into the wastebasket. He pulls out a receipt from the restaurant where his so-called beloved works.

"You wanna read it to me?" Josie cries.

"Josie…"

"You don't wanna read it?" Josie screams. "All right! Allow me!" She snatches the receipt out of Mack's hand.

The Breakfast Nook. Best bacon and eggs in town…"

"Josie, give me that," Mack begs. He reaches for the receipt. Josie pulls away.

"Oh please! Let me finish, please," Josie says trying not to cry. "Sneakaway Inn. 505 Main, Room 13. Your lucky number, Mack?"

"I wrote that for you, Josie," Mack says scrambling for an alibi. "I came back to the restaurant to get something to eat. I remembered that I never gave you the address."

"Why would I need it, Mack?" Josie says. "You were picking me up this morning, remember?"

"Honey," Mack continues his lie. "I thought maybe, you know just in case you came back to the restaurant…"

"Daddy always said this man had an answer for everything." Josie thinks to herself. "I'm supposed to believe you wrote this, Mack?"

"Yes."

"For me?"

"Yes, baby…"

"…with all the little hearts on it?"

"I-I really love you, Jo-."

"Stop it, Mack," Josie says. "I know your handwriting."

"Josie, wait!"

"I also know Millie Cooper's handwriting," Josie says referring to her backstabbing co-worker. Fighting back the tears, a brokenhearted Josie Myles balls up the receipt and throws it in the old liar's face.

"I guess little Belle wasn't as thorough as you thought. And I was afraid of you spending the night alone."

"Josie, I can explain."

"No, Mack. You can't," Josie cries. "I waited all my life for you, and you couldn't wait one night for me."

"Okay, enough damnit," Mack shouts. "Stop with the histrionics…"

Josie's undeterred by Mack's change in attitude. She slaps him.

"Mack Hodges," Josie says. "I left my family for you. Do you understand what that means? My family. I lied to my parents, my brother… and for what? So you could flounce around with some skank you just met."

"All right, Josie. I'm sorry," Mack tells her. "…but you're acting like a child. It was one night. She means nothing."

"Nothing?" Josie says incredulously. "Then I must mean less."

Josie picks up the phone and looks at Mack.

"Josie put down the phone. What are you doing?"

"You better go, Mack," Josie says. "The MP's, remember?"

"You're calling the police? Over this?"

"I'm calling my father. You remember Ol' Grizzly, don't you? You may wanna leave before he gets here."

"I *am* leaving, Josie," Mack says threateningly. "…and you've got five seconds to get in that car!"

"Five?" Josie says slamming the receiver back into its' cradle. "Let's pretend I have just one! Oops! Time's up!"

Mack grabs his suitcase and heads for the door. He looks back and laughs shaking his head. Before he goes, he mutters the one obscenity that boys of his caliber are famous for when confronted by strong women.

Josie's shocked. Mack has never even yelled at his 'Princess' much less cursed at her. Never at a loss for a comeback, Josie fires off a quick one.

"Well, if I am, Mack Hodges I hope I was a *good* one. I'm Jocelyn Myles. Jacob and Dorothy's firstborn. …and I excel in *everything* I do!"

"Josie, look. I'm sorry. I – I didn't mean…"

"Goodbye, Hodges! Have fun in Canada! Be sure to take a coat! I hear it gets cold!"

With that, Josie slams the door in his face. Mack throws his suitcase in the open car and takes off. Josie peeks through the hotel curtain and watches her heart speed away with the only man she's ever loved. Despite her stance and her words to Mr. Hodges, Josie's heart is broken. She sits on the disheveled bed and hangs her head to cry. No one ever said life was easy.

Josie's Dilemma, Part 4—Revelations

"... **AND WHEN** Daddy got through, Mama slapped his hand, jumped in the ring and she took an even bigger chunk out of my butt."

"Hmm. You're right," L'il Daddy says looking at his sister's backside. "There's hardly any left."

"Boy, shut up!" Josie says taking a playful swipe at her brother's head. She laughs.

"Just kidding!" L'il Daddy says kidding his favorite sibling. "There's still a little."

"Hilarious, l'il brother," Josie says. She throws her suitcase on the bed and begins to unpack. "Hey, why don't you try out for Ringling? I heard they're looking for clowns."

"Sorry, sis," L'il Daddy says. "...so they chewed you out all the way home, huh?"

"Boy, you don't know the half of it. First, Daddy told me how much I disappointed Mama. Then Mama told me how much I disappointed Daddy. Then Daddy goes, *"Oh you didn't hurt me at all,"* Josie says lowering her voice and mimicking her father. *"You might have upset your brother or your mother but I'm fine."*

"Oh, he was hurt, Sis." L'il Daddy says. "Big time."

"Yeah, I know," Josie says going through her clothes. "You know how crazy Daddy drives when he's mad."

"Mr. Ten and Two?"

"Um hmm. I was afraid we wouldn't make it home in one piece."

"Pretty bad, huh?"

"Yep," Josie says. Her mood turns somber. "I don't know if he'll get over this one."

"Oh, he will," L'il Daddy says reassuring his sister. "After all, you *are* his favorite."

"Not after today," Josie says sitting on the bed. She closes her luggage and looks at her brother. "I really hurt him, huh?"

"Yep!" L'il Daddy says with a slight smirk. "His baby girl threw him over for another man."

"Don't laugh. I'll never forget the look on Daddy's face when he saw me standing in front of that motel," Josie recounts. "I thought I was gonna throw up. L'il Daddy, I was hoping to avoid that. Why didn't you pick me up like I asked you to?"

"Well, when you called, I went to take the call in your room…"

"In *my* room?" Josie says looking at her brother incredulously. "On the *princess*? Way to go, Einstein. Everybody knows you hate using my phone. You being a man and all."

Brother and sister laugh. She's right. The seventeen-year-old never misses an opportunity to assert his manhood.

"Yeah, yeah. I know," he says.

"There's a name for that, L'il Daddy. I just haven't figured it out yet."

"Give me a break, Sis. They must have listened in on the downstairs phone. When I came down to get the keys to Goldie, they had already left."

"Smooth, L'il Daddy," Josie says. "Smooth!"

"Not one of my better moments, I admit," L'il Daddy concurs. Josie takes her brother's hand in hers. Her demeanor is solemn.

"L'il Daddy, I'm sorry I left the way I did. I wasn't completely honest last night about going to Detroit. I thought I wanted a life with Mack and…"

"Don't sweat it, Sis! If it was Molly Beth…" L'il Daddy says looking away.

"Really?"

"Let's change the subject," L'il Daddy says dejectedly. "Did they tell you about Turner Abernathy?"

"Yep! Turner. Floyd Watts. The Klan looking for Mack. Daddy couldn't wait to tell me that one. Can't say I blame him."

"Look, Sis while we're on the subject…"

"What is it?"

"Sis, I have to ask you," L'il Daddy says holding his sister's hand. "Where did you think Mack was getting his money? For the car, the fancy clothes, and everything?"

"His mama's insurance. Daddy Joseph was in the army so his benefits…" Josie stops in mid-sentence as L'il Daddy shakes his head no. The look on her brother's face tells Josie her world is about to be crushed - again.

"I guess he lied about that, too?"

"Probably," L'il Daddy says.

"What else, l'il brother?"

"Well, there's one thing Cookie told me that I didn't tell Mama and Daddy."

"I'm listening."

"Mack and Turner were passing information 'bout the movement to the Klan."

"What?" Josie says. "…passing information? About what?"

"Civil rights meetings, sit-ins…" L'il Daddy says with anger in his voice. "We always wondered how they got there before us. You know me and Cookie were involved in the movement."

"I know," Josie says hugging her brother. "You two wanted to change the world. You'd be free to marry Molly Beth. Cookie could get with Bobby Matthews."

"Cookie thought she could trust her brother," L'il Daddy says continuing his story. "She told Turner about the meetings. Turner told Mack…"

"…and Mack told Floyd Watts!"

"Yep!" L'il Daddy says. "4F Floyd."

"…and that's how he made his money?" Josie drops her head. "Oh my God!" With that, Josie takes her suitcase and throws it across the room. She sits on her bed and buries her head in her hands.

"L'il Daddy, I'm so sorry," Josie says. "I had no idea."

"Sis, you couldn't have known," L'il Daddy says comforting his sister. "Still can't believe it myself."

"Cookie told you this?" Josie says almost crying. "I can't believe I loved that man. Oh, L'il Daddy, you coulda been killed!"

"Cookie, too. What was Turner thinking?"

"L'il brother, I'm so sorry," Josie says hugging her brother. "I'm so, so sorry!"

"Don't be so hard on yourself, Sis," L'il Daddy says reassuring his sister. "It's over now! Cookie's okay. I'm okay. Hey, did they tell you about Junior Platt?"

"Yeah! How 'bout that?" Josie says sitting back. "That old *'hillwil-liam'* killed his own daddy? ...and himself? ...finally had enough, huh? Think we'll be going back for the funeral?" Josie says sarcastically.

"Daddy, maybe. ...make sure that ol' *'hillwilliam's'* dead!"

"Daddy?" Josie asks. "What do you mean? Why would...? L'il Daddy, you didn't tell Daddy..."

"Didn't have to, Josie. He already knew."

"WHAT?"

"Josie, you never saw how tense Daddy got whenever somebody mentioned Junior Platt?"

"Yeah, but..."

"Remember how Junior told everybody somebody was out to kill him?"

"I heard about it. Wait a minute, you don't think..."

"Josie, Daddy went out hunting with Mr. Matthews that same day."

"So?"

"So Daddy didn't bag any game that day."

"So what?"

"Josie, when have you ever known Daddy to come home empty-handed?"

"L'il Daddy!" Josie says standing up. "Are you trying to tell me Daddy went out looking for Junior Platt? Oh, I can't believe this day. What next? Mama's undercover with the CIA?"

"Josie, hold on," L'il Daddy chuckles. "It's not as bad as you think."

"Not as bad as I think? L'il brother, you can't just sit there calmly and say our daddy tried to kill someone! Even if it's Junior Platt!"

"No, I'm not." L'il Daddy reassures her. "...and keep your voice down."

"Okay! Okay!" Josie says pacing the room. "I'm calm. I'm calm."

L'il Daddy chuckles.

"We're talking about our daddy!" Josie says. "You find this funny?"

"A little bit."

"L'il Daddy..." Josie says about to lose her temper. L'il Daddy gently grabs his sister and sits her on the bed.

"Josie, think! Who won the annual Turkey Shoot five years in a row?"

"Daddy did!"

"Who can shoot a flea off a hound's nose a hundred yards away?"

"Daddy…" Josie says.

"…and who helped me become the marksman you see standing before you?" L'il Daddy says literally patting himself on his back.

Josie beams. She gets it now. Jacob Myles was the best shot in the county. If her daddy wanted to… Still, she can't pass up the opportunity to stick it to her favorite sibling.

"Marksman, huh?" Josie winks. "Now you can't blame that on Daddy!"

"Oh, tee hee," L'il Daddy says mocking his sister's attempt at humor.

"Okay, okay," Josie says. "I know what you're trying to say."

"Um hmm. If Daddy wanted to kill that redneck, he could have. Easy."

"They say whoever took a shot at Junior Platt missed. They shot a bottle of whiskey out of his hand instead."

"Shoot, Daddy could do that blindfolded," L'il Daddy says proudly.

"I know that's right," Josie smiles high-fiving her brother. "So you think Daddy did it to scare the boy? Cause of me?"

"Put money on it!" her brother concurs. "…and knowing Deacon Myles, he had to exorcise himself from the situation. All the way up here."

"…or maybe next time Junior Platt might not be so lucky."

"I have no doubt!"

"…and how do I say thanks? I run off with Mack Hodges. No wonder Daddy was so mad. He hates the boy. He gave up everything for me. …and I just ran off like…"

"…a thief in the night." L'il Daddy says mimicking his father.

"You do that well, L'il…"

Josie stops in mid-sentence and stares at her brother. He cocks his head to one side.

"L'il Daddy?"

"Speaking."

"How come nobody ever said anything?"

"About Mack?"

"Yeah," Josie says sheepishly. She already knows the answer.

"ARE YOU SERIOUS?" her brother says. "I can't remember a day going by when one of us didn't try to talk some sense in that block of cement you call a head. Josie…"

"You can say it!" Josie tells him. "Well, actually you just did. I was over the moon for that man!"

"Your head was definitely in the clouds, Sis! No amount of talking could make you see that something just wasn't right about the man. Brother was way too smooth. Daddy said we'd have to wait until you saw Mack for what he really is for yourself and pray that the lesson won't be too expensive. It wasn't, was it, Sis?"

"What do you mean?"

"You know what I mean."

Knock! Knock!

"Boy, you bad as Mama!"

"*What was that?*" says a voice from the other side of the door.

"Nothing! Nothing! Come in, Mama."

"Hello, sweetheart," Dottie says. She notices the clothing from the suitcase spewed on the floor. L'il Daddy makes an effort to pick them up.

"You okay, baby?" Dottie asks concerned.

"Yes, ma'am!"

"L'il Daddy, give us a moment, please!"

"Sure, Mama." L'il Daddy picks up a belt from the clothes his sister threw on the floor. "Looking for this, Mama?" the would-be comedian jokes.

"For you?" Dottie says sternly.

"…and that's my cue!" L'il Daddy says. He kisses Dottie's cheek and makes his exit. "Later, Sis."

"How are you feeling, baby?" Dottie says taking a seat on her daughter's bed.

"I'm okay, Mama," Josie says as she picks up her clothes from the floor. Embarrassed after all the trouble she's put her mother through, Josie's careful not to look her directly in the eye. After all, she left her biggest cheerleader, her mother, without even saying goodbye.

"Quite a day, huh baby?"

"I guess you can say that," Josie says standing at her dresser. Opening her top drawer to place a few blouses inside, Josie sees her picture of Mack Hodges peering up at her. She almost drops to the floor but catches herself before her mother sees her. She slams the drawer shut, collects herself and speaks.

"I'm a little tired, Mama. …if that's alright with you."

"Sit down a minute, Josie," Dottie tells her. "I want to talk to you."

Josie looks at her clothes on the floor and then her mother. She lets out a half-hearted chuckle motioning to her that she needs to clean up.

"Mama, this room…"

"…can wait," Dottie tells her. She pats the area next to her prompting her oldest to have a seat.

Josie obliges. Dottie takes her daughter gently by the chin. She smiles.

"Now, Josie. I don't want a scene like what happened today to ever happen again. Honey, we're Myles women. We don't run. We talk. You know you can always talk to me. Don't you?"

"Yes."

"Good. Now tell me. What happened with Hodges? Did you ask him about Marilyn Talbert?"

"Yes, ma'am."

"What did he say?"

"Just like you said, Mama," Josie says sarcastically. "He and Marilyn Talbert have a little boy. Just like Aunt Julia and Uncle Joseph said. Probably got a hundred Marilyns and a hundred little boys all across this great country of ours. Happy?"

"You think I'm happy?" Dottie asks. "The boy hurt my child."

"I think you are," Josie says upset. "You and Daddy never liked him."

"Well, baby we obviously had good reason," Dottie tells her. "…and you can ashcan the attitude!"

"Yes, Ma'am!" Josie says straightening up on the bed. Try as she might, she can't hold back her emotions. She drops her head and starts to cry. Dottie takes her daughter in her arms.

"Go ahead, baby. Let it out," Dottie tells her.

"I really loved him, Mama," Josie sobs. "I really thought he was the one."

"It's okay, baby. I know how you feel."

"You can't possibly know how I feel, Mama," Josie tells her. "You've loved Daddy since grade school. How could you know?"

"Well…" Dottie says hesitating.

Josie pulls away from her mother and looks at her incredulously.

"You had another man? There was another man in your life. Does Daddy know?"

"Um hmm," Dottie nods. "To this very day, your daddy can't even stand to look at him."

"What?" Josie says. She's on her feet now and staring at the woman she thought had no secrets. She's afraid to ask but forces herself. "Who Mama? Who?"

"Deacon Fred," Dottie says trying not to laugh.

"What?" Josie says. "Deacon Fred? Deacon Fred Thomas?"

"That would be him," Dottie concurs. Josie bursts out laughing.

"Deacon Fred?" Josie laughs the old man's name. "Mama, he's a hundred!"

"Well, he was quite handsome some years back," Dottie says. "When I was a little girl, Deacon Fred was my Sunday School teacher."

"Mama, he was mine, too," Josie laughs. "All the kids said he knew the bible so well 'cause he was there."

"Now, Josie you stop..." Dottie tells her.

"I always wondered who rolled that stone away..." Josie laughs.

"Young lady..."

"...and he personally chopped the wood for Noah's Ark!"

"Are we finished with the blasphemy?" Dottie says with her hands on her hips.

"Sorry, Mama," Josie says failing miserably not to laugh. "Go ahead, Mama! Tell me 'bout this man who was almost my daddy!"

"You know I owe you one, Miss Josie!" Dottie says.

"Okay, Mama. Okay. I'll be serious." Josie says trying not to laugh.

"Well, when I was in the seventh grade, Deacon Fred made me his Sunday School assistant. I took attendance, collected the offering, read scripture. Everything. The other girls in my class were so jealous. I was Deacon Fred's assistant for two whole years."

"...so what happened, Ma?"

Dottie huffs.

"A little hussy named Abigail Simpson!"

"Abigail Simpson? Who's Abigail Simpson? ...and who names their daughter Abigail?"

"The Simpsons were new in town. Just moved in from Kentucky. I'm guessing they were run out of there, but that's another story. Anyway, Deacon Fred wanted to make Abigail feel at home, so he suggested that she share some of my responsibilities."

"Oh?" Josie smirks. "…and how did that work out?"

"Child had the IQ of lint," Dottie says shaking her head. "Couldn't read, couldn't write. Girl couldn't count to twelve without taking off her…"

"MAMA!"

"Her shoes, Josie. Her shoes. Which, by the way, she seldom wore."

"Mama…" Josie laughs.

"Now you know I'm gonna tell the truth, Josie," Dottie says.

Josie smiles at her Mama. Just like Jacob, they both have a way of tapping 'baby girl's' funny bone.

"I don't remember any Simpsons in Hopskip," Josie says thinking back. "What happened to them?"

"They moved north the following year. Detroit, I think. Hear tell the overall IQ of Georgia shot up ten points the minute Miss Abigail crossed the border."

"Mama, stop!" Josie says laughing.

Dottie continues her story.

"The boys liked her though!"

"Okay, Mama!"

"Child couldn't say no to save her life!"

Just as quickly, Josie's demeanor turns solemn.

"Like Marilyn Talbert, huh?"

"They're probably related," Dottie laughs.

"Okay, Mama," Josie says debating the veracity of her mother's little tale of heartbreak. "That's a very interesting story, but how does a crush on a hundred-year-old Sunday School teacher even remotely compare to my situation with Mack Hodges?"

"It doesn't, actually," Dottie confesses.

"Mama!"

"What can I say? I've been in love with your father all my life."

"Oh, see now you just rubbing it in!"

"Sorry. That's the best I could come up with," Dottie smiles sheepishly. "Your daddy and your daddy alone has been rocking my socks for the last thirty years."

"Oooh, Mama!"

"Baby, come here," Dottie says taking Josie in her arms. "Sweetheart,

I promise you. Once you find your own sock-rocker, you'll wonder what you ever saw in that drug-dealing, draft-dodging, baby-dumping rat, Mack Hodges."

"You think so?"

"I know so. Besides," Dottie says. "Mama understands. I know what you saw in him."

"You do?"

"Uh huh. Superficial as it was."

"Mama…"

"The man was handsome. I'll give him that. He was older. Nothing like the boys you were used to. Nice car, nice threads…"

"Mama, what do you know about threads," Josie says.

"You know your mama's on top of things," Dottie says patting herself on the back.

Josie smiles.

"I also know that the other girls were so jealous of you and that boy that they couldn't see straight. You liked that."

"Oh, Mama…"

"Oh, Mama what? Are we or are we not being truthful, Jocelyn Myles?" Dottie says to her baby. "Don't deny it, honey. You liked the attention. You were Mack Hodges' lady and all of Hopskip knew it. *You* were able to rub it in Marilyn Talbert's face and you *loved* it!"

"I won't deny it, Mama," Josie concedes. "I *loved* the attention."

"Um hmm."

"I especially liked watching Marilyn Talbert seething with envy. Fool got what she deserved."

"Josie, I'm surprised at you," Dottie says looking at her baby.

"Mama, she stole my man," Josie says.

"Honey, no girl deserves being left stranded like that."

"But, Mama…"

"Think of the baby, Josie. Does he deserve to be raised without a father?"

"No, Mama," Josie says dropping her head in shame. "You're right. I shouldn't have said that. It's just that I'll never understand why Mack chose her. He knew how much I hated Marilyn Talbert. I loved that man, Mama. …him *and* his bowlegs."

Dottie laughs.

"...and I really thought he loved me. There wasn't a day I didn't dream of being Mrs. Michael 'Bowlegs' Hodges."

"Unfortunately," Dottie says bringing her love struck daughter back to earth. "Mr. Hodges loved something else a little more..."

"...himself?" Josie concedes.

"Um hmm. Baby, Mack was selfish," Dottie says. "...and let's be honest. All Mack cared about was putting another notch in his belt. Luckily, we got to you in time, huh baby?"

Josie looks away. She remains quiet.

I knew it would come back to this! She laughs to herself.

Taking her daughter's chin, Dottie turns Josie back to face her.

"I said, *'Luckily, we got to you in time, huh baby?'*"

"Mama?" Josie says looking around the room.

"Yes, baby?"

"Do you think Daddy would mind if we re-painted?"

"Now, Josie..."

"Gray is so drab," Josie says purposely provoking her mother. "Now *teal*! That's the color for this room."

"JOCELYN DOROTHY MYLES!" Dottie almost screams. "DON'T YOU PLAY WITH ME!"

Josie chuckles. She looks at her mother and shakes her head no.

Dottie looks at her baby wide-eyed. She cocks her head as if to say...

"Really? Nothing happened?"

Josie nods.

"Really, Mama! Nothing happened."

Dottie grabs her baby and hugs her – a replay of this morning but this time smiles all around.

"I love you, Mama!" Josie says.

"Oh, I love you too, baby!" Dottie says.

"Mama..."

"Yes?"

"Do you think Daddy..."

"He's had quite a day, baby. He's asleep! Let's not wake him," Dottie says anticipating her daughter's question. She gets up and heads for the door. "Besides, your daddy did pick up his baby girl in front of the Sneakaway Inn today. Let's not forget that."

"Mama!" Josie laughs. "I told you nothing happened!"

"I know," Dottie tells her. "Still… Let's wait until the morning."

"You think he'll forgive me by then?" Josie asks apprehensively. "He was pretty upset in the car."

"Well," Dottie says standing at the door. "Once I get some of Dottie Myles' world famous braised sausage, poached eggs, pancakes and cherries with whipped cream, and grapefruit juice in him, your daddy will be ripe for the picking!"

Josie smiles at her mother. She sighs. Dorothy Rosetta Harris Myles, her biggest cheerleader has always had her back. She can't love her any more than now.

"Mama?" Josie says rising from her bed.

"Yes, sweetheart?"

"Did I tell you *I love you*?" she says hugging her mother.

"Couple of times. Never hurts to hear it again. See you in the morning."

Saturday, June 2nd, 1962

"Well, that was quite a meal. All my favorites," Jacob says looking at his wife askance. "L'il Daddy, Savannah, clear the table, please. Frankie, take out the trash. …and don't forget the bedrooms this time."

"Yes, sir." They all say.

L'il Daddy and Savannah clear the table and head to their rooms. Terry stays at the table and drinks his milk while his father reads the paper. Just as quickly, he drops the paper back on the table.

"Now, where's Josie? It's not like her to sleep in on a Saturday."

"Well, she did have quite a day, yesterday Jacob."

"…and the two of you I understand had quite a talk."

"We did."

"…and?"

"Read your paper," she says motioning toward little Terry still sitting at the table. "She'll be down soon."

"Ok, baby," Jacob says. He picks up his paper and buries his head in the want ads shutting out the rest of the world. He's oblivious to the goings on in his kitchen.

"Is there any more coffee, sweetheart?"

No answer. Jacob taps the table – a little joke between him and his wife - waiting for the familiar splash of ground roast in his cup.

"Would you like another cup, M'Lord?"

Jacob gulps. He beams reminded of the days when his one and only girl - his favorite -asked him that same question. He drops his paper smiling at the angel standing in front of him. It's Josie. Her mother stands behind her smiling at her husband bemused and lost in thought. Affecting the same cockney accent she used when she was a girl playing tea party, Josie offers her father a refill. She's dressed in her waitress uniform and holding Nana Yvonne's coffee pot salvaged from the trip north. Full grown and pretty as a picture, she's still able to disarm her loving father with her childlike, angelic smile.

"Another spot of tea, guv'nor?" Josie asks again. She apprehensively bites her lip, trembling. Poor girl's afraid that her daddy may retreat to his paper and shut her out of his life – the way she unthinkingly did when she thought Mack Hodges was *her* life. She wouldn't blame him. After all, the man only moved heaven and earth to make sure his baby girl was safe – a task he performed with pride every day for the last eighteen years.

No way. Jacob's heart melts – and it has nothing to do with the sausage, eggs, and pancakes his loving wife prepared to placate him for his talk with their daughter. Clearing his throat and apparently choking on his happiness, he smiles.

"W-why yes, M'Lady," Jacob stumbles tripping over his tongue. "I'd love some."

Josie pours the coffee. Still trembling, she gets a little help from Jacob who steadies her hand. She places the pot on the stove and runs back to hug her father. They're both near tears. Dottie's already there.

"Daddy, I'm sorry. I-I…"

"It's okay, baby. It's okay," Jacob sniffs. He quickly changes the subject. "Why the uniform? …thought you were quitting."

"Well, if I'm going to night school," Josie says taking the seat next to him. "I'm gonna have to make me some daytime money."

"That's good to hear, baby girl," Jacob says relieved. He looks up at Dottie and smiles. "That's good to hear!"

Terry taking it all in, and quite possibly understanding it all, stands in his chair, reaches over and kisses his sister. He jumps out of the chair, drops his cup in the sink and runs upstairs.

"What was that all about?" Josie asks.

"You're lucky to have him," Jacob jokes. "If it wasn't for him…"

"Jacob…" Dottie says.

"Just kidding!"

Josie smiles. She takes a napkin from the center of the table and dabs her moistened eyes.

"Can you forgive me, Daddy?"

"Baby girl, it's okay. It *is* over. …right? No more talk of that…"

"Right, Daddy!" Josie says. She's tired of hearing the man's name herself. She stands up and hugs Jacob. When she does, an item in her uniform pocket pokes Jacob in his side.

"Honey, what's this," Jacob asks.

Josie pulls out a picture of Mack. The same picture she spoke to every morning and said goodbye to every night. Frankie, still gathering the trash passes by with a wastebasket.

"Honey, what is this," Dottie says. "I thought…"

"Josie!" Jacob says sternly. "I thought we had an understanding, baby girl…"

"I got all the trash, Daddy," Frankie says.

"Not all of it," Josie says. "Come here, Frankie."

Josie tosses Mack's picture in the wastebasket. For emphasis, she stomps it all the way down with her foot.

"Now you can take it out!"

Jacob and Dottie laugh.

Myles, one. Hodges, zero. They hug their daughter. Baby girl's home.

"Come on honey," Jacob says. "I'll take you to work. Maybe the Johnson sisters will be there."

"Oh, I can handle them," Josie says laughing. "Did I tell you what they did last week? Lord, have mercy!"

Lessons Learned, Part 1–
A Case of Schizophrenia

Thursday, June 7th, 1962

2:55 pm. John Robinson Elementary – Savannah Myles and her friend Tamika Jefferson spend the last few minutes talking in class. Mrs. Adkins takes this time to pass out the results of the children's English test. Savannah receives hers first.

"A 'F'?"

"*An* 'F', Savannah!" Mrs. Adkins corrects her. "Didn't you study for the test?"

The entire class looks in Savannah's direction. She's stumped.

"*Do I tell the truth?*" Savannah asks herself. "*...and get in trouble with Mrs. Adkins for not studying?*"

"Savannah?" Mrs. Adkins asks again.

"*...or do I tell a story? ...and look like a dummy in front of everybody?*"

"Wellll..." Savannah begins.

"Yes, Savannah."

"Well," she stumbles. "Actually..."

"Um hmm..."

"My baby brother got sick!"

"Is that right?" Mrs. Adkins asks.

"Uh, yes ma'am!"

"I don't understand, Savannah. How does your brother's illness affect your studying?"

"Well, Ma'am," Savannah gulps. "*What now?*" she thinks searching the classroom ceiling for divine intervention. Nothing. All she sees is a room desperately in need of a paint job. Looks like she's on her own.

"Savannah…" Mrs. Adkins says impatiently.

"Well, ma'am," Savannah says collecting herself. "In my family, we all believe in helping each other."

"That's commendable."

"Uh, yes ma'am. What you said."

"Go on, Savannah."

"Yes, ma'am. So when my brother got sick, everybody had to drop everything we was doing to help him. You see…"

"What did he have?" Mrs. Adkins asks interrupting the little fabulist.

"Ma'am?" Savannah says weakly.

"What did he have, Savannah?"

"What did he have?" Savannah says looking to her friend Tamika Jefferson for help. Tamika shakes her head and shrugs.

"Got nuttin' for you!" her shrug seems to say. At that point the children in room 202 start to giggle. Savannah has to think quickly.

"Quiet, class!" Mrs. Adkins says. "Savannah?"

"Wait!" Savannah says still in her own little world. *"What did that lady on TV have last night?"*

"I'm waiting, Savannah." Mrs. Adkins says. "What did your brother have that kept you from studying?"

"I'm not sure…" Savannah says hesitating. "…but I think it was schizophrenia."

Savannah's classmates look at one another amazed. Tamika and a few others nod their heads up and down supporting the new girl from down south. Luckily for the little Georgia peach, they have no idea what she's talking about but like her anyway.

"Schizophrenia, huh?" Mrs. Adkins says dropping her head and trying not to smile. "Sounds real bad."

"Yes, ma'am!" Savannah says pleased with her tale of woe. "He was throwing up and everything!"

"RIIINNNNGGGG!"

"Okay, class," Mrs. Adkins says. "I'll pass out the rest of the tests tomorrow. Line up!"

"Yes, Mrs. Adkins!" They all say heading for the door. Tamika winks at Savannah thinking her gal pal is in the clear. Savannah grabs her books and runs for the door. Until…

"SAVANNAH!" Mrs. Adkins calls after her. "We need to talk."

"OOOOOOHHHHHH!" Savannah's class exclaims taunting their friend.

Tamika shakes her head as she exits the room with the rest of the class.

"Schizophrenia! Wow! I hope it's not catching."

"Okay, start with the left foot, cross over… then the right, cross over. Three times each, spin and come back. That's the Temptation walk. My Uncle Lloyd taught me. I added the spin."

"What? Git outta here, *Country*! You think we waited 'til you got up here before we learned how to dance?"

"Hey! What I tell you 'bout calling me '*Country*'?"

"Oops! Sorry!" the boy says apologetically. "Franklin Myles."

"Be cool, Arnold," the young girl sitting on the stool tells him. "We're friends now. You can call him Frankie! Right, Frankie?"

"Right, Carmen!" the lad, congenial as always tells her. He slaps Arnold five, once in the palm and twice on the '*black hand*' side. Something he picked up on the playground. "Alright, Arnold. Let's see what you got!"

"Alright, my brother. But don't be too jealous! You asked for it!"

Arnold Mayweather prances to the center of the floor mimicking his would be tutor.

"Watch this!" he brags. Arnold does the Temptation walk for Frankie and Carmen. He gets the crossovers with no problem. The spin however is a bit much and Arnold falls flat on his backside. Baby Terry, sitting on the couch and snapping his fingers doubles over with laughter. Frankie and Carmen, although beside themselves with laughter as well, run over to help their new friend to his feet. Red-faced and a little shaken, Arnold shakes off his friends' guffaws and sits on the couch with Terry. He then runs his hand across the living room floor.

"Did your mother just wax this floor?" he asks.

Frankie and Carmen laugh.

"Ha! Ha! Whatever you say, Arnold!" Frankie laughs. "Looks like I got up here just in time! Huh, Carmen?"

"I hate to say it, Arnold," Carmen laughs. "…but uhhh."

"Okay, okay. Start the record over," Arnold says jumping to his feet. "I'll show you how we do it in Chicago."

"Oh, I can't wait to see this!" Frankie says with a smile. "Get the record player for me, Carmen."

"Okay, Frankie." Carmen jumps off the stool the Myles family uses to cut the boys' hair. Shoeless and in her stocking feet, Carmen glides across Dottie Myles' newly waxed floor in her pink ribboned socks stopping right in front of the Myleses' portable record player. She looks back at the boys and laughs.

"You *jivin'* me, Frankie!" Arnold says. "I knew this floor had wax on it!"

"All right, I admit it," Frankie says. "Hey, I created some of my best moves on floor wax. How do you think James Brown got started?"

They all laugh.

"Okay, Carmen," Frankie says pointing at the record player. Carmen obliges her next door neighbor and places the needle in the appropriate groove. She then takes little Terry's hand and joins the boys on the Myleses' living room/dance floor. The four children laugh and dance together.

"Dottie! I'm home!"

"In here, baby."

Jacob Franklin Myles, home from another hard day of looking for work, kisses the lovely lady he's blessed to call his wife. He moves in for a hug. She gently pushes him away pointing at the children singing, dancing and having fun.

"Well, well," Jacob says admiring the four dancers. "Looks like Frankie finally got his group together. Go, son! Go! Ha! Ha! Take that, Detroit!"

"That's my baby!" Dottie says swaying to the music. She taps Jacob's shoulder and points to a fifth child sitting in the corner - so quiet the rest of the children forgot she was there.

Jacob looks at his wife and whispers in her ear.

"How come Savannah's so quiet?"

"I don't know. She's been like that since she got home. I'll talk to her later."

Frankie, meanwhile full of the soulful spirit, looks up and smiles at his parents. Jacob waves at him, then Carmen's and Frankie's new friend who's waddling around like a certain cartoon character.

"Yeah, Arnold!" Frankie shouts at his friend waddling across the slippery floor. "Do that Duck!"

"*Arnold?*" Jacob says to himself. He does a double take. "Whoa, Dottie! Did he say…"

"Um hmm. Arnold Mayweather."

"The boy Frankie clocked the second week of school?"

"Yep!"

"The same boy that called Carmen…"

"Come with me, baby." Dottie says leading her husband into the kitchen. "I have your dinner ready."

Jacob Myles drives a cab three nights a week. Their neighbor/landlady Johnnie Mae has a friend who owns a cab stand. He lets Jacob drive a cab to make a little money at night while he searches for work during the day. On these nights, his wife Dottie prepares his dinner for him as soon as he gets home from his interviews. Dottie pulls a foil-wrapped plate from the oven. She places the plate in front of her husband as he pulls off his jacket and has a seat at the kitchen table. He removes the foil from his plate as Dottie walks over to the fridge to get her husband a little something to wash it down.

"Hmmm. Looks good."

"Thank you! Milk, sweetheart?"

"Yes, please!" Jacob says with a smile. He says a little prayer. "So they're friends now?"

"Yep!" Dottie says patting her husband on the shoulder. She places a few pieces of silverware alongside the hot plate as she takes a seat across from him. "Turns out they were both looking for somebody to start a singing group."

"Really?"

"Um hmm. Frankie saw Arnold dancing around on the playground. He liked what he saw, invited him to the house…"

"You're not serious," Jacob says cutting himself a slice of Dottie's roast duck. "Well, what about Carmen?"

"The boy apologized," Dottie says stealing the meat from Jacob's fork. She smiles as she kisses it up to God before eating it. "Now, they're the Junior Miracles."

"Well, don't that beat all!" Jacob says. "My son is amazing."

"Uh, uh. Frankie's *my* baby!" Dottie laughs. "You know, Jacob. This reminds me of Frieda Jackson and Earlie Carmichael. Remember them?"

"Who could forget those two?" Jacob says savoring his wife's cuisine. "Could never agree on nothing. Not even the time of day!"

"*Nothing?*" Dottie says checking her husband's grammar.

"Okay, professor. *Anything!*" Jacob says shaking his head. "Good Lord, Dottie."

"Well, how are the kids supposed to learn if they hear their father forming his sentences so haphazardly?"

"Dottie, they're not even in the room!"

"The walls have ears, dear," Dottie says kidding her husband.

"Okay, 'Enry 'Iggins. You finish your story. I'll finish this duck."

"'Enry 'Iggins? I'll pretend I didn't hear that."

"Sorry, baby." Jacob digs into the mashed potatoes. He smiles and winks at his wife, the best cook on earth. She winks back as she gets up to get Jacob a napkin.

"Forget it! Now, do you know what started that fight between the Jacksons and the Carmichaels a hundred years ago?"

"You know?"

"You know your baby knows everything."

"Ha!" Jacob says dabbing his chin. "The all omniscient Dottie Myles. What happened, gorgeous?"

"My Josie happened, that's what!"

"Josie? Baby girl? Woman, what are you talking about?"

"Well," Dottie laughs. "Way back in 1949 when Josie was all of six, Frieda's boy Kevin stole one of Josie's Easter eggs from her basket."

"HE DID?" Jacob bellows. "That little... How come I'm just now hearing about this?"

"Oh, I don't know," Dottie says shaking her head. She laughs at her husband ready to tear off a six-year old's head for something that happened thirteen years ago. "I have no idea."

"Huh? Oh. Well," Jacob says a little embarrassed. "Continue your story, honey."

"Well. Earlie's boy Joe saw him take Josie's egg and tried to get it back for her."

"That was Josie's egg? I remember the fight but I didn't know it was over Josie. Those boys liked to kill each other over that egg."

"So did their mamas. Broke up the Easter pageant that year, too. Remember Brother Lucas had to step in? He sent them both to their respective corners..."

"...and they haven't spoken since," Jacob says finishing his milk. Dottie ever ready, pours him another glass. He smiles. "Thank you, baby."

"Anytime, handsome!"

"My Lord," Jacob says shaking his head. "All this over an Easter egg!"

"You mean over my *Josie*," Dottie laughs thinking back. "So much like her mama!"

"No argument there!" Jacob says blowing his wife a kiss between bites. "So what happened next?"

"Well now here's where it gets crazy. Josie told me later that the boys were actually friends."

"Is that right?"

"Umm hmm. ...made up at school the next day."

"But their mothers never made up," Jacob says.

"To this day, they will not say word one to each other."

"Shameful! ...goes to show you," Jacob says pointing his fork for emphasis. "We keep telling kids to stay out of grown folks' business..."

"Way ahead of you!" Dottie says taking her husband's fork. "Maybe we should tell adults to do the same. Stay out of their children's business!"

"Baby, you ain't never lied!" Jacob says retrieving the utensil.

"The babies make up the next day..."

"...and their parents carry grudges forever!" Jacob says shaking his head.

"Well, Frankie, Arnold, and Carmen are friends now," Dottie glows. "My baby's happy with the move north..."

"...and all's right with the world," Jacob says throwing his beloved another kiss. "So is this duck! Ummmph!"

CRASH!

"All's right with the world, huh?" Dottie cries. "Baby, you might have spoken too soon! FRANKIE!!! What's going on in there?"

"If we're all finished with dinner, I'd like a hand putting the food away and cleaning up."

"Sure, Mama!" Frankie says cleaning his area. "Hey Mama, the chicken was out of sight!"

"Thank you, baby."

"The roast duck. Magnifique!"

"Merci, monsieur!" Dottie says to her oldest son. He picks up his and Baby Terry's plates and takes them into the kitchen.

"Well, somebody put her foot in those mashed potatoes and gravy!" Josie joins in. "I won't say who. I'll just wink at her!"

Dottie blushes. She winks back at her eldest.

"Hey!" L'il Daddy shouts as if just hit with a revelation. "The chicken. The duck. The mashed potatoes. All we need now is green onions!" He laughs.

"You're right!" Dottie says picking up on her son's references to popular music. "Just don't let me catch you with that *One Mint Julep*. Pass me your plate."

"Ma'am?"

"Nothing, L'il Daddy," Dottie says winking at Josie. "You wouldn't get it!"

"Now, L'il Daddy you know Mama's always on top of these things," his big sister smiles proudly. "Wipe the table, please."

"Yes, ma'am!" L'il Daddy tells his sister. "Hey, Mama! What happened to the stereo?"

"Well," Dottie says rubbing her chin. "It's my strong belief – now I could be wrong, so don't quote me!"

"Yes, Mama?"

"I think," she continues. "...somebody in this room - and I'm not pointing fingers – was probably doing back flips in the living room."

"Come on, Mama!" Frankie protests. His mother continues to rib him.

"Was it you, Josie?"

"*Wasn't me, Mama!*" Josie sings.

"How about you, Savannah?"

"Upstairs." Savannah responds tepidly.

"How 'bout you, Brother Myles?" Dottie asks her baby boy.

"No Ma'am!" he laughs.

"Was it you, Dottie?" she asks herself in a low voice.

"*Oh no, I've been in the kitchen all day!*" the soprano answers herself.

Everyone but Savannah laughs. The rest of the Myles ensemble turns and stares a hole in poor Frankie.

"Well now that I think about it," Dottie says searching the ceiling for inspiration. "It couldn't have been my baby. After all, we only told him half a million times about doing back flips in the house. Especially around breakables!"

"It wasn't a back flip, Ma." Frankie says almost inaudibly.

"So what happened?" Dottie asks.

"Frankie!" L'il Daddy interrupts. "Did you break the record player showing off in front of Carmen again?"

"Let me guess," Josie says balling her fists and mimicking her little brother's dancing. She glides effortlessly across the kitchen floor doing her brother's favorite dance. "It was the camel walk, wasn't it?"

"The camel walk?" Dottie asks.

"Um hmm. Only Frankie does it backwards!"

"Boy, how many times I gotta tell you?" L'il Daddy interjects. "Dancing backwards! That ain't going nowhere! Watch where you're going so you won't run into anything!"

"Hey, Savannah," L'il Daddy says trying to bring his cheerless little sister into the mix. "Remember when Frankie poured salt on the kitchen floor?"

"Yeah!" Josie laughs. "...said it helped his *Mashed Potatoes*." She starts mimicking her brother doing the dance.

The Myles clan, save Mother Dottie and Savannah, laugh at poor Frankie.

"Betcha James Brown's family never laughed at him," Frankie says pouting.

"Betcha James Brown never broke any major appliances!" Dottie admonishes the boy. "Just be careful in the future, son," Dottie says hugging her middle child.

"Yes, Ma'am," Frankie concedes downcast. "I won't do it anymore."

"Good!" Dottie says.

They all shake their heads and return to their individual chores. Dottie throws Frankie, her pouting middle child a kiss. It's enough to make him smile. His mother's love has always been enough to bring Frankie out of whatever doldrums he happens to find himself. Eldest daughter Josie then gets her mother's attention. She nods toward Savannah standing quietly against Dottie's library of cookbooks. Dottie nods back.

"Uh Josie, would you give Terry his bath and see that he gets to bed?"

"Sure, Mama!" Josie says. Before she leaves, she pokes Savannah's side to cheer her up. No response. She kisses her sister's head, picks up Terry, and tickles the laughing child while she runs upstairs with him. "All yours, Mama!"

"Frankie, why don't you get started on your homework?" Dottie tells him.

"Okay, Mama!" Frankie drops the rest of the silverware into the sink purposely splashing water on his little sister. She says not a word. L'il Daddy shakes his head at his brother's antics.

"I saw that!" he says.

"So?" Frankie says.

"So, Daddy's not here!" L'il Daddy responds. "That makes me in charge!" He playfully puts Frankie in a headlock and directs him out of the kitchen and toward the staircase. Frankie wiggles out of his brother's headlock and runs up to his room.

"Savannah, you're awfully quiet!" L'il Daddy says. He tightens the tops on the condiment bottles before putting them away. "You had at least three opportunities to signify on Frankie and you missed them all. What's the matter, baby girl?"

"I have to admit, Savannah," Dottie says. "It's not like you to be so unresponsive when Frankie's in trouble. Everything alright at school, baby?"

Savannah looks at the floor.

"Savannah, your mother's talking to you," L'il Daddy says putting a little more bass in his voice than usual.

Dottie smiles proudly at Jacob, Jr. Ever since Jacob, Sr. started his part-time job and began missing a few dinners with the family, her eldest son took it upon himself to take over the tasks his father normally does - with ease at that. He even disciplines his younger siblings when necessary. *They don't call him L'il Daddy for nothing!*

"Mama?" Savannah finally says.

"Yes, baby?"

"They wanna put me back a grade at school."

"WHAT?" Dottie cries.

"What happened?" L'il Daddy says. "Did you do something?"

"I told you to study for that English test," a voice says from behind the kitchen door.

"You're supposed to be upstairs, young man." L'il Daddy tells his brother.

"Don't make me come out there, Frankie!" Dottie says.

"Yes, ma'am!" Frankie says running off. "Good night!"

"Savannah, what happened?" L'il Daddy asks her.

More silence.

"Savannah, baby. Come on," Dottie says. She cups her baby's chin in her hand. She looks her gently into her innocent face. "Tell, Mama. I won't get mad."

"Well," Savannah says. "You know my teacher, Mrs. Adkins?"

"I met her. Sure," Dottie says. "Talk to me, baby. What's going on?"

"Are you sure you won't get mad, Mama?"

"Of course, baby."

"Wellll…"

"Go on, baby girl," L'il Daddy says mimicking his father. "We're family."

Savannah smiles.

"Well, Mrs. Adkins says because I come from the south, I'm not as smart as the rest of the class."

"WHAT!!!!!!!!" Dottie screams.

"Yep, that's what she said."

Dottie takes a wooden spoon from the dishwater and beats it against the edge of the sink, apparently imagining Mrs. Adkins' head on the other end. L'il Daddy gently takes the spoon from his mother and drops it in the sink. He directs her to a chair and sits her down.

"Mama?" he says.

"I'm all right, son. I'm all right!"

"Mama?" Savannah says cautiously approaching her mother.

"What, baby?" Dottie says barely able to control her emotions.

"Can we put a root on Mrs. Adkins? I don't think anybody would care."

Lessons Learned, Part 2—Southern Girls

ONCE UPON A time in the deep south, America's black youth were deprived of the most basic of necessities – Education. For a myriad of reasons, the powers that be put little if any effort into enforcing education for its' Negro children. No one, it seems on either side of the tracks really cared whether young black children attended school or not. Many children found themselves chained to the fields helping their parents relieve themselves of the never-ending debt brought on by that evil institution known as sharecropping. A few of them worked their own farms so they saw no need for education. Those who did attend school did so nonchalantly because Jim Crow would only afford them the jobs 'suited' for the Negro. Many black children who did attend school did so with textbooks so used and outdated they still found themselves years behind their counterparts across the tracks. Schoolhouses for black children in rural areas were overlooked when it came to simple maintenance and necessary school supplies awarded by the city fathers. Truant officers were unheard of in many of those towns giving the unshepherded license to skip school whenever they felt the need. Those who went to college not always found jobs upon graduation – at least not in their desired field. Jim Crow again rearing its racist head.

No wonder that when many children from the South attended Northern institutions of learning, they were immediately held back for fear that they were lacking in the simple basics. More often than not, they lagged behind their Northern counterparts. Southern schools just don't measure up.

"WHAT?!? WHERE IN THE H-E- DOUBLE HOCKEY STICKS…"

"Dottie, what's…!"

"THAT MRS. ADKINS! WHERE DOES SHE GET OFF

TELLING MY BABY SHE DOESN'T MEASURE UP? IS THAT SCHOOL STILL OPEN? I'M GOING DOWN THERE! I'LL SHOW HER WHO MEASURES UP!"

Poor Jacob. He's been here before. His wife Dottie just discovered the reason for their youngest daughter's silence all evening. She was told by her teacher, Mrs. Adkins that due to her southern roots, she would be retained – forced to repeat the fifth grade. Jacob knows full well how upset his sweetheart gets whenever anyone says anything disparaging about southern schools. Somewhere, somehow, people got it in their heads that people from the south are all barefoot, cousin-lovin' farm-raised hicks with mud in their ears who can't read or write as well as people from – well, anywhere else. God help whoever crosses Dorothy Rosetta Myles in this (dis)regard.

"Honey, please," Jacob says trying to calm his wife. "Can I take off my jacket?"

"I'm sorry, honey. Of course. How was work?"

"Oh, it was…"

"JACOB MYLES! YOU EXPECT ME TO BE SILENT WHEN SOME CHICK VILIFIES MY SAVANNAH? HER, EXCUSE ME *OUR* UPBRINGING?"

"No, sweetheart. I don't," Jacob tells her. "Just be calm, honey. Sit down. You're gonna have the whole family up here…"

"MAMA, WHAT'S WRONG?"

"MAMA, ARE YOU OKAY?"

Dottie's so distraught she barely notices her two eldest standing in the doorway of her bedroom.

"*…and now it starts,*" Jacob tells himself. "You may as well come in, you two."

"JACOB FRANKLIN MYLES!"

"Yes, sweetheart," Jacob says wearily.

"I know that woman didn't tell my baby that she's dumb because she was schooled in Georgia."

"Excuse me?" Josie says almost laughing. She kisses her daddy's temple and has a seat on the edge of the bed. "Some of the best historically black colleges and universities are in the south! Anybody heard of Grambling, Spellman?"

"…or Howard?" L'il Daddy says. "Don't get *me* started!"

"I guess I better tell my brother Nate to go back to Fisk and give his Master's back!" Dottie yells sarcastically. "Let that Mrs. Adkins tell it, it ain't worth…"

"MAMA!" L'il Daddy shouts. Josie, shocked as well covers her mouth surprised by her mother's language.

"*Nothing*, son," Dottie says. "I was going to say 'nothing'. Lord in heaven, why do you two always think we're gonna go off the rails whenever we get excited?"

"Sorry, Mama!" They both say with a look of relief on their faces.

Jacob is surprised at his wife's outburst but for a different reason.

"*Ain't?*" Jacob says to himself. "*Did my baby just say 'ain't'? And she used a double negative! Lord, this woman is steamin'!*"

"Close the door, son. …and the transom." Jacob says pointing upward. "I don't want the babies to hear this."

"Right, dad!" L'il Daddy responds. "Just us adults, huh?"

"Boy, close the door!"

"Yes, sir."

Frankie, in his pajamas and seated on his bed, hears the ruckus down the hall. He jumps up and runs down to Savannah's room. He finds her instead listening in at their parents' bedroom door. He drags her back into her bedroom.

"Savannah, what's going on? Why is Mama yelling?"

"They're talking about Mrs. Adkins."

"Your teacher, Mrs. Adkins?"

"No, the mailman Mrs. Adkins. What do you think?"

"Ha Ha," Franklin says drily. "Remind me to use that one. Come on, what's Mama screaming about? What did you do?"

"How come I had to do something? Mama's mad at Mrs. Adkins. She wants to flunk me."

"Flunk you? Over that test? Toldya you shoulda studied."

"Mama's gonna go up to the school tomorrow and beat her up!" Savannah nods proudly.

"What?!?" Frankie shouts. "Parents can't fight teachers. What's wrong with you?"

"That's what Mama said," Savannah says jumping on the bed. "I heard everything. …'til L'il Daddy closed the door."

"Oh?" Frankie says looking down the hall toward his parents' room. "Hmmm."

"What, Frankie?" Savannah says wide-eyed. "What?"

"Savannah…"

"Yeah?"

"Do you remember the human ladder act we saw at the circus last year?"

"There's a couple of brothers in my class who shoulda graduated three years ago," L'il Daddy says.

"Three years ago?" Dottie says.

"Um hmm," says L'il Daddy taking a seat. "They're from Mississippi. I heard they were both put back when they came up here. Sent both of 'em to the fourth grade."

"From the seventh grade to the fourth?" Dottie cries. "That's terrible!"

"Yep! Heard they came to school one day and their books and desks were in another room."

"What do you mean their desks, L'il Daddy?" Josie asks. "Why would they… OH! I get it."

"Um hmm." L'il Daddy says. "They were both too big for the little kids' desks so the teachers made' em bring the ones from upstairs."

"Talk about humiliating!" Josie says.

"My Lord," Dottie says shaking her head. "My Lord."

Frankie squats in the hallway and clasps his hands. Savannah steps from the floor and into her brother's clasped hands with her right foot. She steps onto his right shoulder with her left foot as he hoists her little body into the air. She balances herself against the wall while turning her torso so that the two of them are now facing the same direction. He grabs her by the ankles, balancing his little sister on his shoulders. Voila! The human ladder! Ringling would be proud.

Frankie faces the wall. He holds on tight to his sister's ankles balancing her on his shoulders as he inches down the hall. Savannah balances herself by moving hand over hand along the wall until the *'human ladder'* reaches their unsuspecting parents' bedroom door. Savannah, her pigtails now parallel with the door peeks into the transom window, her little nose pressed against the glass. She sees her mother pacing the floor discussing the day's events. Her brother and sister sit on the edge of their parents' bed trying to calm their mother. Lastly, Savannah eyes her father lying on the bed exhausted. She shakes her head pitying the poor man. He just worked the last four hours driving a cab to put food on his family's table. As much as he would like, Savannah thinks, the poor man would like to get some sleep but now has to worry about some dumb teacher.

"*She deserves a beating!*" Savannah thinks to herself.

"Savannah, what's going on?" Frankie asks.

"If somebody close his mouth, I can hear."

"You're gettin' heavy, Savannah!" Frankie warns her. "Hurry up."

"Shhh!" she responds. "Josie's talking"

"Daddy, this makes no sense. Why would they make Savannah repeat a grade? She's always been a good student. She's keeping up with the new school. I check her homework every night."

"Well, that answers that," L'il Daddy says winking at his father. Jacob smiles but motions to his son to keep quiet.

"This isn't funny, son!" Dottie says still miffed at the thought of her baby being picked on by her teacher. "You saw how distraught your sister was at dinner. Don't make light of this."

"Okay, Mama. I'm sorry. So what do we do?"

"*We* do nothing. *I* am going up to that school first thing tomorrow morning. I can't wait to meet this Mrs. Adkins. Probably one of those sadity Northern chicks never even set foot down south, poor thang! Probably jealous of my baby."

"You tell 'em, Mama!" Savannah says.

"What?" Frankie says.

"Mama's going up to the school tomorrow. She's gonna beat up my teacher! Told you! Wait'll I tell Tamika!"

"Jealous of Savannah!" Jacob says rising from his bed. He tries to restrain himself but he can't help it. He bursts into a fit of laughter. Josie and L'il Daddy fall all over one another laughing at their mother. Mother Dottie tends to get a bit overwrought when one of her babies is in distress.

"What's she afraid of, baby?" Jacob laughs. "That Savannah might take her man? Told that girl to stay out of Josie's lipstick!"

"Oh, you be quiet!" Dottie says laughing in spite of herself. "You all think this is funny but northerners can be a mess."

"Northerners?" Jacob says wearily.

"Remember a few years back at my sister's school?" Dottie says ignoring her husband. "The Battle of the Bands and that school from Missouri?"

"...and the year right after, the one from Wisconsin!" L'il Daddy joins in.

"We did put a strain on 'em, huh Mama?" Josie laughs.

"Those two never came back!" L'il Daddy says.

"Oh, I see!" Jacob laughs. "So Mrs. Adkins is flunking Savannah for revenge *and* because baby girl might steal her man!"

Dottie narrows her eyes at her husband/tormentor.

"I can't stand you, Jacob Myles!" she says trying not to laugh. She grabs a pillow and hits him with it. She throws one to each of her children who join in the fun.

"Savannah, what's going on in there?" Frankie whispers.

"They're having a pillow fight! My teacher's gonna flunk me and they're having a pillow fight!"

"Can't be no worse than what I'm going through."

"What? What's worse than me flunking?"

"Your feet. They're killing me!"

"Excuse me. I wash my feet! Probably your upper lip. I can smell it all the way up here!"

"Oh, really?"

"Yeah, really!"

The two siblings squabble unaware that their voices can be heard through the partially closed transom. Josie is the first to hear them. Getting her brother's attention, Josie points to her mother's makeup mirror – particularly the reflection of her sister's head bobbing up and down just outside the transom. She puts her finger to her lips as she and L'il Daddy creep over to their parents' bedroom door. Josie snatches open the door.

"Hey, Savannah! Whatcha doing?"

Savannah screams losing her footing. L'il Daddy, always at the ready catches her and throws her still screaming onto his parents' bed. Jacob, Dottie, Josie, and L'il Daddy circle the little conspirator lying on the bed. Josie and L'il Daddy try in vain to stifle their giggles. Their parents are not so joyous.

"Mama! Daddy!" Savannah cries. "You see what Josie and L'il Daddy did? I could have died."

Dottie's beside herself. Not as angry as she could be, but angry nonetheless.

"Girl, you gonna wish you died when I get through with you! Frankie, get in here!"

"Yes, ma'am."

"How long you two been listening in through that transom?"

"It's the first time, Mama!" Frankie cries. "Honest. I swear."

"What did I say about swearing in my house, Franklin Myles?" Jacob bellows.

"Uh, only you and Mama can do it?"

"Boy, go to bed!" Jacob tells him.

"See what you did, Savannah?" Frankie says. "Always gittin' me in trouble."

"You wanna see real trouble, Frankie?" Jacob says.

"No, sir!" Frankie says zipping down the hall. Jacob shakes his head and laughs. He always wondered which of his precocious children would be the first caught peeking in on him and his wife.

"You, too Miss Eavesdropper!"

"Yes, ma'am!"

"…and tomorrow we're going up to your school. I have a few choice words for Mrs. Adkins."

"Yes, ma'am!"

"Savannah!" Dottie says stopping the little girl. "By the way. Where did you get the idea that I know anything about putting a root on people?"

"Well, I heard Daddy say one time your mama tried to put a root on him!"

"SAVANNAH!" Jacob says. "That was years ago! You always gittin' me in trouble!"

Jacob runs out of the room laughing. Dottie, trying not to laugh chases her stand-up comedian of a husband down the hall with the pillow.

"You gon' git enough talking 'bout my mother, Jacob Myles. Maybe somebody oughta put a root on *you*!"

Friday, June 8th, 1962

"Good morning, Mrs. Adkins."

"Good morning," Savannah's teacher responds. The young educator, putting the finishing touches on her lesson plans for the day, continues writing at her desk. She doesn't bother to look up since she recognizes the child's voice.

"Savannah, the morning bell hasn't rung yet. Shouldn't you be on the playground?"

"Mrs. Adkins?"

Hearing a more mature voice this time, Mrs. Adkins looks up from her workspace searching for the owner. Expecting someone under four feet tall, she instinctively looks in the direction of the doorknob. She sees instead a pair of balled fists. She looks up to see her student's very concerned mother standing at the door. She immediately jumps up to greet her.

"Hi, you must be Mrs. Myles?" she says extending her hand to greet her. "Savannah, you didn't tell me your mother was coming."

"Uh, yes ma'am," Savannah says hesitating. After last night's debate regarding northern teachers, she half-expected her mother to come out swinging. Now she just wants to go outside.

"Well, come in Mrs. Myles," Mrs. Adkins says. "Please have a seat. Savannah, you can wait on the playground while we talk."

"Yes, Savannah!" Dottie tells her. "That's probably a good idea!"

"Okay, Mama!" Savannah says running out the door.

The two ladies wait until Savannah is heard running down the hall.

"That Savannah!" Mrs. Adkins says smiling. "She's something else. You have two children here, don't you Mrs. Myles?"

"Let's dispense with the formalities, Mrs. Adkins!" Dottie says in that no-nonsense tone that's been known to instill hesitancy (yes, fear) in anyone in her proximity.

"I beg your pardon, Mrs. Myles. Is there something wrong?"

"Something wrong?" Dottie says barely concealing her disgust for the woman. "I can't believe my ears. You're from the South, too!"

"COBBS!"

"What?"

"You don't know cobbs, Frankie?"

"Girl, what are you talking about?" Frankie asks pulling a bag of wine candy from his jacket pocket. Carmen snatches the bag.

"Hey, what…"

"If somebody sees you on the playground with a snack, they can call 'cobbs' and take it from you."

"What! Carmen, that's nuts!"

"You have to call *'no cobbs'* to keep it."

"NO COBBS!" Frankie shouts.

"Too late!" Carmen says taking a piece of candy from the bag. She unwraps it and pops it in her mouth. "I'll just take one since you're new." She smiles and hands the bag back to him.

"Hilarious!" Frankie says returning the smile. Little does Carmen know, Frankie would hijack a truckload of wine candy for the little heartbreaker.

"Hey!" Carmen whispers. "Here comes Arnold. Hide your candy."

"Hey, Frankie!" Arnold shouts. "You in trouble?"

"Naw, Man. What are you talking about?"

Arnold throws his books in a corner of the schoolyard and walks over to Carmen and Frankie.

"How come Mrs. Myles is here, Frankie?" the boy asks.

"She's here to see Savannah's teacher. That's all."

"Oh! Hey, Frankie," Arnold laughs. "Did you get a whipping for breaking your record player? Man! That was ugly!"

"How would you know?" Frankie asks. "You were out the door before it hit the floor!"

Carmen laughs.

"Yeah, Arnold!" Carmen says pushing the boy. "Who knew you could run so fast?"

"We don't get whippings in my house!" Frankie replies. "Just a record player."

"Me, either." Carmen concurs. "Not over a record player."

"Well, in my house everybody gets it when somebody's in trouble!" Arnold says.

"Everybody?" Frankie and Carmen ask incredulously.

"Yeah!" Arnold says. "My ol' man calls it cleaning house. He figures we must've done something somewhere down the line we got away with, so..."

Frankie and Carmen give each other that *'That's nuts!'* look - a look perfected in the few weeks they've come to know young Mayweather.

"Frankie," Carmen says tugging her friend. "Here comes Savannah."

"Savannah, what happened?" Frankie asks. "Are they gonna hold you back?"

"Hold her back?" Arnold says. "Oh yeah, that's right. You're from Georgia. They hold everybody back a grade when you come from the South. It's the law."

"THE LAW?" Savannah cries. "NOOOOO!"

"Why yes, I'm from the South! Alabama born and bred. What gave me away? My Alabama twang? Mr. Adkins is from New York. He always says..."

"Mrs. Adkins, please!" Dottie says restraining herself. "I came here for my daughter, Savannah."

"Of course, you did, Mrs. Myles. I'm sorry. Please go on."

"Well..."

"Oh, would you like some tea?"

"TEA! Mrs. Adkins..."

"I brought some hot water from the cafeteria," she says. She opens her bottom drawer and reaches all the way into the back of it searching for her special blend. "I'm sure I have some Orange Pekoe here somewhere. Ah, here it is!"

"Mrs. Adkins, I did not come here to drink tea! You're from Alabama..."

"Yes, Mobile. East Mobile. Ever been?"

"Lord, what is with this woman?" Dottie thinks to herself.

"Mrs. Adkins, if we can dispense with the Orange Pekoe, your husband, and the geography lesson, I want to talk to you about your making my daughter repeat the fifth grade."

"Excuse me?"

"Mrs. Adkins!" Dottie says. She's now on her feet and circling the poor woman's desk. "What kind of school policy approves placing a child with my daughter's intelligence and ability back a grade simply because of her state of birth? I don't know about you, but where I come from Mrs. Adkins, that is unconscionable. I don't know about the other parents who moved here from the south but my name is Dorothy Harris Myles, straight from Georgia and proud of it. And I'm not about to allow the backward thinking on the part of this administration stereotype my baby and keep her from advancing to the next level. She's earned it. My daughter will graduate with the rest of the class as she should and I won't hear another word about it!"

"Mrs. Myles."

"WHAT? I-I mean yes."

"I never said I was going to hold her back."

"THE LAW?" Savannah cries. "The police are gonna make me repeat the fifth grade?"

"No, Savannah," Carmen says comforting her new friend. "Arnold doesn't know what he's talking about. Arnold never knows what he's talking about."

"Do too!" Arnold shouts.

"Then how come they didn't send me back?" Carmen challenges the boy. "I'm from Florida."

"That's not the south!" Arnold dares back.

"What?" Frankie says. "Florida is further south than all the contiguous states put together."

"You tell 'em, Frankie!" Carmen says.

"Yeah, but Carmen's from Miami," Arnold argues.

"So?" the kids shout.

"That's where they grow oranges. Everybody likes oranges."

"What?" Carmen says.

"If you come from a state where they grow corn and cotton," Arnold says. "they automatically put you back."

"Arnold, they grow corn in Illinois," Carmen says wearily.

"Riiigghtt!" Arnold says patting himself on the back. "The *southern* part of Illinois."

"Arnold?" Frankie says once again giving Carmen that patented *'That's Nuts'* look.

"Yeah, Frankie?"

"*SHUT UP!*"

The kids laugh. Even Arnold joins in the frivolity although the poor boy has no clue why. Just then, Christopher Champion, a classmate of Savannah's passes by carrying a violin case. Carmen points him out to Savannah who turns her way and blushes. The two girls giggle.

"Hey Savannah," Arnold says watching the girls carry on. "You know if you joined the band with the rest of the nerds, Mrs. Adkins might give you a break."

"The band?" Frankie says with a smirk. "No way you'd catch me in the band. Carrying a violin around like a girl."

"What's that supposed to mean?" Carmen demands.

"Yeah!" Savannah shouts. "What's wrong with the band?"

"Nothing," Frankie says. "If a *girl* wants to play the violin or the piano, it's okay. I got no problem with it. But dudes? Real men? Naaahhhh!"

"Frankie…" Carmen says.

"*…except for Ricky Ricardo!*" Frankie says interrupting his friend. He pretends to play the bongo, entertainer Desi Arnaz' signature instrument. Frankie high-fives Arnold. *"Babalooooo!* Yeah! That's my man!"

"Franklin Joseph Myles, that's ridiculous!" Carmen says shaking her head. "There are plenty of boys in the band…"

"Yeah, and they're all, well let's say they'd look better in dresses."

He and Arnold laugh and slap each other five.

"So you wanna be a singer, but you don't want to learn music?" Carmen says. "Now you sound like Arnold!"

"Yeah!" Arnold says. "Now you sound like me!"

"Need I say more, Frankie?" Carmen says. Frankie shakes his head.

"Carmen," Frankie laughs. "Nobody pays attention to the band! As long as I can sing, and you know I can dance!"

Frankie does a little twirl. A few girls behind him watch the would-be entertainer and giggle. He does a little dance around his admirers and blows them a kiss. He looks Carmen's way and smirks.

"Need I say more, Miss Hamilton?"

"Well, I have one thing to say, *Mr. Ricardo!*"

"What's that, *Loocie?*" Frankie responds mimicking his TV hero.

"COBBS!" Carmen yells. She opens Frankie's jacket revealing his candy to the world. The little girls he tried to impress with his moves grab Frankie's bag of candy and run across the schoolyard laughing.

"Hilarious, Carmen," Frankie says. "Hilarious."

"You're not flunking Savannah?" Dottie says sheepishly.

"No!" Mrs. Adkins responds. "Of course not. I think her friend Tamika Jefferson must have told her that. A mind like Savannah's? Oh, no! That girl's going places. I wanted to talk to you about her study habits."

"Her study habits?"

"That's right," Mrs. Adkins smiles. Dottie returns the smile with one of her own - careful not to show the crow between her teeth.

"May I sit down, Mrs. Adkins?" Dottie says red-faced.

"Of course." Mrs. Adkins replies. "How about that tea, now?"

"That would be nice, Mrs. Adkins," Dottie says.

Mrs. Adkins hands Dottie a large Dixie cup filled with water from the table behind her. She hands her a packet of tea.

"I am so embarrassed," Dottie says dipping the bag into the water. "I promised myself I would never be one of those parents."

"Girl, please," Mrs. Adkins assures her. "If it was my daughter, I'd do the same thing. Besides, we Southern girls have to stick together."

"Well, well. You *are* from the South."

"Alabama and proud of it!" The two women toast one another.

"Georgia girl!" Dottie says with a shake of the noggin. She takes a sip of her tea. "Thank you, this is good."

"You're welcome," Mrs. Adkins says. "Hopskip, Georgia. Savannah talks about it all the time."

"That's my baby!" Dottie says proudly.

"Now, as I said I have no intention of holding Savannah back. I do however want her to re-take the test. I don't know what children have against diagramming."

"Diagramming? That's very important. My Jacob – junior, that is - loves English. He can tutor her."

"Wonderful!" Mrs. Adkins proclaims. "Will she be ready next Thursday?"

"Oh, she'll be more than ready, Mrs. Adkins."

"Good!"

Dottie gets up and heads for the door. She tosses her cup into a nearby wastebasket.

"Thank you for the tea, Mrs. Adkins."

"My pleasure."

"Mrs. Adkins, I am so sorry," Dottie says turning around. "I'm afraid I get a little crazy when I think my babies are being mistreated. They're good kids. All of them. I came here ready to…"

"I know."

The ladies laugh.

"Oh, one thing Mrs. Adkins. If you have time."

"I do. What is it?"

"Last night, my oldest boy told me about two seventh graders from Mississippi. He said they were put back three grades after moving north."

"I think that's a bit extreme."

"So, it's not true."

"Well, Mrs. Myles," Mrs. Adkins explains. "If a child is reading at a lower level, it would be detrimental to the child's education to pass him because of his age. As much as it hurts, I've had to retain a few children from the south. Sit down, please."

Dottie sits in one of the student's chairs. Mrs. Adkins takes the seat next to her.

"Unfortunately," Mrs. Adkins continues. "There are some children from the south who get left behind for various reasons. We have no choice but to place them back a grade or two when they're not performing at their grade level. It's a shame – no, a sin I think that some children who aren't performing at their level are allowed to progress through the system less than equipped. He or she will get progressively worse and drop out in high school."

"Oh, I'd hate to see that!" Dottie exclaims. "Especially now."

"*Now*, Mrs. Myles?"

"Oh yes!" Dottie says. "As you know, a lot of opportunities are opening up for our babies. Opportunities you and I could only dream about."

"Amen!" Mrs. Adkins concurs with a smile.

"Thanks to Dr. King, a lot of doors that were nailed shut are finally opening up to our children."

"And they *must* be prepared."

Dottie nods her head. "I agree, Mrs. Adkins. Still, it must be awfully demoralizing to put a child back a grade where he towers over the other children. It must be a terrible blow to the child's self-esteem."

"It is. But it's also unfair to let a child continue if he's not mentally prepared. It's best to get to them early. BETTER HEARTBREAK AT SEVEN THAN SEVENTEEN."

Dottie smiles. "I like that. I'll be sure to share that with my husband."

"Oh, let *me*, Mrs. Myles." she winks.

"Excuse me?" Dottie says puzzled.

"PTA meeting! Next week! See you then?"

"It's a date!" Dottie says with a smile.

"You know what, Mrs. Myles. It's ironic."

"What's that, Mrs. Adkins?"

"I've seen some teachers with absolutely no regard for the child's welfare, send a southern born child immediately to a lower grade upon arrival to the city…"

"Really?"

"…and some of the children born *upsouth* are promoted even though they are nowhere near as prepared as they should be!"

"That's unfair, Mrs. Adkins," Dottie concurs.

"It is. That's why the teachers here at John Robinson give our children assessment tests."

"Really?" Dottie says impressed. "…and the test determines where they should be? That's more than fair."

"Thank you. I appreciate your saying that."

"I don't recall Savannah taking a test?"

"No need. Your baby was off and running as soon as she sat in that chair!"

"My Girl!" Dottie says literally patting herself on the back. "But if she's doing so well…"

"Way ahead of you, Mrs. Myles. For some reason, Savannah is sloughing off. She's talking just a little bit more in class than necessary. She's not as focused as when she first arrived."

"Oh, I can fix that," Dottie assures her. "…and I'll have her ready for that test next week."

"Excellent!" Mrs. Adkins says rising from her chair. "Mrs. Myles, we need to do everything in our power to nurture a mind like Savannah's.

No telling what she can become. You should have heard the story she gave me for not studying."

"I know my baby. I bet it was a doozie."

RIINNNGGG!!!

"I better let you get to your class," Dottie says grabbing her things. "Thanks, Mrs. Adkins. I'm so glad we had this talk."

"So am I. Oh, by the way."

"Yes, Mrs. Adkins?"

"How's little Terry's schizophrenia?"

"...so Mrs. Adkins says she'll let Savannah re-take the test."

"Great!" Jacob says. "You hear that, Savannah? Frankie, pass the hot sauce."

"Yes, sir."

"L'il Daddy," Jacob continues. "You don't mind tutoring your sister, do you?"

"Not a problem, Daddy!" he answers. "Hot sauce, please!"

"...and she said nothing about retaining you, baby," Dottie continues.

"For real?" Savannah beams.

"Um hmmm."

"Alright!" Savannah says almost jumping out of her chair. "Pass the hot sauce!"

L'il Daddy passes the bottle to his little sister only to have Dottie snatch it away.

"Mama..." Savannah says.

Dottie looks at her baby.

"What, Mama?"

"She also said that you and Miss Tamika have been running your little mouths in class."

"Oh no, Mama!" Josie winks. "Not Savannah!"

The rest of the family laugh.

"What's that about, Savannah?" Dottie asks.

"*Oh, oh!*" Savannah thinks. "*I can't tell her about Christopher Champion. I'll never hear the end of it!*"

"Make it good," Jacob says nonchalantly between bites. He's been here before. Nobody tells a story like Baby Girl No. 2.

"Well..." Savannah says.

"Um hmm?" the whole family says.

Savannah comes up with a good one.

"Well, Mama," she says. "If a person asks you a question, no matter where. Wouldn't it be rude to ignore her?"

"Savannah…" the family says wearily.

"I bet that's in the bible somewhere. Huh, Daddy?"

Jacob looks up as if he's thinking. He taps his chin and then answers his daughter.

"You know what, Baby Girl…"

"Yes, Daddy!" Savannah answers gleefully thinking she's made headway with her daddy.

"You need to stop talking in class."

"Yes, Daddy," Savannah responds. "Can I have the hot sauce now, Mama?"

"Sure you won't get schizophrenia?"

"What?" Savannah says soaking her chicken breast. *"Boy, teachers sure have big mouths!"* she says under her breath.

Josie continues the conversation.

"So, Mama, Mrs. Adkins is not gonna flunk Savannah, huh?"

"No, baby. Apparently, somebody's been listening to certain people."

"Don't look at me," Frankie says. "That was Arnold!"

"Um hmm." Dottie winks at Frankie and smiles. "Mr. Eavesdropper. Don't think I forgot about last night."

Frankie smiles back. He knows his mother well enough to know she's not upset.

Josie elbows L'il Daddy.

"…so Mama," she laughs. "Mrs. Adkins gets to keep her head?"

Her brother and father laugh.

"Okay, okay! So I misunderstood the woman. She's okay. Real smart. I can tell she cares. Alabama girl, Jacob!"

Jacob perks up.

"Say what?" he smiles.

"Um hmm," Dottie says with a smile. "You'll meet her at the next PTA meeting." Dottie then snatches a piece of her famous hot water cornbread from her husband's plate.

"Cobbs!"

"Hey!" Jacob cries.

"That's for talking about my mother last night."

The family smile at Jacob's predicament.

"Mama, you know cobbs?!?" Frankie asks incredulously.

"Boy, you know your mama knows everything," Dottie smiles. "There's more in the oven, Jacob."

"Good one, Mama!" Frankie says.

"Thank you, baby!"

"So, Daddy!"

"Yes, Frankie?"

"Now that we've solved Miss Savannah's issues…"

Savannah licks out her tongue at her brother.

"Um hmmm." Jacob responds.

"There's still the matter of getting my group together."

"His group?" L'il Daddy whispers to Josie.

"The Junior Miracles," she responds.

"Oh, right," L'il Daddy shrugs. "That group."

"Since tomorrow's Saturday…" Frankie continues.

"Um hmmm…"

"…and you're not working yet, right?"

"WHAT? BOY!" Jacob says almost choking on his food.

"Can we go downtown this time for a record player?"

"EXCUSE ME?" Jacob says coughing.

"Too much hot sauce, Daddy?" Frankie says. "That happens to me, sometimes. Anyway, Arnold Mayweather said we could get a more expensive record player downtown."

"Oh he did, did he?" Jacob says.

"Yes, sir," Frankie says. He's oblivious to the stunned looks on his family's faces- especially Jacob's.

"Yes, sir," Frankie continues. "If we get one of those floor models – Arnold says they're pretty sturdy – we won't have to worry about it falling over like the portable one you got on Maxwell."

Josie and L'il Daddy, trying desperately to hold in their laughter, kick one another under the table waiting for Jacob to lower the boom on their clueless little brother. Dottie cradles her forehead in her palm shaking it back and forth. She's constantly amazed by her middle child's naiveté.

"Sounds like you got it all figured out, son," Jacob says feigning interest.

"Yes, sir! ...and Mama, guess what?"

"What, baby?" Dottie says wearily.

"You can close the top and put flowers on it!"

"Really?" Dottie says listening to her son's spiel.

"Uh huh. I mean *Yes, Ma'am!*" Frankie says correcting himself. He's trying to get a new stereo. No sense in getting sloppy with the manners.

"Oh, and Daddy..." Frankie says.

"Yes, son?"

"Can we go around twelve?"

"Twelve?"

"Yes, sir," Frankie says never missing a beat. "That's when the cartoons go off."

At that moment, L'il Daddy sputters his milk back into its glass. Josie drops her fork on the floor laughing along with the rest of the family.

"What's so funny?" Frankie asks innocently.

"Boy, do you really expect me to just get up, go buy a new record player – a console - and leave it at that?"

"Well, yeah," Frankie says. "They don't cost that much. Do they?"

"Son, that's not the point."

"It's not?" Frankie says with his head down.

"No," Jacob says patiently. He's been here before. Frankie's always been the child who needs a little more explanation than the rest. No problem. No one's going anywhere – especially not downtown.

"Frankie," Jacob explains. "Whenever you break something, you can't just expect me or your mother to reach into our pockets and replace it no questions asked."

"We're not rich, sweetheart," Dottie explains.

"So what do I do, Daddy?" Frankie asks. "Whenever Josie and L'il Daddy wanted something back home, you had 'em do chores around the ranch. Not that much to do around here."

"YOU THINK NOT?" Jacob says pointing his fork at his son. "I COULD THINK OF A FEW THINGS..."

"Now, now Jacob," Dottie says playing the arbitrator. She places a calming hand on her husband's arm. "Frankie, I know how we can get you a record player, ...*and* a tutor for Savannah!"

Lessons Learned, Part 3—
Will the Real Savannah Myles Please Stand Up

Saturday, June 9th, 1962

"I'M NOT GOING to ask you again, Savannah! Get out of the car!"

"No, Mama! I can't stand Tamara! She thinks she's better than me! She thinks she's better than everybody!"

"I know that's right!"

"You're not helping, Frankie!"

"See, Mama!" Savannah says. "Frankie agrees with me! Josie and L'il Daddy, too! How come L'il Daddy can't tutor me? It's not fair, Mama!"

"Savannah!" Dottie says wearily.

"Mama, she thinks she's better than everybody. She wears a dress everywhere, and she talks all high and mighty like she's Cleopatra or somebody."

"Savannah, baby please…"

"…and she talks with a southern accent!"

"I know baby, but…"

"Mama! She's from Chicago!"

"I know baby, I know."

"How can I argue with these children?" Dottie says to herself. *"Tamara and Freddie, are well, different. Little do they know that I promised my sister-in-law I would try and get my children together with hers once we moved north. I thought Frankie would be the problem. I don't understand Savannah. She usually gets along with everyone. …never thought I'd be in over my head with an eleven-year-old."*

"Uh, Mama," Frankie says. "Are you okay?"

"Yes I am," Dottie says snapping out of her daydream. "Alright, Savannah Vernell. I've had enough. Frankie! Go ring the doorbell."

"Yes, ma'am!" Frankie says. He grabs his backpack full of 45's and his little sister's textbook and runs gleefully to the Duprees' front door.

"...and Savannah," Dottie warns her insolent daughter. "If you're not out of the car by the time your Aunt Lucy comes to the door I'm coming in after you. ...and it won't be pretty!"

Frankie rings the doorbell to his aunt's home. The Duprees live in an upscale section of Chicago known as Pill Hill. Lucy's father-in-law, orthodontist Fredrick P. Dupree, the second moved his family into the south side bungalow in the 1940s as the area found itself increasingly becoming a haven to factory workers from the city's nearby plants. Dr. and Mrs. Dupree remained in the area when many of those factory workers left and the community was replaced with residents from nearby South Chicago Hospital. Hence, the name Pill Hill. The elder Duprees have since passed leaving the family stead to their only child, Fredrick P. Dupree, the third. The neighborhood is quickly earning a reputation for wealth and high society – a fact Lucy's arrogant husband never fails to mention to his select group of friends. All two of them. Unfortunately, his penchant for braggadocio has rubbed off on his daughter Tamara. No wonder the Myles children find the little diva difficult to endure.

"No one's answering, Mama!" Frankie yells.

"Good!" Savannah smiles. "We can go!"

"You hush, little girl!" Dottie says. "Try it again, Frankie."

As soon as Frankie reaches to press the buzzer, the door opens. A little girl, whose haughty attitude belies her young age, peeks outside.

"Well, it looks like ignoring you doesn't help," the twelve-year-old says in a condescending tone perfected over the years. "Apparently, you're not going anywhere! What are you doing here?"

"Hello to you too, Tamara!" Frankie says drily. He shakes his head. Truth be told, he'd rather be anyplace else.

"Must I repeat myself, little boy. What are you doing here?"

"Little boy?" Frankie says offended. "Girl, don't act like you don't know me! Open the door, Tammy!"

"*Tammy?*" the child says with a smirk. "My, aren't we overly familiar!"

"Girl, if you don't..."

"Who is it, Tammy?" says a voice from inside.

"Well, if I had to guess..." Tammy says looking her cousin up and down.

"Girlll!" Frankie says boiling.

"I would have to say…"

"TAMMY!" Frankie yells.

"…the Salvation Army. Are you looking for donations for your clothing drive?"

"Aaaagggh!!!" Frankie screams.

"Is that you, Frankie?" his aunt says coming down the hall. "Hi, baby!"

"Hi, Aunt Lucy," Frankie says exasperated.

"Tammy, open the door and let our guests in."

"Yes, ma'am," Tammy says with a look of condescension that would rival even that of her arrogant father.

"I'll talk to you, later!" her mother tells her. She looks out onto the street and sees her sister-in-law exiting the car.

"Dottie! Hi! Where's Savannah?" Lucy asks.

"SAVANNAH!" Dottie yells looking behind her.

Savannah jumps out of the car and slams the door behind her. Arms folded, she stomps down the walkway and up the steps to her Aunt Lucy's home. Lucy manages a smile. She understands. Daughter Tamara isn't the most loving of children. She grates on everyone's nerves. Still, she's hers and well, someone has to love her.

"Fredrick had to work today," Lucy stammers. "He's going to be so upset he missed you."

"No he isn't, Mother," Tamara says. "He's in the garage."

"He's working from home, sweetheart!" Lucy says sheepishly. "Let's try not to bother him okay, baby?"

Frankie and Savannah look to their mother. The looks on their faces say the same thing.

"In the garage? Wow, he doesn't wanna be here either! How come we…"

"Savannah! Tammy and I are so happy to finally have you over. Aren't we, Tammy?" Lucy says staring daggers at her tactless offspring. "Give your Aunt Lucy a hug, baby!"

Savannah forces herself to hug her aunt. Not that she dislikes her. She loves Lucille Dupree and would do anything for her. She just can't understand for the life of her how her daddy's sweet baby sister had Lizzie Borden for a daughter.

"Hi, Aunt Lucy," she says.

"Hi, baby! Tamara, you remember Savannah." Lucy says pushing the two girls together. Dottie smiles at her daughter's distress. Frankie is beside himself with laughter but restrains himself admirably.

"Hug your cousin, Sis!" Frankie says with a grin. Savannah sneers at her brother's attempt at humor.

"Savannah," Dottie says looking to the Lord for relief. "Say hi to your cousin Tamara. Aren't you happy to see each other again? What's it been, now? Two years? My, how time flies!"

Two years.

It was only two years ago that the Duprees travelled south on one of Fredrick's business trips. Lucy brought the kids by the ranch to visit the Myleses while Fredrick stayed at the hotel. Little Freddie studied his music (Frankie conveniently had other plans) while Savannah took Tamara out to the stables to see Spirit - her new horse. Caleb Wright, a friend of the family and long time crush of Savannah's happened to stop by that day. Tamara unfortunately caught the eye of Savannah's young crush. He spent the entire time trying to impress the young diva from Chicago ignoring little Miss Myles. Savannah was heartbroken. She hasn't spoken to Tamara (or Caleb either, for that matter) since.

"Say hi to your cousin, Savannah!" Dottie says.

The two girls oblige their mothers but look past one another.

"Hi."

"Hmm…"

Umph! Silk dress and patent leather shoes, Savannah thinks to herself. *On a Saturday? …and why does this child have a ribbon in her hair? Going to the opera, Lady Jacqueline?*

Tamara looks her cousin up and down and then smirks.

Will you look at this child's hair? Tamara thinks. *Looks like a Brillo pad! Jeans and a t-shirt? In public? Looks like somebody's been cleaning out the garage. Helping Mama in the kitchen, Beulah?*

"Well," Dottie says after what seems like an eternity of silence. She hugs her niece and kisses her forehead.

"Tammy, your Aunt Lucy says you're a real whiz when it comes to English. We were so happy to hear that you were anxious to help Savannah with her test next week. Weren't we, Savannah?"

Savannah looks straight ahead. She's quiet.

"SAVANNAH!" Dottie almost screams. She pushes her daughter.

"Mama, my stomach hurts!"

"Get over it!" Dottie finally says.

"You have to push, Savannah?" Tamara smirks. "Is that it?"

Frankie covers his mouth. He knows if he laughs…

"TAMARA LUCILLE!" Lucy says admonishing the child. "THAT'S ENOUGH!"

"Mother…" Tamara protests.

"Enough, Tamara! Take your cousin upstairs. Now!"

Frankie hands Savannah her textbook.

"Don't wanna forget this," he teases.

Tamara takes the book from Frankie and opens it. She reads the inside front cover of the book and smirks.

"John Robinson Elementary? Isn't that a public school?"

Savannah bristles. She snatches the book from her cousin and rolls her eyes at her. Tamara smirks.

"UPSTAIRS, TAMARA! NOW!"

"OK, Mother! OK! You don't have to shout," Tamara says dismissing her mother. She turns toward the staircase and looks back at her cousin. "Follow me. Cousin!"

Frankie covers his mouth chuckling at his little sister's dilemma. Savannah punches her brother in the shoulder and licks out her tongue at him. She grudgingly follows her cousin up the stairs. Frankie shakes his head. He can't wait to tell his older siblings about today. Suddenly, he remembers why he agreed to come along.

"Aunt Lucy, where's Freddie?"

"Oh, I'm sorry, baby," Lucy says. "Freddie! Frankie's here, baby. Come on down!"

"Coming, Mother!"

Fredrick Dupree the fourth, as wide as he is tall, scampers down the Duprees' spiral staircase. Landing on the bottom step, he trips and runs smack into his Aunt Dottie. She falls against the wall and almost knocks over a planter. Frankie shakes his head at the poor boy. His mother Lucy is humiliated. She helps Dottie to her feet.

"What a spaz!" Frankie thinks to himself.

"Freddie, honey," Lucy says a little embarrassed. "What did I say about running in the house? Where are your glasses?"

"Upstairs, Mother."

"Oh, Freddie!" Lucy says. "Dottie, are you..."

"It's OK, Lucy. I'm all right," Dottie says regaining her composure. "Come here, Freddie. Give your aunt a hug."

"Kay!" the boy says lumbering over to his aunt. He gives her a big hug. Dottie tries to return the hug but can barely get her arms around the boy.

"Freddie's gained a little weight," his mother concedes sheepishly.

"No kidding!" both Dottie and Frankie say to themselves. Freddie cheerfully turns to his cousin.

"Hi, Frankie! Give me five!"

Frankie obliges.

"Up high!" Freddie says holding his hand in the air. Frankie slaps the boy's hand.

"Down low!" Freddie says holding his hand to his side.

Anticipating the little butterball's joke, Frankie obliges. He takes his time slapping Freddie's hand. Freddie gleefully snatches his hand away.

"Too slow!" Freddie shouts jumping up and down. 'I got him, Mama! I got him!"

Lucy, ever conscious of her son's 'geekiness' lets out a nervous chuckle.

"Yes, baby. Heh! Heh! You did. Uh, why don't you take Frankie upstairs and show him your room?"

"Okay, Mama!" Freddie says. "Walk this way, Frankie!"

Frankie watches his cousin walking ahead of him and imitating a runway model. Freddie looks back at his bewildered cousin and lets out a Curly Howard-type laugh.

"Nyuk! Nyuk! Nyuk! Like the Three Stooges! Right, Frankie? Get it! Get it! Walk this way, right? Ha! Ha! Come on Frankie, let's go upstairs."

Frankie looks at his mother. He turns and heads for the door but one look from Dottie stops him in his tracks. She does not want a replay of Tamara and Savannah. He reluctantly turns and follows his cousin upstairs.

"If this boy didn't have his own record player..." Frankie tells himself.

"That Freddie," Lucy says to her sister-in-law. "Always kidding. Ha ha!"

"Must be a handful!" Dottie says offering a sly reference to her nephew's weight.

"Uh huh! Just like Tamara!" Lucy says missing the reference entirely. Poor Lucy. Not a day goes by that her children don't embarrass her in some form or fashion. Why else would she have to arrange for her kids to have play time?

"Tea, Dottie?" Lucy asks. She directs her sister-in-law toward the dining room.

"Love some!" Dottie replies. "Walk this way!" she says imitating her nephew.

Lucy takes a playful swing toward her brother's wife. That swipe was loud and clear.

"Not funny, Dorothy Myles!"

"So I have to help you with your English," Tamara says as she sashays down the hall to her bedroom. "I guess being from Georgia puts you at a disadvantage grammar-wise! What's the name of your sleepy little town? Hop? Skip? How quaint."

"Look, Tammy!" Savannah yells as she follows Tamara to her room. She points her textbook at the pretentious girl to make a point. "I didn't ask to come here! And you got one more time to, to..."

"Oh, relax child," Tammy says dismissing her cousin. She opens the door to her room. "It's not like I care. Just making conversation."

Savannah stops just short of her cousin's room. She's motionless. Her book falls out of her hand and to the floor.

"Savannah? Savannah? Girl, are you okay?"

Savannah's in shock. The little Georgia peach sees something that, up until now she's only seen in the movies. Her cousin Tamara has a princess canopy bed – pink no less. Tamara's bed is adorned with matching pink pillows and a large pink comforter. Pink teddy bears of all sizes smile at Savannah from every corner of her cousin's immaculately decorated room. A silk robe (with matching slippers, of course) is draped over one of the bears sitting in a pink chair in the far corner of Tamara's room. Her pink bureau (the masses would probably call it a dresser) blends in perfectly with the teddy-bear themed wallpaper. In a corner adjacent to the window overlooking the street sits the little princess' vanity (pink, of course) with a lighted glamour mirror. A crystal chandelier hangs over Savannah's head. Savannah is awestruck. Her cousin's room looks like the inside of Barbie's dream house.

"This is your room? This is all yours?" Savannah gasps.

"Well, who else's would it be? Fredrick's?" Tamara says with a smirk. Tamara gathers her robe and slippers and heads for the closet. She opens the closet door.

Savannah gasps.

"OH MY LORD!"

"Do you play chess, Frankie?" Freddie asks anxiously. He runs to his closet and pulls out a chess set from the top shelf. He snatches the plastic wrap off the brand new box.

"I could teach you, Frankie!"

"No, thanks."

"How about Monopoly? I got crazy eights, dominoes…"

"Where's your record player, Freddie?"

"It's in the closet, I'll get it."

"Don't sweat it. I got it." Frankie retrieves the record player from the top shelf of his cousin's closet. He moves a few items from Freddie's desk and sets the record player down. Frankie dumps his 45's onto Freddie's bed.

"Hey, where's the disk?" Frankie says looking around.

"The what?"

"The disk. Little plastic thing. How else do you play your sides?"

"Sides? What are sides, Frankie?"

"Your 45's, Freddie!" Frankie says shaking his head.

"I don't," Freddie says. "All of my music comes on albums. "I got Mozart, Bach, Brahms. Beethoven, of course! We could play some while we play chess!"

Frankie shakes his head at his poor cousin.

"Like I'm gonna be caught dead listening to a bunch of old farts." He thinks to himself. *"This boy is such a nerd!"*

"You have so many sweaters!" Savannah says awestruck. "Cashmere!"

"Daddy purchased them for me on one of his many business trips to New York City," Tamara says. "I tell him to stop but you know how daddies can be. Anything for his little girl."

"*Lew-is Vit-ten...*" Savannah says reading the tag on the dress in her cousin's closet.

"That's *Louis Vuitton!*" Tamara says correcting her cousin. "I guess I shouldn't be surprised..."

Savannah, still awestruck hasn't heard a word her snooty cousin has said.

"It's beautiful..." Savannah says stroking the fabric.

"That old thing? Just something Daddy brought me back from Los Angeles. I keep telling him he doesn't have to, but..."

"OH MY GOD!" Savannah screams.

"What?" Tamara shouts. "What is it? Did you see a mouse?"

"YOU HAVE A PHONE!"

"Well, of course!" Tamara says relieved. "Doesn't everyone?"

Savannah picks up the phone. She's in total shock.

"A dial tone! It's real! My big sister Josie didn't get one until she was sixteen! Wowwww!"

"Of course it's real," Tamara says shaking her head. She watches as Savannah, mouth agape checks out her closet. She's speechless.

"*My poor disadvantaged little cousin,*" Tamara says to herself. *What does Uncle Jacob do with his money?*"

Sensing that she has the upper hand with her overwhelmed younger cousin, Tamara barks an order to Savannah.

"Brush, please!"

Savannah hurriedly looks around. She sees the brush – crimson, this time – on Tamara's bureau. She watches as her cousin has a seat at her very own vanity. Tamara reaches for the brush.

"I – I'll do it!" Savannah offers. She takes the brush and methodically brushes her cousin's hair, counting each stroke. Tamara notices Savannah in the mirror brushing her hair and watching her with awe.

"Um, Savannah," Tamara finally says. "How long are you gonna be here?"

"I don't know! Eleven, twelve ..." Savannah says dutifully counting the strokes. "Why?"

"Disk, please!"

Freddie reaches into his desk drawer for the adapter.

"Here it is," Freddie cries. "I always wondered what that was."

Frankie looks at his cousin and shakes his head pitying the clueless child.

"How in God's name did he make it this far?" Frankie asks himself. He snatches the adapter from his cousin, clicks it into his favorite 45 and places it onto the spindle. Frankie turns on the record player and places the needle into the outermost groove of the spinning disk. He breathes a sigh of relief, grinning like a man who was just rescued from a deserted island.

"Hey, Frankie," Freddie says. "You wanna play dominoes while we listen to music?"

Frankie turns up the volume on his host's record player. He then turns his back on the lad and practices his dance steps.

"How about Bingo?" Freddie asks.

Frankie drops his head and bops to his music. He has totally zoned out his poor cousin. Freddie, dejected and disappointed, plops anguished on the bed. He grabs a candy bar from under his pillow and buries the food in his jaws.

"Oh, my Lord. Look at the time! Time to go, kids! Frankie! Savannah!"

"Coming, Mama!"

After a few minutes, Frankie runs down the stairs. Freddie trudges behind him.

"Frankie," Dottie says. "Did you thank your cousin for inviting us over?"

"Huh? Oh yeah. Thanks, Freddie." Frankie tells him. He doesn't even bother to look his cousin's way.

"Did you have a good time, baby?" Lucy says hugging her son.

"I guess so."

"Savannah!" Dottie yells as she searches her purse for her keys. "Come on baby! Time to go!"

Silence.

"Savannah?"

"Coming, Mother…"

Savannah walks slowly down the Duprees' spiral staircase. She stops at the foot of the stairs waiting for her mother to look up from her purse and look her way.

"Well, Mother…"

"It's about time," Frankie says turning around. "Girl, what in the…"

Dottie looks up at her baby girl.

"SAVANNAH!"

"SURPRISE!" Savannah screams. With a southern accent to boot.

"Good Lord, Savannah! What have you done to your hair?"

"It's a perm, Daddy."

"I know what it is, Josie!" Jacob says incredulously. "I'm gone for two hours…"

"Jacob," Dottie says. "Have a seat. I'll get your dinner."

"Aren't you a little young for a perm?" Jacob asks. "Dottie!"

"Don't look at me, baby. I turned my head for five minutes, and poof! My daughter turned into Jacqueline Kennedy. In the flesh!"

"Savannah," L'il Daddy laughs. "I thought you said you wouldn't be caught dead with a perm."

"Yeah, Sis!" Josie laughs. "You said anybody who puts relaxer in her head wasn't down for the cause."

"Yeah!" L'il Daddy says mocking his baby sister. *"Only sellouts use relaxer."*

"It never hurts to look your best, Jacob. Jocelyn."

"Jacob?"

"Jocelyn?"

"Savannah…"

"Yes, Father?"

"Father?" Frankie frowns. "You sound like Tamara. I don't think I can take two of you."

"Well!" Savannah cries. She puts her hand on her hip - a sign of defiance to a family that just doesn't understand.

"Look at me, Savannah," her father tells her. "Now baby girl, this morning we had to drag you out of this house kicking and screaming to go see your cousin. Now…"

"Well, Father," Savannah says dabbing her chin with her napkin. She folds it and sets it on the table. "I discovered to my surprise that there are benefits to having a cousin like Tamara."

"Benefits?" Dottie says.

"Why yes!" Savannah says haughtily. "My dear cousin has travelled our great country extensively. Seen many of the great landmarks in this great land."

"Has she now?" Jacob says.

"Why yes!" Savannah continues. "The Duprees have dined in some of the finest restaurants Chicago has to offer. I understand her father has met the mayor. Isn't that exciting?"

"I suppose," Jacob says. He looks around at his family shaking their collective heads in disbelief. The family's revolutionary has been taken over by the devil's spawn, and her name is Tamara Dupree.

"Well," Jacob says. "Let's not forget the reason your mother took you to my sister's in the first place. How's the studying coming?"

"Oh fine, Father," Savannah says sounding like Scarlett O'Hara. "I'm gonna demolish that old test! You just watch."

The whole family looks at Savannah incredulously. The transformation of Baby Girl Number Two has left them flabbergasted. Jacob looks at Savannah. He then looks at his wife.

"Honey…"

"Let it be, baby," Dottie says anticipating her husband's anxiety. "It'll pass. Trust me. It'll pass. Pass the ketchup, sweetheart?"

"Mother," Savannah says. "You really should try horseradish. Tamara says…"

"I'll keep it in my mind," Dottie says interrupting the little princess. "Grace, Jacob. Please."

Over the next few days, Frankie and Savannah ride their bikes to the Duprees after school. Under her cousin's influence, Savannah becomes more indoctrinated in the ways of Chicago's very own Southern Belle, Miss Tamara Dupree. The children at John Robinson notice the change in Savannah. She wears a dress every day and sits in class brushing her hair. She even refuses to participate in her favorite sport – kickball. She doesn't want to ruffle her dress. Worst of all, Savannah pays little to no attention to her best friend Tamika Jefferson, whom she now feels is beneath her. The old Savannah has disappeared from the face of the earth.

Meanwhile, Frankie continues to pay regular visits to his Cousin

Freddie's; more so his cousin's turntable. Freddie's only permitted a few hours an evening to play it, of which Frankie consumes every minute. While Frankie monopolizes the record player, Freddie spends the time sitting on the bed playing chess with himself and devouring chocolate bars. No wonder poor Freddie has gained so much weight.

Wednesday, June 13th, 1962

"Hey, Mama! what's for dinner?"

"Boy, you know what's for dinner," Josie says. "It's Wednesday. Time for Mama's... Gimme a drum roll, L'il Daddy."

L'il Daddy beats the table.

"SPAGHETTIIIIII!" they all shout.

"All right, Mama." Frankie shouts.

"... *and* pork chops," Dottie says exiting the kitchen with a huge platter. "Don't forget the pork chops. Get the salad and the tongs from the kitchen, L'il Daddy."

"Yes, Mama."

"Jacob!" Dottie shouts. "Come down, honey. Time for dinner."

"Right here, baby," Jacob says taking a seat.

"Josie, fix your daddy a plate, please."

"Sure, Mama. Daddy, you look tired. How was work?"

"Not bad. Not bad. I'm learning the city at least. Where's Savannah?"

"You mean Scarlett O'Hara?" L'il Daddy says. "I passed her room. She's changing into her evening wear."

"Boy, please!" Jacob laughs.

"I'm not joking, Daddy. Wait'll you see Miss Scarlett!" L'il Daddy says impersonating Clark Gable. "She's ravishing."

The family all have a good laugh until they hear Savannah descending the staircase.

"Is she wearing heels?" Josie asks.

"She'd better not be!" Dottie says.

Savannah comes down the stairs and sashays into the dining room a la Tamara Dupree. She stops in the doorway to model her dress. Jacob gasps.

"Hey, look!" Frankie says. "It's Mary Tyler Moore!"

"Quiet, Frankie," Jacob admonishes his son. "Savannah, where did you get that dress?"

"Is that a Louis Vuitton?" Josie shouts. "Where did you..."

"From Tamara," Savannah says taking a seat next to Baby Terry. "She thought, well why not. I should look the part. Such a dear friend!"

"So she lent you her dress," Dottie says. "Savannah, this is too much. The dress goes back."

"But, Mama..."

"The dress goes back. Tomorrow!"

RINNGGGG!

"I'll get it," Dottie says. She gets up and heads for the living room. "...and take that off before you spill something on it."

"Daddy..."

"What?" Jacob says. "You heard your mother. Dinner will be here when you return. Pass the rolls, son."

Baby Terry passes the basket of rolls to his father. In doing so, he knocks over a glass of milk - right onto his sister and her new dress. Savannah jumps up from the table screaming.

"TERRY! YOU CLUMSY..."

"SAVANNAH!" Jacob admonishes her. "That's enough. It's not the end of the world. This is why I don't want you borrowing your cousin's clothes. Look at you."

"Well, I wouldn't have to if you had a job like Uncle Fredrick," Savannah says. "He can buy his daughter anything she wants. He has an important job while you drive a cab all day!"

Jacob drops his fork. Startled and shocked, he stares at his baby girl. Josie and L'il Daddy both fall back in their chairs. Frankie almost chokes. Terry, not sure what's going on but still hurting from his sister's berating of him starts to cry. Josie takes the lead.

"Uh, Daddy," she says. "I don't think..."

Jacob raises his hand signaling for his eldest to remain quiet. He stares again at Savannah for what seems like an eternity. Savannah looks around dumbfounded. She can't understand why everyone is so upset. Finally, Jacob gets up from the table and walks quietly upstairs.

"What did I do?" Savannah asks in her faux southern accent. "I just told it like it *t-i-tis!*"

"Are you nuts?" Frankie asks.

"Must be!" L'il Daddy says. "Do you know how hard Daddy works?"

"What is the big deal?" Savannah says dismissing her siblings.

"Quiet!" Josie says getting up from the table. "Upstairs!"

"Jocelyn…" Savannah pleads.

"NOW!"

"What is it, Savannah? Is it the relaxer? What?"

"What are you talking about?"

"That mess in your hair! Did that stuff seep into your brain?"

"Jocelyn…"

"How dare you talk to Daddy like that? Comparing our father to Fredrick Dupree? Fredrick Dupree? Have you lost your mind?"

"Oh, Jocelyn…" Savannah says turning away from her sister.

"Hush up, Miss Scarlet!"

"Miss Scarlet? Jocelyn, I resent…"

"Lose the accent, Savannah! *I'm* talking now! …and wipe that condescending smug look off your face. If you don't, I'll do it for you!"

Savannah starts to pout. Her bottom lip starts to quiver. She knows big sister means business.

"Jocelyn, why are you yelling at me?"

"I said lose the accent, Savannah. This family has had enough!"

Lessons Learned, Part 4—Mouths of Babes

"JOSIE! I – I don't know what came over me. Tamara said…"

"Tamara!" Josie says exhausted. "If I hear that name again…"

"I'm sorry, I – I…" Savannah looks in her sister's face and sheds a tear. She sits on her bed and starts crying. This is the baby sister Josie knows. Her heart melts.

"Honey, come here," Josie says sitting next to Savannah on the bed. She reaches out to her. "Talk to me, baby. What's this all about?"

Savannah shakes her head no.

"Savannah?" Josie says with a loving smile.

"Yes?" Savannah replies.

"You know you can talk to me."

"You'll laugh!"

"I promise I won't," Josie tells her sister.

Savannah looks up at Josie and then looks away.

"His name is Christopher."

"What?" Josie says pulling her sister back to face her. "*Whose* name is Christopher?"

"A boy in my class. Christopher Carlton Champion. He has brown eyes and curly black hair. Frankie doesn't like him. He called him a nerd 'cause he's in the band."

"Christopher Carlton Champion," Josie replies. "Boy, that's a mouthful! So you mean all this, the hair, the dresses, and that God awful accent…"

"You said you wouldn't laugh!"

"I'm not laughing, sweetheart! Savannah! I didn't know you even liked boys. Does he know you like him?"

"NO!" Savannah screams. "Not after what happened with Caleb…"

"Caleb? Caleb Wright? You mean freckle-faced Caleb Wright back home?"

"You remember Caleb?" Savannah says optimistically.

"Yeah!" Josie says thinking back and chuckling. "That boy had so many pockmarks they used to play connect the dots with his face!"

"YOU SAID YOU WOULDN'T LAUGH!"

"No, no sweetheart!" Josie says catching herself. "I'm not at laughing at you. I'm laughing at Caleb. Wait a minute! You and Caleb were boyfriend and girlfriend?"

"Yep! Me and Spots!" Savannah concedes. "...until Tamara Dupree showed up with her pressed hair and Lewis Vitten dresses."

"Louis Vuitton," her sister corrects her.

"He said he was coming over to see my new horse. I had my hair combed, new pair of jeans and everything."

"But the high society chick from the big city turned his head, huh?" Josie says.

"Uh huh..." Savannah says trying not to cry. "He made a fool of himself trying to impress Tamara."

"Boys are such idiots," Josie says supporting her baby sister.

"I thought if I could be more like Tamara..."

"...then this Christopher Champion would like you the way Caleb liked Tamara."

"He didn't even look at me!" Savannah says through her tears.

"Don't cry, baby."

"Okay," Savannah says wiping her eyes with her sister's sleeve.

"Look at me, Savannah," Josie says turning Savannah's cherubic face to hers. "You, my sister are the real deal! If this Christopher Carlton Champion doesn't like you for you, then he's not worth the space. Besides, the perm and the designer clothes... That's not you, sweetheart. People can tell when you're putting on an act."

"They can?"

"Sure! They figure if Savannah's not being true to herself, then how is Savannah gonna be true to them."

"But Tamara..."

"Tamara Dupree is another story altogether. She gets away with it 'cause she's been like that all of her life."

"I made a fool of myself trying to be like Tamara, didn't I?"

"Nothing that can't be fixed, honey," Josie smiles. "I wouldn't sweat it."

"My friends at school won't talk to me…"

"They'll be back," Josie assures her. "Give it time."

"For real?"

"I guarantee it."

"What about Daddy?" Savannah says wiping the tears from her face. "Daddy hates me."

"Savannah! How can you say that?"

"After what I did," Savannah says. She starts crying again. "I wouldn't blame him if he *never* talked to me again!"

"Savannah, stop! Baby, look at me! Nobody hates you. Especially Daddy!"

"But I compared him to Uncle Fredrick! He hates Uncle Fredrick."

"Daddy doesn't hate Uncle Fredrick."

"He doesn't?" Savannah says incredulously. "Could've fooled me!"

"Savannah, Daddy would never waste that kind of emotion on someone he doesn't even respect. He's not overly fond of the man. That's the truth. But he doesn't hate him. And I guarantee you. Daddy does not hate you."

"He doesn't?"

"Girl, please!" Josie says hugging her little sister. "Didn't you know?"

Savannah shakes her head no.

"You're his *second* favorite!"

The two Myles girls laugh.

"Savannah… Let me let you in on a little secret."

"What?"

"Do you know why Uncle Fredrick buys Tamara so much stuff?"

"He's scared of her?"

"What? No. At least I don't think so. Uncle Fredrick buys Tamara all those things to make up for the time he's away. I'm guessing for a man like Fredrick Dupree, it's easier to buy her things than to give her what she really needs."

"What's that, Josie?" Savannah asks innocently.

"Attention. Aunt Lucy loves her, but a girl needs her father, too. Didn't you tell me that when you went to see Tamara and Freddie, their father was hiding out in the garage?"

"Yeah!" Savannah says. "What was that about, Josie?"

"Hard to say. Fredrick Dupree is one strange bird. But I bet Tamara and Freddie wish otherwise. I can't imagine a parent who won't spend time with you. ...can't communicate. ...can't even say I love you on a regular basis."

"Me either, Josie," Savannah says. "We're lucky to have Daddy."

"I know that's right!" Josie says high-fiving her sister. Josie looks over at Savannah's display case. She picks up a picture of Savannah's horse from the bottom row.

"Hey, remember when you got Spirit?"

"Um hmm," Savannah says caressing the glass frame. "I still miss him, Josie. Daddy says he'll be alright without us."

"I miss him, too. I remember Daddy used to spend hours teaching you how to ride. He bought you your very own saddle, showed you the proper way to brush a horse. Daddy used to say he wanted his little equestrian to be the best Hopskip ever saw!"

Reminiscing about Spirit and the Saturday morning riding lessons brings a wistful smile to Savannah's face. Josie smiles, too. She puts the picture back in Savannah's display case. Savannah's favorite doll Rosa, named after Civil Rights activist Rosa Parks, sits on the top shelf. Josie points at her.

"Remember when she joined the family?"

"Kinda. Aunt Bree Bree gave her to me."

"Nope! Daddy."

"Daddy? I thought Aunt Bree Bree bought it."

"I'll let you in on another secret. Aunt Bree Bree did promise you a doll for Christmas, but was overseas and couldn't get it to you in time."

"Daddy?"

"Yep! He didn't want you to be disappointed come Christmas morning. Daddy and L'il Daddy traveled a hundred miles to Jessup County to get it."

"They did?"

"Um hmm. You see, they didn't sell colored..."

"Black!"

"Sorry, *black* dolls at the department store in Hopskip."

"They didn't? That's not fair. What did little girls like me do?"

"Nothing. It's what their daddies did. Aunt Julia told Mama about a store she knew that had a few of 'em left and that's all Daddy had to hear. He jumped in Ol' Goldie and took off. Got the last one, too!"

"For real?" Savannah says beaming.

"Oh yeah!" Josie says reminiscing.

"We got a good daddy!" Savannah grins.

"The best, baby girl!" Josie says. "The best!"

Savannah's grin disappears. "Only…"

"Only what, sweetheart?"

"Only how do I get Daddy to talk to me again? He was real mad, Josie."

"I wouldn't worry about it. Daddy never stays angry with his girls for long. Just those bean-head boys. Go talk to him. He always listens."

"'Kay," Savannah says. She hugs her sister. "Thanks, Josie!"

"No problem, Sis," Josie says returning the hug. "Only first, let me have that dress. I can get that stain out for you."

Savannah pulls off her dress and jumps into a pair of jeans and a t-shirt. She and Josie look at Savannah in the full-length mirror on the back of her bedroom door - courtesy of Jacob Franklin Myles. Her sister looks her up and down.

"Now there's the Savannah we know and love. Looking good, Miss Myles."

Savannah looks at herself in her mirror. Not a lighted one like Tamara's, but a good one just the same. She turns and heads for her father's bedroom.

"Thanks, Josie!" Savannah says stopping at the door. "I love you,"

"Love you more, baby girl!"

Savannah smiles and shakes her head no.

"Nahhh!" she says. "I doubt it."

Knock. Knock.

"Come in."

"Hi, Daddy."

"Hello, Savannah."

"Daddy, can I talk to you?" Savannah says looking at the floor.

"You can always talk to me, Savannah."

"Wow!" Savannah says to herself. *"Just like Josie said!"*

"Savannah…"

"Uh…Daddy, I…"

"Come closer."

"Sir?"

"Closer, baby," Jacob says. "I can't hug you way over there."

Savannah runs to her daddy and jumps in his arms. She hugs him – harder than she ever has before.

"I'm sorry, Daddy!" Savannah says crying.

"It's okay, baby girl," Jacob reassures her. "I know you didn't mean it. Have a seat."

"Yes, sir," Savannah smiles. She jumps on the bed and sits next to her father.

"Easy to get lost in all of that."

"Sir?"

"The sweaters and dresses. ...brand name shoes and purses," Jacob says referring to Tamara's wardrobe. "Personally I think she's too young for all that jewelry."

"You've seen Tamara's room?"

"Oh no! Your mother told me. She said a lot of the clothes still had price tags on 'em. Not like you to get overwhelmed by something like that, baby girl. What happened?"

"He doesn't need to know about Christopher," Savannah thinks to herself. *"If I know Daddy, he'll be sitting in the back row of all my classes!"*

"I know, Daddy," Savannah says. "Uh, Josie talked to me. It won't happen again."

"Oh? Well, I see no need in reprimanding you twice."

"Thanks, Daddy!" Savannah says relieved.

"... *however!*"

"What, Daddy?"

"Your mother and I went to the PTA meeting last night..."

"PTA?" Savannah says to herself. *"I smell trouble!"*

"Uh, Daddy you shouldn't go to those things. You work hard enough already."

"Savannah?" Jacob says holding back a smile.

"Yes, sir?"

"We had quite a talk with your teacher."

"You did?"

"Um hmm."

"Did she say I wouldn't have to take the test?"

"Hardly. Still scheduled for tomorrow. Are you ready?"

"Yes, sir!"

"Good!"

"Daddy, you look hungry," Savannah says jumping off the bed. "Let's…"

"Not yet! Now, Sister Adkins…"

"Sister?" Savannah says to herself. *"Oh, God! The lady goes to church. That means Daddy likes her. I'm doomed!"*

"Yes, Daddy…"

"Sister Adkins says you've stopped talking in class…"

"She did? That's a good thing, right? Let's eat!"

"…only because your recent behavior has alienated you from the rest of the class. Sit down and don't get up."

"Yes, sir." Savannah says. She takes a seat across from her daddy.

"Now, we're not upset with you, Savannah," Jacob says sternly. "Your mother took you to your Aunt Lucy's because she hoped that you and Tamara could become friends."

"Yes, sir."

Jacob smiles.

"If I knew you would become her evil twin, I would have never agreed to it. One Tamara Dupree in this family is enough. Get my drift?"

"Yes, sir!" Savannah chuckles. "I get it."

Father and daughter have a good laugh. All of a sudden, Savannah stops laughing.

"Wait a minute!" Savannah tells herself. She squints her eyes and then looks up at her father. *"I've been had!"*

Savannah jumps off the bed. She walks over to her parents' bedroom dresser. She turns around head tilted and glares at her bewildered father. She taps her right foot on the floor, folds her arms and looks her father squarely in the eyes while drumming her fingers on her elbow - much like her mom does when she knows something's not quite right. Jacob recognizes (and dreads) the gesture.

"What's wrong, Savannah?" Jacob asks cautiously.

"You and Mama sent me to the devil's lair?"

"Girl, what are you talking about?"

"I thought you sent me there to do homework! You sent me there to make friends with Tamara? Tamara Dupree? Daddy, she's Lucifer! The devil incarnate!"

"Looks like the old Savannah's back," Jacob says to himself. *"Lord, help us!"*

"Daddy, how could you? Do you know how close I was to becoming Tamara Dupree? I could've made a morphus and never come back."

"Savannah, please!" Jacob says. "...and the word is metamorphosis."

"Yeah, right. That!"

"Oh hush, girl," Jacob says hugging his baby. "You loved it over there. You went every day this week! Now granted, Miss Tamara has her issues but you can handle her. Right?"

"Well," Savannah says. "...with the Lord on my side..."

Jacob shakes his head. *"Lord, give me strength! This child is too much.!"*

"Anyway," Jacob continues. "...as I was saying. One Tamara Dupree in this family is enough. I want you to change your attitude. Give Tamara her dresses back. ...and wash that stuff out of your hair. Tonight!"

"It's a perm, Daddy! You can't just wash it out."

"Well, cut it out or something. I don't care what you do! I want my Savannah back! I think..."

"DADDY!"

"Come on, baby girl," Jacob says with a smile. "Let's get something to eat!"

"Okay!" Savannah says. "I love you, Daddy!"

"Not more than I love you!"

"You think so?" Savannah says running down the stairs.

"I know so!" Jacob laughs. "I know so!"

"Hi, Daddy," Josie says. "We put your plate in the oven. I'll get it."

"Thanks, baby."

"How's Miss Scarlet?" L'il Daddy chuckles reprising his Clark Gable impression.

Jacob raises his hand.

"No more of that, son. The old Savannah is back!"

"Yayyy!" they all cheer.

"Your mother's still on the phone?" Jacob asks. "Who's she talking to?"

"Aunt Lucy, I think," L'il Daddy says. "Sounds kinda heated."

"Really!" Jacob says.

At that moment, Dottie comes storming back into the dining room.

She has a seat next to her husband and looks at no one in particular. She folds her arms, drumming her fingers on her elbows.

"Not again!" Jacob thinks.

Dottie is beet red! The children all look at one another stunned. Finally, Josie approaches her mother.

"Mother, can I fix you a plate?"

"Don't bother!" Dottie says. "I can't eat right now! Finish your dinner!"

Dottie stands looking around. She grabs the salad tongs from the bowl in the center of the table. She grabs the bowl and slams it on the table in front of her. She vigorously begins mixing the already tossed salad. She tosses a few carrots in the air until one plops into Jacob's cup splashing milk onto his face. Baby Terry covers his drinking glass while the rest of the family covers their mouths at their daddy's dilemma.

"Dottie," Jacob says wiping his face. "Is everything okay?"

"How *dare* she!" Dottie says.

"How dare who, Mama?" "Frankie says trying to add a little levity to the situation.

"Quiet, son," Jacob says. "Dottie! What's the matter?"

"How dare she accuse my baby!" Dottie says pointing the salad tongs. "My baby would never…"

"Which one, Mama?" Josie says. "Accuse who of what?"

"Dottie, sweetheart. Calm down," Jacob says gently taking the tongs from his wife. "What happened with you and Lucy?"

"Your sister, my supposed favorite sister-in-law accused my baby of taking advantage of her child!"

"What, Savannah?" Jacob says. "Honey, didn't you say Tamara gave you those dresses…"

"I'm not talking about Savannah and Tamara!" Dottie says. "I'm talking Frankie and that roly-poly tub of lard, Freddie!"

"Wait! Wait! Now hold on, honey!" Jacob says. "Dottie, sit down and tell us what happened."

Dottie takes a seat next to Jacob. The children stop eating. They're rapt in their mother's tale of anguish and betrayal. Everyone that is, but Frankie who continues to slurp his spaghetti.

"Your sister had the nerve to say after all she did to show my babies some culture…"

"CULTURE?" Jacob interrupts. "That doesn't sound like my baby sister."

"You think I'm making this up!" Dottie shouts.

"Oh no!" Jacob says backing off. Jacob Franklin Myles knows full well that discretion is the better part of valor. Why fight the battle when you could lose the war?

"Tell us what happened, honey," Jacob says calmly.

"All she did for me! Hmph! All I did for her! Did she forget where she came from? You know that child practically lived at my house when her mother passed. I was like a mother to *her*! I taught her how to cook. How to clean. How to dress. *I raised her*!"

"Mama," Josie says.

"What?"

"I think Daddy means what happened *today*."

Brave girl. Hell hath no fury like a black woman who's been told to get to the point.

"Honey, sit down," Jacob says. "What happened?"

"Lu-*cille* Du-*pree* had the nerve to say that after all she did to bring our sons together...that Frankie...my baby ignored that fat little butterball Freddie! She claimed Frankie played his records and wouldn't let Freddie play his! She said all Frankie did was send Freddie back and forth for snacks! That Frankie wouldn't even play checkers with him! I told her little citified cultured tail that my son was raised better than that! My baby don't have to take advantage of nobody! My baby, uh, uh..."

Dottie, finally coming up for air looks at her family at the table. She notices everyone looking at Frankie. Jacob, L'il Daddy, and Savannah look at the boy askance. Josie's arms are folded (fingers drumming, of course) and looking at her little brother sideways. They know him. Even Baby Terry taps his fork on the side of the plate waiting for his brother to respond.

"Well?" Jacob says.

"Well, what?" Frankie says. "What did I do? Why's everybody staring at me?"

"Mama and Daddy have had enough drama tonight, Frankie!" L'il Daddy says. "Don't sit there like you don't know what's going on."

"Well, son," Jacob says. "Is it true? Did you take advantage of Freddie's hospitality?"

"Mama, Daddy, I know what you're gonna say."

"Oh, do you?" Jacob says.

"Um hmm," Frankie says wiping his chin. "I'm not apologizing. Pass the milk, L'il Daddy."

"Excuse me?" Dottie says. "Boy, do you realize I just had an argument with your Aunt Lucy over you? My best friend? I just defended you over something you actually did, and you won't apologize?"

"Mama, Freddie's a nerd," Frankie says. "All he does is play the piano and listen to garbage by some old white dudes. I betcha he's in the band, too."

"Boy, do you hear yourself?" Jacob says. "He's in the band. So what?"

"Daddy, everybody knows the band is full of nerds."

"Boy, are you crazy?" Josie asks. "Marching bands down south got some of the finest brothers – *on earth*. I can guarantee you they're not nerds."

"*Speaking from experience, Sis?*" L'il Daddy whispers to his sister.

"*Hush, boy!*" Josie says elbowing her brother.

"Can I be honest with you, Frankie?" L'il Daddy says. "Truth be told, Freddie has a better chance of making the big time than you do."

"What?" Frankie shouts. "He can't sing half as good as me?"

"Frankie, there are hundreds of thousands of singers looking for their big break," Jacob says. "Every street corner in Black America has 'em. Freddie plays an instrument and studies music. Possessing an extensive knowledge of music theory increases the odds that he'll make it."

"Did you know Smokey Robinson plays the piano?" Josie says.

"No," Frankie says sheepishly.

"Even I knew that!" Savannah chimes in.

"Did you know Ray Charles loves and plays classical music?" Jacob says.

"Ray Charles?" Frankie says incredulously. "Daddy, for real?"

"For real, son!"

"Okay," Frankie says. "Smokey and Ray Charles are good musicians but they're men. Freddie's a kid. He should be out playing baseball or something."

Dottie shakes her head. As usual, her middle child needs more convincing than the average bear. No problem. Frankie's loving family will not let him leave the table until he understands. Dottie takes her son by his shoulder.

"Come here, baby. Let me ask you something."

"Ma'am?"

"When do you suppose Smokey started singing?"

"I don't know."

"What about Ray Charles? When did he start playing the piano?"

"I don't know. Twenty? Twenty-five?"

"Twenty-five?" Jacob says incredulously. "Son, both those men started when they were children. Ray practiced every day. Smokey kept a lyric pad with him just in case..."

"Like me, Daddy?"

"Like you used to do, Frankie. What happened with that? I know you haven't given up."

"No sir," Frankie says sheepishly. "Just took a break, that's all."

"Frankie," Dottie says. "These so-called nerds you're making fun of. They're laying down some serious track for the future."

"Um hmm," Jacob says. "...and I bet they never took a break!"

Dottie nods her head.

"Frankie, I'm betting Mr. Robinson and Mr. Charles got teased by a few folks coming up themselves. Who's laughing now?"

"What's your point, Mama?" Frankie says with a little arrogance.

"Her point, young man," Jacob says grabbing Frankie gently by his arm. "Is that all your so-called heroes were just like your cousin Freddie - putting their heart and soul into their craft. You laugh at Freddie son, but chances are, and I don't say this to be cruel but L'il Daddy's right. Freddie has a better chance of making it than you do. I've never seen anyone so devoted to something he loves. Look at me, Frankie."

"Yes, sir," Frankie says.

"You could learn from your cousin."

"I guess I never thought about it," Frankie says.

"Think a little harder before you make up your mind about some-body you barely know. And Frankie..."

"Sir?"

"Give a listen to those old white guys. Some of 'em aren't half bad."

"Yes, sir."

"Frankie, baby," Dottie says. She takes his chin into her cupped hand. "All Freddie wants is a friend. Somebody he can play with. Tomorrow, I'll pick you and Savannah up from school. And I want you to apologize to Freddie. 'Kay, baby?"

"Yes, Ma'am."

"My little man," Dottie says.

Frankie blushes.

"Looks like everyone's finished," Jacob says looking around. "Why don't you all take your plates in the kitchen? Put the food away while your mother and I enjoy our meal."

"Okay, Daddy!" They all say. Josie gets up and holds the door to the kitchen while her four siblings take in their plates and silverware.

"I'll take out the trash, Daddy!"

"Thank you, Frankie."

Dottie watches as the last child, Savannah takes her plate into the kitchen. She winks at her daddy as she closes the door behind her. He winks back.

"Love you some Savannah, don't you?" Dottie says.

"Um hmm. Love you some Frankie, too!" Jacob says. "A whole lot!"

"What?" Dottie says.

Jacob touches his wife's hand. Apparently, he dismissed the kids so that he and Dottie could talk. He tilts his head expecting a response regarding the phone call.

"So, Dottie..."

"Nothing to talk about, baby," Dottie says anticipating her husband's thoughts. She's embarrassed enough about her talk with her sister-in-law. "Let's eat. ...wouldn't want the food to get cold."

Jacob sets his fork on the table. He folds his arms and drums his fingers on his left elbow. He squints his eyes, tilts his head and winks at his wife.

"Hmm! He does a great me!" Dottie concedes. *"...and Savannah."*

"So which one are you?" Jacob smiles. He gets right in his wife's face while she tries to eat. "Frieda Jackson or Earlie Carmichael?"

Dottie drops her fork. Recalling their conversation about the two battling women from church, Dottie drops her head. She can't help but smile.

"I can't stand you, Jacob Myles!" Dottie laughs. "Okay, okay! I'll talk to Lucy tomorrow."

"Okay, baby!" Jacob laughs. "Pass the salad, please. Gently, this time."

Thursday, June 13th, 1962

"Hey, babies! How was school."

"Fine!" Savannah says.

"Great, Mama!" Frankie says. "Hey, Mama! When are you gonna let me drive?"

"We're not in Georgia, Frankie," Dottie says. "...and this isn't your father's tractor. Be patient. You'll be driving before you know it."

"I can't wait," Frankie says.

"*I can*," Dottie says under her breath. "Savannah, baby. How was the test?"

"Good, Mama!" Savannah cries. "I passed!"

"Oh baby, that's wonderful. I guess the devil incarnate knows her English, huh baby?"

Savannah and Frankie both shake their heads.

"*Lord, have mercy,*" Savannah whispers to her brother. "*Mama and Daddy tell each other everything!*"

"*Um hmm!*" Frankie concurs.

"What was that?"

"Nothing, Mama!" the two say in unison. Savannah and Frankie giggle.

"Hey, Frankie!" Savannah says nudging her brother. "What were you talking to Christopher Champion about?"

"Christopher Champion?" Frankie chuckles. "You must be mistaken. Why would I talk to him?"

"Come on, Frankie. I saw you."

"What's it to you? Why do you care?"

"Huh?" Savannah says caught off guard. "Uh... No reason!"

"I don't talk to nerds, Savannah."

"He's not a nerd, Frankie. Why were you talking to...?"

"We're here!" Frankie yells. Frankie jumps out of the car and runs up to the Duprees' front door.

"Frankie, wait!" Savannah yells after him. "Wait!"

Frankie rings the doorbell. He looks back at Savannah and grins mischievously.

"Boy makes me sick!" Savannah says to herself.

"Savannah, what's the matter?" Dottie asks.

"Nothing, Ma," she says getting out of the car. Savannah grabs the bag with Tamara's dress. She's halfway up the walk before she realizes Dottie is still in the car.

"Aren't you coming, Mama?"

"Sure," Dottie says a little hesitant.

"Dorothy Myles, don't you make me come in after you!" Savannah laughs.

"Yep!" Dottie says to herself. "The old Savannah is back!" Dottie turns off the family car and gets out. Slowly.

"Right behind you, baby. Right behind you."

"Hey, Aunt Lucy! Freddie!" Savannah says running up the steps and inside the house. "Tammy! I got my test paper. Mrs. Adkins gave me an 'A'."

"That's my girl!" Tamara shouts. She high-fives her cousin and gives her a hug. Dottie and Frankie follow Savannah inside. Unbeknownst to the two friends, their mothers and brothers have yet to speak to one another.

"Let me see your test, Savannah," Tamara says taking the paper. "100 %! Girl, I knew you could do it. What's in the bag?"

Savannah pulls out her cousin's dress.

"Savannah," Tamara says. "You didn't have to bring it back. I gave it to you."

"It was a gift, Savannah," Lucy finally says. "Your mother wouldn't let you keep it?"

Dottie starts to tense up. In light of her promise to her husband, she remains civil to her sister-in-law.

"Jacob and I thought it was a little too much for a girl Savannah's age," Dottie responds. "Maybe next year."

Lucy rolls her eyes and turns away. Tamara takes the dress.

"Tell you what, cousin," Tamara says. "I'll pack it away until next year. I'll wear mine and we can be twins!"

Savannah gushes.

"Wow, Thanks, Tamara!"

"No sweat! Let's go upstairs."

Tamara and Savannah run upstairs arm in arm and in synch. As if they were from the same womb. Tamara stops her mid-way and lays a surprise on her.

"Girl, guess what?"

"What?"

"Daddy bought me a doll today."

"He did? Wow, is it your birthday?"

"No, but guess what?"

"What?"

"I made him buy two!"

"Two?"

"Yeah. One for me! ...and one for my girl!"

"Ooh, Mama," Savannah screams. She looks back at her bewildered mom. "Can I?"

"Uh, yes baby," Dottie says somewhat embarrassed. "But just for a little while. Your father's waiting dinner for us."

"Okay, Mama. Thanks!"

Dottie and Lucy watch the two new friends run upstairs. Dottie hears Savannah and Tamara giggling all the way. She looks at her sister-in-law and drops her head.

"I guess they're friends, now."

"I guess so," Lucy says with half a smile.

"Well, I brought Frankie over to talk with Freddie," Dottie says. "He has something he wants to say. Frankie?"

Frankie, quiet and pensive shakes his head.

"No, Mama," he says quietly.

"Frankie." his mother says. "I brought you here to apologize."

"No, Mama. I can't do it. It wouldn't be right!"

"WELL!" Lucy shouts. "I guess Savannah takes after her father's side!"

"EXCUSE ME?" Dottie says.

"It's okay, Mama," Freddie says. "I wanna go to my room."

Dottie takes her son's arm and swings him around. They're now face-to-face.

"Franklin Myles, you apologize this instant!"

"Mama... Freddie," Frankie says turning to his cousin. "Look, you're not a bad guy. We're family. Cousins. And I got your back. I can apologize today, but so what! What about other people? What happens when *they* walk all over you?"

"Frankie…" Dottie says still boiling from her sister-in-law's comment.

"Mama, please. Freddie, Cuz… Man, I can apologize all day long but nothing's gonna change unless *you* make some changes. You need to stand up for yourself. Stop being a punk, man."

"A PUNK?" Lucy shouts. "If this is what you call an apology, Dorothy Myles…"

"I can handle my own son, Lucille Dupree!" Dottie shouts. "Frankie, that's enough! Apologize! Now!"

"No, Mama," Frankie says. "Dr. Martin Luther King said *'Whenever men and women straighten their backs up, they are going somewhere, because a man can't ride your back unless it is bent'*. Nobody can ride you unless you bend over, Freddie. ARE YOU A PUNK, FREDDIE? HUH, ARE YOU A PUNK?"

"I'M NOT A PUNK!" Freddie shouts.

"Then stand up for yourself, Man!" Frankie says pushing the boy. "STAND UP FOR YOURSELF!"

Freddie, getting angrier by the moment, pulls off his glasses. Lucy and Dottie are stunned. Lucy walks over to her son and takes his hand.

"Freddie, sweetheart…"

"I'M NOT A PUNK!" he cries. With that Freddie swings. He punches Frankie square in the nose. Frankie falls to the floor. Freddie lunges at Frankie only to have his mother pull him back. Lucy's ecstatic. She's waited for this day for years. She's watched her son back down from bullies all his young life. She's happy but she can't let her sister-in-law know she approves. Poor Lucy's caught between doing a handstand and making her son stand in a corner.

Dottie, however, is nowhere near jubilant. Her son, her heart and soul is lying at her feet with a bloody nose. She picks him up. Remembering her talk with Jacob the night before, she tries desperately to restrain herself. She and Lucy stare at each other. She's always loved this woman and was thrilled when they became family. Now their children are fighting. How do they handle this without fighting themselves? Fortunately for the ladies, Franklin Joseph Myles has the answer.

"That's right, Freddie! My dog! My main man! Dog, you can fight!"

Both mothers, bewildered beyond words have the same look on their faces. Utter confusion.

"That's my man!" Frankie shouts. He holds up Freddie's arm the way a referee announces the winner of a championship bout.

"Mama!" Freddie shouts triumphantly. "I can fight! I can fight!"

"I'm sorry, champ," Frankie says hugging his cousin. "I took advantage of you. I shouldn't have..."

"That's okay, Frankie," Freddie says. "Hey! Mama bought me some records! I got Smokey, The Supremes... everything!"

"Wow!" Frankie shouts. "Yeah, man. We can listen while we play chess. Let's go!"

"Frankie," Dottie says. "Your nose..."

"Freddie, get Frankie some tissue from the bathroom!" Lucy says with a smile.

"Okay, Mama!"

"Hey, cuz?" says Frankie.

"Yeah, cuz!" says Freddie.

"We can play some Mozart, too! I heard he's the bomb!" Frankie laughs.

"Okay!" says Freddie grinning wider than all outdoors.

The two boys run upstairs to Freddie's room laughing and playfully punching one another. They slam the door behind them leaving their mothers in a confused but jovial state.

Dottie looks at her sister-in-law. Lucy, mouth still agape manages to speak.

"Did you..."

"Um hmm..."

"Can you...."

"Uh, uh!"

The two women fall onto one another laughing. They look at one another somewhat sheepishly. They both shake their heads and smile.

"Oh, Lucy! I'm so sorry..."

"No, it's my fault..."

"No. No. I should have never..."

"My kids drive me crazy!"

"Oh, me too sister-in-law! Me, too!"

"Would you like some tea, sister-in-law?" Lucy says taking Dottie's arm in hers. Dottie happily returns the gesture. She gives her a hug.

"Love some, sister-in-law!"

The women walk into the kitchen arm in arm laughing. Lucy mimics her son.

"Mama, I can fight! I can fight!"

Dottie joins in the fun.

"My main man! Got any of that Mozart? He's the bomb!"

"L'il Daddy. Josie. Set the table please."

"Yes, Mama."

Jacob, Dottie, and Baby Terry sit at the dining room table while Dottie tells her husband about her visit with the Duprees.

"So what happened next?" Jacob asks.

"…so these two fools run upstairs joking and playing."

"Um hmmm…"

"…punching each other. Frankie's bleeding all over the place…"

"Um hmmm…"

"Lucy's overjoyed that the boys are getting along. Tamara and Savannah…."

"Um hmmm…"

Dottie Myles, in recounting the day's events notices that her husband is just a bit too smug for his own good. She feels like setting him and his plate on the back porch. If only she didn't love him so much.

"I know that grin, Jacob Myles."

"What grin is that, Precious?"

"Oh hush up! Okay, I went overboard. You've had your moments too, Mr. Perfect."

"I have no idea what you're talking about."

"Oh, really?"

"Really."

"Okay, Jacob Myles," Dottie says. "Oh, Josie?"

"Yes, Mama?"

"Question for you."

"Ma'am?"

"Who was it decided his rifles needed cleaning whenever you had a boy over?"

"I'm not sure," Josie says placing a table setting in front of her father. She gives him a hug. "Does his name rhyme with 'Bacob'?"

"Ah, that was just a coincidence," Jacob laughs looking away.

"Coincidence?" Dottie laughs.

"Uh huh."

"Come here, L'il Daddy." Dottie positions her boy in front of his father.

"What's up, Ma?"

"Tell me, Jacob Myles," Dottie says pinching her son's cheek. "Was it just a coincidence when you were ready to jack up your best friend Johnny Hargrove when his son pushed your precious baby boy on the ground? In his new Easter suit?"

"When did this happen?" L'il Daddy frowns.

"You were all of four," Dottie says. "Your daddy pulled Mister Hargrove out of Sunday School to have a word with him outside."

"Wow, Daddy! You were 'bout to fight Mr. Hargrove over me?"

"No, son," Jacob says. "I wasn't. If you recall, Dorothy Myles... I only had a conversation with the man. We settled it like the gentlemen we are."

"Like gentlemen?"

"Yes, like gentlemen."

"Well, Mr. Diplomat," Dottie says with a grin. "I never mentioned it but Johnny's wife Daisy listened in on that so-called conversation between you and Johnny. He said you threatened to pull his heart out through his throat."

"Daddy!" Josie laughs. "You didn't? Is that even possible?"

"His heart through his throat?" Jacob stammers. "Dottie, I..."

"Daisy said if Johnny wasn't so easy going, he'd have thought you were serious. Actually, he got a good laugh out of it."

Jacob chuckles.

"Johnny was always a good friend!"

"Yes, he was!" Dottie says. "Family! Dinner!"

Savannah and Frankie run upstairs from the basement and join the rest of the family at the table. Savannah has her new doll. It's black. Looks like Fredrick Dupree isn't all bad.

Doorbell rings.

"Now who can that be?" Jacob asks.

"Oh! Frankie invited a friend to dinner," Dottie says. "I said it was OK."

"Carmen from next door?" Jacob asks.

"No, a friend from school," Dottie replies. "Frankie calls him C3. Get the door, Frankie."

"Yes, Ma'am." Frankie runs to the door. "Hey, man! Come on in."

Savannah, with her back to the door, pours herself a glass of milk. She doesn't even bother to look up when they enter the dining room.

"A friend of Frankie's huh?" Savannah says. "Well, don't let him sit by me? Whatcha bet he left his table manners at home?"

"Be nice, Savannah," Dottie says. "Hi, Frankie. Who's your friend?"

"Everybody," Frankie says entering the dining room. "This is C3. Christopher Carlton Champion."

Savannah fumbles with the pitcher upon hearing the boy's name. Josie, sitting next to her little sister grabs it just in time. She uses her napkin to wipe up the spill.

"CHRISTOPHER!" Savannah shouts. "WHAT ARE YOU DOING HERE?"

"Hi, Savannah," the boy says with a smile. "Frankie told me about his group. He said I could come by for dinner and then go over some steps. Are you in the group, too?"

"I – I was thinking about it…" Savannah stammers.

"I'll get some more milk," Josie says. "Nice to meet you, Chris!"

"Thank you," Chris says with a disarming smile. Savannah melts into her seat. While Christopher meets the rest of the family, Josie kisses Frankie's forehead before leaving the room. She gives her baby sister a thumbs up and mouths a message to her.

"He's fine, girl!"

Savannah grins.

"I saw you and Tamika playing kickball today, Savannah," Chris says. "You have strong legs."

"Strong legs?" Jacob says to Dottie. "What's he doing looking at her legs?"

"Thank you, Chris," Savannah says blushing. "Can I fix you a plate?"

"The boy can't fix his own plate?" Jacob almost shouts. Dottie pats her husband's hand – a signal that he's getting a little loud. L'il Daddy laughs.

"That would be nice!" Chris says. "Thanks!"

"Your plate, Frankie?" Savannah asks. Her way of saying *'I love you, brother'*.

"Sure, Sis!" Frankie says. His way of saying *'backatcha, Sis'*.

"Oh, now she's fixing Frankie's plate? Dottie," Jacob whispers. "What's going on here?"

"I'm not altogether sure," she whispers back. Dottie notices her daughter smiling broader than she has all week.

"Jacob?"

"Uh, huh?" he says watching Christopher like a young Mack Hodges.

"Do you think your rifles might need cleaning?"

Lightning, in a Bottle, Part 1—
You Just Don't Qualify

IT'S SIX AM in the Myles master bedroom. The alarm clock rings. Jacob was always the first to get up when they were living in Georgia so the clock was always on his side of the bed. He usually turned it off before disturbing his beautiful wife. Some mornings, Dottie would wake up and find her husband watching her sleep. This always made her day. This morning, however, Dottie finds herself reaching for the alarm, ostensibly to throw it out of the window. Reaching around in the still dark room, she touches her husband instead whose sitting restlessly on the edge of the bed.

"Jacob?" says Dottie. "Honey, are you up already? Jacob?"

"Oh, I'm sorry honey," he says turning off the alarm. "Lost in my thoughts."

She rolls over and kneels behind him. As with most wives who know their husbands better than they know themselves, Dottie can tell when something's wrong. She hugs him.

"What's the matter, baby?"

"You know, Dottie. They can send a man into space. Orbit the earth…"

"Jacob, you're not still …"

"…worried about my job? Yep!" says Jacob turning on the lamp next to the clock on the stand. "Or lack of one." He looks her way and points his finger at his wife.

"Your brother-in-law…"

"Oh, no! Fredrick Dupree is *your* brother-in-law," says Dottie getting up and walking around to Jacob's side of the bed. She sits next to her despondent husband. "I would never let any sister of mine marry *him*. He's *your* sister's husband, poor thing. Don't throw him off on me."

"I'd like to throw him *some*where." Jacob jumps from the bed and starts pacing the floor. "He promised me a job at his plant, that no good..."

"I know, honey," says an exasperated Dottie. "You've told me three times already. First when you came in last night. You couldn't even get your jacket off talking about it. Then all through dinner. You couldn't even stop to eat. I bet the children got a show they'll never forget. Then when we went to bed," says Dottie pulling her husband down on the bed and next to her. "Well, you were quiet then. For awhile anyway..."

"Dottie, please," says Jacob red-faced but smiling nonetheless.

"But after that..."

Dottie lowers her voice and paces the floor mimicking her husband.

"That no-good, pointy-headed imbecile – lying to everybody about his so-called connections. Everybody at that plant cafeteria was laughing behind his back. Boy if I could just..." she says balling her fists and swinging at an imaginary punching bag. "Dottie, he's just a figurehead. He can't do nothing for nobody. Puppet on a string, Dottie. Puppet on a string!" says the animated Mrs. Myles dancing like Charlie McCarthy, the television marionette.

"Well, now you had me until then," says Jacob staring at his wife and pulling her down on the bed beside him. "I don't recall dancing around like one of Edgar Bergen's dolls. You do that well, by the way."

"Sorry, baby. You know how easy it is to get carried away when you're telling a story," she says winking an eye at her husband.

"Okay, okay I get your point," says Jacob smiling at his wife. Dottie chuckles, sighs, and then rests her head on her husband's shoulder. They sit silently until Jacob jumps up and bellows.

"...and did you know he only got *his* job to keep the picketers off the front gate? He only got it because the Negro workers were protesting and..."

"Aaaargh!" screams Dottie.

"What's wrong?" says Jacob with a puzzled look on his face. He sits next to Dottie on the bed. "Did I tell you this already?"

"Oh no, Jacob," says Dottie sarcastically. "This is my first time hearing it! Please tell it again!" Dottie starts laughing.

Jacob throws his head back and laughs along with his wife. He grabs her hand. "Oh, my Lord! I needed that. Thanks, baby."

"For what?"

"For lightening the load honey," Jacob says kissing Dottie on the cheek. He puts his right arm around his wife and then takes her left hand with his own. He looks down and then back at Dottie.

"Honey, the money my brother Joseph sent us, for my half of the ranch – it's running out. The last thing I wanted to do was give up my half of the ranch…"

"You did what you had to do, honey."

"I know, I know. Driving a cab a few times a week won't put the kids through college. If I don't find something soon…"

"Oh, you will, baby. You will. I have faith…"

"…in God?" interrupts Jacob turning his head away.

"Oh that goes without saying," replies Dottie turning her husband's head back her way and kissing him. She then stands. She goes over to the other side of the room and takes a rolled up pair of socks from the chifferobe her talented husband built for them.

"I have faith in *you*, Jacob Myles." Dottie stands in front of her husband. She cups her hands over her mouth as if making an announcement to a crowd of people.

"Ladies and Gentlemen, now approaching the pitchers' mound for the Mavericks. Hopskip, Georgia's greatest living pitcher, Jacob 'Lightning' Myles," says Dottie harking back to the old days when her husband pitched for the local Negro team. "Lightning Myles, a fan favorite…"

"Dottie, please!" says Jacob almost blushing.

"Lightning Myles takes the mound. Oh, oh," says Dottie. "He appears to be signaling to his *backcatcher*."

"Catcher, baby, catcher! Why do women always say *backcatcher*."

"Catcher, backcatcher! Whatever! This is *my* story. Okay?"

"You have the floor, Mrs. Myles."

Dottie now takes the stance of a baseball pitcher. She bends over at the hip and puts her hand with the balled sock behind her back. She looks Jacob right in the eye. She frowns comically as she mimics a pitcher 'signaling' to the catcher.

"Are we staying in Hopskip?" says the ersatz pitcher. She responds to her own question by shaking her head no as a pitcher would to his teammate behind the plate. "Am I letting my man go to Chicago alone?" She shakes her head 'no' again but this time more vigorously. "Do I have faith… in my man?" she says slowly. "…as a husband, and a provider… for me and our children, as God intended?" Dottie nods emphatically. It's a big YES. She winds up and fires the rolled up 'sockball' with all her might. Daydreaming and a million miles away, Jacob catches the 'ball' without even blinking. Apparently, the ex-pitcher's still got it. He's obviously on cloud nine reminiscing about his younger days on the baseball diamond he used to call home.

"You sure looked good in that uniform, Lightning!" says Dottie.

"Was I sweet, baby?"

"Oh, you were dripping honey!"

The two of them laugh. Dottie sits back on the bed.

"Jake, the Mavericks always called on you in the last inning to clean up. They depended on you and you never let them down. Your wife and your loving children came to this cold, windy, city by the lake, Jacob Myles" says Dottie almost crying. "…because they have faith in you. You never let us down. We love you."

Jacob stands up and smiles at his wife. If there was no light in their darkened bedroom ten minutes ago, there's more than enough now. Even with the shades drawn, she's generated enough light in his once dismal soul to light up a hundred rooms. He beams as he starts to recall all the reasons he married this woman; and not one why he wouldn't have. He grabs her and kisses her so hard she's almost off her feet.

"You know, Dottie. You haven't called me Lightning in years." He starts to lean back toward the bed. "How 'bout you and me…"

"Uh, uh Lightning," smiles Dottie gently pushing Jacob away. She grabs her robe from the hook on the door. She ties her robe while she playfully admonishes her husband.

"None of that. Not now anyway. Besides", she says patting her husband's tummy, "you need your strength. You hardly ate last night."

Dottie looks off to the side smiling and heads toward the bedroom door.

"Family! Time for breakfast!" she yells heading toward the hallway. Jacob ties his robe and follows his wife. He catches up with her, pinching her bottom. She tries to contain a mild shriek but breaks into laughter instead. She playfully taps her husband's arm as they head downstairs hand in hand.

Saturday morning breakfast with the Myles clan is like watching a well-orchestrated ballet. Everyone has a role to play and they do it flawlessly. Dorothy Myles, matriarch, master chef, and hostess extraordinaire treats every one of these breakfasts like a royal banquet. Every Saturday, since she and Jacob were married, Dottie has brought out the lace tablecloth that Mother Harris received from Dottie's grandmother when she married. Except for a spot in the center of the cloth (which the lady of the house covers with a religious centerpiece), Dottie has managed to keep it neat, clean and without a tear. Not an easy task while feeding five kids and one hungry husband. Everyone in the Myles family has their own table setting; a plate, a saucer, a bowl for fruit or cereal, a glass for juice or milk, a fork, a spoon, and a knife. The adults also have coffee cups. Four-year-old Terry has two spoons; something he insisted on having since his mom wouldn't let him have a knife. He also has the distinction of drinking his juice from his very own Flintstone mug. Juice seems to go down easier with Fred and Barney. After Dottie and Frankie set the table, Mrs. Myles selects the meat.

When the family was in Hopskip, Dottie's Saturday morning feast started with chicken – fresh from the coop. "Chase that yard bird," she said. "Snap its' neck, pluck it, clean it, cut it up, and toss it in that hot grease before it wakes up!" she jokes. "The only way to cook a good chicken. Oh, and keep a hammer nearby. Just in case." Dottie loved regaling her city friends with her barnyard exploits. Those who weren't squeamish always came back for more. Now that the family has moved north, preparing breakfast has become less adventurous - it's bacon, ham, or sausage. Fresh from the butcher.

Dottie fries the meat. She uses an old cast iron skillet, an heirloom from Mother Harris that she salvaged from the trip north. This Saturday morning, it's bacon. Two strips for everyone. She adds a little brown sugar to it. She thinks no one knows her secret. Every southern cook south of Tennessee and above knows that little trick. Except Dottie adds one other ingredient. She puts in a little…

"Frankie, how do you want your eggs?" says oldest daughter Josie.

"Cooked, of course," jokes her little brother.

"Cute, Frankie, cute. You should be on Ed Sullivan," Josie replies. Josie prepares the eggs. She wears the same apron she wore as a little girl, though no longer stepping on its' straps. She's prepared eggs for the whole family since she was ten, sometimes utilizing a hot plate kept on the counter. Watching her baby girl prepare three types of eggs in three skillets at once gave Dottie bragging rights at Big Mama's Hair Emporium back home in Hopskip, Georgia. Scrambled, fried, or over-easy, "Short Order Josie" has yet to burn the hen fruit. On Sundays, she fixes pancakes with her eggs while mom gets the little ones ready for church.

"Did Daddy say what he wanted for breakfast, Mama?" asks L'il Daddy.

"Oh, the usual," says Mother Dottie. "A little bit of everything. Try not to burn anything this time," she jokes.

"Ma, please!" he answers.

L'il Daddy makes the oatmeal and/or toast, depending on what each family member prefers that day. He fixes the toast in the oven and the oatmeal on the top back burner. He thinks that particular burner gets hotter than the others. At one time in his young life, Jacob Jr. wouldn't be caught dead near any kitchen appliance. "Women's work," he would say scornfully watching his mom and sister. After his dad informed the little chauvinist-in-training that some of the best chefs in Europe are men, he decided that the kitchen wasn't such a horrible place after all. L'il Daddy cooks almost as good as his mom, though you won't catch him bragging about it in the locker room at school. L'il Daddy hasn't even **singed** the toast in years and big sister Josie no longer compares her brother's oatmeal to Plaster of Paris. Those European chefs would be proud.

Each cook has timed his/her individual preparation to the nanosecond. By doing this, everything is ready at the same time so that all the food is hot and ready when the family sits to eat. Imagine. Three cooks on one stove (and a hot plate) all at one time. How the three of them can work at the one appliance without scalding or burning themselves; or even one another baffles even Jacob. Talk about synchronization.

"What'll you have, L'il Daddy?" says Savannah.

"Coffee, Savannah. You know me and Daddy always drink coffee."

"Since when?" says Dottie. "Give him orange juice. Boy gets a piece of a mustache..." Dottie mumbles to herself.

Savannah is in charge of liquid refreshment. There's always milk and the three juices; apple, cranberry, and orange, in the Frigidaire. She takes everyone's drink order and pours 'til they say stop. The younger children drink apple juice and milk. Josie likes cranberry while L'il Daddy drinks orange juice. So do his parents. Dad likes the new fresh frozen concentrate. Dottie prefers fresh squeezed. No doubt the only thing on which the two disagree. Savannah keeps glass pitchers of the different drinks on her side of the table in case anyone wants seconds. Dottie (using Josie's hotplate) brews the coffee in an old pot she got from her Nana Yvonne as a wedding gift nearly twenty years ago. If Savannah's careful, she gets to pour the coffee, too.

Frankie scavenges the Myles home for chairs for the feast. The last tenant left a kitchen table with four chairs. Since a lot of their kitchen furniture was left down south after the move, the family uses a few chairs from the dining room. Frankie likes the barstool his Dad bought for the basement. Jacob and Dottie found most of their kitchen furniture (including the barstool) in an open-air market on Maxwell Street near Chicago's downtown Loop area. It is said that when Jacob negotiated an unbelievably low price for the untagged items, he and L'il Daddy hurried the pieces out to the borrowed pick-up before the proprietor changed his mind. On Saturday afternoons, the barstool is used by Jacob when he cuts the boys' hair; a practice at which he's grown quite adept these days in his attempt to save the family money. This Saturday, however, Jacob will drop Josie off at her job at the *Breakfast Nook* after breakfast, and continue his search for employment.

Even Baby Terry performs his task with ease. He says grace. Actually, Jacob says grace. Little Terry mouths his dad's every word in synch and almost as flawlessly as the rest of the family does in preparing their buffet of love.

Everyone is seated.

"Let's say grace," says Jacob. They all bow their heads and clasp hands while Jacob petitions the Lord on the family's behalf.

"Amen," say both Jacob and the little parrot sitting next to him. "Mmm. Everything looks good. Everybody ready to eat?"

"Yessss!" "Yes sir." say the children.

"Coffee, Daddy?" says Savannah already pouring the brew.

"Thank you, honey."

"Fix up your toast, Daddy?" says L'il Daddy reaching for the butter and jelly.

"Please. Butter the baby's too, son" says Jacob. "Only one slice for me though, I'm not that hungry," says Jacob unconvincingly.

Dottie can see that the love of her life is making sure that the kids are fed first. Just one more reason why she's still in love after twenty years.

"Now, now Jacob," says Dottie slipping him one of her strips of bacon. "You need your strength. You have a big day today."

"Thank you, sweetheart," says Jacob beaming recalling the last time she remarked that he needed his strength.

Savannah, who likes her bacon crisp, breaks one of her strips in half. She surreptitiously passes the half strip around the table by way of Frankie, her brother, and partner-in-crime who sneaks it onto their father's plate. Savannah crumbles the rest of her bacon and sprinkles it onto her oatmeal. Unbeknownst to all, Baby Terry has slipped his own piece of the brown sugared concoction into his daddy's jacket pocket.

Everyone quietly eats their meal. Dottie feeds the baby a slice of toast. L'il Daddy is reading George Orwell's *1984*, a novel for his English Lit class while Josie devours a pamphlet for a nursing school she wants to attend downtown. Savannah thumbs through a copy of Jet magazine. The issue is two months old but the Myles' little *'Rosa Parks in pigtails'* never tires of reading about Adam Clayton Powell. *'You don't find too many activist/heartthrobs'*, she's been known to say. Of course, not around Jacob. Frankie, finishing his SuperSpy comic book and his breakfast before everyone else, decides to break the silence - a decision he later regrets.

"How's the job hunt, Daddy?" says Frankie absentmindedly. "Did you talk to Uncle Fredrick?"

"FRANKIE!" shouts Josie and L'il Daddy in unison. Dottie, dropping the baby's toast, heaves a sigh of dread preparing her for a repeat of last night's tirade by her beloved. Savannah shakes her head at Frankie as if to say *'you're gonna get it now'*.

"Where were you last night, big mouth?" says Josie.

"I'll tell you where he was." says Savannah. "He was listening to his transistor radio at the table again."

"Was not!" says Frankie.

"Was too!" says Savannah.

"Was not! Was I Josie?" Frankie replies dolefully looking to Big Sis for help.

"Yeah, you were." she says nonchalantly without looking up from her eggs. "Someone pass the hot sauce."

"Don't worry about Uncle Fredrick, Daddy." says L'il Daddy slapping Frankie's head. "Us Myles men have always made it on our own. You don't need him. Right y'all?"

"Right!" they all say.

"Amen to that." says Dottie.

"Amen." echoes little Terry.

"Must be true if Terry says so, Daddy!" says L'il Daddy.

They all laugh.

"A toast!" says Savannah lifting her glass of apple juice. "To our Dad!

"Wellll!" says Josie taking the family to church.

"He's hipper than…" Savannah pauses and then raises her magazine. "Ooh! Adam Clayton Powell!"

"Tell the truth, l'il sister!" Josie says waving her hands in the air. "Tell the truth!"

"Tougher than '*Big Brother*,' says L'il Daddy raising his novel.

"Say it my brother, say it!" says Josie pointing at Jacob, Jr.

"…and cooler than, *Ooooohh!*" says Frankie getting from his seat, twirling around and singing in falsetto. "My man Smokey Robinson!"

"Yaaay!" they all laugh and shout.

"Fred Flintstone!" chimes in Baby Terry holding up his mug.

The rest of the family lifts their individual glasses and cups. Frankie lifts two.

"Well, Lightning," says a smiling Dottie. "It's unanimous."

Jacob nods in accord. He is visibly moved. A man not easily frightened by the evils of the world, Jacob Myles chokes up when publicly embraced by the spirit of love. He clutches his coffee cup. He looks at the six beautiful, adoring faces smiling and winking his way. Talk about a Kodak moment. He smiles at his wife. Evidently, he and Dottie did something right!

"Backatcha!" says Jacob lifting his cup and smiling broadly. "Besides, who needs that pointy-headed…?"

"Jacob!" reprimands his wife. She shakes her head and throws him a quick smooch.

Everybody laughs. The boys slap one another five.

"Ooh, Daddy!" says Josie looking at the clock on the wall. "We have to go. I don't want to be late for my appointment." She finishes her juice, gets up and hugs her little brother Frankie; her way of atoning for leaving him drifting in the wind seconds ago when he begged for her support. He smiles at his big sister.

"Right behind you, baby girl. L'il Daddy?"

"Sir?"

"You and Savannah clear the table when you're finished. Terry, you're in charge while I'm gone."

Baby Terry looks at his dad and laughs.

"And you, Mister Robinson…" says Jacob getting up and grabbing his jacket from the back of the chair.

"Yes, Daddy?" Frankie responds.

"Leave the transistor in your room."

"Yes, sir." Jacob rubs his son's head. They smile at each other. Jacob kisses Dottie and the baby goodbye and waves to the others as he and Josie head for the door. "Love you!"

"Backatcha!" they reply.

"Oh, and Savannah," says Jacob winking at his baby girl. "Loved the bacon; nice and crispy, like I like it".

Jacob and eldest daughter Josie arrive downtown at the Amlin School of Nursing. She plans on registering for classes to become a Licensed Practical Nurse like her Aunt Julia – maybe even a doctor. Julia Chapman Myles, Jacob's brother Joseph's wife was a bit of a celebrity back home. She was offered a job in a hospital on the white side of town back in Hopskip. She would have been the first but she turned it down. Julia was offered a considerable raise in pay too, but she said no. '*Her people came first.*' Josie learned from her aunt that money means nothing if you're not happy with the person looking back at you in the mirror every morning. After Josie has finished her meeting with the administrator, she'll walk over to her job on State Street where she waits tables at *The Breakfast Nook*.

"Get me a paper, honey," says Jacob pointing at a newsstand. "I want to check the want ads."

Josie exits the car and grabs a copy of the Sun-Times from a nearby newsstand. She offers to pay but the young man at the stand says no.

He asks Josie her name. Josie smiles and begins a conversation with the young man until the dungeon master that is her father yells from the car.

"Jocelyn, leave the money on the stand," Jacob bellows. "Get back in the car".

Jacob reminds his impressionable daughter when she gets in the car that nothing is free. He doesn't like the look of the young man anyway. He left Georgia to get his daughter away from lecherous scalawags like him but apparently they have a nationwide brotherhood.

"Fathers", says Josie to herself with a smirk.

"I know that look," says Jacob, self-proclaimed *'King of all Fathers'* and protector of fickle daughters everywhere. "...and I know that look on *his* face, too. Wouldn't be the first pimp disguising himself as a paperboy. Pointy-headed..."

"Here's your paper, Daddy," says Josie interrupting her father before he starts his rant. "Actually, we should have waited until tomorrow," says Josie holding back the newspaper. "The want ads section is much bigger. I guess more people pick Sundays to look for work, huh?"

"They *should* be in church. Paper, please." His daughter hands him the paper.

"Oh, and here's your resume," says Josie thumbing through her new attaché case. "It gives you that professional look for your interview. You really should let me punch this baby up for you", says Josie holding the document.

"This is fine, baby girl," says Jacob. "Thanks". She hands him her lovingly typed document in a neat yellow manila folder.

"Daddy," says Josie apprehensively. "Can I ask you a question?"

"Can I stop you?"

"How come you never finished school? You're the smartest man I know. You read all the time. You know the answer to everything. You could have easily..."

"Baby, these things happen," says Jacob regretfully. "I dropped out of school when the ranch became too much for Papa Myles to handle. Your Uncle Joseph was only a few months from graduating so it was left up to me. The following year I married your mother. You came along right on time, pretty as a button; then your brother. After that, it just made sense to keep working the ranch. I never found the time to go back. Don't *you* make that mistake, baby girl! I see great things ahead for you, your brothers; little Savannah. Times are getting better for Negroes but we have to be ready for it. Nobody's gonna just hand it to you and I wouldn't want it if they did."

"You're right, Daddy," says Josie. "Times *are* changing for us, so don't you think…"

"…and speaking of time, you have an appointment to get to," says Jacob interrupting what he knows will be a lengthy speech from his daughter turned lecturer. "You better get going. See you at home."

"Okay, Daddy!" says Jacob's eldest resignedly. "See you at home." Josie kisses her father on the cheek and exits the car. "Good luck, Daddy," she yells over her shoulder.

"Thanks, and stay away from that news vendor!" Jacob jokes trying to lighten the mood.

Josie smiles and waves at her dad as she walks toward the school. Jacob quickly notices the vendor walking toward her. He leans so hard on the horn that the young Lothario drops his papers. Jacob watches his baby girl until she's in the building. He's now eye-to-eye with the vendor as he slowly pulls away. The vendor laughs half-heartedly trying to regain some dignity only to drop his papers again. Jacob smiles and takes off.

Round 1 – Jacob Myles, King of all Fathers and Eradicator of Wannabe Pimps everywhere.

Jacob Myles has always missed the tranquility of life on the farm. Caring for the ranch and the family farm kept his family away from city life and the 'slicksters' he abhorred. The closest semblance to those rolling hills and farmland (in his mind, anyway) is the many parks that dot the city's landscape. Since he was near the Loop, he drove himself to Grant Park to relax his mind and read his paper. Although a painful reminder of the life he had to leave that he shared with his brother Joseph and his family, the park is still a friendly and comparatively quiet place where Jacob could go and collect his thoughts. It is here that he decides to scope the want ads and continue his search for work.

"This looks like a good spot," thought Jacob to himself as he throws his jacket on the park bench next to an empty baseball diamond. Just as he was about to sit down, a ball rolls on the ground towards him and lands at his feet. He scoops it up instinctively expecting the orb to be a baseball thrown from the diamond behind him. He looks around for a kid with a baseball glove but is surprised instead to see an officer with a police dog. The young officer signals for Jacob to throw the ball. He complies but to his surprise, the policeman stands still. The police dog sitting at the officer's feet watches the ball as it sails over their heads. Jacob watches with a smile as the young officer beckons the reluctant canine to go after the ball. The dog refuses to budge. Jacob smiles and returns to the park bench to read the want ads.

Preparing to circle an ad that interests him, Jacob searches his pockets for a pencil. He finds instead the bacon strip that baby Terry dropped into his dad's pocket at breakfast. Jacob is initially surprised but remembers that with five children in the house, nothing is beyond reason.

Jacob waves the newly found treat in the dog's direction. The dog, a German Shepherd named King, runs over as if he's known Jacob all its' young life.

"Sit!" says Jacob. King immediately obeys. Jacob snaps off a piece of the bacon strip and stuffs it in the obedient hound's jaws.

"Jump, boy! Jump!" commands Jacob holding another bit of the treat inches above the dog's nose. King leaps into the air three times. He grabs the bacon bit in its' mouth on the third try.

"Shake hands, boy! Walk! Rollover! Stay!" commands Jacob as the submissive pooch responds to his every command. Jacob gives King the last piece of pork and rewards him with platitudes he honed while training hunting dogs on his father's ranch. "Good boy! Good boy! Who's a good boy, huh?" says Jacob as his new best friend licks his face.

Unbeknownst to Jacob, a crowd has gathered around him and the now obedient German Shepherd. Many of the onlookers start to clap. Another officer has joined the first and the two walk over to Jacob who's now returned to the bench where he's laid his jacket and newspaper. King sits at the feet of his new master oblivious to the two approaching officers.

"Amazing. Absolutely amazing, Mister...?"

"Myles. Jacob Myles," responds Jacob arising from the bench and shaking the young officer's hand.

"Officer Madison," says the young man still beaming after the floor show Jacob put on for the park and its' denizens. "Alfred P. This is Officer Ballotti."

"Carrie," says the policewoman. "Myles, I'll get right to it. Would you happen to be interested in working with the Chicago Police Department?"

Working. The word resonates with Jacob like a gong in one of those Saturday morning cartoons he forced himself to watch while caring for Baby Terry. The word is barely out of the officer's mouth before a usually reserved Jacob Myles responds in the affirmative.

"Yes, I would," he responds smiling broadly.

Officer Ballotti describes the position to Jacob. The Chicago Police Department is looking for experienced men and women for its' K-9 unit to train dogs. The animals will be used to sniff out drugs, a growing problem in Chicago, and accompany officers on their beats. Jacob is ecstatic. Not only will he be doing something he loves – working with animals, he'll be out in the open; taking in the fresh air. God's sweet breath, he calls it. Jacob secretly wished for a job outdoors. He hated the thought of sitting at a desk all day doing paperwork. Most important, he can put his fears about having to return south to rest.

"Here's my card," says Officer Ballotti. "The address is at the bottom. Ask for Mr. Daniels. He's working today. I'll give him a call; let him know you're coming. They're real anxious to hire someone".

"I don't doubt it," muses Jacob to himself as he watches young Officer Madison fall to the ground entangling himself in the playful dog's leash.

"Thank you!"

Jacob arrives at the address on the card given to him by Officer Ballotti. There's a parking space right in front of the building. Jacob jumps out of the old station wagon with his jacket in one hand and resume in the other. He reaches into his pocket for change for the parking meter. There are still thirty minutes left on it. He takes this as a sign from God.

"Could things go any better?" thinks Jacob as he runs up the courthouse stairs to see the interviewer.

The interviewer's office is on the third floor. Jacob's in such good spirits he takes the stairs – two steps at a time. Not bad for a father of five who's pushing forty, Jacob assures himself. O. H. Daniels, according to the foyer directory is in Room 309, last door on the left. Jacob sprints toward the end of the hall almost dancing. He opens the door to see a balding, fifty-something-year-old male hovering a flower pot on the window sill.

"Hello!" says Jacob. "I'm looking for Mr. Daniels."

Dead Silence.

'Maybe he didn't hear me', thinks Jacob to himself.

"Are you Mr. Daniels?" Jacob queries the man's back.

Standing with his back to the anxious interviewee and giving more attention to the fern on the window sill, Oliver Herschel Daniels, pompous in attitude, stance, and even moniker finally turns to face the now bewildered Jacob. Mr. Daniels looks over his desk at Jacob. Not the friendliest man on earth thinks Jacob to himself, but right now the only thing in the world standing between him and his family's future. Daniels eyes Jacob from head to toe a full minute before the silence is broken.

"Good morning, I'm Jacob Myles," says Jacob extending a hand to the arrogant interviewer. "I believe Officer Ballotti called…"

"Oh yes, Ballotti. How nice of her." Daniels says ignoring Jacob's offer of a handshake and sitting down. "Well, you're already here. You may as well sit down," he says motioning toward a wooden, rickety chair in front of his desk. "Let's get this over with".

"Excuse me?" says Jacob sitting in the noisy chair. He's caught off guard by the man's patronizing demeanor.

"Let me guess. You don't have a resume," says Daniels smirking and leaning back in his padded comfortable chair.

"As a matter of fact I do," says Jacob taking the requested document from its' folder. "Hot off the presses," he says trying to lighten the mood. He places it on the crotchety cynic's desk.

Daniels rolls his eyes frowning. He leans forward snatching the paper from the blotter on his desk. The condescending old man retrieves his glasses from his inside jacket pocket. He blows them twice forming enough condensation to wipe them clean.

'Humph. Cold heart, cold breath', Jacob thinks to himself. No surprise there.

The interviewer reads the top line to himself. *Jacob Myles – Rancher, Hopskip, Georgia.*

He looks over the top of the paper and shakes his head at the interviewee sitting across from him. He stares at Jacob as if the man just disembarked a spaceship.

"You're from Georgia?"

Only Daniels' eyes are visible to Jacob now and Jacob has seen that look before, especially since moving his family north. For some strange reason, a lot of Northerners consider anyone below the 'Mason-Dixon line' to be a few centuries behind the times. *'Their schools don't compare'.* *'They spend more time at the fishin' hole than the library'. 'No one wears shoes if they don't have to'.* Jacob Myles has heard it all before - more times than he can count.

"Yes," says Jacob calling on all the restraint he can muster. "I'm from..."

"Hopskip!" interrupts Daniels with a barely concealed smirk. "How quaint."

"Mr. Daniels," says Jacob trying to maintain civility, "I'm here for the job opening in your K-9 unit. Training police dogs. Officers Ballotti and Madison said that..."

"I see you didn't finish high school. HIGH SCHOOL?"

"No, I did not," says Jacob tiring of the old man's pretentiousness and feeling his blood starting to boil. "Sir, if you just listen..."

"I'm sorry, uh Myles," says Daniels glancing at the resume and sliding it to the other side of his desk. It falls to the floor at Jacob's feet.

"I believe you know my name," says Jacob picking up the resume.

"I'm sorry, sir! The rules are clear," says the interviewer barely concealing his contempt. You must have at least a high school education."

"Mr. Daniels..." says Jacob rising out of the rickety seat.

"Mr. Myles. Sorry. YOU JUST DON'T QUALIFY! Goodbye!"

"What?" says Jacob slamming his resume on the desk. He hears Daniels' final words echo in his brain. *'YOU JUST DON'T QUALIFY!'* He stares at him for what seems like an eternity.

"Sir? Sir?" says Daniels trembling. "Do I have to call security?"

"No, you don't," says Jacob suddenly snapping out of his trance. "... and you can come from behind your desk." He storms out of the interviewer's office. In doing so, he brushes past an elderly Japanese gentleman just walking in Daniels' office.

"Excuse me," says Jacob still walking and staring straight ahead.

"That's alright. Bill Okuda." says the man extending his hand to Jacob. "Are you…?"

Distraught and angered by his confrontation with Daniels, Jacob doesn't see the man extend his hand nor does he hear him speaking. He's so upset about the row with Daniels that he slams the door behind him breaking the glass inside it. Pieces of the glass fall to the floor at Mr. Okuda's feet.

"Well," says Daniels coming from behind his desk and still shaking. "Quite the revelation, eh Mr. Okuda?"

"Daniels, what *are* you talking about!" shouts Mr. Okuda. "Was that Jacob Myles? Did you insult that man?"

"Uh, no sir! No sir! See for yourself, Mr. Okuda." Daniels clumsily picks up the resume and shows it to his boss hoping to redeem himself. "Not even a twelfth-grade education," says Daniels laughing nervously. "So typical of the South. Unbelievable!"

"Yes, Daniels it is," says Mr. Okuda quickly tiring of his employee's arrogance. "Unbelievable. Clean this up!" he says pointing to the glass on the floor. "Now!"

Mr. Okuda steps over the glass to exit the room and look for Jacob. Unfortunately, the hallway is empty.

Lightning, in a Bottle, Part 2—
Stop. Think. Be Blessed

FOR A DAY to have started off with so much promise, Jacob Myles can't believe he's back where he was before his day began; jobless, despondent, and no hope for employment. His whole adult life, (and a few years before) Jacob Myles has always worked. He knew the satisfied feeling a man - a real man gets from putting in a full day's work. Getting up before the sun to do his chores. Wiping the sweat from his brow after threshing an entire field of wheat. Feeding the chickens, slopping the hogs, and baling hay for the horses. Funny thing about those *'critters'*; every morning when Jacob opened the barn door to feed them, they all seemed to gather in concert (vocally, that is) to greet him. Jacob always said that the barnyard noises he heard after feeding them were their way of saying thanks, like a standing ovation from the animal kingdom. Their contented neighing, mooing, and other assorted sounds soothed him immensely. Brother Joseph and Papa Myles laughed the first time Jacob confided in them those weird and wonderful feelings. Deep down, they both felt the same way. When Dottie moved in and the kids came along they all agreed, there was nothing like it. They all loved the ranch, farming, and living down south. Now they were all 'UpSouth' and Jacob was having doubts about taking his family from the only life they've ever known.

He was back in the ballpark now, somewhat oblivious to the cheers and shouts from the baseball game going on behind him. He sat pondering his decision to move north. Just about everyone he knew in Chicago had once lived somewhere in the south. His landlady, brother-in-law, other cab drivers. Since the Great Migration of 1919, Negroes have made the trek north in search of a better life; escaping the cotton fields, sharecropping, and old Jim Crow. Jacob knew people who flocked to the steel mills of Gary, Indiana; the rubber plants in Akron, Ohio and the glass factory in East St. Louis, Illinois. He even had friends in Detroit, Michigan where the largest percentage of migrants settled, working in the auto industry.

"Maybe *we* should have moved to Motown," Jacob mused trying to cheer himself. "At least Frankie would be happy."

Jacob started to smile, but then he thought about Daniels and the great job that could have been. He saw red just thinking about it. Daniels' words kept ringing in his ears.

YOU JUST DON'T QUALIFY! YOU JUST DON'T QUALIFY!
CRACK!

Jacob stood up as the sound of bat against ball awakened him from his reverie. The fans in the nearby ballpark shouted. If anything could offer respite from the tension of this morning's melee, it would be the thought of a quiet game of the national pastime. The frown plastered on Jacob's face since leaving the interviewer's office slowly dissolved. He sat back and folded his jacket in his lap in front of him. He then clasped his fingers behind his head as he always did when relaxed and reminiscing. Jacob's thoughts drift to another park (a little smaller than Grant), to a memory he stores in the recesses of his mind.

"Time out!" yelled Charlie Wright, the old baseball coach. "Lightning! Baxter threw out his shoulder. Take the mound!"

Jacob Myles, nicknamed 'Lightning' for his fast curveball, exited the dugout. Although a little worn from pitching the first five innings, he happily trotted out to the diamond as if being called to play for the first time in his life. His family and friends cheered as he waved to them. Jacob had pitched for his team every Sunday during baseball season for three years now. This Sunday, however, was different. All of West Hopskip, the Negro side of town, talked about this game for the last two weeks. Jacob's team, the West Hopskip Mavericks usually hosted Negro teams from nearby towns for friendly games on week-ends after church. Last month, a few white men from North Hopskip took in the game. They had just returned from Germany protecting the world from the Third Reich. They served alongside a few Negro soldiers from West Hopskip – without incident – and were quite proud. They thought it would be fun to take in a game on the Black side of town with their fellow soldiers. All went well until one of the spectators, Tate Spindler, a ballplayer himself and self-proclaimed separatist got a little drunk. He yelled to anyone within earshot that no Negro could ever stand his ground in Germany, much less a game of baseball. He was then challenged by one of the white soldiers, 'enlightened' by his experiences overseas to bring in his own team to play the Mavericks; no money on the table, just bragging rights. One day we'll all play as one, thought Jacob. Just not today. Jacob knew whatever the outcome of this game, he would be hearing about it for many years to come.

The score was six to five. The Mavericks were up by one run. Their opponents, the Orioles had a man on first. Two outs. Bottom of the ninth. It wasn't lost on Jacob that if he struck out the last man, the Mavericks would officially be the best Negro team in the South, not counting, of course, those teams playing in the Negro League. If Jacob failed, however, and the next batter hit a homer, his team would be down by one, the Mavericks would lose and the image of the Negro player in the game of baseball would be tarnished forever thanks to their glorious pitcher. At least that's how it appeared to the Negro denizens of Hopskip, Georgia. This would be one Sunday afternoon none of them, particularly Jacob Franklin Myles would ever forget.

Jacob watched as his team threw the ball around the infield. He signaled for the catcher, Milt Paulsen to throw him the ball. Milt, a lifelong friend of Jacob's and fellow baseball enthusiast, worked the land with his father on the farm adjacent to the Myles ranch. When they weren't working the land, the two men brushed up on baseball, their families, and whatever concerns they had in the world. Most recently, their tete-a-tetes were about Tate Spindler and today's game, the most important game either of them ever played in their young lives.

Jacob warmed up by throwing the ball back and forth to Milt until he felt his pitching arm had loosened up. He then nodded to the umpire, Jeff Stukel who signaled for the game to resume. A veteran of the game with no allegiance to either team, Jeffrey James Stukel, a Northerner now living in Atlanta, was brought in to ensure impartiality on both sides. It was that important. He signaled for the next and hopefully, thought Jacob, the last batter. Jacob felt a stinging in his right bicep; after all, he had pitched the first five innings and had expected to sit out the remainder of the game. No such luck.

His bad luck tripled it seemed when he recognized the Orioles' pinch hitter crouching over home plate - Tate Spindler. Tate Spindler, the drunk who belittled his team and the Negro soldier with his outbursts about white supremacy now faced Jacob ready to prove his point. Striking out Spindler would be ever so sweet thought Jacob. Sweeter than the maple syrup and whipped cream on his wife Dottie's strawberry pancakes. But letting Spindler hit even a single would in Jacob's mind verify all the trash about Negroes and their so-called shortcomings that somehow found refuge in the weary pitcher's head.

"Come on, Lightnin'," mocked Spindler. "Let's see whatcha got." The Orioles' man on first jumped back and forth preparing himself for a steal. Jacob winds up. He throws the ball with all his might. Stukel calls it.

"Ball!"

"Ha!" Spindler laughed. "That's it? That's all you got? Come on Lightnin', gimme somethin' I can hit. Come on, son," says Spindler hitting home plate with the bat. "Right here!"

Jacob stiffens. "Apparently alcohol wasn't the only source of his bigotry," thought Jacob. "He's just as ignorant without it."

Jacob winds up. He pitches. Stukel calls it.

"Ball two!" says Stukel staring at Spindler and shaking his head.

Spindler falls on one knee laughing. Paulsen, the catcher throws the ball back to Jacob. Spindler gets up and continues his mockery of the frustrated pitcher.

"Hey, 'Short Circuit'! Yeah, that's my new name for you. 'Short Circuit'. Cause you got no juice." A few members of the Orioles chuckle at Jacob's distress. One of the Mavericks comes out of the dugout but Coach Wright motions for him to sit down.

"Look here," mocked Spindler. "I'm gonna help you out. See this right here," he says hitting the plate with his bat. "That's home plate." He holds the bat between his knees and forms a box with his hands in front of the catcher's mask. "Your mission, 'Short Circuit', is to get the ball right in here. All you have to do is to pitch. That is…*if you qualify*. Do ya qualify, 'Short Circuit'? Tell me, huh? **Do? You? Qualify?**"

"Qualify?" screams Jacob inside himself. "What? Who is he to tell me I don't qualify?" Jacob angrily throws the ball but the pitch is wild; so wild that Paulsen, the catcher jumps up, catches the ball and lands on his back. He throws the ball to third base just as the Orioles' man on first slides into second. The Mavericks' second baseman throws down his glove in disgust. Jacob's teammates sitting in the dugout begin to groan. So do many of the fans. Jacob's coach, Charlie Wright calls a timeout. He and the catcher walk out to the mound to speak to the exasperated pitcher.

The two men surround Jacob discussing the situation. "That's three balls, Jacob," says Wright. Charles Jackson Wright, a transplant from New Orleans and former coach with the Negro League's '*Black Crackers*', lived and breathed the game of baseball. Memories of his old team's exploits sustained him through old age and many a hard winter. Wright was there two weeks ago when Spindler spewed his gibberish about Black inferiority. Ol' Charlie felt he had as much to lose as Jacob, if not more.

"I don't have to tell you how important this is, do I?" continued Wright.

"All of Hopskip's depending on us, Jake" chimed in Milt.

"Come on man! Shake it off!" reiterated Coach Wright.

"Don't let this fool idiot get in your head, son," says Papa Myles.

"We've come back from tougher games than this," says Dottie beating her fist into her catcher's mitt.

"*Wait! What? Dottie? Papa Myles?*" says Jacob to himself. "*When did she get on the field? ...and Papa Myles? Papa Myles? Papa's been gone...*"

By this time, Jacob wasn't sure who was speaking or where he was. Two of the most important people in his life were now standing in place of Coach Wright and Milt, the catcher. They were both suited up and clearly ready to play. Milt and Charlie were talking but he couldn't hear a word they were saying. Disoriented, tired, and still feeling the strain in his biceps, Jacob shook his head. He rubbed his eyes and focused on his surroundings. His late father, Joseph Myles, Sr. was now standing in place of his coach. Papa Myles, as he was known to his family and friends, speaks to Jacob.

"How's your head, Jacob? Full, I bet."

"What?"

"Why would you let that knucklehead Spindler take up space in your head? Rent free at that?"

"Papa..."

"Son, we've dealt with his type before. You can't let people like him get to you. Once he's in your head, the game is lost. You don't think straight. You don't make the best decisions when you're frazzled. Now, you can get mad and throw balls all over this park; or you can collect yourself and show this man who *qualifies* and who doesn't."

"Listen to your daddy, baby," says Dottie pulling her mask over her face and crouching over an imaginary home base.

"Jake?"

"Sir?"

"What we do in this life is not about us, but about God. When someone vexes your peace, stop. Think. Be blessed. Understand me, son?"

"I do."

"Good. Now. Show him who qualifies. Understand, Jake?"

"I understand, Papa."

"Excuse me?" says Coach Wright.

"Papa?" Jacob says shaking his head and looking around.

"Jake, are you OK, man?" says Milt.

"I'm fine."

"You're sure?" says Coach Wright scratching his head.

"I'm sure. I'm fine. Let's play."

"Jake…," says Milt still looking a little worried.

"Milt, I'm okay," says Jacob reassuring his friend. "Let's get this boy gone!"

Jacob stands on the pitcher's mound. He surveys the spectators seated in the stands. His wife Dottie waves at him from her seat. She blows him a kiss. Toddler Jake Jr. sits in her lap. His three-year old daughter Josie stands at her mama's side eating popcorn. Jacob smiles. His wife smiles back. He looks at his team on the field and then in the dugout. Tate Spindler, court jester for the visiting team, walks back to the plate and winks at Jacob. He then points in the sky toward the outfield in the style of Babe Ruth. He points at Jacob, swings his bat, and then laughs at the beleaguered pitcher. The three men discussing Jacob's situation a few moments before are now ready. They nod at one another. Stukel, the umpire signals for the game to resume.

The ballpark is quiet. Jacob stands alone at the mound. He digs the toe of his right foot into the mound kicking a little dirt in front of him. Jacob stretches trying to relieve the tension in his right bicep. He rolls his neck. He begins to wind up. Spindler, finally behaving like an adult swings his bat back and forth anticipating Jacob's next pitch. Jacob eyes the plate. The batter eyes Jacob. Milt, the catcher signals to Jacob. He nods as Jacob begins his wind up. He's halfway in his follow through when he hears...

"GIT HIM, DADDY! KNOCK HIS HEAD OFF!"

Jacob somehow is able to interrupt his pitch before letting go of the ball. He recognizes the voice of course. He looks back at his wife to see her muffling his biggest fan. She escapes her mom, a very embarrassed Dottie, and yells again.

"Hi, Daddy! It's me, Josie!" she screams. The apple of his eye, little Jocelyn Dorothy Myles has decided to join the game. The once quiet park bursts into laughter. The umpire calls time – again.

"This has got to be the longest inning in history," Stukel thinks to himself.

"Be still, little girl," says Dottie red-faced and grabbing her daughter. Dottie looks around at the audience her baby girl has generated. "I'm so embarrassed," she says.

"No more than I am," says the woman sitting next to her. "I'm the one who has to go home with him."

"I'm sorry, what?" says Dottie.

"Katie. Katie Spindler. Babe Ruth's wife?"

Dottie is visibly taken aback. "Hi! Dottie Myles. The pitcher's wife."

The two grab hands as only women do and start laughing. Mrs. Spindler picks up Jake, Jr. and rocks him in her lap. The spectators in their area laugh along with them. Jacob looks up and sees his wife laughing and talking to Mrs. Spindler. She's even holding Jake, Jr. The enemy? Holding my son? Even Spindler's laughing. Jacob scratches his head. He has a bewildered look on his face.

"Am I dreaming again?" Jacob asks himself. "No. Of course not."

He drops his head and smiles. Papa Myles, as always was right. It's only a game. The fate of the free world does not rest with one man's ranting. You can't let somebody take up space in your head – rent free. Hopskip, and the world is gonna keep on moving – whether I win or not. Jacob nods to the ump. He signals to Milt. He's ready to play. Even better, he feels qualified. The catcher pulls down his mask. Spindler steps back to the plate.

"Can we play now, Lightning?" asks Spindler.

"You better believe it," says Jacob. "You better believe it!"

Jacob eyes Milt. He winds up, throws a pitch and gets it right over the plate. Spindler connects. He hits it directly to Myles knocking him to the ground. Dottie along with everyone else jumps to their feet. Spindler tosses the bat and bows to his teammates in the dugout. He looks at the spectators and waves. Everyone in the stands is out of their seats and cheering. Spindler takes off his hat and waves to the crowd as he trots to first base. As he rounds first, he notices his man on second hasn't moved. Spindler's teammate on second is standing there applauding. At first he thinks the applause is for him until he turns his attention toward the pitcher's mound. Jacob is still on his back. He raises his gloved hand. Spindler's ball, which he assumed was sailing over the horizon, is firmly in Jacob's grasp.

"Out!" yells Stukel the umpire. "Yep, I was right. Longest inning in history," he mumbles to himself as he heads off the field.

The spectators cheer. Even the Mavericks' opponents, the Orioles are applauding. Jacob's team storms the field. Milt and a few players hoist him on their shoulders. A few of them do a little dance. Spindler walks over to the crowd of men. The ballpark turns quiet. Jacob's teammates put him on the ground. He and Spindler are now standing face-to-face. Dottie and her new friend Katie hold each other's hand. A worried Josie looks up at her mom as Tate Spindler steps closer to her father.

"Tate!" yells his wife.

Spindler waves behind him. "I got this, honey." Without batting an eye, he beckons two of his teammates.

"Holloway! Jessup! Get out here!"

Jacob clinches his fists expecting the worst. He and Spindler are still eye-to-eye. Two of the Orioles run out to the mound. From the corner of his eye, the worried and exhausted pitcher notices them carrying something. An ice chest? They place the chest at Spindler's feet. He opens it and takes out two bottles handing one to Jacob.

"Good game, Lightning. Good game," Spindler says. He winks at Jacob and clinks the pitcher's bottle with his own. He shakes Jacob's hand as the rest of the Mavericks throw up a cheer for their illustrious pitcher. Spindler shrugs his shoulders, smiles and walks off to his dugout. Jacob smiles as he watches him walk away.

"I guess there's some hope for us after all," thinks Jacob to himself. Players on both sides smile at one another as beers are passed out all around. The opposing teams shake hands and slap one another on the back. Everyone laughs. Jacob hoists his bottle to his wife. She smiles. He looks at the bottle in his hand.

"Papa Myles was never one for alcohol," he thinks to himself. *"But I think today, he would make an exception. Thanks, Papa."*

Back to the present.

Jacob smiles.

"Thanks, Papa," says Jacob who's now so caught up reminiscing that he doesn't hear a kid yelling at him.

"Wake up, old man. Throw the ball." says a little boy balling his fist and slamming it into his glove.

Jacob now in a calmer state and empowered by his memories stands up. He picks up the ball and stares at the little boy. He winds up. The boy holds up his glove and starts to shake anticipating what he thinks is going to be a hard throw. He steels himself for the catch. Jacob lobs the ball instead to the insolent little brat and laughs. Jacob runs to his car, jumps in and speeds off. He drives to a building on State Street, parks, and runs inside.

Jacob speaks to a woman at the front desk. She directs him to a young man scanning a pamphlet outside his office.

"Good morning, I'm Jacob Myles. I know I don't have an appointment but if you could spare a few minutes it would mean a lot to me."

"Of course, sir," says the administrator. "I'm Mr. McGill. Step right in."

The two men sit at Mr. McGill's desk. Within twenty minutes, the men have finished their business. The administrator hands Jacob a pouch with important documentation inside. Jacob runs out of the office with a sprint in his step. The administrator steps from behind his desk and watches as Jacob leaves the building. He has the same sprint in his step as he did when he first went to see Oliver Daniels.

"I think he's gonna do all right," McGill tells the young woman at the desk.

"Mr. Daniels."

Daniels is on his knees sweeping when he notices two big shoes in front of him.

"Come to break another window, Myles?" says Daniels rising from the floor.

"No, sir and I'm sorry about that. I let my anger get the best of me. I'll be happy to pay for it."

"I'm sure," replies Daniels. He puts the rest of the broken glass in a wastebasket. The old man then goes back to his desk and sits in the padded chair. The smirk on his face tells Jacob that he's barely listening. He appears to be content to let poor Jacob grovel. He doesn't even offer him a seat.

Remembering his father's words, Jacob refuses to give in. He continues.

"Mr. Daniels, I have a proposition for you."

"Proposition? Mr. Myles, as I said before, you need at least a high school education for this position. Now you seem like a nice man but I'm afraid you just don't er, uh, um…" Daniels stumbles remembering the last time he dared broached Mr. Myles' qualifications.

"Qualify?" Jacob says calmly. "Mr. Daniels, no one knows my situation better than me. I'm not looking for a free ride. I've always made my own way and I don't intend to stop now."

"Excuse me?"

"After our talk this morning, I realized something was missing from my life. Education. I insist on it from my children but in actuality, well I was shortchanging myself. Times are changing. When the world changes, you change with it or you get left… Sorry, Mr. Daniels. I tend to prattle a bit. Dottie, my wife…"

"Mr. Myles, what does that…?"

"Let me finish. I understand there's a six-month probationary period for this position."

"So…"

"So I've just signed myself up for a program downtown. I can go to school and get my high school degree by taking courses at night.

That coupled with 'life experiences', I will have my degree at the end of the probationary period. I can do the job, Mr. Daniels. I only ask that you..."

"Make an exception?" says Daniels muffling a laugh. "Mr. Myles, surely you don't..."

At that moment Mr. Okuda, who has been viewing the proceedings from across the hall enters Daniels' office. William Scott Okuda, born and bred in California, came to Chicago just before the United States entered World War II. Mr. Okuda had the foresight and good fortune to sell his home and businesses before the government relieved America's Japanese citizenry of their property and assets and sent them to internment camps. Bill Okuda always suffered from survivor's remorse. He felt guilty escaping to Chicago with his fortunes when so many of his brethren were unjustly imprisoned. To 'atone for his leaving', he and his immediate family helped others of his culture who made their way east get settled and find work. It always pained him to watch men like Daniels abuse their power and station in life to belittle those whom they believed for some reason didn't measure up.

"Daniels, what's the matter with you?" queries Mr. Okuda. "Why don't you offer Mr. Myles a seat?"

"I beg your pardon," says Daniels obviously stunned by the request.

"And get us some coffee," orders Mr. Okuda.

"But Mr. Okuda," he stammers.

"Mr. Myles, how do you take your coffee?"

"A little sugar," says Jacob relaxed and a little taken aback by the change in Daniels' nature.

"A little sugar," the interviewer says under his breath.

"What did you say?" asks Mr. Okuda.

"Nothing sir, nothing."

Mr. Okuda sits in the flustered interviewer's chair shaking his head. He looks at Jacob and points his finger towards Daniels who's now in the outer room making coffee.

"Now see, that's why I'm against cousins mating. No good can come from that!"

Jacob looks at Mr. Okuda surprised and shocked. He almost drops the pouch he received from Mr. McGill. That was one line he did not expect from the gentleman. He tries to stifle a laugh but almost chokes.

"What's the matter?" says Mr. Okuda laughing. "A man of Japanese descent can't play the dozens?"

"*Apparently*, Mr. Okuda!" says Jacob still laughing. "Very well at that." Okuda straightens his tie and motions for Jacob to have a seat.

"Sit down, Mr. Myles! Sit down."

Jacob sits in the rickety old chair.

"I read your resume," says Mr. Okuda sitting in Daniels' chair. "Played a little ball, did you? Love the game. Love the game. Centerfield," he says pointing to himself. "Nothing got past 'Ol' Sharp Eyes'. We'll definitely have to get together some time."

"Sounds good!" Jacob says smiling.

"I spoke to Mr. Madison," says Mr. Okuda. "He and Officer Ballotti were quite taken with your command of ol' King. He's a tough one – or was. They say your mastery of dogs is nothing short of amazing. Even without the high school degree, most impressive. Most impressive."

"Thank you, Mr. Okuda. I appreciate that."

"Bill."

"Bill it is," Jacob replies.

"May I call you Jacob?"

"Call me Jake."

"Here's your coffee, Bill!" says Daniels as he sets the two paper cups on his desk.

"Excuse me?" says Mr. Okuda.

"Uh, *Mister* Okuda…sir! Your coffee. Sir."

"Jake," Mr. Okuda continues and turning his attention back to Jacob, "Life experiences *are* very important. I believe in life lessons playing a role in a man's character as much as I do in structured learning. Maybe even more."

"Thank you, Bill," says Jacob.

"Oh, no problem. A man of your age and experience willing to go back to school for a position he's more than qualified to handle? We're impressed, aren't we Daniels."

"Yesss!" says Daniels begrudgingly. He looks at his boss sitting at his desk as if he expects Mr. Okuda to get up. Okuda looks at Daniels as if he expects him to leave. Guess who wins. Daniels returns to his station at the coffee kiosk.

"Lord, Lord!" whispers Okuda across the desk to Jacob. He motions for Jacob to come nearer. Jacob, still drinking his coffee moves closer. "What do you bet Daniels' mama was dropped on *her* head, too?"

Jacob almost chokes on the brew. He shakes his head and holds it down trying to muffle his laughter. He hasn't enjoyed himself this much all day. He puts his cup on the desk and laughs.

Mr. Okuda smiles back. He leans back in Daniels chair and drums his fingers on the desk. A moment of silence passes before Jacob hears the words he's been waiting to hear since he moved his clan to Chicago.

"How soon can you start, Mr. Myles?"

"Right away, sir! Uh, Bill."

"Good! Daniels!" shouts Mr. Okuda. "Get in here! Say hello to Jacob Myles, our new employee."

"But sir! Mr. Okuda. We're not in the habit of making exceptions."

"Exceptions?!?" exclaims Mr. Okuda. He comes from behind the desk and stares at Daniels; starting with his cheap toupee down to his Buster Browns and back to the minion's trembling lips. Mr. Okuda stares him right in his eyes.

"Exceptions, is it? I make one every day. Do I have to tell you about it?"

"Noooo." says Daniels holding his head down. He's goes to a file cabinet and takes out a piece of paper. "Here." says Daniels handing the paper to Jacob. "Take this to Ms. Walcott. 2nd floor, 205. She'll get you settled in."

"Thank you," says Jacob taking the paper from Mr. Daniels. Daniels nods. Mr. Okuda escorts Jacob to the door.

"And we'll need that diploma at the end of six months, uh… sir, Mr. Myles," says Daniels fumbling for the right words after realizing that he's put his foot in his mouth - again.

The two men turn simultaneously to face Daniels, whose face has now turned pale. Mr. Okuda shakes his head disapprovingly as if a child has just broken a vase he was told to avoid.

Jacob approaches Oliver Daniels. The two men are now face-to-face.

"That won't be a problem, Mr. Daniels. Jacob Myles is a man of his word, and I've never broken a promise to anyone. Not even to myself. Besides," he says rolling the document Daniels gave him and tapping the man's chest with it. "I've been known to come through in the last inning." Jacob winks at Mr. Okuda as he exits the office.

"Of that," interjects Mr. Okuda, "I have no doubt. See you Monday."

"AAAAHH! L'il Daddy! What did you do!"
"Frankie, calm down," says L'il Daddy. "I told you to be still."
"What's all this noise?" says Dottie entering the living room. "L'il Daddy, what's going on in here?"
"Look what L'il Daddy did to my head, Mama!"
"You kept wriggling in the chair, Frankie. Dancing and bobbing. I told you not to wear those earphones while I'm cutting your hair."
"Who told you to cut his hair?" says Dottie. "Your daddy is not gonna be happy."
"Mommy, Daddy's home!" says Savannah running to her father.
"You might wanna retire to your room, young man," says Dottie looking at her eldest son. "Hi, honey, you're late. I was starting to worry about you. How did it go?"
"Hello, family! Good news, Dottie!" says Jacob taking off his jacket.
"Daddy," says Josie. "Is that an 'Amlin' pouch?"
"Why, yes I believe it is," says Jacob proudly.
"What's going on, Jacob?" asks Dottie. "Baby, are you going back to school?"
"Why of course!" says Jacob kidding his wife. "I need it for my job on Monday."
"All right, Dad!" "My Daddy can do anything." "Wow." say the Myles children.
"I'll be training dogs for the Chicago Police Department," says Jacob smiling proudly.
"Jacob, that's great!" says Dottie. "Training dogs? I am so proud of you!"
"Thank you, baby."
"Now, what was I saying this morning about faith?" Dottie winks. "God got you that job!"
"Yep." Jacob concurs nodding his head. "God, you, and Papa Myles."
"Come again?" his wife replies with a puzzled look on her face.
"I'll explain later."
"Yeah, you better," says Dottie chuckling. "Family! Dinner!" she says herding the kids toward the dining room.
"Wow, me and Daddy going to school together!" says Josie to herself

taking a seat at the table. *"At this rate, I'll never get a husband!"* she chuckles. She's kidding. Jacob's eldest is more than happy to see the *'greatest father on earth'* get his high school diploma.

L'il Daddy pats his father on the back. "If you need any help Daddy, I'm right here. I got an A in English last semester."

"...and an 'F' in cutting hair!" says Frankie.

"Daddy doesn't need any help, L'il Daddy," says Savannah confidently. "He knows everything." She believes this with all her heart.

"Don't worry about your hair, Frankie. I'll take care of it," Jacob grins rubbing his son's head. He heads for the kitchen drawer where the clippers are kept.

"Well for now, it's time to eat," Dottie reminds her husband. "You're gonna need your strength."

"For school? My new job?" queries Jacob.

Dottie whispers to Jacob. "Among other things."

Jacob smiles. His smile is almost as wide as when Mr. Okuda offered him his new job. "Somebody say grace," Dottie says to the table. "Your father looks hungry."

Life is good.

Meanwhile, on the other side of town...

"OLIVER! THESE DISHES AREN'T GOING TO WASH THEMSELVES!"

"Y-Yes, Dear..."

Yes, indeed. Life is good.

Our Day Will Come, Part 1–
Bobby Loves Brittany

Intermarriage between whites and blacks is repulsive and averse to every sentiment of pure American spirit. It is abhorrent and repugnant to the very principles of Saxon government. It is subversive of social peace. It is destructive of moral supremacy, and ultimately this slavery of white women to black beasts will bring this nation a conflict as fatal as ever reddened the soil of Virginia or crimsoned the mountain paths of Pennsylvania.

... Let us uproot and exterminate now this debasing, ultra-demoralizing, un-American and inhuman leprosy

—*Congressional Record, 62d. Congr., 3d. Sess., December 11, 1912*

THIS IS THE day which the Lord hath made. Let us rejoice and be glad in it. Jacob Franklin Myles, Jr. (also known as L'il Daddy) has heard his father recite this verse all his life. In good times or bad, father Jacob believes that every day is a gift from God and one worth celebrating. Unfortunately, in matters of the heart, neither young Jacob nor his sister Josie has had much to celebrate since arriving in Chicago. Josie and her former beau Mack Hodges have called it quits. She's accepted it. L'il Daddy hasn't seen or heard from his beloved Molly Beth Brand since his family left Georgia for the Windy City. That, however, is about to change, for Jacob, Sr.'s oldest son is about to undergo the most heartbreaking, yet eye-opening day of his young life – a day that will definitely need the love of his family - and the Lord - to survive.

Josie Myles is ecstatic. Her best friend Brittany Abernathy, from her hometown of Hopskip, Georgia, is coming to Chicago for a visit. Brittany, better known as 'Cookie' has stayed in touch with Josie since the Myles family left Georgia a few months ago. The two best friends have made plans to meet at Josie's job, *The Breakfast Nook* for a bite to eat. Brittany has a surprise for her friend. Josie is going to surprise Brittany by having her brother L'il Daddy meet them for a late lunch. Josie has five minutes left on her shift. Her boss, Mr. Triplett, and co-worker Millie Cooper are also at the restaurant taking inventory.

"Uh, Miss can I get some coffee over here?" says a customer.

"Be right with you, Mr. Tannen," Josie says grabbing the pot. "Did you want cream and sug--,"

Josie screams.

"COOKIE!!!"

"JOSIE!!!"

"Oh, my Lord, Cookie," screams Josie almost dropping the pot of hot coffee on her customer. "Sorry, Mr. Tannen!"

"No problem," says the customer. "Who's your friend?"

"Cookie!" Josie says hugging her friend. "Girl, I can't believe you made it up here!"

"Cookie! Nice name!" says the customer extending his hand. "Mark. Mark Tannen."

The two friends are oblivious to the old man's imposition. Neither of them has heard a word he's said.

"Well, I'm here," says Cookie hugging her friend. "It was a long ride but I had to see my girl!"

"I'm so happy to see you!" Josie says setting the glass coffee pot on the counter next to Mr. Tannen. She whips off her apron and throws it behind the counter.

"Okay, Tannen," says the customer to himself. "Pour your own coffee. Got it!"

"Oh, me too, Josie. I'm so happy to see you!" Cookie says hugging her teary-eyed pal. "I've missed you so much!"

"I've missed you, too," says Josie wiping her eyes. "We have so much to talk about! What's this big surprise you have for me?"

"Well, give me your hand," says Cookie grabbing her old friend's hand and placing it on her stomach.

Josie holds her hand to her mouth. She gasps.

"Oh my God, Brittany! You're pregnant!"

"…and that's my cue," Tannen says leaving the counter. "I'm out!"

"Oh, I'm sorry Josie. He didn't leave you a tip."

"Don't worry, girl. He never does," Josie says dismissing the customer. "Cookie, you're pregnant! How did this happen?"

"Uh, the *usual* way, Jocelyn Dorothy Myles!"

"B-But you said you would never…" Josie stammers. "I mean…we made a pact."

"Well, my *husband* and I made another pact," Cookie says holding out her left hand. She flashes her wedding ring under Josie's nose.

"*Your husband?*" Josie says incredulously.

"Bobby." Cookie says.

"*Bobby?*" Josie responds. "*Bobby Matthews? You and Bobby Matthews got married?*"

"Yep." Cookie says taking her friend's hand. She leads her over to the restaurant window and waves for her husband Bobby to come inside. Bobby Matthews, a tall and slender young man with chiseled Greek features, wavy hair, and chestnut brown eyes to boot, waves at the two friends from his car. He gets out and runs toward the restaurant.

"Oh, my God!" Josie says heading for the nearest booth. "I better sit down. No, *you* sit down. Oh my God, *Bobby Matthews!*"

"Josie!" Bobby Matthews screams. Bobby's dimples seem to appear out of nowhere every time he smiles. Cookie's been known to melt whenever he does.

"Bobby, hey! Oh, my God. It's so good to see you," Josie exclaims hugging the young man. "Cookie told me! You're married…and *expecting*. I'm gonna faint!"

"Let's all sit down," Bobby says.

"My two best friends. Married!" Josie says catching her breath. "I can't believe it!"

"I can't believe we're sitting in the same booth." Cookie says instinctively looking around. Bobby nods his head in agreement.

"It's a little different," Josie concedes. "Oooh, Cookie. Girl, you're married now. Tell me. What did Big Mama say? And Daddy Turner? Child, they must've flipped out. No offense, Bobby."

"None taken, Josie."

"Our parents didn't know, Josie," Cookie confesses dropping her head. "We called them once we hit Indiana. Told 'em we was going to Illinois, getting married and can't nobody stop us!"

Bobby, holding his new wife's hand continues their story.

"We knew if we tried to get married in Georgia, our parents would find out. Plus we knew everybody was scared of breaking that stupid 'anti-miscegenation' law," Bobby says quoting with his fingers. "Stupidest thing I ever heard of. We finally found a minister in East St. Louis. Cookie has people there. He had no problem getting us hitched!"

"Oh, keep thinking Bobby. This world is full of stupid laws," says Josie. "You two are so brave. Weren't you scared?"

"Yep, no doubt," says Bobby. "But we felt, as long as it feels right, you know? We got each other's back. That's all that counts."

"I'm sure God's got your back, too!" Josie says.

"Amen, my sister." Cookie says. "Amen!"

"*Of all the gin joints in all the world…*" L'il Daddy says sneaking up on the couple.

"Choo-Choo!" Bobby yells jumping up. "My main man!"

"Bobby! C'mere, boy!" L'il Daddy says hugging his old friend. "You still doing the worst Elvis Presley known to man?"

"Me?" Bobby laughs. "I haven't heard a worst Humphrey Bogart…"

"Oh, Lord here they go," Cookie says laughing.

Robert Matthews, Jr. and Jacob Myles, Jr. have been tight ever since Robert Matthias, Sr. moved his family to Georgia. The senior Matthias changed the family name to Matthews and opened Matthews' Groceries in the middle of town. He brought his nine-year-old son Bobby, Jr. in one Saturday to help stock groceries. He and L'il Daddy met and became lifelong friends. Although the boys couldn't attend school together, they always found time to get together afterward and hang out. Bobby and L'il Daddy used to talk football, music, movies, girls, and whatever teenage boys talk about for hours on end in the alley behind the grocery store. Charlie "Choo Choo" Brackins was a quarterback for the Green Bay Packers during the 1955 season. Being the first Negro to play that position for the team, L'il Daddy couldn't get enough of him. Impressed by his hero's achievements, Jacob Myles, Jr. adopted Brackins' nickname as his own. Actually, it was his good friend Bobby who first started calling his pal 'Choo Choo'.

"Cookie! My girl!"

"Hey, Choo-Choo! How's my *boyfriend*? Hope you don't mind my gettin' married on ya?" Cookie says kissing his cheek and showing off her ring.

"Girl, please! Come here!"

L'il Daddy and Cookie hug one another. Seems like old times. Brittany 'Cookie' Abernathy was known around Hopskip, Georgia as the girlfriend of Jacob 'L'il Daddy' Myles, Jr. Margaret Elizabeth Brand, also known as Molly Beth pretended to be Robert 'Bobby' Matthews' girlfriend. The four friends concocted this ruse so that they could be together and pass messages to one another without creating suspicion among their parents and the unenlightened of their little town.

"Well," L'il Daddy says looking at his '*girlfriend's*' tummy. "Looks like you finally went and did it."

"CHOO-CHOO?" Cookie says incredulously.

"JACOB MYLES, JR.!" Josie says pulling her brother's shirttail. "Do you hear yourself?"

"What? I mean they finally went and got married!" L'il Daddy says. "What are *you* talking about, JOSIE?"

"Boy, shut up! You mean already knew?"

"Course I knew," L'il Daddy says hugging his two oldest friends. "Bobby's been promising to marry Cookie since the sixth grade. Shoot! One of the reasons I got in the movement... so me and Molly... and these two..."

L'il Daddy starts to well up. He hasn't spoken to Molly since they left Hopskip. Josie is a bit stunned. She knew her brother always had a weak spot for the underdog but this? A hopeless romantic?

"You never cease to amaze me, l'il brother," Josie says with a tear in her eye. She kisses him on the cheek.

The four friends huddle around one another. Josie wipes her tears with a napkin and then does the same for her brother and Cookie. Even Bobby is beside himself with emotion. It's like a dream come true. One that Josie knows Cookie has always wanted.

"Honey," Cookie says to her new husband breaking the silence. "Why don't you show Choo-Choo our new car while me and Josie catch up?"

"Good idea! Chooch," Bobby says pointing his thumb toward the parking lot. "Come see our new car."

"New car!?"

"Pontiac Grand Prix! Cookie and I got it for the trip. Uh, **Mrs. Matthews**," Bobby says smiling. "Order us up some sandwiches, would you? We'll be right back."

"Okay, **Mr. Matthews**," Cookie says beaming.

"Girl, he's still got those dimples!" Josie says.

"It was those dimples that made me say yes!" Cookie says laughing.

"To what?" Josie says slyly.

"Now girl, don't you start." Cookie says blushing.

"Wow, **Mrs. Matthews**!" says Josie still stunned. "I can't believe it."

"Oh, believe it girl," says Cookie. "Did I--"

Cookie is momentarily distracted. She spots another waitress standing at the counter. She's pretending to wipe down the counter but is obviously eavesdropping on the two friends. Cookie taps Josie's wrist.

"You know this chick's been eyeing me and Bobby since we walked in. Wait a minute, Josie! Is that..."

"Um hmm. Millie. Honey, she's quitting in a couple days. Can't wait 'til she's outta my face."

"Millie, huh?"

"One and only."

Cookie looks at her friend and winks a knowing eye. Millie continues to wipe down the counter.

"You know, Josie..." Cookie says in a loud voice. "Mack Hodges came back to Georgia."

"Did?" Josie says.

"Um hmm. Right before we left."

"Oh, really? How is ol' Mack?"

"They say the boy's sick."

"Oh my Lord!" Josie says feigning concern. "I hope it's nothing serious."

"Girl, they say that boy got V.D.!" Cookie says watching Millie shake.

"Oh no," Josie says suppressing a laugh. "If he's got it, then that means..."

Cookie and Josie turn to look at Millie. The look on her face is priceless. She pulls off her apron and runs to Mr. Triplett. Her words inaudible to Cookie and Josie, Millie pulls on his shirt and whispers in the boss' ear. He drops his clipboard and runs over to Josie.

"Uh, Myles," he says nervously throwing on his jacket. "I have to go! Uh, Millie too!"

"Problem, Mr. Triplett?"

"We're out of straws," the old man says nervously. "Lock up when you're through."

He and Millie run out the door and jump in the old man's car. Josie and Cookie run after the pair. They stop at the door.

"Shall I tell *Mrs.* Triplett where to find you?" Josie yells.

The two old friends laugh. They slap one another a high-five.

"Wow!" Josie says. "Didn't see that one coming."

"You never know, child," Cookie laughs. "You never know."

"Now!" Josie says. "…back to us. You and Bobby married. I still can't believe it."

"It's real! Let's sit down, Josie," Cookie tells her. "There's something I have to tell you."

"So, Bobby my man," says L'il Daddy. "Where you two headed?"

"Either Canada or California. Don't know yet."

"Canada or California?" says L'il Daddy puzzled. "You better make up your mind before you take off. They's both a way's from one another, you know."

L'il Daddy and Bobby run to the east end of the parking lot. Bobby's on cloud nine. L'il Daddy hasn't smiled this much since before leaving Hopskip. The two old friends stop at a 1962 candy apple red Pontiac Grand Prix. L'il Daddy looks at his buddy admiring his new car.

"Umm, Bobby this is sweet," L'il Daddy says beaming. "This year?"

"You always did know your cars," Bobby says. "Yep, 1962! Take the wheel, my man!"

L'il Daddy obliges his buddy's offer. Bobby received the car as a gift for his nineteenth birthday from his father, Robert Matthews, Sr. Bobby's dad was a friend and hunting buddy of Jacob Myles, Sr. Matthews' Groceries was the only market the Negro denizens of Hopskip felt comfortable patronizing. All of West Hopskip, the Negro side of town, liked Bob Matthews and his family.

"Nice color, too. You must've stacked a lot of canned peaches to get this baby," L'il Daddy grins. "Speaking of peaches, did I ever…"

"A million times, my man," Bobby says anticipating his buddy's question. "A million times. Forget about it, it's over."

L'il Daddy is referring to the time Bobby Matthews came to his sister Josie's rescue a year or so ago. He prevented local bully Evan Platt, Jr. from attacking Josie in the alley behind the Matthews family market. Bobby beaned Platt with a can of peaches right before Mack Hodges, Josie's then boyfriend disposed of him with a few rights to the chin.

"How's your brother, Cookie?"

"He's gonna be fine, Josie," Cookie says. "But there's no place for him back home. Soon as he's well, he'll be leaving Hopskip, too."

"I expect he will," Josie says.

"Josie," Cookie says her head down. "When I gave my brother your location and your new job address and all, I knew he'd tell Mack but I had no idea... I mean, when he told me what they did...What Mack did..."

"Girl, don't even sweat it," Josie says holding her best friend's hand. "You couldn't have known. Actually, you did me a favor."

"A favor? How?"

"Well, I finally got to see Mack just for what he was. People kept telling me he was no good. L'il Daddy, Mama, Daddy... It took your doing for me to finally get me to see for myself. Girl, you had my back and didn't even know it! Yeah, it hurt, I won't lie. But, well..."

"It's over," Bobby reiterated. "Josie's safe up here. From Mack Hodges *and* Evan Platt. You know, before the accident ol' Evan was keeping a pretty low profile. They say somebody tried to kill him. Even took a shot at him."

"Oh, really?" L'il Daddy says mockingly. "How sad."

"So sad!" Bobby responds.

They slap one another five. If ever someone deserved being used for target practice...

"Jacob, I have to tell you something."

Jacob. L'il Daddy thinks to himself. Bobby Matthews had a way of moving from the sublime to the deadly serious in a matter of seconds. L'il Daddy remembered that whenever Bobby called a person by his given name, he was setting the tone for some unpleasant news. He turned to his friend.

"What is it?" L'il Daddy said bracing himself.

"Have you talked to Molly Beth, Jacob?"

L'il Daddy looks at Bobby. Fearing the worst, he takes his time responding. The longer he waits, the longer his beloved is safe and out of harm's way – at least in his mind. Yet he knows that he can't pretend everything concerning Molly Brand is peachy keen. Whenever he tried to call her, her brother Cletus answered the phone. L'il Daddy wasn't sure if it was bad timing or if she was using her brother to avoid talking to him. He broaches the subject gingerly.

"...haven't heard from Molly Beth since we left Hopskip," L'il Daddy says fiddling with the radio. "What's she been up to?"

"Well..." Bobby says hesitating.

"Don't tell me she got married, too?" L'il Daddy says restraining his anger. "Come on Bobby, spill it! What happened?"

"It's not like that, Jacob."

"Then what?"

"Molly Brand had a miscarriage." Cookie tells Josie back at the diner. "She was about four months along."

"*Miscarriage?*" says Josie. "*Molly Brand was pregnant?*"

"We were with her," Cookie tells her. "It was *Jacob's.*"

MISCARRIAGE. Bobby's words hit L'il Daddy like a runaway train. He's speechless. '*My Molly? Pregnant? A miscarriage?*'

'This can't be real," L'il Daddy thinks. Bobby's joking. L'il Daddy searches his friend's face frantically for the slightest semblance of jocularity. Not even a smile.

"Man, you and your jokes. You almost had me," L'il Daddy laughs nervously. "Hey, let's hear some tunes. Let me find the Rock 'n Roll station for you..."

"Jacob, come on. I wouldn't joke about a thing like that!" Bobby says grabbing his friend's shoulder. "'Specially with Brittany expecting our first. Poor Molly miscarried your baby. Nobody else knows..."

"...but me and Bobby!" says Cookie. "We took her to that hospital over in..."

"I know the hospital, Bobby," L'il Daddy bemoans. "Is she...?"

"She's hangin' in there," says Cookie. "A little depressed..."
"Who wouldn't be?" says Josie. "Poor Molly Beth, I feel so bad for her. This is gonna kill my brother. Are you sure no one else knows?"

"I think her brother Cletus knows," says Bobby.
"Why do you say that?" L'il Daddy asks.
"He used to come in the store and stare daggers at me. Like he was always mad about something."
"Why would Cletus Brand be mad at...?" asks L'il Daddy puzzled. "Oh, right! She was supposed to be your girlfriend. Do you think her father...?"

"GOD NO!" Cookie shrieks. "Marvin Brand? He would come after my Bobby!"
"Come after Bobby? For what?" Josie asks. "Oh, yeah that's right. Everybody thought..."

"...that me and Molly was seeing each other...and that you and my Cookie were a couple. Hah! We fooled everybody, didn't we, Choo-Choo?" Bobby laughs. "Anyway, I hope you don't plan on going back to Hopskip. If the Brands find out..."

"My brother could get – I don't even wanna think about it," says Josie. "Don't worry, Cookie. I'll make sure he stays put. And girl, thanks."
"No problem, Josie. No problem."
"What is holding up your sandwiches?" Josie says looking toward the kitchen. "You only ordered them a half hour ago. Be right back."

L'il Daddy gets out of the Matthews' new car and gently closes the door. He looks over the roof of the vehicle at his friend's smiling face.
"*This could have been me and Molly, too,*" he thinks to himself. Depressed, he starts to walk away in the opposite direction of the diner.
"Hey Chooch," Bobby yells after his friend. "Chooch, where you going, man? Aren't you going to say goodbye to Cookie?"

"I'm sorry, man," L'il Daddy says with a lump in his throat. He comes back and hugs his friend. "I gotta be alone now. Say goodbye to Cookie for me...and good luck. California, right? Stay in touch!"

Bobby watches L'il Daddy take off down the street. He looks back at the diner where his new wife, Cookie is watching from the window. She sadly shakes her head. They just broke their best friend's heart. Cookie runs outside to Bobby standing beside their car.

"Honey, did you talk to Choo-Choo?" she says taking his hand.

"Yeah. He had no idea. He took it pretty hard, poor guy."

"Okay, I got two turkey subs and a couple cans of pop," Josie says walking up to the pair.

"Pop?" says Cookie.

"Yeah, that's what they call soda up here," Josie laughs. "...even got the chef to throw in some deep dish pizza. Real big around here. You'll like it. Hey," Josie says looking around. "Where's my brother?"

"He took the news about Molly pretty hard," Cookie says hugging Josie. "Probably just needed to be alone."

"Choo-Choo's strong," Bobby says. "He'll pull through. Probably just headed home. Speaking of which, Mrs. Matthews, I think it's time we headed out ourselves."

"Oooh, do you have to go," says Josie.

"I'm afraid so, Josie," Bobby says taking the bag of goodies. "It was great seeing ya!"

"Lunch is on the house," says Josie. "Oh, and I got you something else."

Josie pulls out a stuffed doll from the pocket of her skirt. She purchased it for her own baby when she thought that she and Mack Hodges would get married and have children. She puts it in both their hands.

"A little something I found in my locker. For my goddaughter," she says crying.

Cookie bear-hugs her friend and starts crying with her. She then goes around to the passenger side of the Pontiac and gets into the car. Bobby follows her. He puts the bag of sandwiches and pizza in the back seat and then buckles up his wife. He kisses her, closes her door, and then comes back around to Josie.

"Take care of Chooch, for me would ya, Josie," Bobby says hugging his best friend's sister. "Tell him I never had a better friend."

"I will," says Josie. "I know he feels the same about you."

"Bye, Josie." Cookie says through her tears. "I love you!"

"Love you back," Josie waves. "Bobby?"

"Uh huh?"

"You two got a big job ahead of you," she says kissing him goodbye. "Please. Take care of my Cookie."

"You kiddin'?" he says getting in the car. He turns on the engine and smiles at the love of his life. Brittany 'Cookie' Matthews, lost in her husband's big brown eyes and dimpled smile kisses his cheek. She blushes. She's never been happier. Robert Matthews, Jr. has been waiting for this day for years. He kisses the palm of his beautiful new wife's hand and squeezes it. He then turns back to Josie and smiles.

"Don't worry, Josie," Bobby assures her. "I was made for *this* job."

"Is anyone sitting here?" the sixteen-year old Jamaican beauty asks.

"What? No, sorry," the young man says picking up his jacket from the seat next to him and placing it in his lap. He hadn't noticed that the bus is half empty.

"Thank you," she says. "What's *your* name?'

The young man is quiet. He stares ahead, barely noticing the comely teenager.

The pretty young woman with the Colgate smile is Angela Cunningham. Angela is sporting a short, black mini - sure to catch any man's eye. She wears her hair in the new afro-centric 'natural' style. Her 'do, perfectly round and neat, glows in the sunlight. She sports an afro pick right in the center of her hair. Her knee-high go-go boots, black and shiny like her mini, accents her shapely legs.

"My name is Angela," she says. "People say I look just like Angela Davis. Funny, huh?"

"Uh huh," the young man says obviously occupied with other matters. His mind is elsewhere.

"Would you look at that?" says a gray-haired gentleman to his equally gray-haired buddy sitting in the back row of the noisy transit bus.

"Girl is fine. Fine! And all *that* boy can do is look out the window. If that was me..."

"You'd be tripping over your tongue," says his riding companion.

"That's what you'd be doing. What would you know 'bout '*fine*', anyway? I've seen the kinda women you pull, and ain't none of them *Jet Beauty of the Week*! Still, fox like that. Young blood *must* be having issues. Better be careful though. She's dressed like one of them militants! Can't have that."

"Um hm," says his friend ignoring the warning. "Love me some big legs!"

Jacob Franklin Myles, Jr., (also known as L'il Daddy) oblivious to the world around him, has barely noticed the pretty teen sitting next to him. And with good reason; he just got the worse news of his young life. His girlfriend back home, Margaret Elizabeth Brand also known as Molly Beth has suffered a miscarriage. Jacob wasn't aware of her pregnancy, nor was he there when she needed him.

Young Jacob is overcome with guilt, and in his mind there's plenty to go around.

"*Thanks a lot, Daddy,*" he says to himself. "*I shoulda been back in Georgia with Molly!*"

"…and after the meeting," the young Jamaican says proudly. "We're going to the set next door. To celebrate our independence. Sounds like fun, huh?"

"I suppose," L'il Daddy says feigning interest. "What's a set?"

"It's a dance, 'bama!" the old man from the back replies bluntly. "Even I know that!"

"I'm from Georgia," L'il Daddy replies wearily to the old man. The old man shakes his head piteously and turns away. L'il Daddy turns his attention back to the young teen sitting beside him.

"If you don't mind, I…"

"Here!" she says interrupting him. "Take a flyer. Be there or be square."

L'il Daddy takes the flyer from the pretty young lady. He returns to his daydream - one that includes his dream girl Molly Brand. L'il Daddy reads the flyer and then places it on top of a stack of leaflets that Molly secretly printed for him.

"It's a good thing the janitor doesn't clean up the stacks like he should," Molly says referring to their school's old abandoned library and her and L'il Daddy's secret hideout. "If he found us up here…"

"Don't wanna think about it!" L'il Daddy responds. "Shoot, I'd hate to

think what your father would do if he knew you were using his mimeograph machine to make flyers to get out the Negro vote."

"Yes, I know," she replies. "Mr. Brand would not be too happy with his baby girl."

Molly looks at her boyfriend with anticipation. She's been anxious to change the subject for awhile but has been dreading how L'il Daddy might respond to the news she has for him. She broaches the subject cautiously.

"You like coming up here, L'il Daddy?"

"Molly, don't call me 'L'il Daddy'. At least not in public. People might think something's going on. Like we're closer than we should be. You know what I mean?"

"Yeah, I guess."

"You guess? A white girl helping a Negro print up flyers for colored people to vote? I don't know who got more to lose, you or me. Believe that!"

"Oh, you know I would never say anything. My daddy would kill us both."

"Yeah, but your daddy would kill himself, too!"

"Oh, Daddy's not that bad," Molly says pushing her boyfriend. "He could change a little, sure. But he still loves me. Which is more than I can say for my mama."

Molly Brand's mother, Elizabeth Josephine Brand left Hopskip in the middle of the night eight years ago. Her whereabouts are unknown to her family. It has been long rumored that Molly's father Marvin Brand, a sympathizer to the local Klan was somehow responsible for his missing wife's disappearance. Although he speaks of her in the past tense, as if she'd died, he's assured his children that he had nothing to do with her disappearance and that she will return when she's ready. Molly has her doubts. It's been eight years. The years go by slowly when they're as agonizing as they've been to Molly Brand.

"You'll see her again, Molly Beth," L'il Daddy assures her. "I know you will."

"Do you think this will do any good, L'il Dad- uh, sorry," Molly says correcting herself. "Jacob Myles, Jr.? The flyers, I mean. People down here are so set in their ways."

"My granddaddy, Papa Myles used to say the smallest drop of water can wear away the biggest stone."

"We don't have that much time, Jacob," she says taking his hand. She pats her stomach but he doesn't notice.

"Speaking of which, I need to get over to the church," Jacob says staring at the clock on the back wall of the library. He stashes the flyers in an old knapsack. "I appreciate the flyers. Any money we can save the movement is always a help."

"Jacob, I – uh…" Molly stammers. She's unable to find the words to tell Jacob what he needs to know.

"Yes, Baby Girl?"

Molly stares at Jacob. She can't tell him.

"Be careful!" she tells him instead.

"I know Molly Beth. I know."

"Jacob, you still didn't answer my question."

"What question was that?"

"Do you like coming up here? Do you like being with me?"

"Well, yeah. It's like we're in a whole 'nother world," L'il Daddy says taking her in his arms. "Another planet. No parents asking questions, no teachers, waitresses sitting me on one side of the room and you on the other. Is it OK for me to even come in? No stupid rules up here. It's like when we were kids, Molly Beth. Nobody but you…and me."

He starts to kiss her but stops short. He hears the janitor milling around in the hallway. He puts his finger to his lips motioning for Molly to stay quiet.

"Wait a few minutes and then come down," L'il Daddy tells her. "I'll see you tomorrow."

Tomorrow, unfortunately never came.

Molly Beth Brand intimated living in a world where people, particularly her and Jacob Jr.'s baby would be accepted for who they are. She was trying to tell him that she was with child. His son, she hoped. L'il Daddy, unfortunately never caught on until now – on a bus, a million miles away from his heart.

L'il Daddy's bus pulls up to a stop a block away from his house. He excuses himself as he moves past the young beauty with flyers in her hand. She winks at him. Indifferent to the lovely Miss Cunningham and her advances, L'il Daddy politely and nonchalantly waves back. He hasn't even noticed that she wrote her name and number on the flyer.

"Now don't you lose that," she says.

L'il Daddy nods, folds the paper and puts it in his jacket pocket.

"Hey, young blood!" yells the old man from the back of the bus. "If you not goin' to the set, tell Angela Davis up there I'm available!"

The few people on the bus start to laugh. L'il Daddy smiles at the two old men and steps aimlessly off the bus into the street.

Six o'clock. Dottie Myles calls everyone to dinner. Normally there's a stampede whenever Mrs. Myles rings the dinner bell but tonight a few family members have other plans.

"Your father has class tonight," Dottie tells her children. "I am so proud of your Daddy taking these night school classes. You two could learn from him. Got your favorite, L'il Daddy. Meatloaf, broccoli, and creamed corn. Better eat up before your father gets home."

L'il Daddy sits quietly at the table. He's in another world. He doesn't even acknowledge his mama, baby brother Terry or his sister Josie nudging him under the table trying to bring him back to reality.

"Where are Frankie and Savannah, Mama?" Josie asks now pulling her brother's sleeve. "Not that I miss 'em. Right, L'il Daddy?"

L'il Daddy is miles away, on another planet no doubt, thinking about the day's events and the shocking news about his sweetheart Molly Beth.

"They're spending the night with Aunt Lucy and the kids so it's just us four," Dottie says. "Sit up, Terry. L'il Daddy? L'il Daddy, would you say grace please?"

"I'm sorry, Mama," L'il Daddy says getting up from the table. "I'm not hungry."

"Not hungry? Now baby, you know I know when something's wrong," Dottie says. "You've been quiet as a mouse since you came home. Talk to me, son."

L'il Daddy gets up from his chair and pushes it under the table.

"I'm sorry, Mama. I can't."

He looks at Josie. She takes her brother's hand. She knows what he's about to say.

"Can't what?" Dottie says. "What's going on?"

"I'm sorry, Mama," L'il Daddy says. "I have to pack. I'm moving back to Hopskip."

"Hop- what? Moving back?" Dottie says. "Boy, what are you talking about?"

L'il Daddy leaves the table and runs upstairs. Dottie starts to follow. Josie takes her mother aside.

"Mama, wait. I have to tell you something."

"This better be good, Jocelyn Myles," Dottie says.

Josie explains what happened to her brother and about her friends. She tells her about Bobby, Brittany, California, and the awful news about Molly Beth Brand.

"I already know about Molly Beth, honey," Dottie says.

Josie is stunned.

"You do? Mama, how…"

"Fix the baby a plate. I need a minute with your brother."

Dottie goes upstairs to find her son packing.

"I know about Molly Brand," Dottie tells her son. "I'm sorry. It's sad. For all of us."

Josie runs up the stairs after quickly fixing her baby brother's plate. Trying to defuse what she knows will be a tense confrontation between mother and son, Josie goes over to talk to her distraught brother.

"Josie!"

"I'm sorry, L'il Daddy. Mama needed to know"

"She didn't have to tell me," Dottie says to her grieving son. "After the miscarriage, Molly Beth started to develop complications. Your Aunt Julia called and told us."

Julia Chapman Myles is the wife of Joseph Myles, Jacob, Sr.'s brother. The two met as young adults when Joseph went to visit a friend at Bethlehem General Hospital. Built in the late 1920's, Bethlehem General is Hopskip, Georgia's leading care provider for its Negro citizens. Julia started there a candy striper when she was just eighteen. She worked her way up the ladder as a nurse's aide and became the youngest Head Nurse to walk the halls of Bethlehem General. She and Dottie have remained in touch since the family moved north.

"She went to Aunt Julia's hospital?"

"Boy, white folks been sneaking over to Bethlehem for years! *Hiding out*," Dottie says quoting with her fingers. "They don't mind *us* knowing they need a shot. Heaven forbid, their own family members would know what kinda trouble they're getting themselves into."

"Molly Beth's not like that." L'il Daddy says defending her. "Why did Aunt Julia tell you about Molly, Mama? How did you know it was her?"

"I found your locket a few weeks before we left Georgia."

"Mama!"

"Well, it's not like you were hiding it. Who else washes your clothes?"

L'il Daddy frowns. He thought he was careful hiding the locket Molly Beth gave him last year.

"Well, good," L'il Daddy thinks to himself. *"Everyone should know the truth."* He goes over to his dresser and dumps the contents of the top drawer onto his bed. His mother shakes her head pitying her young son's foolish intentions.

"You talking about going back?" Dottie says. "How long have you been black? What do you think is going to happen when you get there? You think they'll throw you a parade?"

"I'm sorry, Mama," L'il Daddy says stuffing his clothes into his suitcase. "I have to see Molly Beth!"

"Are you forgetting she's Marvin Brand's daughter, little brother?" Josie says. "Marvin Brand?"

"Marvin Brand's daughter," Dottie reiterates. "Oh, there'll be a parade, alright."

"I'm not afraid of Marvin Brand, Mama." L'il Daddy boasts. "I can handle myself. I'm not afraid of him or Cletus."

"You should be," Dottie reminds him. "I don't know which is worse, him or his daddy."

Cletus Brand is Molly Beth's only sibling and older brother. Cletus leaves nothing to the imagination regarding his feelings about Negroes and race-mixing. Cletus misses his mother as much as his sister does. Although he believes his father's friends are responsible for his mother's disappearance, he has somehow resigned himself to the belief that his soft-hearted mother, given her tolerance for Civil Rights may have unintentionally contributed to her own undoing. Cletus enjoyed a peaceful, yet distant friendship with Jacob, Jr. until a disagreement occurred between their fathers. He respected the younger Jacob for protecting his sister, Molly Beth during a ruckus between two drunks brawling in the street. Jacob, Jr. protected the young beauty from getting hurt although Cletus never knew the real reason for the attack or the true relationship between his sister and young Jacob. The two drunks swear they saw Molly throw L'il Daddy a kiss. Cletus *knew* they had to be drunk. *'Northern rabble-rousers and the so-called movement have upset the peace of the South,'* he'll say to anyone who'll listen. Unfortunately for Molly and L'il Daddy, that number has grown exponentially.

"Son, it's not just them," says Dottie. "Everybody black down there ain't your friend, either! You ticked off a lot of our people back in Hopskip, too! Remember? The sit-ins, that voter registration drive. Even some of our church members stopped coming by for my pies."

"Who needs 'em," Josie says with a wave of dismissal.

"Son, you have to think about this," his mother pleads. "At least wait until your father comes home."

"I have thought about it, Mama," L'il Daddy responds. "...and I can't wait for Daddy. I have to see Molly. She needs me."

L'il Daddy grabs his hastily packed suitcase and puts on his jacket. Despite his mother's and big sister's pleas, he runs downstairs ready to leave home and reunite with his beloved Molly Beth. He looks behind him to see Dottie and Josie standing at the foot of the staircase. They're heartbroken. He can see it in their faces. He hesitates for a moment but remembers that his true love needs him and is just a few days away. He waves goodbye to his family. L'il Daddy opens the door to walk out but is immediately stopped in his tracks. Thunderstruck by the vision standing before him, L'il Daddy drops his suitcase to the floor with a thud. A vision - with hair as red as a Colorado sunset - stands demurely in L'il Daddy's doorway. The poor boy, disoriented by the apparition standing before him, shakes his head. He blinks. No change. She smiles, refusing to comply with the belief that he must be dreaming. He blinks again not believing his own eyes. Still there. He opens his mouth but his tongue won't cooperate. The source of the poor boy's physical deprivation speaks.

"Hello, Jacob. I was just about to ring the doorbell. It's good to see you."

For an apparition, Margaret Elizabeth Brand has a considerable command of the English language.

To Be Continued

Lightning Source UK Ltd.
Milton Keynes UK
UKHW021023071218
333626UK00009B/329/P